Clytemnestra's Bind

Clytemnestra's

Bind

THE HOUSE OF ATREUS

Susan C Wilson

NEEM TREE
PRESS

Published by Neem Tree Press Limited, 2023

This edition, 2024

1 3 5 7 9 10 8 6 4 2

Neem Tree Press Limited
95A Ridgmount Gardens, London, WC1E 7AZ
United Kingdom
info@neemtreepress.com
www.neemtreepress.com

A catalogue record for this book is available from the British Library

Hardback
ISBN 978-1-911107-59-0
UK Paperback
ISBN 978-1-911107-60-6
UK Ebook
ISBN 978-1-911107-61-3
USA Paperback
ISBN 978-1-915584-58-8
USA Ebook
ISBN 978-1-915584-57-1

Printed and bound in Great Britain

For Jacqueline,
We shared such happy times immersed in the magic of Greece.

And it is the eternal rule that drops of blood spilled on the ground demand yet more blood.

Aeschylus, *The Libation Bearers*
(Translator: Herbert Weir Smyth)

BRONZE AGE
GREECE

LAND OF THE ACHEANS

AEGEAN SEA

Troy

CYCLADES

EUBOEA

Aulis
Athens
SALAMIS
Thebes
BOEOTIA
LOCRIS
Delphi
Mycenae
ARGOLIS
Phthia
THESSALY
PELEPONNESE
Lacedaemon
LACONIA
Pylos

ACARNANIA

ITHACA

IONIAN SEA

N
W E
S

CHARACTERS APPEARING IN THE HOUSE OF ATREUS TRILOGY

HOUSES OF ATREUS & LACEDAEMON

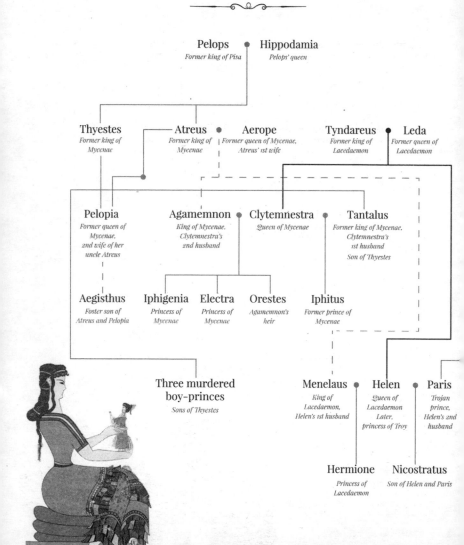

Pelops
Former king of Pisa

Hippodamia
Pelops' queen

Thyestes
Former king of Mycenae

Atreus
Former king of Mycenae

Aerope
Former queen of Mycenae, Atreus' 1st wife

Tyndareus
Former king of Lacedaemon

Leda
Former queen of Lacedaemon

Pelopia
Former queen of Mycenae, 2nd wife of her uncle Atreus

Agamemnon
King of Mycenae, Clytemnestra's 2nd husband

Clytemnestra
Queen of Mycenae

Tantalus
Former king of Mycenae, Clytemnestra's 1st husband Son of Thyestes

Aegisthus
Foster son of Atreus and Pelopia

Iphigenia
Princess of Mycenae

Electra
Princess of Mycenae

Orestes
Agamemnon's heir

Iphitus
Former prince of Mycenae

Three murdered boy-princes
Sons of Thyestes

Menelaus
King of Lacedaemon, Helen's 1st husband

Helen
Queen of Lacedaemon Later, princess of Troy

Paris
Trojan prince, Helen's 2nd husband

Hermione
Princess of Lacedaemon

Nicostratus
Son of Helen and Paris

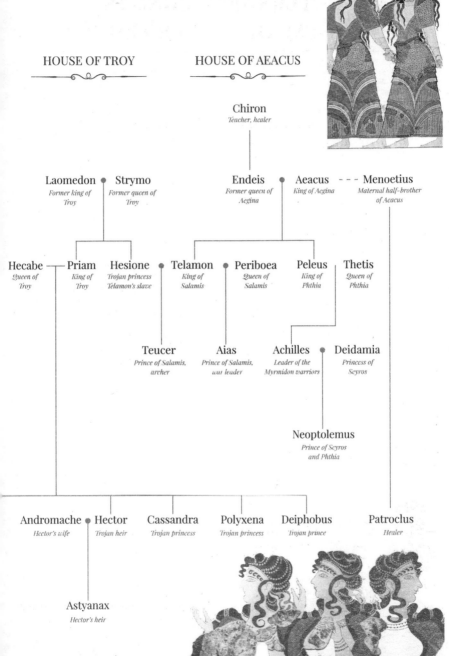

HOUSE OF TROY

HOUSE OF AEACUS

Chiron
Teacher, healer

Laomedon
Former king of Troy

Strymo
Former queen of Troy

Endeis
Former queen of Aegina

Aeacus
King of Aegina

- - - **Menoetius**
Maternal half-brother of Aeacus

Hecabe
Queen of Troy

Priam
King of Troy

Hesione
Trojan princess Telamon's slave

Telamon
King of Salamis

Periboea
Queen of Salamis

Peleus
King of Phthia

Thetis
Queen of Phthia

Teucer
Prince of Salamis, archer

Aias
Prince of Salamis, war leader

Achilles
Leader of the Myrmidon warriors

Deidamia
Princess of Scyros

Neoptolemus
Prince of Scyros and Phthia

Andromache
Hector's wife

Hector
Trojan heir

Cassandra
Trojan princess

Polyxena
Trojan princess

Deiphobus
Trojan prince

Patroclus
Healer

Astyanax
Hector's heir

TABLE OF CONTENTS

PART ONE

CHAPTER 1

Sometimes I hear murdered children in the corridors of the palace. I told my husband once. He said it was only foxes crying on the hillside below the citadel, pigs squealing within the walls. He hates to be reminded of his family's crimes, but the murdered children beg for justice. They sob and whisper, and I make plans.

My husband is waging war overseas. How natural it feels to rule in his place, instead of listening from the shadows while he decides our destinies. When he returns, I'll arrange a celebration feast. He will not attend it.

A homecoming marked the first of his family's crimes, and his homecoming will end them.

*

His father, Atreus, plotted the atrocity that began our troubles. Long years have seared it into my mind as if I'd been there. I heard it from Thyestes, Atreus' brother, who told it over and over in his drunken waking hours and in his screaming, nightwalking sleep. Thyestes and Atreus had cherished a bond of mutual loathing, which Thyestes considered unbreakable. A throne, of course, was the source of their enmity – the throne of Mycenae. Small wonder, then, that Thyestes experienced a pang of misgiving when Atreus invited him back to Mycenae for a reconciliation feast, after a spell in exile. But a man who takes no risks makes few gains.

The scene: Atreus' hall. A log fire crackles on the hearth. All else is silence – no bard, no tumblers, no guests attend Thyestes' homecoming celebration, besides his hard-faced host Atreus and, occupying a separate table, a boy of eight cheerless winters and a cringing lad of six.

Atreus' lips twitch in a rare smile. "Fill a bowl for my brother."

A slave lifts a lid from a tripod cauldron over the hearth, releasing a waft of something piggish, and carries a steaming bowl to Thyestes.

Thyestes raises the rim of the bowl to his mouth, tips a stew of some description down his throat. Greasy globules scald his oesophagus. He belches, offers his verdict: "Stinking. Still, I've known worse dangers than bellyache since you flung me into exile."

The smile doesn't reach Atreus' eyes. "That's enough of our quarrel, Thyestes. Our family is reunited, and more closely than ever. I've been thinking, if I made you Guardian of the Host would you stop hankering after my throne? You'd have landholdings second only to my own."

Thyestes scratches his neck, shrugs. "Might consider it. Not having any stew, Atreus? What about the whelps? Your youngest lad looks used to first and second helpings, third too, and licking the cauldron clean."

The younger boy rises, trots towards the hearth with his empty bowl.

"Sit down, greedy little turd!" shouts Atreus. "You'll eat when I tell you."

Crimson-faced, the boy shuffles back to his table. His brother quiets his sniffling with an elbow in the ribs.

The feast continues, hardly a feast at all. Atreus nibbles bread dipped in olive oil, and his sons do the same. The two boys and two men glance up at the sound of footsteps pattering on the balcony overlooking the hearth, the swish of tiered skirts, plumage of a bird in flight.

"Aerope, you spying bitch," Atreus bellows, and the bird – his queen – steals back to the balcony. "Get down here and show my brother your famous hospitality. I'm sure he's missed it."

While they wait for the queen to make her way downstairs, Atreus watches Thyestes, and Thyestes watches him back. An age seems to pass before the scarlet curtain in the doorway peels open and Aerope, stalked by an armed guard, enters the hall. The youngest boy jumps up and squeaks a filial greeting; the elder grabs the child's hand, jerks him back to his stool. The guard sets a third stool at the children's table, and the queen accepts it. She sits with her head bowed. She wears a traditional open-fronted jacket designed to expose bare breasts, the nurturing potential of womankind. A thin blouse disappoints Thyestes' probing eyes.

"She covers her tits these days," says Atreus. "I'd make her veil her sly face too, if it didn't betray her secrets. Well, Aerope, aren't you greeting Thyestes? Doubtless you'd be friendlier if I left you alone together."

The queen murmurs, "Atreus, why don't you ask the bard to sing?"

"Woman, why don't you eat something? Perhaps I'd find you more palatable with some meat on your skeleton. What about you, Thyestes, how do you like my wife?"

"Just spit out whatever you have to say," says Thyestes.

"Oh, I won't be the only one spitting something out tonight. You've always wanted what was mine, haven't you, Thyestes?"

"If you mean the throne of Mycenae, it was never your birthright."

"No!" Atreus' fist crashes against the table. "I won it through merit. The Mycenaeans wanted me, they didn't want you. Our nephew was a fool to name us his joint successors when he went to war. If we'd ruled together, we'd have torn this kingdom apart."

"Only one arse can fit on a throne," agrees Thyestes.

"His Followers begged me to rule alone after he got himself killed. We were strangers in Mycenae, but the Mycenaeans knew you for what you are. And, be sure of this, they will always remain loyal to me. They have men's faithful hearts." Atreus tips his cup, tosses the contents in his wife's face.

Aerope sits frozen, makes no sound. Then she rises, dabs at her blouse with fluttering hands. Her younger son whimpers. The elder gnaws a hunk of bread.

"Did I give you leave?" shouts Atreus, and the queen falls back to her stool. "You took it anyway. Whore! I know what you did."

He gestures brusquely at the slave to refill Thyestes' bowl. Thyestes forces down another mouthful of stew. The seasoning is pungent, probably to disguise rancid meat. His stomach, though, has tensed for a different reason. Somehow his brother has learned the truth at last.

"It was you who stole the fleece of kingship," Atreus accuses Aerope.

Her gaze fastens on the flexing and unflexing of his fingers.

"You gave it to Thyestes so he could wear it on my coronation day. Because of your treachery, the Mycenaeans decided the gods had chosen him instead of me. We spent years in exile before I won back my throne and exiled him. Did you think he'd seize you too, make you his queen? Stupid bitch. Well, Thyestes, was she a good tumble before you threw her away?"

Thyestes picks a sliver of gristle from between his teeth with his thumbnail and flicks it at a hound padding hungrily around the hall. "As you say."

Soundless tears mingle with the wine on Aerope's cheeks. A womanly mistake, to imagine a lover must love her in turn, to believe he will deliver her from a miserable marriage bed. Some women see only what they long for, raise towers on foundations of wax.

"A scribe told me of her whoredom after I caught him trying to crawl inside her skirts himself," says Atreus. "He saw the two of you, all those years ago, sprawled over a bench in her throne room. Seemed to think his tardy information would save him. I cut off his cock and watched him bleed to death in the courtyard."

"Can't blame a man for trying," says Thyestes.

Veins bulge in Atreus' neck. "Blame? If I'd known how far you'd betrayed me, I'd have killed you when I won back my throne, not let you fornicate in exile with other men's wives."

"It certainly hasn't all been bad," says Thyestes. "But enough now, stop flirting with me. Return my spear and we'll decide this as men, or else I'll take my leave. Your wife's hospitality is always my pleasure, but I've other beds to warm."

At last a smile reaches Atreus' eyes. "Oh? Thinking of visiting another old lover or two, catching up with some stray pups? I always say a man should acquaint himself with his children. Yet you haven't recognised yours tonight."

Thyestes frowns at the two boys seated with their mother. The elder has Atreus' dirty-bronze hair and sunburned complexion. The younger is paler, lentils and curds. Thyestes himself is dark as an Egyptian.

"They're your brats, Atreus."

"Agamemnon and Menelaus? No doubt. Well, off you go, Thyestes, and take some stew with you."

Before Thyestes manages a scornful rebuff, the queen's sword-wielding guard seizes him. He considers resisting, but he didn't survive in exile by acting the hothead. The guard steers him to the tripod cauldron over the hearth. The slave raises the lid. Cold bronze presses against the nape of Thyestes' neck, makes him bow. Steam stings his eyes. His cheeks swell against a strange familiar reek. He peers through the swirling vapour, roars, falls back, clutches his mouth.

The heads of his sons have an amber sheen. Their hair sways in the bubbling sauce like tentacles. It catches at three pairs of armless hands, which bob around the children's faces as if girlishly directing attention towards pretty lips, a dimpled cheek.

Thyestes grapples with the guard, screaming, kicking, lashing out. He thinks he will die tonight, would welcome death, if first he kills his brother. Atreus has doomed them both, made them abominations in the eyes of the gods. He has daubed a circle in blood, a prison for the generations, a cycle of eternal destruction. Fathers must avenge murdered sons, and sons avenge murdered fathers, brothers will kill brothers, nephews kill uncles, and on and on it goes.

When men plunge a family into self-destruction, women must find a way to break the curse.

CHAPTER 2

Thyestes had another son, fathered on a peasant woman while he wandered in exile once more after the murders of his innocent children. This boy, Tantalus, became my husband.

We married when Tantalus was fifteen and I was three years his senior. Thyestes, by then, had returned to Mycenae at the head of a mercenary army and toppled Atreus from the ivory-plated throne for the final time. My parents had known about the brothers' feuding, though not that gruesome supper, but with Atreus now dead I overcame their objections to Thyestes' proposal of a marriage alliance. Mycenae was too glittering a prize to refuse.

Only when I became pregnant did the misgivings set in.

Like any girl new to motherhood, I dreaded something happening to my baby. A jealous spirit might steal his breath as he slept in his cradle. A god might strike him with sickness to punish an offence I'd unknowingly committed. I fretted over my abilities as a mother, despite the cousins, nephews and short-lived siblings I'd cared for. Most of all, I feared the ruthless family into which I'd delivered my son.

Though his birth festivities passed auspiciously, I felt no peace till Tantalus, cradling our baby in his arms, ran three times around the hearth fire at the naming ceremony. Some of the spirits who prowl around unnamed infants would now flutter away, despairing of easy prey. But, even as Tantalus returned our son to my outstretched arms, I wondered if we could ever keep him safe.

"The little one needs his rest," said his nursemaid after the guests had presented their name-day gifts.

I pretended not to hear her. Clutching my child, I sidestepped into the throng of Followers – nobles of the land – who were formerly Atreus' loyal men and were now subject to the joint rule of Thyestes and Tantalus. They milled around while cooks and carvers prepared the name-day feast over the hearth fire.

Tantalus touched our son's flushed cheek. "This heat and smoke isn't good for him. He should go to the nursery, my love."

He was right, of course. The nursemaid reached for my child, and with a pang of envy and regret I surrendered him. It was our first parting since he tore from my body amid so much pain and blood. He was seven days old.

The garlanded Followers sat in pairs at small round tables throughout the hall. They picked at the meats and fruits before them with as little enthusiasm as for the earlier rites. Never had I longed for my parents as I did now, surrounded by these men. My mother and father hadn't travelled to Mycenae for the birth celebrations. Father had broken his leg while hunting and Mother was still polluted from another miscarriage.

"Try the squid; it's excellent," said Tantalus, with an encouraging smile.

A hovering server placed a stuffed squid on the table. I straightened my back and composed myself. My parents would expect me to mask my fears, to be queenly. I mustn't think of dead children, mustn't imagine them weeping in the corridors of the palace. I mustn't think of warrior princes in exile: Agamemnon and Menelaus and their foster-brother, those three young men who'd escaped when Thyestes retook Mycenae. More thoughts than mine, I was certain, had dwelled on them while my belly swelled with child.

Tantalus' father squeezed the backside of a passing flute girl. "Tell the musicians to shush their bellowing, gorgeous." He grinned sourly at the Followers around the flower-bedecked hall. "Well, ladies? Your looks could curdle water. I think I know why."

I grasped Tantalus' hand under our table. Surely not even Thyestes was crass enough to say what we all must be thinking? He wouldn't acknowledge, on my son's name day, that my baby wasn't the only claimant to the throne.

Thyestes squared his jaw, his black beard jutting. "Musing on the sons of the potter, painter and piss-pot emptier, are you, ladies? Atreus was a cuckold. His sons could be anyone's. But Tantalus is true born, and now he's given Mycenae an heir of his own."

"A queen too, to rule over us," said a Follower.

Thyestes glowered at me. "Little Clytemnestra? My boy alone shares my throne, and no bony-arsed girl will ever sniff the cushion. He'll learn soon enough to reward her delusions with his belt."

"If I may speak?" I ignored the heat rising in my cheeks. "The gods favour men with thrones and women with sons. My only ambition is to raise my child to be a wise ruler of this kingdom."

"Well said," agreed Tantalus.

"Enough said." Thyestes tossed a gnawed bone to the floor, where snarling hounds fought over it. "Now, ladies, no more scowls. No muttering in the corridors where you think I haven't ears. Serve me loyally and you'll never be short of land or rents, your store cupboards will overflow. Atreus was never so generous." He banged his cup on the table. "What happened to the music? Bring out the dancing girls!"

But not even somersaulting women, their skirts as short as men's, could lift the mood in the hall. The Followers spoke in such a broken hum that I caught few of their words – except, once or twice, the names of Atreus' sons.

Thyestes grew increasingly drunk. His bleary gaze kept drifting to a tripod cauldron steaming on the vast central hearth, then he'd bounce a dancer or two on his lap and drain his cup. Sweat beaded on his forehead.

I whispered to Tantalus, "Let's go to our chamber." Close the door against these men.

Thyestes slurred a song and fondled a Nubian dancer's thigh as we approached his table to bid him goodnight.

"Who's that?" Red-eyed, Thyestes peered at Tantalus like a man half blind. "Which one is this?"

"Father, it's me," said Tantalus.

The Nubian sprang aside as Thyestes flung his arms around my husband in a fierce embrace and winded him with pounding fists. "I can't bear your pretty little face," he said, and shoved my husband away.

Tantalus turned mournful eyes to me. Tonight, they said, we would hear Thyestes roar in his chamber; the nightmares would return.

Tonight, dead children would scream in the palace.

*

We entered the wide vestibule, the painted floor cool beneath our feet. Night muted the vivid colours of the wall frescoes all around us. The bronze-plated door to the porch stood open and, behind us, the guards kept the scarlet curtain swept aside to draw out some heat from the hall.

Parched from the smoky hearth fire, I inhaled a breath of soothing air. Tantalus wrapped his arm around my shoulders and pressed his cheek to mine. If Thyestes was watching us from the hall, he'd mock us in the morning. Still, I let my body sag into Tantalus' side and we made our way upstairs.

Thyestes had insisted our marriage chamber should be next to his apartments. Not only must we endure his nightly grunting with slave girls, but he often burst in on us, open-eyed yet trapped in nightmares. We never told him, next morning, of his hours spent weeping like a baby in his son's arms.

Yearning ached in my breast. "I should check on Iphitus."

Tantalus drew me onto our bed. "Not now, my love. You'll only wake his nursemaid."

"But he's my baby."

He smiled at the peevish tone of my voice. "And he's the luckiest in the world to have you as his mother."

He reached into my hair, which I was growing from the shaven style of maidenhood. He plucked out the combs and pins used by my servants to create the illusion of tamed womanly locks, leaving me self-conscious, girlish again, as the ends of my curls tickled my neck.

We lay in our ceremonial clothes, too weary to undress – he in his long tunic, me in tiered skirts and a short-sleeved jacket.

So little time had passed since my mother led our wedding celebrations, since those first shy nights of discovering each other's bodies and discovering ourselves. After Mater Theia blessed my womb, we feared to harm the blossoming seed. And now, on our first night since my purification from childbirth, my body hurt too much to even imagine joining with Tantalus in love.

His fingers trailed up and down my arm till his touch, for once, grew absent as Thyestes with the dancing girls. "I'm afraid, Clytemnestra."

I stiffened. My tranquil husband rarely sensed the lurk of danger. "Why?"

"Father. I can't help him."

I could have reassured him – what harm, to lie? But no one could free Thyestes from the past. "Oh, Tantalus. How ever did you spring from such a family?"

On my wedding night, I learned the extent of my new family's depravity. Flushed from our marriage celebrations, Tantalus had summoned the nerve to untie my girdle, when his father tore, howling, through our chamber. An age seemed to pass while I waited, alone and shaken, for my husband to settle the sleepwalking Thyestes back into bed.

When we lay again in each other's arms, desire snuffed out by the interruption, we talked and shivered into the grey hours of morning. He told me of that ungodly supper and the years Thyestes spent gathering an army to storm Mycenae. Atreus hadn't fallen to Thyestes' spear, but he fell all the same, and Thyestes sent for Tantalus to keep him safe from Atreus' ousted sons.

And now we'd given another child into this family.

"We'll keep Iphitus safe," said Tantalus, reading my thoughts as if they were frescoes on a wall. "We'll rule Mycenae together, you and I, even if the Followers don't approve. We'll be a brilliant king."

His words thrilled me. He looked so young, smiling at me with his trusting dark eyes. He was, to me, like a beloved brother and precious charge. How wise of Thyestes to claim him after fourteen years of absence from his life. Thyestes bargained on Tantalus' youth and modesty to disarm the Followers – and so did I.

With our fingers entwined, my husband fell asleep. I watched the flutter of his eyelashes against his hairless cheeks. Deep within the palace, a woman shrieked and a man laughed, slaves and Followers playing love games as the night deepened. All else was silence, except for Tantalus' gentle breathing.

I rose and tucked the bedcovers around my husband's shoulders. What a burden those shoulders bore. To a boy of barely sixteen summers, raised by his mother's family of shepherds, fell the duty of defending the kingdom and our helpless child from circling vultures. We would bear that duty together.

Soft rugs brushed my feet as I walked to the window seat. Through the window slit I gazed up at Arachne's Peak, the highest of the two sacred mountains between which our citadel nestles, together known as the Mother's Bosom. "Mater Theia," I whispered, "embrace no more of your children too soon."

Wind gusted down the scrubby slope. From somewhere beyond the citadel came a scream, high and mournful, ghostly in the darkness. It came three times. Foxes, or Mater Theia crying out for her children.

Three murdered sons of Thyestes, unburied and restless. Three sons of Atreus, eager to avenge their ills in turn. It must end here. I must stop the wheel of retribution from spinning, mould a lynchpin of wax. Thyestes might jeer at me for being ambitious, "a king with pretty tits." He should call me, rather, the mother of a son.

With a last look at my peaceful husband, I crossed the chamber and opened the door. I wouldn't disturb Iphitus. I just needed to hear him breathing, to see his sleep-dewed face peep from his swaddling. To brush his lips with the lightest of kisses.

Guards rarely patrolled the upper floors of the palace, but tonight they stole along the corridors, alert as weasels. A necessary precaution, I supposed – thanks to Thyestes' generosity with the wine, more than a few fights had erupted between guests bedding in the palace for the birth festivities.

Thyestes, despite my protests, had insisted on placing Iphitus in a nursery at the far end of the domestic quarters, so he wouldn't be woken in the night by a bawling infant. Out of pity, I'd bitten back a retort. As I neared my destination, the occasional crimson-cloaked Follower brushed past me, though most would sleep tonight in the hall. Some faces I recognised; others escaped me. I ignored everyone and pushed down the memory of Thyestes' coarseness towards me in front of these men at the name-day feast.

Head down, a Follower almost collided with me. There was something in his glance as it darted from mine. "Forgive me," he muttered.

I swept past him. I was queen of Mycenae, and a king's daughter too. These men might dislike the new rule, but the gods allowed it. Mortals must accept the will of the deathless ones.

"At your service, lady, O queen," sniggered another Follower, further along the corridor. He bobbed his head sycophantically.

A swell of laughter rose from the hall and swallowed my rebuke. I'd meant to quicken my pace at the balcony over the hearth. Now, I drew away from the wall's protective shadow and stood at the railing, as Aerope once did during that terrible feast. I gazed down into the hall through the wispy smoke of the ever-burning hearth fire.

Tables were overturned. Food lay trampled into the floor. A horde of Followers blocked the curtained doorway. More Followers crowded around Thyestes, chanting his name and jostling each other for a better view. He held a huge silver rhyton above his head and drunkenly tried to balance on one leg. Instead of pouring a libation to the gods from the sacred horn, he aimed the spout at his mouth. He seemed not to know what he was doing. He swayed like a rotten tree, prevented from toppling by the Followers' shoving, grabbing hands.

I turned away with a sickened stab of pity. This was a king? But at least he'd sleep soundly tonight, too far gone for dreams.

I met no one else till I reached the nursery. Two guards stood outside the door, heads together, whispering: ". . . gods. . . abandoned. . ." Their heads snapped up, eyes blinking stupidly at my approach. Without another word, they slunk off down the corridor.

On any other occasion, I'd have ordered them to stop, to explain themselves and pay me respect. Instead, I flung open the door, which my maids had smeared with pitch to ward off evil spirits. I needed no time to adjust to the darkness inside. I could have reached the cradle blindfolded.

Iphitus lay swaddled and still. My stomach lurched. I touched his cheek, and his sleepy coo was almost lost in my sigh. My fears drained like the rush of wine from Thyestes' rhyton.

His nursemaid groaned and stirred in her bed.

"Go back to sleep," I told her.

I drew a stool to the cradle and sat admiring my baby. Was there any living creature, even a god, so perfect? But such thoughts anger the deathless ones and must be quickly renounced. "Ugly boy," I said, though I couldn't help smiling, since I didn't mean it.

I longed to unwrap Iphitus from his swaddling. Already, during his short waking hours, he tried to wriggle his arms when he saw my face or heard the jangle of my jewellery. Such early awareness was a sign of high intelligence. And the way he seemed to focus on the sway of my seal ring, which hung on a cord around my neck, suggested an instinct for authority. This ring, a wedding gift from Tantalus, was engraved with the guardians of Mycenae, Mater Theia's twin lionesses. The guardians reared at either side of an altar, over which coiled a snake, symbolising my rebirth into my husband's house.

I reached up to touch the golden ring. My hand met with bare skin. The cord must have worked loose as I lay beside Tantalus.

In the corridor, a woman screamed.

I sprang to my feet and gathered up Iphitus. The nursemaid tumbled from her bed. She reached for my child.

I turned from her. "Go see what's happening."

She opened the door a crack. "It's Followers, with a maid. I think they mean to…to…"

Disgusted, I threw wide the door and hurried into the corridor, followed by the nursemaid. "Let her go at once!"

Three Followers froze in their efforts to drag a writhing slave girl into a chamber. One smirked and said, "Just having a bit of fun."

His disrespect stunned me. "Are you drunk, to speak to me this way?"

Iphitus chose that moment to give a lusty cry.

"Go give your child some tit, woman," said the Follower, "unless you want to join us."

One of his accomplices stared into the shadowy corridor. "Pan's cock! It's time."

Feet pounded towards us. Before I could see who approached, the Followers dropped their victim. The one who'd addressed me so rudely grabbed my collarbone and thrust me backwards into the nursery. He slammed the door in my face as the nursemaid tried to follow me. I heard someone strike her, the thud as she hit the floor.

Iphitus bawled. I clutched him too tightly, I knew, but my muscles had spasmed. All along the corridor, doors opened and slammed. A pair of swords scraped.

A lone male roar shocked me into action. I laid Iphitus in his cradle and dragged the nursemaid's bed to the door. It was too light for a barricade, oxhide stretched over a wooden frame. I glanced desperately around the room. What other furniture? A table. A three-legged stool. I set them on the bed, heaved a chest on to the overturned table and placed the cradle beside the chest.

"Father will come," I whispered as I lifted my howling baby from the cradle. I clasped him to my breast. "Grandfather will come."

I thought of Thyestes swaying on one leg in the hall, swilling the gods' portion as the Followers crowded around him. This was no surprise invasion: the Followers had planned a revolt. I imagined my husband waking in our bed, Tantalus the shepherd boy, who'd never fought a battle in his life. Oh, let them not hurt him! Let them oust Thyestes and set Tantalus alone on the throne.

"Father will come." A sob caught in my throat.

Something slammed against the door. The wood creaked, the bed jolted. A muffled curse outside.

I shrank back and shielded Iphitus between the wall and my body.

Another thud. The stool went flying. It rolled towards us. A third. The door split. Cradle, chest and table crashed to the floor.

A man burst into the chamber. Even in the dim lamplight from the corridor, his face and corselet gleamed with blood. He reached me in a few strides.

"Tantalus?" I heard myself say.

"Dead." His muscular arms reached out. He ripped Iphitus from my breast. His voice came gruff through my screams: "They gave me no choice."

No choice. Time and my heart froze.

He caught my baby by the swaddled feet. Iphitus choked on a scream. I threw myself against the man. He might have been granite. He clamped a hand over my face and shoved me to the floor.

"Look away," he said.

He swung Iphitus as though my baby were a hurling stone, as if the unyielding wall were an endless, empty sky. I tried to scramble up. My arms and legs gave out, my body pitched forward.

I will not describe the sound I heard next, though I hear it over and over in my dreams. Then came only a woman's screams, my own.

CHAPTER 3

I lay in an unfamiliar bed; someone must have carried me there. A night passed, or two, three. I curled into a ball. Perhaps I could curl up so tightly I'd disappear and no one could call me back.

Always there came a woman's voice: "Eat something. Drink. You must sit up."

Sometimes wine moistened my lips, barley gruel was spooned into my mouth. I let it dribble out.

"We heard you were a sensible lady," persisted the voice, "so summon your strength."

Leave me to my memories of my child, I told it silently. Leave me to my nightmares.

Once, a draught rippled the bedcovers and the chamber door opened. A man spoke, gruff, rapid – whether a guard, a slave or a son of Atreus, I didn't care, though if the latter I ought to have torn his heart out. I knew, of course, that no other than Atreus' sons had destroyed my world.

He asked if I was ready.

"Give me a few more days with her," answered the woman, softer than with me, "please."

"Sooner we get this done, the better," grumbled the man.

Another time, I heard Tantalus whisper in my ear, "Look away." Fingers stroked my bare arm. I opened my eyes to see my baby's killer thrusting above me in his bloodied corselet. *Hymen, O Hymenaeus*, sang a chorus of children's voices. I turned my face and wept.

"Tut, lady. What good do tears ever do?" said the woman. "It's time to bathe."

"Get him off me," I sobbed. "I smell him."

She gathered me in her arms, efficient as my mother, though lacking tenderness. Till now, I hadn't really seen the woman. She was slightly older than me, narrow face, narrow hips, narrow everything, with an expression neither kind nor unkind. She took a kylix from the bedside table, held the rim to my mouth and tipped my chin, forcing me to swallow sour wine. She broke a few crumbs from a seed cake and pushed them between my lips.

"That'll do it," she said. With her arms around me, she steered me to a clay bathtub in the middle of the floor, and into cool water.

My weakness should have shamed me; my instinct wasn't the natural one – I didn't think of my duty to live and gain vengeance. I bent my knees and let my back slide down the glazed interior until the water covered my face. The woman drew me up, her hands beneath my armpits. I slid down again. She drew me up. I slid down.

And so we continued, till she tried to haul me from the bath. I made my body like stone – easy to do – and she ran into the corridor. Her shouts faded as my head sank, as water filled my mouth and nostrils.

My body betrayed me, or else the gods wanted me to live, for my throat sealed up. I could only weep at my failure, my tears futile as raindrops in the Sea of Aegeus.

A man, not a god, plucked me from the tub and carried me back to bed as if I were an infant. His eyes were wide and blue in a full-moon face; I met them with all my hatred for the world. He blinked at me and shifted his gaze to my naked belly. His cheeks flamed brighter than his red-gold hair. He turned away.

"Will she be all right?" he asked.

"She has to be," replied the woman. "Lord, won't you…?"

"Oh, pardon me! Well, I'll be going." Above his festive kilt, the man's fleshy back muscles twisted as if he would face me again. He froze. "If you're quite well, lady?"

Laughter bubbled up from my throat, convulsing my body as he hurried from the chamber. He stumbled once, over his own boots. Everything had become startlingly clear, as if I'd emerged from a cocoon, from suffocating darkness. I knew who this man was and what today would bring.

"I'm quite well!" I shouted hoarsely, though by now he was probably downstairs and halfway across the courtyard. "But you've had a fright!" I rose, dripping wet. "Is it unlucky, Helen? My bridegroom's seen me naked."

She stared at me. "My name isn't Helen, it's Harmonia. Come, I'll dry you and anoint you."

I held out my arms, so she could rub me down. "Don't play silly games, little sister, not today. Hurry up and dress me. And promise you won't make eyes at him during the wedding feast."

She dried me silently.

I lifted my hair while she massaged perfumed oil into my neck and shoulders. "I must admit, I'd hoped Tantalus would be handsome, but we women must love our husbands just the same. Oh, I do wish you were coming with me to Mycenae."

She led me to a table littered with ivory pyxides. I touched one of those small boxes and snatched back my hand. "Where did these come from?"

"From your old chamber. Sit, lady."

She lied, of course. Mama would have considered such beautiful pyxides too extravagant for an unmarried girl. I sank onto a stool and closed my eyes, while the lids of those familiar boxes clacked open and shut, releasing acrid odours of powders and paints. A brush fluttered over my face, breasts, arms and hands. I hardly knew if I was awake or dreaming. If this... this *person* – who seemed not to be Helen after all, who called herself Harmonia – hadn't kept pausing to grip my shoulders, I might've keeled slowly from the stool.

At some point, she pinned up my hair and raised me to my feet. She shrouded my legs in heavy skirts and forced my arms through jacket sleeves. My body felt numb, swaddled. She set a wreath of flowering myrtle on my head.

The chamber door flew open and a gaggle of maidservants poured through – some vaguely familiar, others strangers.

"Did you bring the jewellery?" the woman asked them.

A maid held out a casket and lifted the lid, so the woman could pluck out a few items. I stood as motionless as an idol being adorned by its priestess – hollow, aloof – till the woman hung around my neck a golden seal ring. I grasped the ring, ran my finger over the engraving. Rearing twin lionesses, forepaws poised on an altar…a coiled snake, emblem of rebirth…rebirth into my husband's house. The House of Thyestes.

Tantalus, the beautiful shepherd boy, gave me this heirloom on our wedding day, to stamp my authority as queen of Mycenae.

I ground the seal into my breastbone and willed Mater Theia to witness the mark of a widow whose child is slain. *Take my beloved ones to your bosom, Lady of the Black Earth. Do not let their deaths go unpunished. Avenge them, Mother. Avenge me.*

But Mater Theia's lionesses were more than a symbol of my authority. They guarded the citadel and whichever king ruled over it.

My arm fell to my side. The woman, Harmonia, took it and led me into the corridor. The maids followed us.

*

Guards patrolled the domestic quarters, as they had on the night I left my sleeping husband's side to visit our child. For a heart-stopping moment, I wondered if Zeus had turned back time to grant us another chance. Some say he reversed the course of the sun for Atreus when Thyestes first seized the throne. Others deny this and claim the sky dripped blood. But gods rarely take such trouble over the plight of mortals.

As we passed downstairs towards the porch outside the hall, I remembered walking with Tantalus in the opposite direction after our baby's name-day feast. I still felt his warm hand on my shoulder, smelled his faint rose-oil scent. But beautiful Tantalus was gone, a mere shade, a ghost. He was gone. And Iphitus, more precious than the breath in my lungs, was gone.

I pulled free from Harmonia and ran past the pair of guards who stood between the two blood-red columns in the porch. Beyond, in the courtyard, the sun sent up such a glare that I thought the white patches on the brightly patterned floor were a trick of the light. Later, I learned that a few loyal Followers had fought for us on the night of slaughter, and their blood had to be scrubbed from the floor. But most of our fallen defenders had been slaves – men, women and little children, armed with sticks.

I stopped before Protectress Athene's shrine, a replica of the one in my father's courtyard, which I'd commissioned on my arrival in Mycenae. This shrine has three niches, each with a short pillar around which the snake Agathos Daemon, our physical manifestation of the Good Spirit of the Household, likes to coil. And there he was, in the shadowy central niche, sleeping.

"The Protectress hasn't abandoned me," I whispered. "Agathos Daemon hasn't abandoned me." Yet those guardians hadn't spared us the night of slaughter.

Harmonia took my arm, gently enough but brooking no more resistance. I glanced over my shoulder as she led me back towards the hall. The snake's glossy head twisted in my direction, his eyes flickered open, and I believed my guardians remembered me still.

The two guards leaning against the porch columns were more interested in grinning at my maids than investigating whether we had permission to intrude on the men's inner sanctum. Garlands still decorated the bronze door to the vestibule, as they had during Iphitus' birth celebrations. Had no one thought to take them down? One of the guards opened the door. I passed through, with the sensation of falling into the maw of a beast.

"Why did you bring me here?" I asked Harmonia, wondering if the words even left my lips.

She answered tonelessly, "Because the king demands it."

The king. A jolt passed through me, like a violent awakening from sleep. Thyestes lived? But this couldn't be. Mycenae had a new king. A wolf, a jackal, a killer of children. Was I still its queen?

"Walk tall," said Harmonia, and for the first time her words seemed to be less an order than an encouragement.

Clutching her arm, I stepped into the smoke and heat of the hall. Tables were set for feasting, as on that last occasion. Joints of meat roasted on spits over the flame-patterned central hearth, between tripod cauldrons large and small. The cooking odours mingled with the stink of so many Followers, who sat clustered around tables, sweating in their white-tasselled crimson cloaks.

Harmonia led me towards the dais, where a man sat on the throne, the golden sceptre of Mycenae across his knees. My legs buckled.

A Follower threw out his arms to catch me.

Iphitus' killer, ripping my baby from my breast.

The Follower clasped my clawing hands, while the maids fussed over me. Harmonia put her arm around my back and I leaned into her.

"He killed my baby," I whispered.

Yet she steered me towards him, the monster on the throne. He no longer wore his bloody corselet. Gold and carnelian beads hung over his shaggy chest, above a purple and white kilt. A gold diadem covered his brow. Heavy armlets of every precious metal encircled the muscles that had stretched to snatch my child. Stony-faced, he fidgeted with a finger ring, less at ease in baubles than in armour.

A flustered voice broke the silence: "Hear me, noble Mycenaeans. In the absence of this lady's father – that would be Tyndareus – Tyndareus, son of Oebalus – Agamemnon and I stand as her relatives and guardians. That is to say, we, Agamemnon Atreides and Menelaus Atreides, are her kin through her ill-famed marriage to our cousin, Tantalus, son of Thyestes."

Agamemnon, son of Atreus, destroyer of my family, glowered a challenge around the hall from the throne. No one took it up.

I forced my attention back to Menelaus, who was standing beside the dais – the man who'd lifted me from the bathtub. He flinched as our eyes met, but this time he didn't look away.

"It pains me to remind you all that my uncle and cousin were usurpers," he said. "Traitors to their kin. They brought the gods' wrath on themselves and on their…their –" he bowed his head, and I swallowed rising gorge – "progeny. Ungodly men cause the gods to deal justice. The godly weep and obey."

"And now the ungodly lie unburied, food for birds," said Agamemnon, "a lesson to all men."

"Lady," said Menelaus quietly, "are you quite well?"

My limbs trembled so violently that my arm had wrenched from Harmonia's. I forced it behind my back and used my fumbling fingers to pull the other arm behind me too. Rather the Followers than the sons of Atreus witness my emotion.

Iphitus, Tantalus and Thyestes lay unburied, beyond Mater Theia's embrace. Trapped between the realms of the living and the dead.

My voice sounded as if from the grave that my dead didn't share: "Quite well...guardian."

Though he grimaced, Menelaus pressed on: "Our desire is to protect this lady, our kinswoman. And so I, as her guar – her kinsman, offer Clytemnestra, daughter of Tyndareus, to Agamemnon, son of Atreus. May she give splendid sons to our house."

I crumpled. I would have screamed, but no sound came from my throat. Through the fussing of my maids, I heard Agamemnon say, "See? She submits."

I tried to rise. My legs might have been hamstrung.

He added, "I too am willing."

Menelaus sounded shaken: "Let the wedding feast begin."

The maids and Harmonia half dragged, half carried me to an unoccupied table by the hearth, where they bundled me on to a high-backed chair. Agamemnon approached and lowered his bulk on to the chair opposite mine. He snapped his fingers for a slave to serve him. Harmonia, standing behind me, held me in place by the shoulders. She pressed a kylix to my lips. Perhaps the wine she gave me earlier had been drugged too. Conversation no sooner began to fill the hall than my eyelids drooped. I caught my face in my hands, my elbows dug into the table.

Hypnos, Giver of Sleep, spare me the final rite of this mockery. You showed no mercy at the bridal sacrifice, nor let me slip beneath the water of the nuptial bath. Spare me the marriage bed and the rebirth it brings.

CHAPTER 4

Agamemnon didn't come to me on our wedding night or in the nights that followed. I lay entombed in grief, trapped within the blackness of its walls. My dead gathered around me. I felt their touch, heard them breathe, whisper, babble and weep. They couldn't understand their strange, unburied existence. They didn't know they were dead.

Harmonia washed me in bed. She forced me to take sips of wine and spoke of the duties and trials of women. I lay there, silent and unmoving, as if a sculptor had carved me. How much time passed, I couldn't say. At some point, Harmonia seemed to be warning me about something. Agamemnon? Yes, Agamemnon – he grew impatient. He had expectations. He wouldn't put off visiting his wife for ever. His *wife*.

I dreaded him walking in and finding me naked, so I began to let Harmonia dress me. I returned to bed each morning, fully clothed, wrapped not in blankets but in memories of Tantalus' embrace and of Iphitus' milky scent.

When my limbs started to ache, I moved from the bed to a chair. Harmonia coaxed me to take honeyed wine for my hoarse throat. Sometimes I tried some morsel or another. More than a mouthful was too much effort.

One day, I asked a question and caught myself by surprise: "Is the sun shining outside?"

Harmonia turned sharply from the window. In measured tones, she said, "Always. The priests of Zeus sacrifice for rain."

Longing seized me to walk in the citadel, to retrace the steps Tantalus and I once took. He and I used to stroll around the terraces each morning, hand in hand, till the sun drove us back beneath the echoing colonnades of the palace courtyard.

Harmonia read my thoughts: "If you'd like to take air, I'll speak to the king."

A queen required permission to leave her chamber? But I was Agamemnon's queen, and of course I did.

"He wants to make sure you're strong enough," said Harmonia.

He wanted to ensure I posed no danger to him. Shrewd, suspicious Agamemnon. The absurdity almost made me laugh. I was young, female and friendless. Not even my father had come to my aid. The men of my native Laconia were no match for the might of my enemies here in Mycenae.

That day passed slower than any other. My thoughts kept straying from my prison chamber, along paths familiar as the bones now protruding from the backs of my hands. My mind led me down cobbled ramps and past the houses of the nobles, counsellors and gods. It carried me out through the Gate of the Sacred Lionesses and far beyond the citadel walls, whose massive heights once reassured me. I saw myself as a speck on the slopes of Arachne's Peak and Holy Mountain, searching frantically for my dead so I could sprinkle their bodies with earth and pour libations, rites that would bring peace to their restless, sundered shades.

I rose and wandered to the window where Harmonia stood. To the cloudless sky, I made a silent vow: I'd leave my prison, but only by my own cunning. Not by the permission of the man who murdered my child.

"Do you know why he didn't sell me as a slave?" I said.

"The king? Why, lady?"

From Zeus' bright sky, my gaze travelled to Arachne's Peak and the vast sun-scorched dominion of two generous, terrible queens: Mater Theia and her daughter, whose name is never spoken – She Who Reigns in Her Mother's Womb.

"The conqueror marries the queen and redoubles his claim to the soil. We women, who possess so little of our own, bestow so much."

Harmonia waited for me to continue, doubtless intending to make a report to her master. Let it be worth hearing.

"Women deliver kingdoms and kings," I said, "and whether my womb resists Agamemnon's seed or quickens, he means to make sure no son of mine will topple him from Tantalus' throne. But blood-ties are no hindrance to some men, and sceptres can be snatched from grasping hands by even stronger fists."

She studied me. When I didn't speak again, she opened the door. A guard waited outside.

"The day wears on," she said. "Will I request anything special for supper while I'm downstairs?"

I returned to staring out of the window.

*

Harmonia's duties, it seemed, were to loosen my tongue, encourage me to eat and prevent me from harming myself. She lacked the charisma to excel in her role, but her eyes and ears missed little and her memory never faltered. She was a clay tablet primed for the stylus, and I confess I took some satisfaction in playing the scribe. Vague shows of conformity encouraged her to leave the chamber for longer periods, giving me peace to muse on escape plans. Always, a guard remained outside.

One morning, Harmonia's voice snapped me from my absorption as she slipped back into the room. I'd been pacing around a table in the middle of which stood a rock-crystal vase. With a faint shock, I realised I was pondering whether the vase, swung with force, might split a man's skull.

"With guards, of course," she was saying. "Would you like that, lady, to go outside today?"

Outside. Today. In an instant, all my escape plans seemed a foolish distraction from grief. A vision came to me, as if I were a bird perched on a branch of the oak tree below the palace. Tantalus and I were sitting on the grass, under the branch, sheltering from the sun. He held out a fig and I bit into it. We giggled like the children we'd so recently been. I saw us again, dressed as the proud god and goddess – Earth-Encircler Poseidon and Mater Theia of the Black Earth – leading the dance out through the Gate of the Sacred Lionesses, to Holy Mountain.

How could I retrace our steps and allow Agamemnon's guards to sully those precious places, those memories?

"You must exercise," said Harmonia. "You'll need your strength."

My hand closed around my seal ring, around the serpent poised above the altar. I hesitated for only a moment, then crossed the chamber and opened the door.

*

At first, I was painfully aware of Harmonia and the two guards who followed me. Did they notice my faltering steps, weak as I was through lack of food and exercise? But soon my memories carried me back to those halcyon days as Tantalus' bride. So recently, I'd passed through these same corridors on Tantalus' arm, trying to walk tall, my belly big with child, my ankles swollen and heart even more so. How full of hopes we'd been.

I lingered in the little forecourt leading to the double-porticoed main entrance of the palace, and tipped my face to Zeus' bright sky. The air tasted like the crystal waters of the Perseia Spring a short way east of the citadel. But only a sip, before the bitterness returned. My boy-husband should be by my side; my child should be in my arms. Were the gods punishing my pride and ambition? A sparrow, tiny herald of Zeus the Sky Father, wheeled through the air. It landed on the god's altar, cocked its head and blinked its clever black eyes at me. What its message was, I couldn't say. I walked on.

One can never be entirely alone in the citadel, even without an escort of guards and spies. Administrators and Followers hurry about on official business; sentries patrol the paths and wall-walks; slaves of the gods, free and captive alike, perform their duties in the sacred quarter. The circuit wall of the Circle of the Ancestors at least offers a little privacy, and this would be my refuge today. In the Circle, I'd entreat the ancient ancestors to intercede with the Two Queens – Mater Theia and her only daughter, the Lady Who Receives Many – to pity my unburied dead.

The clomping of my guards' boots dogged me all the way down the great ramp to the lower acropolis. At the entrance to the Circle, I stopped so abruptly that Harmonia had crossed halfway over the three massive threshold slabs before breaking her stride.

I slammed my hand against the shell-studded doorpost. "Am I a spirit? Do you think I can escape through solid wall? Give me peace."

"We've orders not to leave you," said one of the guards.

"There's no other way out," I said. "You will wait outside. Respect this sacred place."

As I stepped into the Circle, the guards' footsteps crunched behind me on the bone splinters of some long-ago funeral feast. I spun around in confrontation. From the corner of my eye, I glimpsed a figure emerge from behind one of the grave markers. Agamemnon's brother, red-haired Menelaus. The man who'd given me to my child's killer at the mockery of a wedding.

"It's all right, men. I'll look after the queen from here," he said.

The guards blinked stupidly at the sandstone wall, as if assessing whether it could be scaled by fingernails and sandalled feet. At a nod from Harmonia, they returned with her across the threshold. Half of me wanted to sweep after them; the other half to claw ribbons from Menelaus' white cheeks.

The younger Atreides studied the carvings on the grave markers with exaggerated attention. He traced a spiral pattern with his plump finger, nodding and clucking like a foreign envoy flattering a royal guide. I drew a silver pin from my hair and placed it before the grave marker of a dead queen. Palms lowered in communion, I held out my arms and tried to ignore Menelaus' presence. His little noises jarred me.

"How many did you kill that night?" I asked.

He gaped at me like a speared fish.

"Did you murder Tantalus?" My surprise probably exceeded his, for until now I hadn't considered who took my husband's life. A hundred times or more, I'd imagined a faceless invader standing over his bed. "At least I know you didn't kill Iphitus."

Menelaus found his voice: "My cousin died in a duel, the most honourable way for a young man."

I clutched the seal ring around my neck. Better than the fate of his child. "Was he…? Did he…?"

"He was courageous to the last. Agamemnon had him brought unharmed to the hall, and they both took up spears. It was a fair fight, a warriors' fight."

Agamemnon. Deep down, I'd known he'd killed everyone I loved.

"An untried youth and a warlord – you call that a fair fight?" I said.

Menelaus mumbled something and returned to feigning interest in the graves.

"I asked you, was that a fair fight?"

He hunched over to examine a votive offering. His mouth tried to work a reply.

"Murderers!" My accusation screamed across the distance between us. "Kin-killing, baby-killing murderers! Sons of a kin-killing, child-killing father. You murderers!"

Without knowing how, I was standing before him. My fingers raked at his moon face. A clump of hair came away from his scalp, in my hand. I spat on it, flung it down, ground it underfoot. Garbled curses tore from my throat in someone else's voice. My fists pummelled his chest.

And all the while, he let it happen. He just stood there, head bowed, waiting.

When my violence gave way to tearing sobs, he patted my hand. He hesitated for a few moments, before wrapping his arms around me. "There now, lady. All will be well, you'll see. All will be well. There, there. You'll—" He held me away from him. "You're smiling?"

Not merely smiling. Laughing through my tears. All would be well – he actually believed it. All would be well!

"It's been so long since you last left your chamber," he said. "This is too much for you. Let me take you back to the palace."

"No." I gripped his arm, the arm of a man who'd speared and sliced his way into my world, a man whose brother murdered my husband and child, who gave me to that brother – and yet I found I didn't hate Menelaus Atreides. A bitter feeling, for he deserved to die.

I released him and we watched the imprints of my fingers fade from his skin.

He said, "I'm sorry you're suffering. That was never our wish."

"And Iphitus, what of his suffering?"

Menelaus sighed. "Nothing I say will ease your pain. The throne is rightfully my brother's."

"Thrones belong to the strongest?"

"Yes." His voice held no hint of triumph.

"An illusion, in your case. Agamemnon killed your kin. A miasma hangs over your house. You're tainted if you don't avenge your family, tainted if you do. The gods curse you twice over. You're lost, Menelaus."

"What must be, will be," he said wearily. "To keep one law, sometimes we must break another. The error isn't in choosing wrongly. It's in not choosing at all."

"A riddle?"

"The Followers gave my father a throne. Twice, Thyestes defied their choice, and he paid for his hubris at their hands in his hall. The gods hate kin-killing, it's true, but they also hate disorder and too much pride. I had a duty to help Agamemnon regain his throne."

"What a burdensome duty, to help yourselves to the wealthiest citadel in Achaea." My words rang hollow. What warrior prince wouldn't fight for what he considered to be his god-given right?

But Menelaus' words rang hollow too, and he at least believed them: "Yes, the gods pity Agamemnon. What a terrible burden, to regret everything but know you'd do the same again. May gods and men never leave you in so hopeless a position."

"Family would always be my choice."

He touched my hand. "You didn't ask to be in this situation, I know, but the gods allowed it. Order had to be restored, and now our house can finally be at peace. No more blood need be spilled."

"You think it ends here?" Didn't my son require vengeance? Tantalus too. Even drunken Thyestes, cut down in the hall while guzzling wine from the gods' rhyton.

Menelaus' brow furrowed. "What can you do? Make the best of your situation. Mortals mustn't resist the will of the gods. Don't pine away in grief."

There were moments when such a thing seemed likely, but now I had no intention of going into the earth weeping. Agamemnon had murdered every male who might have avenged my dead. Their blood demanded justice all the same.

And if I should die in the accomplishment?

"What must be, will be," I said.

"If you don't care for yourself," said Menelaus, "at least consider what Tantalus would have wanted for you. I've heard he was a gentle youth. His father led him astray."

"I'll never forget his goodness. He honoured the living – and the dead."

"I'm glad he was kind to you. Who else can a woman turn to in times of need, if not to her husband or king?"

"She turns to the gods."

But the deathless ones don't always trouble themselves with the cares of mortals. Menelaus had reminded me of how alone I was. No friend would aid me in what I must do. No one would speak for me when the blood stained my hands.

So be it.

I walked from the Circle.

The sentries at the Gate of the Sacred Lionesses were closing the bronze-ornamented double doors, locking them with the huge crossbar. A man stood before the shrine, which belonged to Mater Theia, dedicating a thank-offering of pine cones. He wore a coarse travelling tunic and carried no spear. From his shoulder belt hung a sword with a distinctive gold hilt, fashioned to resemble the claws of an eagle grasping the blade.

I raised my gaze to the man's face and a dull ache throbbed in my chest. Olive skin. Dark eyes. Curling black hair brushing his shoulders. Grief curses us to see the shadows of lost lovers in the faces and forms of others. To see our dead children in every newborn child. To hear our parents calling to us from another lifetime.

But this man lacked Tantalus' quick smile. He was taller, too, and his age was closer to mine. His gaze swept over my clothing and took in my seal ring.

"You're from the palace," he said. "Were you Queen Clytemnestra?"

Menelaus emerged from the Circle of the Ancestors. He raised his arm in greeting and strode, beaming, towards the newcomer. "A ram to Hermes of the Wayfarers for guiding you home! Welcome, welcome."

The man submitted briefly to his embrace, before stepping back to release himself. "I rejoice to be home."

"How it warms my heart to see you." Menelaus squeezed the newcomer's shoulder. "Two years, and no messenger."

"I had no message."

Menelaus' hand dropped to his side. Then, remembering the courtesies, he took my elbow to offer my wrist, which the newcomer dutifully clasped. "Forgive me, Aegisthus – I present Clytemnestra, daughter of King Tyndareus of Lacedaemon. Lady, this is my brother."

So this was the foster-son of Atreus, the third head on the chimera, though whether the lion, goat or snake I couldn't tell. Still, at least he was untainted by the family blood.

I'd heard the story of this man's origins from Tantalus, who learned it from the Followers. As a healthy baby, Aegisthus had been abandoned outside the palace. Atreus would have let nature take her course, the usual fate of exposed infants, or allowed the slaves to rear the child to serve in the palace if they wished. But the young queen, Aerope's successor, took pity. As a former priestess of Protectress Athene, she divined that her goddess desired Atreus to raise the child as his own. The shrewd king, no doubt spotting an opportunity to atone for past offences against the helpless, agreed.

"Greetings, Aegisthus. Have you travelled far?" I said.

"Yes." He stalked off towards the low, broad ramp that connected the lower and upper terraces of the citadel.

Menelaus winced in apology. He offered me his arm and we followed his boorish foster-brother, barely able to match Aegisthus' long stride. Aegisthus made no reply whenever Menelaus' bland pleasantries jarred the silence, but his jaw clenched when Menelaus began humming a self-conscious snatch of song.

At the summit of the citadel, instead of continuing around the palace to the official propylon entrance, Aegisthus made for the nearby ceremonial stairway leading directly to the forecourt of the main courtyard. He ignored the guards at the foot of the stairs and on the landing, who struck their spear shafts against their chests in salute. In the forecourt, he halted sharply and stared out across the great courtyard, as if expecting the ancient walls and colonnades to have somehow altered during his two-year absence.

Menelaus sagged onto a stone bench. "Bathe and eat, brother," he panted. "Once you're refreshed, we'll hear all about your adventures."

"Didn't you follow your brothers into exile when Thyestes retook his throne?" I asked Aegisthus.

"I'm no Follower," he said.

I couldn't help smiling. Unlike Menelaus, who would have walked with Agamemnon into the belly of Python, this one seemed less loyal.

"I'll enjoy hearing about your time abroad," I said.

He continued to stare across the courtyard. "I doubt you'll be allowed into the hall to hear it."

"I doubt I'd enter." Without another word, I walked into my throne room, which overlooked the forecourt.

Menelaus' voice carried after me: "Should I send your woman? Or would you rather be alone?" I was already halfway across the saffron-yellow floor and didn't bother to reply.

Time stood still in the throne room, as if the deeds of the last weeks had never been, yet there was a desolate air. A layer of dust coated the tables, the stuccoed benches and the little shrine to the Two Queens. On the crimson wall opposite the throne, the painted figures of Mater Theia and her terrible daughter gazed impassively at a female worshipper whose expression had faded to indecision. The worshipper reached out to the Two Queens, less in homage than as if choosing between Mater Theia, the Lady Who Gives Life, and her daughter, Who Receives Many. My own choice was clear, but the path remained hidden, as if by the dust around me.

I picked up the throne cushion and beat it clean. A different woman sat here last, a queen learning kingship. Not that my ambitions made me neglect the responsibility of managing the household, unlike my ladies during my absence. How strange the throne room was without their chatter, how sterile the air without the rivalry of their perfumes. Usually they worked at looms or sat on the benches along the walls, sewing or playing guessing games or knucklebones. Their younger children spun tops and chased each other; their elder daughters carded wool. It was all so tediously pleasant that I often wished myself elsewhere. What I'd give now for a child's bubbling laughter to warm the chill from my flesh.

How long I sat staring at the walls, scarcely blinking, I couldn't say. At some point, the tangled colours of the wall-hangings turned grey. A slave entered with a torch. He lit the floor lamps on either side of the door. I ordered him not to approach any further. Alone in the darkness, I waited for a sign, a sensation, a revelation as to how a friendless woman could overcome and slay a pitiless warlord.

A sign, Mater Theia, give me a sign.

None came. At last I rose, numb in body and mind.

He spoke so softly, he didn't startle me: "Queen."

Aegisthus stood in the doorway. The flickering lamplight cast his face in light and shadow.

I sat back down. "What do you want?"

"You asked about my time abroad."

"I was being courteous. It's what well-bred people do. But I've other things to think of now."

He took a step into the room. "The poets say the troubles of another can distract from our own, at least for the time taken to tell them."

I halted him with a raised hand. "I'm not seeking distractions, though maybe I should be grateful for the attentions of Agamemnon's brothers. Such kindness from usurpers."

His expression melded with the gloom. "I didn't usurp anything."

"True, you came late, but you're here now to ask for your share. First the conqueror, then the diplomat. What are you? The spy?"

He walked to the bench beside the door and set down his eagle-talon sword and a dagger from the belt around his waist. He sat beside his weapons, not heeding the dust that would dirty his fresh white tunic.

"If I wanted to spy," he said, "I'd have got your measure at the Circle of the Ancestors and you'd be meeting me for the first time right now."

"Well, we're acquainted all the same. Shouldn't you be making up for lost time with your foster-brothers, or are you always so cold when Menelaus opens his arms to you?"

"We're not close."

"Perhaps you'll have more time for Agamemnon. Crumbs fall from kings' laps."

Aegisthus' olive skin darkened in the shadows. "You think I'm a table hound, greedy for scraps?"

"A wolf, if you learned anything from the House of Atreus."

He rose, thrust his sword into his belt, and strode to the throne. "You think you know so much, don't you? A girl a few years gone from clinging to her mother's skirts."

I held up my arms, expecting him to strike me, a good son of his foster-family after all. "You haven't seen what I've seen! You haven't had your child ripped from your breast."

We fell silent. The blood pounded in my ears.

At last he said, "Is that how it happened?"

Now he meant to intrude on my grief, my only refuge? Was there nothing these sons of Atreus wouldn't sully? I said, "Get away from me."

His face hardened like the stiff linen masks worn in sacred dances. "As you like, but let me leave you with a piece of advice.

Agamemnon says he's married you. You should consider where your duty lies. Goddesses and farm wives can grieve endlessly – they aren't bound by restraint. But you are a queen. Wake up from your stupor and act like one."

His words stunned me, and he wasn't finished.

"Go to your husband. He's in Atreus' old apartments. Your former life has gone. You loved your son, of course – any mother would – but he was only a few days old. Most women lose children. Start again. Agamemnon will give you others."

A fit of trembling seized me. I couldn't raise my arm to strike him or force my lips to form a reply.

Grim-faced, message delivered, he turned and stalked from the room.

I waited for the thumping of my heart to steady. When I trusted my legs to support me, I rose and walked to the door. A gleam caught my eye from the bench where Aegisthus had sat. My heart started thudding once more. He'd left his dagger.

CHAPTER 5

I was a bridegroom on my wedding night.

I crossed the moon-washed courtyard, sure that every patrolling guard must sense the bronze blade beneath my skirts, secured to my thigh by my belt. I avoided the colonnades, lit as they were by flickering torches in sconces, in case the guards detected a flush on my face, a new gleam in my eyes.

With my dagger, I'd consummate my marriage to Agamemnon, and the spray would bring not life but death to us both.

And when his body lay still, what then? Turn the blade on myself? Or exult? Show myself to the people and offer thanksgiving sacrifices? Such thanksgiving.

No, there would be no time for celebrations. At their king's screams, his guards would burst into the bedchamber and drag me from his gore, toss me from the citadel walls with his blood on my face. I was ready to die; I welcomed death. Only, let them leave me unburied out on the mountainside to search for the shades of my dead.

I knew Agamemnon couldn't put off visiting me for ever if he wanted heirs, but my lost ones would wait not a day longer. They demanded justice. Tantalus, gentle shepherd-king, dragged from his bed and murdered in his hall. Iphitus, who'd never babble sweet baby-words, never be weaned from my breast, never clutch his first wooden sword carved by his father's hand. Even Thyestes shouldn't have died so wretchedly. Momentarily, I leaned against the wall for support. I mustn't weep now. I'd weep afterwards, if I still lived.

A guard approached me. "Are you hurt, lady?"

I touched my thigh through my flounced skirts, half expecting my fingers to come away wet with blood. The material was soot-black in the darkness.

"I'm stiff through lack of exercise, that's all," I said.

"Would you like me to help you upstairs?"

I toyed with the idea of a traitor – for these men were all traitors – escorting me to the killing of his king. But this one merited no special punishment. He mattered nothing.

"Not especially," I said.

He grimaced and slipped away.

I tried to walk naturally, past the guards in the porch outside the hall. My heartbeat pulsed in my ears as I entered the side doorway and picked my way upstairs. The walk seemed endless through the long Gallery of the Tapestries – where, in a former life, I'd sat around the hearth fire with my ladies, in colder weather. Onwards I went, to the second flight of stairs. Up, to the domestic quarters. I could hardly believe my ambition was at hand.

There were no more guards until I reached the apartments where Thyestes once roared in his sleep for his murdered boys, next to the room where his remaining son dreamed a last dream. They'd hauled Tantalus past the spot where I now stood, along the passageways I'd just walked through, to meet his death at Agamemnon's hands. My heartbeat slowed, my euphoria dissolved.

Another beat and it returned. The guard outside the bedchamber door said, "You've taken a wrong turning, lady."

My voice seemed to radiate from outside myself, as if my goddess spoke through me: "Isn't this my husband's chamber?"

"He's not expecting you."

"Then announce me."

He crossed his spear over his body, as if an empty-handed woman might try to force a way past him. The bronze dagger goaded me, pressing against my thigh like a lover's insistence. But Protectress Athene whispered a warning in my head: I had only one chance. Agamemnon wouldn't suffer a failed executioner to live.

"The king says he's not to be disturbed," said the guard. "You'll have to turn back."

His impassive expression didn't falter, even when a gasp shuddered behind the door, high and girlish. Even as it quickened, accompanied by a male grunt.

Heat flamed my face. The slaves, it seemed, had a new master worthy of the goat Thyestes. I forced a cold smile. My stomach knotted. "Very well. He can have his whore tonight. Tell him his queen shares his bed tomorrow."

"I can't tell him anything, but I'll be sure to repeat your words."

I swallowed the sickening disappointment and turned away. Summoning the reserves of my dignity, I stiffened my back and retraced my steps along the corridor.

CHAPTER 6

The following evening, the same guard still barred my way to Agamemnon's bedchamber. Every few nights, I returned with my dagger; but some guard or another always turned me away, as if I were of no account, so their master could plough his serving slut without his pleasure being cut short by a wife. How proud Thyestes would have been of such a nephew, if that nephew hadn't murdered him.

But my time would come, I was certain. Agamemnon was beginning to trust me. I now moved freely around the palace, without Harmonia or an escort of guards. Sometimes I met Agamemnon's brothers in the corridors. Aegisthus slipped away like a shadow; but Menelaus, bustling about on errands for the usurper, would pause to ask after my health. Menelaus might have proved a useful ally – might perhaps have secured me an audience with Agamemnon – but his bashfulness irritated me. I always managed to send him scurrying off in a fluster. Wisest, I decided, to depend only on myself.

Accordingly, I hatched a plan. I rose one morning before the sun and wrapped myself in a glittering skirt embellished with rows of gold discs. I paired the skirt with a jacket cut to display my bare breasts and tied a wide belt around my waist. With a scarlet paste of crushed beetles, I painted my forearms, nipples and feet. My face I powdered with lead, my eyes with malachite and charcoal. Finally, I teased my dark curls up on my head, secured them with jewelled pins, and let a few locks fall loose. After studying my reflection from all angles in a bronze mirror, I left my apartments.

Slaves emerged from the half-light of the corridors like lizards scuttling from hiding places. They lit oil lamps and swept floors, dusted balustrades, and polished wooden pillars with beeswax. Their master would by now be alone in his hall, staring into the hearth fire. Agamemnon spent little time in his bedchamber; according to the whispers of my ladies, he took his pleasure quickly with whomever he fancied, then rose long before dawn. Perhaps ghosts plagued his sleep, as they had the sleep of Thyestes. Perhaps Erinys, daemon of vengeance, shrieked through his dreams. In his waking hours, did he see his victims in the writhing of the hearth fire? Did they lurk in the shadows beneath the gallery?

From his throne, he could see three sides of this gallery, but a listener might remain hidden on the fourth. I slipped above him now, my heart racing, yet curiously light. When the moment came to reveal myself, I must not allow myself to freeze under his gaze, as I had in Iphitus' nursery and at our sham wedding. I would appear before him in the finery of a queen, painted like a goddess or a whore. Whichever he desired – queen, goddess, whore – I'd be, till we entered his bedchamber. Then, I'd be the wife and mother of his victims.

His voice rumbled through the silence: "Not much of a hunter, are you?"

Icy sweat broke out on my back. My throat dried up.

"You could hold the reins while we men spear the boar," he continued. "Or perhaps you'd rather work wool with the queen's ladies? I hear my wife doesn't spend much time at womanly pursuits. You two could swap skirts."

I leaned against the wall to stem the rivulets trickling between my flesh and the panels of my jacket. Once again, I'd permitted him to affect me, as he had twice already.

Aegisthus answered him – another who had difficulty sleeping? "She's too preoccupied to weave and sew. She's grieving, Agamemnon."

"She's had weeks."

"Yes – to dwell on her ills, as she sees them. She's not a horse you can just break in."

"She's hardly the first woman to be claimed by the warrior who defeated her family. And how many spear prizes are given the status of wife and queen? I've been more than generous, yet she repays me like a bitch pining for its dead master. She's weakening, though." Agamemnon chuckled, a humourless sound. "She's been creeping around outside my chamber. Women need husbands far more than any man ever needs a woman."

"Has she?" said Aegisthus.

"She has, and I don't trust her. Still, I can be patient. If I learned one thing in exile, it was patience. While you spent your days moping about on mountainsides, buggering goats and singing hymns to the moon, the rightful king of Mycenae was travelling the length and breadth of Achaea, winning men to his cause and making warriors of farmers who couldn't tell one end of a spear from the other. Every fibre of me longed to march home and take back what was mine. But I bided my time, I waited to strike, and it's time to strike now—" footsteps thudded on the dais; the back of Agamemnon's head came into view – "straight through the throat of a fat tusker. Well, are you joining the hunt or will we men leave without you?"

"I'll join you. No one else will bring the boar down."

"Keep talking like that and I might start to like you." Agamemnon, hand on Aegisthus' shoulder, steered his foster-brother from the hall.

Once they were gone, I let myself breathe. Agamemnon had again escaped my ambush. No matter. A man's blood runs hottest when he returns from the hunt with new tusks for an ivory war-helmet, while the palace women crowd around him, admiring his bravery and prowess.

I made my way to the courtyard.

Followers in coarse hunting tunics and linen greaves waited in the dawn light, noisy hunting dogs lolloping around their legs. Agamemnon ignored me when I raised my arm to him in greeting. He continued a low-pitched conversation with Aegisthus, whose glance kept slipping to me. At Agamemnon's signal, the hunting party swept past me in a roaring, barking cacophony.

Only one man remained. Until now, I hadn't noticed Menelaus.

"You're not hunting?" I said.

He smiled shyly. "Agamemnon asked me to stay behind in case you needed anything."

I returned his smile. Clever Protectress Athene had inspired me with a plan. "How thoughtful. There is something you could do to cheer me. I'm so melancholy here, in the palace. Take me for a chariot ride."

"I don't think Agamemnon—"

I laid my hand on his arm. "You don't know how bleak my days are. I dwell on my hurts, on things been and gone. If only I could see how the world carries on." I gazed at him imploringly. "Does it carry on, Menelaus? Wouldn't the king want me to see it and believe it?"

And I could intercept Agamemnon as he drove home with his ivories, ensure he returned to me and not one of his serving sluts.

Menelaus rubbed at the bridge of his nose with his knuckles. "Yes…yes, I suppose you're right. Well, if you really think it'll help you, wait here; I'll speak to a groom."

*

When Atreus extended the walls of the citadel, he built a shrine to Mater Theia within the inner court of the Gate of the Sacred Lionesses, a limestone hollow for the goddess whose womb is the vessel of all earthly abundance. Here, worshippers and travellers leave suitable offerings, such as flowers, fruits, sheaves of grain, and figurines fashioned to represent worshippers, lions, pigs and snakes.

"Give me your knife," I ordered Menelaus as our chariot rumbled towards the shrine.

He frowned at me.

"My hair," I said, pulling a curl that spilled over my headband.

He reined in at the shrine. Instead of handing me the knife, he sliced through the strands and placed them in my palm. I tossed the dark lock into the low-burning flame in the sacred hollow, and the tang of sulphur mingled with incense. Holding my palms downwards, I made a bargain with Mater Theia that would have made Menelaus shudder if spoken out loud.

Shadows swayed along the shrine walls, as if my silent words had unsettled the clay devotees and little votive beasts.

When I finished, Menelaus drove the horses out through the Gate of the Sacred Lionesses. He hadn't any need to make an offering to the Mother or seek her aid. He wasn't setting out along an unknown road or hunting dangerous prey. He was no outsider in a hostile land.

The relief sculptures of the Mother's guardian lionesses reared behind us above the gate lintel, forepaws poised on adjacent altars. Between the altars rose a pillar symbolic of the reigning house, the House of Atreus. The lionesses' black steatite heads, facing out from their limestone bodies, seemed to snarl at our departing chariot. I turned away and stared ahead.

*

We continued along the narrow ridge known as the Crone's Spine, which curves past the ancient and recent hill tombs outside the citadel. The air danced around us, lightly ruffling my skirts. Birds shrieked overhead in the dazzling sky, sharper than usual, yet lovelier, as if carrying reassurances from above. For a while, I emptied my mind of all that had happened and all that must be, of the man beside me and the monster I must soon confront, and I thought of my sister, Helen. I remembered how she and I would ride from dawn till dusk, over hills and across the Eurotas Valley; how she sulked when I, her elder, refused her the reins; then she'd catch sight of a pretty hare or bird and laugh again. Should I snatch the reins from Menelaus, drive all the way back to Lacedaemon, to my family, to life?

"Over there! What's she doing out by day?" Menelaus pointed towards a bushy tail disappearing into a den. "What could it mean?"

Foxes on the hillside. The cries of murdered children.

I gripped the chariot rail. "I expect it's an omen. Of sorts."

He didn't seem to think it a bad one. Keen as a scribe at his inventories, he kept up a commentary of trifling remarks about the swooping birds and darting insects. He drew my attention to plants he thought might please me: elegant larkspur, fragrant heliotrope with flowers turned to the sun. He pointed to the hollow trunk of an ancient oak, his secret childhood den. I found myself imagining Menelaus as a boy: shy and inquisitive, more at ease in the company of nature than with playmates and men. At last, he ran out of words. He hummed a tuneless song as we returned towards the citadel.

The most imposing of the hill tombs loomed ahead: Atreus' self-commissioned monument to hubris. For some days I'd observed, from the citadel above, slaves clearing the earth-and-rubble fill from the long dromos leading to the doorway of the tomb. This could only mean one thing: they were making the burial chamber accessible for a new funeral. Briefly, I dared to hope that Agamemnon was making me a wedding gift – the burial of my husband and child – till Harmonia told me about the second funeral planned for Atreus. Agamemnon suspected Thyestes of scrimping on the grave goods for Atreus' westward journey to the Underworld, after he buried him following their final battle.

If Agamemnon had spoken to me, I could have told him how Thyestes boasted of the weapons, jewels and beasts he'd given Atreus. Thyestes was too shrewd to set a bad precedent for the burial of kings. A pity his murderer had no such qualms. Somewhere on the scrubby slopes of Holy Mountain or Arachne's Peak lay the unburied remains of Thyestes and Tantalus. Foxes would have long since dragged away my baby's tiny body, left no trace.

Menelaus stopped humming. "Lady—?"

"Stop the chariot," I cried. "Just stop."

He threw out a hand to catch my arm as I stumbled from the still-moving vehicle. I spun with the force of the rolling wheels, tumbling backwards when the momentum forced him to release me. The baked earth and jagged grass did little to cushion my fall. I raised my wet eyes to Atreus' tomb.

Menelaus reined in the horses and jumped from the chariot. He knelt beside me. "Are you hurt?"

He steadied me while I pushed myself up on grazed palms. I freed myself from his arms. My grief was all I had; I could not allow him to intrude on it, this man whose brother was its cause. I limped a little way along the dromos, grateful for the shade of the retaining walls that rose with the slope of the mound. The gaudy façade of the burial chamber, its crust of red, green and white crystals, blurred with my tears. Such a grand tomb. So few permitted to share it.

A pair of guards stood between the two massive half-columns of green marble that flanked the bronze-ornamented tomb door. They levelled their spears in challenge, before changing the gesture to a startled salute. The door they guarded was high enough to admit a Titan, but a man lay behind it. Next to Atreus lay his second wife, the former priestess Pelopia – the only known daughter of Thyestes. Pelopia's marriage to her uncle ensured she produced no son likely to avenge her three murdered brothers on their killer. Her marriage and mine served much the same purpose.

I halted some distance from the burial chamber. Unwise to approach the dead without offerings.

"Where does your mother lie?" I asked Menelaus, who'd followed me at a respectful distance. I'd asked Thyestes the same question once, but he didn't know where his former lover, Queen Aerope, was buried or even how she died.

"Lady, I don't like to speak of her," said Menelaus quietly.

"Don't you see?" I said, infuriated by his bovine passivity. "Why should they go unpunished, the ones who defile our dead? Is she in a poor woman's grave? Or no grave at all? Agamemnon condemns your cousins and uncle to the same."

Menelaus' face hardened. "Don't expect me to pity Thyestes. My mother's bones lie unburied, somewhere, because of him. Did he boast to you about how he seduced her, how he persuaded her to steal the fleece of kingship from my father?"

He knew the answer before I could hide it from my face. The entire palace, from the bath girls to the highest officials, heard Thyestes' brag of the trick he'd employed to win the throne. On the eve of Atreus' coronation, Thyestes persuaded Atreus and the Followers to swear the most dreadful and binding of oaths – where each man stands on the bloody pieces of a butchered horse

– to accept the possessor of the sacred fleece as rightful king. Everyone swore gladly, believing Thyestes had finally accepted Atreus' claim over his own. But when Atreus stood before all the nobles the next day, the Keeper of the Golden Fleece opened the cedar-wood chest to present him with the sacred garment… and found the chest empty. Thyestes, still dripping with sweat from the processional dance to the palace, peeled off his long cloak to reveal sodden lambswool shot through with gold.

"Thyestes stole the throne, but my father took no revenge," said Menelaus. "Even when the Followers brought Father back after the sun changed its course, all he did was exile Thyestes. Then he learned how the traitor beguiled my mother, how she'd given Thyestes the fleece, and the news brought on a fit of…madness." He stared at the carving above the door lintel of the tomb, two bulls frozen mid-leap in eternal combat. "Thyestes bears the blame for everyone he used and discarded. For his sons. For my father. And for my mother – my poor, poor mother."

He fell so silent and motionless in the gloom of the tomb walls, I fretted over whether to return him to the present with a touch of my hand.

"It was a fit of madness," he said at last. "And Father made us…watch."

"Those murdered boys, the sons of Thyestes? You were at that horrible supper?"

"Mother, he made us watch Mother."

His words tumbled out, a monstrous family secret. Not enough for Atreus, the gruesome revenge he took on Thyestes. I listened, transfixed, though I pitied Menelaus the telling.

"At the end of that awful supper, the guards threw Thyestes from the palace and Mother sat sobbing. Father went to her, wrapped his fingers in her hair. 'There, there,' he said. He told her to get up, and she tried to obey, she really did. But she stumbled, like after a beating. She would have fallen if he hadn't held her up, his knuckles white in her hair. He dragged her from the hall. And her screams, her screams…"

He heard them now, the undying screams of the dead.

"I could hardly stand either, but Father ordered us to follow. Agamemnon kept me upright. Father led us upstairs to the Red Bathroom. The water in the bath was steaming. How it must have scalded. 'Watch how we repay our enemies,' Father said. 'Your mother prepared herself for her lover in this bath.' He pushed her. Her skirts caught at her feet like nets. She fell down the steps into the water."

"Menelaus, you don't have to—"

"Agamemnon held my head between his hands, forcing me to watch. 'They gave him no choice,' he whispered, over and over, his lips pressing into my ear. I barely heard him through my screams. I thought my neck would snap from trying to escape the hands pressing into my temples. Father was glistening like Poseidon. He cursed me for a coward but was too busy holding Mother under the water to deal with me. She thrashed and twisted; then, after a while, she didn't struggle so much. Agamemnon let my face go. He held me to his chest. 'Look away,' he said. 'I'll look for us.' Then Father was standing over us, rubbing his fingers. 'Take that weakling away,' he panted. 'I'll think of a punishment later.'"

"He punished you?" I cried, appalled.

"No, he punished Agamemnon. He often did, for my mistakes – to make us strong. If I cried, Father beat him even harder. But I didn't cry when he whipped him the next morning. I felt nothing, and neither, I think, did Agamemnon. It took a long time for the numbness to pass. We never spoke of our mother again."

Yet he'd spoken to me. "Oh, Menelaus."

And after today, the numbness would return, Menelaus would mourn. I hadn't forged the knife that the men of his family passed from one bloodstained hand to the next, as if it were the sacred flame in a relay race, but I would wield it in turn. If those men believed they had little choice in their deeds, I had far less. Was I to betray the tormented shades of my dead, who cried out for justice? Should a mother forsake her murdered son as no father ever would? The blood of my dead was worth more than a throne or a cuckold's wounded pride.

But it was bitter indeed, this knowledge that I'd bring more grief to gentle Menelaus.

He'd fallen silent and I had no words of comfort. The image wouldn't leave my mind: two boys in a bathroom – my bathroom – watching their mother drown. Then I realised my arms were around Menelaus' back, and his chin rested on my shoulder. I wondered how to separate our bodies without embarrassing us both. Menelaus sighed and shuffled, as if he'd step away. He resettled his chin. His soft cheek quivered against mine.

I said, "No child should know such suffering at the hands of brutal men."

He pulled back, startled. "Forgive me. I didn't mean to…I'd never try to…"

I took his hand and squeezed it in futile sympathy.

*

We passed the short drive back to the citadel in a heavy but intimate silence. I felt closer to Menelaus than I'd ever imagined possible, and I'm certain he felt the same. Underneath his meekness was a man of dignity and quiet strength. When all of this was over, I hoped he'd begin a family of his own, a happier one, and rule Mycenae wisely and well. By then, he'd despise me. He'd pour no libations to quench the thirst of my shade. But my execution and barren womb would break the cycle of vengeance. Menelaus' reign would bring peace for the first time in generations. He was not a warlike man.

Chariots rumbled behind us on the pathway.

"Stop here, let them pass," I said.

A snaking dust cloud hid the returning hunters and barking dogs. I hardly dared breathe while we waited for the first chariot to catch us up. Aegisthus was driving the horses, while Agamemnon stood beside him in the car, holding the head of a young boar by its tusks, his weather-beaten face flushed with victory.

"Lord," I greeted him, forcing awe into my voice. I let my fingers linger at my throat, a favourite gesture of my sister's for directing a man's attention.

Agamemnon's expression remained stony, even as his gaze dropped from my throat to my breasts. His torso resembled a stinking, matted mongrel left out in the rain.

"Why isn't she in the palace?" he asked Menelaus.

"I've grown weary, since my lord doesn't visit me," I said coyly. Sickened.

He glared at me. I knew my blunder at once: my revelation embarrassed him in front of his men. The hunters in the nearest chariots feigned deafness. Aegisthus, with a distracted air, patted the rumps of his restless horses.

"A man decides when he'll visit his wife or when he prefers someone else," said Agamemnon. "Be where you should be, and I'll visit when I will."

His horses started forward at Aegisthus' prompt.

Menelaus managed a comforting if anxious smile for me as we waited for the last chariot to pass by. I beamed back at him. My blunder was fortunate. I'd shamed Agamemnon into visiting my chamber.

*

We returned once more to the walled and subdued citadel. In the palace, I ordered my maids to bring a bathtub to my apartments. I was loath to enter the red-floored bathroom where Queen Aerope died.

The maids bathed and anointed me, then dressed me in a simple regal purple tunic and applied a light touch of powder to my face. Agamemnon, I now suspected, might find a demure wife more to his taste than the painted, glittering version he'd met earlier today. The notion almost made me retch.

When the maids finished spreading the bed with fresh, inviting coverlets and scattering it with extra cushions, I dismissed them and rummaged through a chest crammed full of rolls of cloth for dressmaking. My hand closed around a linen package. I sat on the edge of the bed, stiff and sore after my earlier fall from the chariot, and peeled the wrapping from the bronze object inside. Aegisthus' dagger. I selected a particularly plump cushion, slipped the dagger underneath, and waited for Agamemnon.

Alert to every step in the corridor, I waited, and waited. And I thought again of two boys waiting for their mother to drown. Gentle Menelaus forgave his murderous father, as he now excused Agamemnon's crimes, but he'd hate me for this night's work. I couldn't spare his pain. My duty lay with the dead, as his did with those who still lived. We each had a duty to our family, and it was sacred.

Dusk descended impossibly slowly beyond the narrow window. Grey gave way to black, and still Agamemnon did not come. My expectation turned to despair. I sank on to my side on my bed and wept, uselessly clutching the dagger's hilt beneath the cushion.

Once before, I'd anticipated a consummation that wasn't to be, when Tantalus and I prepared to gift each other our virginity on our wedding night. Thyestes' night terrors had interrupted us, but the next evening I helped my young husband from his tunic while his trembling fingers plucked at my laces, clasps and pins. His lips awakened in me a warm rush of pleasure. He kissed my neck and shoulders, asked if I was ready, and we made clumsy, tender love. How were we to know our first embrace would be one of our last?

I blinked away my tears. Agamemnon mustn't find me weakened, if he found me here at all.

A heavy tread sounded in the corridor. My heart froze. The door swung open, and Agamemnon's repulsive bulk filled the doorway. His fleecy chest, above a short kilt, glistened in the light of the wall lamps, freshly oiled. My stomach churned as he approached the bed. The sinews in his thick legs stood out like cords. His shoulders were broad as Poseidon's.

Atreus, glistening like Poseidon, holding Aerope beneath the bathwater.

I tried to rise on my elbows, light-headed. Did I have the strength to deliver the blow, with such a body crushing down on mine?

"Lie still," he ordered.

He gripped my shoulders and I tasted bile. His torso loomed over me, too close for my eyes to find a spot where muscle didn't plate his innards like armour.

He tugged at the knots of my girdle. "Get this thing off."

"Then get off me!'

Instantly, I regretted my harsh tone. I rose and undressed with my back to him. The dimness of the chamber masked the scrapes and bruises from my earlier fall. When I stood naked, he seized my shoulder and turned me around. He nodded in approval as I hid my groin behind my hands.

His bull neck – I'd strike there. And if he saw the blow coming? One chance. I had only one chance.

He groped and prodded at my flesh, as if choosing choice cuts of meat at a sacrificial feast. When he shoved me back down on the bed, I couldn't prevent my whole body from twisting and recoiling. He seemed unoffended. I think he smiled. His weight bore down on me, pinning my arms to my sides and preventing his attempts to knee my thighs apart. He shifted on to one elbow, hoisted my leg and stabbed into me.

I screamed. I threw back my arm and fumbled under the cushion for the dagger. He grabbed my forearm and slammed it down by my side. "Don't play the slut. I like you modest."

I waited, bracing myself against each thrust, until he seemed absorbed in his pleasure. I slid my arm upwards. He seized my wrists and clasped them against my shoulder without breaking his rhythm.

I focused on easing one hand free, ignoring the pain inside me. My hand reached the pillow. He smacked my face and folded my arms beneath him.

At last, his body buckled and his girth rolled off me. My arms were paralysed, pierced through by numberless pins. Winded, eyes stinging with tears, I watched him stride from the chamber.

CHAPTER 7

Twice daily, I sank into a clay tub in my bedchamber, yet still I felt polluted. Every step in the corridor made me sweat in the cool water. My maids shrank from assisting me, skittish as deer at the barking of hounds. Strange to say, since I trusted no one, Harmonia's stolid presence was my mainstay. Before long, she was the only maid who dared to wash me and dress me, the only one I tolerated.

Shortly after Atreus' second funeral, which I wasn't asked to attend, she broke the news of the departure of Agamemnon and Menelaus.

"Where are they?" I said, though I couldn't have cared less, at least for Agamemnon's whereabouts. Then, more urgently, "When will they be back?"

"They don't confide in me, I'm sure," she said, tying an embroidered girdle over my skirts. "I only know that you should take some air, restore balance to your body." She didn't need to add, *And to your mind.*

Now that Agamemnon was gone, I needed no further prompting to leave the room where he'd consummated our hateful marriage.

Down in the courtyard, two guards loitered under the colonnades, while a third wandered back and forth and yawned up at the morning sky. A cook, frying flat cakes on a griddle over a brazier, turned his frowning face to the heavens. A few drops of rain splashed onto the painted floor. Oil hissed in the pan as the cook flipped his cakes. I caught the aroma of warm honey, but it did nothing to revive my appetite.

To my chagrin, the Protectress' courtyard shrine lay neglected. Harmonia cleared away the withered flowers and spoiled fruit, then went to fetch fresh offerings for the goddess and a drinking-saucer of milk for Agathos Daemon. The snake had abandoned his niches in the shrine. He'd likely be basking in some sunny spot away from the pacing of the guards, but I couldn't see him anywhere.

While waiting for Harmonia's return, I considered how to spend the day. A visit to the herbwife, the crone from the town below the citadel, would be prudent. My women often sought her remedies for problems they didn't dare reveal to the palace herbcutters. But such a trip might attract attention. Best to avoid the herbwife and her dangerous cures till I knew whether or not I needed them. Instead, I'd summon my ladies to my throne room. We'd work at our looms and enjoy the brief return to pleasant, dreary normality while it lasted.

A rustle distracted me from my thoughts. In the porch outside the king's hall, the graceful tip of a red-blotched tail uncoiled and whipped from view. Agathos Daemon. No sentries stood between the pillars of the porch. One guard was now dozing upright on a bench in the courtyard, while the other two ate flat cakes and chattered like laundry women. I slipped unseen between the pillars and through the open bronze door. In the almost lightless vestibule, Agathos Daemon snapped his slender head towards me. His eyes gleamed with preternatural fire, coaxing me to follow him. He glided beneath the scarlet curtain.

I drew the curtain aside, and Aegisthus stepped through; a series of expressions flitted across his olive-skinned face, before it settled into a bland mask. "Lady, you look well."

Stomach sinking, I peered around him, expecting to see Agamemnon seated splay-legged on the throne. The hall was empty.

"You're back?" I said.

"I never left. What did you want in the king's hall?"

The truth, that the snake led me here, would have sounded ridiculous. "Not to sit on his throne, but how did you find it?"

He grimaced. "I suppose he told you his plans before he left?"

He surely knew Agamemnon had done no such thing. "If he did, I wasn't listening. Where is he?"

"Lacedaemon." Though Aegisthus' manner was quiet, he might as well have struck me.

"What…what business could he have there?"

Gently, as if speaking to a highly strung child, he said, "To settle your dowry with your father."

"Dowry? It carries over from my first marriage! He should be paying my father compensation, not renegotiating dowries."

Aegisthus glanced over his shoulder in time to see the serpent slither beneath the legs of the empty throne. "He's left me to guard over Mycenae in his absence. That's why you found me in his hall. Is there anything you need? Can I do anything for you?"

"Only if you're prepared to be as treacherous a brother as Atreus or Thyestes."

"I'm not them. Listen, Clytemnestra, I know we got off to a bad start. I was unkind to you. I didn't know you. And returning to Mycenae after everything that's happened…" His excuse trailed off.

The thought struck me as I studied his handsome, guarded face: what if he and Agamemnon had plotted together to test me with the dagger?

"You're alone." He gave an awkward shrug. "I can at least try to be a friend to you."

The offer was as unexpected as it was unwanted. I'd sooner trust a wolf in a sheepfold.

"I want nothing from you." I nodded politely and returned to the courtyard, where Harmonia waited with Agathos Daemon's milk.

*

Aegisthus was the least of my concerns as the weeks drifted by. The thought of Agamemnon's presence defiling the little palace in Lacedaemon citadel, my peaceful childhood home, nauseated me. I feared for my gentle parents and pretty sister. I fretted for Laconia, the land ruled by my father, our rich plain and abundant valley. I only hoped Menelaus would curb the greediest of Agamemnon's demands.

Something else troubled me too. My bleed hadn't come.

Mater Theia often spared me the tyranny of my cycle. Girlhood feuds with Helen were enough to disrupt me, as were the months of preparation for my wedding to Tantalus. Before I left for Mycenae, my mother made me sacrifice to Mater Theia for the return of my menses; a woman needs a store of blood, it's said, to nurture her husband's seed. If only I'd remained bloodless and barren, Iphitus needn't have been born, and I needn't fear now that Agamemnon's seed had taken root in my womb.

Harmonia noticed my missed bleed. To my astonishment, she proposed a visit to the herbwife in the lower town. In the pragmatic way I was coming to know so well, she suggested I might not be ready in body and mind to carry Agamemnon's child. I was young, she said; I'd have many sons in time. Besides, better to consult with a woman who specialised in women's bodies than the palace herbcutters who cared more about men's wounds than women's bleeds.

Was she testing me, gathering evidence to make a report? What did it matter? So long as no one tried to stop me. Yet it seemed as if something had passed between us, an understanding that only women can share, of a reality no man ever knows.

I ordered her to fetch some long cloaks and good sandals, and we set out.

*

I'd never before had any reason to enter the town below the citadel. The sight of it was so familiar from the palace high above, I paid it no more mind than I would a rug beneath my feet. From the citadel, it resembled a cluster of dolls' houses within a winding fortification wall. I'd imagined it could be crossed from end to end, densely populated though it was, without pausing to catch one's breath.

The reality, I now discovered, was a disorientating labyrinth of crowded alleyways. Hammers rang incessantly. Smoke billowed from smithies. Incense drifted from shrines. The overpowering stink of dyes and perfumes wafted from workshops. We raised our skirts to avoid soiling them with the dung of the braying, grunting, bleating livestock, which carters and herdsmen drove past us. Townsfolk hurried about their business or loitered in groups, their clothing stained by earth or dye, grease, soot or blood. Still others wore the pristine robes of slaves of the gods.

Too many stares came our way. Our cloaks felt too clean, too expensive with their fine stitching, and I hadn't thought to wipe the paint from my face or remove my jewellery. But surely, cloaked as I was, no one would recognise me from the few ceremonies I'd presided over before Tantalus persuaded me to take more rest during my pregnancy. Or might one or two have glimpsed me in the palace when they presented their tithes to the inventory scribes? Met me in the king's hall when I sat at Tantalus' side to hear petitions?

To my relief, the cramped alleys eventually broadened and the traffic thinned. The jumble of buildings gave way to spacious houses with twitching shutters. Harmonia pointed to a pillar topped by a bronze sculpture of a squatting woman, whose enormous belly shone from the touch of countless hands. It stood outside a handsome two-storey house of stone and mud-brick. I rubbed the statue's belly for luck. Harmonia knocked at the door.

An answering maidservant probed our cloaks with a penetrating stare. "Who will I say is calling, and why?"

"Tell your mistress…" Like a libation from a spilled cup, my mind emptied of the name and background I'd dreamed up for myself during the walk through town. "Just tell her to receive us, and quickly. I'll discuss my business with her alone."

The girl shrugged. She led us across an altar-filled courtyard and into a waiting room decorated with frescoes of maternity. A painted clay idol of the Lady of Childbirth occupied the centre of the room, on a plinth between two stuccoed benches. Gold and bronze armlets covered the goddess's arms; a necklace heavy with beads of carnelian, amber and blue lapis draped her neck. Suggested offerings, I presumed. The herbwife's clients might be anxious enough to relinquish their trinkets while they waited an eternity for the old woman to see them.

"Oh, where is she?" I rose from the bench, where I'd been sitting with Harmonia, to pace the small waiting area.

"All will be well," said Harmonia, gazing at the goddess.

"She's waiting to hear my jewellery rattle." I shook my bracelets.

The maid stuck her head through the doorway. "My mistress will see you now."

The girl took us to a hall adorned with wall frescoes illustrating the three stages of womanhood: from graceful maidens dancing at shrines, to heavy-breasted mothers nursing infants, and stout crones teaching granddaughters to weave. Likenesses of flowers and herbs decorated the floor. I wondered which of these matched the ingredients in the head-swirling bouquets rising from a variety of burners and boilers that smoked and steamed on portable hearths throughout the hall. I half regretted not sending Harmonia alone for the medicines, but couldn't have risked an unsuitable prescription by not letting the herbwife examine me.

The witch herself stood at the fixed central hearth, stirring a tripod cauldron. Her lips stretched into a foxlike grin. "What an honour! Ah, yes, I'd know your noble face anywhere. And if I'd only known you desired my services...Can it be, you have excellent news, great lady?"

I threw a glance at her maid.

"Oh, she's trustworthy," said the herbwife. "That's why I pay her so generously from the little I have. I guarantee the utmost discretion, and I'm sure such a lady as you will do the same, if necessary."

"Tell her to leave," I said.

The old woman flicked her fingers and the girl slipped from the hall. She balanced her ladle against the inside of the cauldron and wiped her hands on her apron. "I am Eritha, as you doubtless know, the most esteemed practitioner of my calling. Well-born women come to me from near and far. In my vast years of experience, I've assisted queens and commoners alike – anyone who can cover my modest expenses. My medicines and charms will deliver whichever effects you require, as will my services when the joyous day arrives. Which, of course, you anticipate with gladness?"

"You'll examine me," I said. "You'll prescribe a tonic to wilt the seedling in my belly, a charm to ensure the tonic works, and a prayer to speak over the charm. Say nothing of this to anyone, and I'll reward you handsomely."

The loquacious witch patted her pot belly with a scrawny hand. "Come this way."

We followed her into a side chamber furnished with two stools and an oxhide bed. A disturbing array of instruments were spread across tables, along with alabastrons of every size, which sent up aromas of herbs with underlying noxious notes.

"I don't expect extravagant payment," said Eritha. "It's my honour merely to serve you. Just pay what you believe my faultless expertise deserves."

I gritted my teeth, lay on the bed and raised my skirts. "As I said, handsomely."

The woman prodded and poked at me, while asking a string of questions about my last pregnancy and delivery, my health, and my relations with Agamemnon. Finally, she straightened up, bony limbs creaking. "Your womb has indeed quickened. The seed's been lodged fast for some time, not much chance of a natural miscarriage. Exposing the living child would be the safest option, though my special purging draught is more discreet. It's a precious elixir made from the rarest ingredients, a formula passed down through the wise women of my family for generations."

A new hope struck me. "Could it be possible…? Might a seed lie dormant before it blossoms? Perhaps all my nurturing blood went to Iphitus, but all along I carried twins?" I'd only lain with Agamemnon once. Surely I wasn't one of those women cursed with a fatal womb that quickened every time?

The herbwife pressed her fingertips together and considered. "True, I've known of long-delayed births, even among widows whose husbands died years earlier. But never with twins. The trauma of labour expels the unhatched seedling along with the living twin. No, this is new seed, lady. Female, judging by the signs, so you needn't feel too much regret."

My hopes turned to ashes in my stomach. "Just give me the remedy."

"Ah, but first I must travel the plain to locate all the ingredients – time and skill, that's why my business is such an expensive one. It's not as if I'm giving you wormwood to sprinkle in your bathwater – nothing so crude for you. When the potion's ready, I'll send my girl for payment and the cure will follow. Which brings me back to the delicate matter of price."

"You won't receive a bauble until I have the cure. I'll pay the equivalent of a roll of saffron-dyed cloth on delivery. When the cure succeeds, I'll send the cloth. And I warn you, under no circumstances come to the palace yourself or tell anyone what you're doing."

The crone folded her thin arms above her bulging belly. "Well! Of course, I'd never expect the full price from my queen, even if I'll be chewing asphodel roots for lack of a decent meal – what with the taxes I pay to the palace. So be it. It's to your good, after all." She managed a sour little smile for Harmonia, whom I'd quite forgotten. "If any of the palace folk recognise my girl, just say the potion's for your maid, here. Though if you want a dose for her, I'll have to charge extra."

Harmonia's hands flew to her belly.

The herbwife chuckled. "Well, if I wasn't certain before, I am now."

I turned sharply to my serving woman. "Have you something to tell me?"

She bowed her head. "There's a young man. He's fond of me, lady, and I'm fond of him. He'll provide for me."

I sighed. I'd begun to rely on Harmonia, at least a little. The pregnancy was an inconvenience. "Does he want to marry you?"

"He can't," she admitted.

"I suppose you could go to his household, if his wife needs a maid and doesn't resent you too much."

"Let me stay with you. Please, lady. The child will be no burden. I'll make sure it's well trained."

I patted Harmonia's narrow shoulder. I'd have regretted losing so efficient a servant. "Very well, though you should have told me sooner."

"Haven't you enough to think of?" she said. "I can serve you right up till the birth and return to my duties as soon as I'm purified."

Eritha nodded. "As indeed she should, if she's to be worth the bread you feed her. But if you're fond of her, and if you value her health, you'll want an amulet to protect her, at the very least. A spell, too." She extended a bony finger to tap an unguent jar on one of the tables. "And this balm, rubbed over her belly, will ensure a beautiful child – more valuable to you, as its owner."

"Keep your overpriced remedies," I said, as Harmonia helped me back into my cloak. "Send the cure in seven days, and remember to tell no one. Good day, herbwife."

CHAPTER 8

I spent the day of the promised delivery in my throne room, working at my loom with Harmonia while waiting for Eritha's maid. Since childhood, I've always prided myself on my skill as a weaver – a woman should excel in the practical virtues when her sister excels in charm. But my mind was far from my web, and far, too, from the chatter of my ladies, who carded and spun wool.

"Where *is* the girl?" I whispered to Harmonia, who separated the warp threads while I plied the shuttle. "What if something's happened?"

"The herbwife won't risk losing the fee," she replied, "unless of course the gods have other plans."

Harmonia's mind, to my disquiet, was travelling down the same dark path as mine.

"No woman can thwart divine will," I said gloomily.

"True, but there's nothing to be gained from fretting. We can only do what we can, then it's out of our hands."

Unlike the faded worshipper on the wall opposite the throne, who dithered between the Two Queens – between Mater Theia, Who Brings to Blossom, and the terrible daughter Who Reaps, I knew what I must do. Gods and men had brought me to this. I only hoped my guardians would remember me when the time came to drink the cure. Earlier in the morning, I'd made offerings at Protectress Athene's courtyard shrine and implored her to watch over me. Agathos Daemon was coiled in one of his niches. His head glided towards me like a whip, his tongue darting defensively. A film covered his red eyes; dullness marred his brilliant scales. Never before had I seen an ailing serpent, for we kept no house snake in the palace at Lacedaemon. His sickness seemed ill-omened, though I judged it unwise to seek an explanation from the palace diviners.

The day wore on. When the boy came to light the lamps, I set down my shuttle and dismissed my ladies. After a while, I dismissed Harmonia too, weary of her serenity, of the way her hand kept slipping to her still-flat belly. I'd known that sense of anticipation once. Certain Eritha's maid wouldn't come, I sank on to the throne. I was half musing, half dozing when footsteps roused me.

A guard in the doorway saluted me with a tap of his short spear against his chest. "A herbcutter to see you, lady. Says her name's Eriphyle. She's come about your woman."

"Erith-Eriphyle?" My voiced sounded too sharp in the empty hall. "I don't know an Eriphyle. I haven't sent for her. Still, I suppose you'd better show her in."

He ducked into the vestibule and returned with the herbwife Eritha, who flashed me a simpering smile. Though he kept his distance from her, he asked, "I'll wait here, will I, lady? These witches – she could be trouble."

I waved my hand in dismissal and imagined it cracking across Eritha's face. "No need; she looks more like a fool than a sorceress. Is that what you are, old woman? A fool?"

Eritha tittered. She said nothing until the guard's footsteps faded, then launched into her explanation. "I'm sure you'll consider me most prudent, lady. You see, I could hardly leave the delivery to a silly maid, who might—"

"Step closer."

She kept up her prattle as she followed the crook of my finger. "You know how these girls are. She'd have stopped along the way to hear the love-talk of some handsome herdsman returning from the fields, or ended up in the guardhouse with one of your young men here. Why, a woman in my business knows these things. And if you're wondering why I'm late, you can't imagine the trouble I went to, securing all the ingredients. Then there's the art of preparing and blending the elixir. And all in seven days!"

"Do you realise the trouble your visit might cause me? What if someone recognises you? Half the ladies in the palace have used your services."

She tapped her chin with a bony finger. "Half? That's something of an exaggeration, as my storerooms confirm."

"Your storerooms are the real reason you're here. You want to make sure you get everything I promised. You're afraid I'll change my mind or your maid might take a fancy to a shiny pin, a couple of beads."

The herbwife sucked in her cheeks. "Nothing could be further from my mind."

"Good. Because whether the cure works or not, you can forget the second half of your payment if your visit sets tongues wagging."

Scowling, the witch opened the bag tied around her plump waist and fished out a stoppered flask, which she gave me. "You couldn't buy a gentler or more effective cure than this. It can't possibly fail – unless the goddesses want it to, then there's nothing you or I can do about that. Just make sure to take it as soon as I leave, while I'm sending prayers for your success." She dipped into the bag and pulled out a copper talisman on a leather cord. "And wear this while you drink the elixir. It's a thing of beauty in itself, and that's not counting its extraordinary power. Don't remove it for three days, not even in your bath."

I held up the talisman, a crude thing embossed with a plant. The thick phallic stalk and frothy blossoms, clustered above several pairs of arm-like leaves, suggested fertility rather than miscarriage, yet what else could I do but trust Eritha? I slipped the cord over my neck. The pendant clacked against my seal-ring from Tantalus.

Lastly, she produced a cheap alabastron. "I can't deny you'll have some pains, but rub this unguent into your belly and you'll think a lover's caressing you. You'll be up and standing at your loom in no time." She smiled, revealing a row of flat little teeth, doubtless ground down through years of testing the purity of ingots. "Now, returning to the matter of my fee…"

I placed the flask and alabastron next to an empty kylix on the table beside me. The previous night, Harmonia and I had selected Eritha's payment from among my jewels, dropping rings and necklaces into a wooden casket. I now instructed the old woman to wait while I made my way through the draughty corridors of the palace to the storeroom where I'd left the casket.

Which items should be deducted? Oh, the jewellery mattered little to me. It announced a person's status, and mine as queen of Mycenae was a curse. But I was loath to reward the herbwife for marching through the palace with her bag of cures.

Her face fell when I returned and dropped the casket into her outstretched hands. It was half as light as before. Forgetting all decorum, she shrieked, "You're robbing me! Didn't we agree—?"

"We agreed you wouldn't come to the palace. You broke our agreement, and now you may leave. And if the king learns about your part in this, a few jewels will be the least you'll lose."

She bent her head over the casket, breathing hard, until she composed herself enough to speak. "As you wish. And I won't forget to pray for you. No one can say I'm not generous, poor woman though I am, with no husband or child to support me in my winter years."

I turned my back and stood motionless while an age seemed to pass, waiting for Eritha to be clear of the palace, clear of the citadel gates.

At last, I reached out with a trembling hand for the flask. The herbwife was gone, and the danger was only beginning. What if Eritha had miscalculated the dose? Even if she hadn't, would it hurt very much? My mother hurt every time her body rejected the bloody matter of pregnancy or a tiny infant who'd never known life. I used to mop her legs, while her ladies fussed over her and my sister wept.

The stopper fell to the floor from my fumbling fingers. I watched my hand pour the liquid. How dark the cure gleamed in my silver kylix. It smelled of bedchamber spices, of cinnamon and myrrh, masking decay.

My throat closed up as I raised the kylix towards my mouth. Strange, I'd never before noticed the artist's intricate handiwork all around the cup, the embossed borders of sacred knots, the rows of double-headed axes.

I held the rim to my lips. If I didn't drink, the seed might still pass from me. If I drank, I might be poisoned, and Agamemnon would live.

The heady scent clouded my senses. The barrier at the back of my throat opened. I tipped the cup.

It flew from my hand and clattered to the floor.

Aegisthus stood before me, gabbling, gesturing at the fallen kylix. His face was grey. I couldn't understand what had happened or what he wanted.

He swept his hand across the table and knocked the flask to the floor, where it shattered into three large chunks. The last of the cure formed a sticky pool around the broken pieces. I dropped to my knees and scooped at the liquid with my hands. Aegisthus' fingers dug into my shoulders.

"Woman—" he shook me; his words came disjointed to my ears – "might – killed you – fool." Then, more clearly: "... know how dangerous these potions are?"

"How did you…?" Eritha couldn't have betrayed me. She'd never have risked her payment.

He lifted the amulet from my chest, where it lay over Tantalus' seal ring. He let it fall back down and pulled me to my feet. "I saw the witch from town leaving your throne room. She said your maid was with child, you'd bought a sickness remedy." He laughed scornfully. "A girl like that isn't worth a casket of jewels. So I tested her. I said I knew why she was here: to ensure you wouldn't bear my child."

Stunned, I couldn't speak.

"She swallowed the lie. I offered to double what you'd paid her, if she told me what she'd prescribed. But I swore I'd hang her with my own hands if any harm came to my seed."

I struck his face.

He cupped my cheek instead of his. A pulse fluttered in his hand and travelled through my clammy skin. I could neither breathe, nor pull away.

"What have I done?" he whispered.

His voice released me. I stumbled from the throne room and into the courtyard. At the Protectress' shrine, I fell down and clasped the pillar in the central niche as if it were the goddess's knees.

"Lady, hear me. Hear me, hear me," I cried.

Did she mean for me to fail, my own protectress, for my womb to nurture the child of my child's killer? Was Aegisthus her instrument? Had goddesses no sympathy for their sex?

"Is there no justice?" I sobbed. "Can this really be your will? Show me a sign, goddess, show me what to do."

Silence.

"Give me a sign! I must do what you will."

A rustle. Agathos Daemon slithered from the right-hand niche of the shrine and glided towards me. Even in the twilight, his tawny scales gleamed like jewels. Fire rimmed the black obsidian of his eyes. In his wake, he trailed a sheath of diaphanous skin.

Not that sign. Now I understood his earlier strangeness. The serpent was reborn. Sleek and sinuous, he glided around my knees. I thrust out my hand and willed him to strike.

"He killed my baby," I wept, in accusation – in plea. "Oh, my guardians, must I become the mother of his?"

A little boy laughed. I turned to see Iphitus totter towards me across the courtyard, on unsteady legs. He grew taller. He brandished a training sword, yelled at an invisible opponent. He strode to the grand stairway in the costume of the Young God, Dionysus, eager to preside over his first festival.

I saw Aegisthus, his unfathomable eyes, his confusion. *What have I done?*

I saw another child. Naked, without a face.

"Would you deny my dead their blood-price?" I implored the goddess.

Soft as the promised caress of Eritha's unguent, Agathos Daemon twined around my wrist. He coiled his way upwards, his embrace tightening, loverlike. When his head reached my shoulder, he blinked his ancient bright eyes at me.

I ground my palms into the floor in communion with my goddess, but she had nothing more to say. I rose on shaking legs, weeping, broken. I watched Agathos Daemon slither away.

The goddess had willed that a child would be born. Broken things must mend or else be swept away – this, alone, remained my choice to make.

CHAPTER 9

Harmonia knew of a cave a short journey from the citadel, with a natural altar and a stone cradle carved by a kindly god's hand. We loaded a pack mule and made our way to this place, three mornings after Protectress Athene's intervention.

We set lamps on rocky ledges inside the cave; we burned incense of precious myrrh. On a bed of moss, I placed a love token from Tantalus, a lily-shaped pendant from which tiny pomegranates dangled on delicate twists of his hair. Close by, I placed a cutting of Thyestes' hair; I'd retrieved this a lifetime ago from the dustheap, in case I ever needed it for a spell. It was black, flecked with grey – just as the hair of Tantalus and Iphitus might one day have become, if only they'd lived.

A roll of swaddling cloth took the place of my baby's body. I held it to my breast, then laid it in the stone cradle. At the head of the cradle, I set a clay warrior to guard over the swaddling. It stood no taller than Iphitus might by now have grown. The warrior held a little sword, since a spear would remind him of how his father died.

We made offerings to my dead that wouldn't have been recorded in the palace inventories, that wouldn't be missed: trinkets, simple utensils, jewellery given to me as wedding gifts. I placed the ash-wood shepherd's crook of Tantalus' boyhood to one side of the lily pendant. In life, he'd held this crook with a surer hand than he held the golden sceptre of Mycenae.

"Use it, gentle one, to guide our son," I told him.

Harmonia placed a small cauldron next to a channel in the floor. She filled it with honey, water and wine from three amphorae, then tipped the cauldron over. We watched the liquid seep into the earth. Whether my dead would taste the libation, I didn't know. Nor did I know how to commune with them, whether to lower my palms as one did with those below, or raise my arms as to those above.

I held out my arms before me. "Thyestes and Tantalus, kings of high-walled Mycenae. Darling Iphitus, blameless prince. Accept this drink of forgetfulness and take comfort from these gifts as you seek a path back to the Mother's womb."

There are four kinds of restless dead, so it's said: those felled by violence, justly or unjustly; those who never married or had children; those who died unnaturally, before their allotted time; and those deprived of their lawful funeral rites. My baby was all of these. I had done what I could to right this last injustice, though I feared it wasn't enough. I'd washed Iphitus' swaddling as if it were his milk-sweet skin; anointed the hair of Tantalus and Thyestes with perfumed oil until it gleamed; wept until I was empty; scratched my face and torn my hair; made offerings; appealed to Mater Theia, in her pity and outrage, to guide some honourable stranger to my unburied dead, so he might cover their bones with earth or raise a tomb.

Harmonia and I ate a simple funeral feast of nuts and barley cakes. She didn't complain, pale and trembling though she was from the nausea of our shared condition. I pressed her hand in comfort, and she returned the pressure weakly.

"You can come here to commune with them," she said.

I nodded, but knew I never would. She must make libations in my place. The one thing my dead most required of me, I couldn't give: the price for their blood. If the seed in my womb would know life, I couldn't kill Agamemnon, couldn't condemn his child with the unspeakable duty of gaining the blood-price for its dead father.

I must live and be a mother. Lock away the grief and horror, put it in a casket in a lightless cupboard, behind a door never to be opened. A child would be born, and so once more must I.

PART TWO

CHAPTER 10

Every day, I made offerings great and small to the goddesses and begged them not to let me give birth to a brutal boy. This family needed no more of those. My husband – it still jarred to think of Agamemnon as such – would have little enthusiasm for a daughter, but she'd never be short of love. She would be my child, my hope.

Eritha, whose services I retained to keep her fox-mouth from barking, believed the child would be a girl. She instructed me how to make doubly sure, though she grumbled that a princess would ruin her self-declared unmatched reputation for delivering boys. Accordingly, I slept on my left side, stopped eating nuts and seeds, and avoided overheating my blood through too much activity or by sitting too close to the portable hearths in my throne room. In case these precautions failed, I prayed that a mother's nurturing love would prove stronger than the seed of the father.

"He'll be glad, won't he?" I asked Harmonia.

She was running her finger over the lids of jewellery boxes spread across a table in my chamber. She paused on an ivory casket carved with deer frolicking in long grass while griffins wheeled overhead. A pretty piece, a wedding gift from Thyestes. She opened the casket, selected a pair of gold sun-disc earrings, and held them against my ears. "When he learns of your condition? Certainly, the king will be glad."

A herald had arrived the evening before to announce Agamemnon's imminent homecoming and request my attendance at supper on his arrival. A clamour a short while ago in the courtyard signalled his return. The thought of the joy that might crack his granite face when he learned of my pregnancy made me more bilious than the pregnancy itself. Still, at least he might stay away from my bed, since he'd no reason to be there. And, if not, I could pretend sickness to ensure he satisfied his lust elsewhere.

Harmonia selected a handful of amethyst and carnelian finger rings from the ivory casket. "He'll bring news of your parents and sister," she said, slipping the rings onto my fingers.

"If I'd known he was visiting them, I could've sent a message."

"Well, it can't be helped now and there's nothing to gain from brooding." She picked up a comb from the table and attempted to make light-hearted chatter while she styled my hair. Hairdressing was a skill she excelled at; chatter was beyond her realm of expertise and no great pleasure of mine. We soon fell into silence.

My hair still held a curl from the fire-heated tongs she'd applied a few days earlier. She pinned up most of the ringlets and let others fall loose, securing the style with rows of jewelled headbands. Though the process wearied me, I dreaded the moment I must approve my reflection in the mirror and exchange the sanctuary of my apartments for Agamemnon's hall.

Too soon, the moment came. I refused Harmonia's persuasions to escort me downstairs. Instead, I made my way slowly through the corridors, gathering my thoughts and emotions, and pushing them down. The palace seemed smaller and darker tonight. Shades flitted across the walls. The spiral-patterned dados made me think of sword gashes exposing red and blue tumbling innards. With each step, I felt closer to an abyss into which I'd no choice but to plunge – a wide-eyed sleepwalker, separated from everyone I'd ever loved.

Tonight, the sons of Atreus and I would take supper together for the first time, as a family. I froze, gripping the handrail in the gallery above the courtyard. Then I moved on.

*

A king's homecoming might be considered a cause for celebration, but only one little table had been set up in the hall, with three stools placed around it. Two were occupied: Agamemnon slouched opposite Aegisthus, drumming his fingers against the table edge. Dismayed, I peered around the hall and willed Menelaus to melt out from the frescoes of battle and the hunt. I saw only cooks and servers through the pall of mutton smoke spreading from the hearth.

Aegisthus rose. He uttered a polite greeting and pulled out the third stool. His foster-brother's flinty stare went straight to my belly, the flatness of which I'd perversely emphasised with an embroidered apron.

I accepted the seat and took my place between the two men, within elbow-distance of both. A grumbling hound shifted beneath the table and crammed its warm body against my shins. I waited till an attendant finished pouring water over our hands, tipping it from a silver pitcher above a basin.

"I trust your visit to my father passed peacefully?" I asked Agamemnon.

He swatted away the question as if I were a child or slave. "Still thin, I see. From now on, you'll be eating for a prince."

I might have been glad to be spared the task of breaking my news, if someone else's tongue hadn't waggled with such haste. I shot a glare at Aegisthus. With a sickening lurch, I wondered what else Agamemnon might have learned.

"I'm pleased with you," Agamemnon said.

"I'm touched," I replied.

He squinted at me suspiciously. The scales seemed to tip in my favour. He called out for wine.

"Enough!" he barked when the wine steward had filled my dainty kylix halfway. "Moderation at all times, that's what a wife needs."

We sat in silence as attendants placed baskets of bread, cheeses and olives on the table, and a carver sliced the roast mutton. Agamemnon rose to spill a few drops of wine over the hearth and drop a hunk of bread in the flames. At least he was pious enough to pay the gods their due.

"Isn't Menelaus joining us?" I asked when he returned to his seat.

"He's staying on in Lacedaemon. I'll summon him for the birth celebrations." He didn't seem inclined to elaborate.

This revelation would have cost me my appetite, if I'd one to lose. While Agamemnon and Aegisthus spent the meal making

terse attempts at conversation, I brooded over possible reasons
for Menelaus remaining in my father's kingdom. If Agamemnon
wanted him to be his eyes and ears, I was glad of Menelaus'
decency – and afraid of his brotherly loyalty.

After the servants cleared the table, Agamemnon called for
the bard, who sang about my homeland in formulas borrowed
from a common bardic stock. A sickness of longing came over
me for the fertile valleys of Laconia, for the crystal waters of
the Eurotas River where I used to cool my feet, on whose banks
so many of our rites take place. Behind my closed eyelids rose
Mount Parnon, majestic seat of our citadel, where nymphs play
in forests of pine, juniper and fir. I heard the bellowing of satyrs
and drunken centaurs, who fight and carouse on fertile Mount
Taygetus while Zeus' eagles circle the peaks high above. I heard
the rumble of chariot wheels, Helen whooping the way she did
when we followed the hunt or pursued our own careless hearts.
How free our lives had been. How I envied my sister now.

Agamemnon sighed throughout the performance and
snapped his fingers for refills of wine. Moderation, it seemed,
wasn't a virtue required of husbands. He swilled from his cup
like a hound at a puddle. At last, he blinked away the glaze from
his eyes. "Sing something pleasing."

Without breaking his metre, the bard switched to Atreus'
accomplishments on the battlefield and at the hunt. Never had I
suspected my husband's father of such heroic feats.

Agamemnon knocked my arm with his elbow. "You've
conducted yourself well, after…such a start as ours. How did
you find Aegisthus while I was gone? Enthralling company, eh?"

Aegisthus pretended not to hear. A muscle twitched in his
cheek.

"We rarely saw each other," I said.

Agamemnon lowered his voice: "Our union got off to a
miserable start, it's true. I didn't wrong you, let's make that clear.
My uncle and cousin wronged me. Your father wronged me too,
by marrying you into a family of usurpers. Now, don't interrupt
– I didn't go to Lacedaemon to punish Tyndareus, if that's what
you're thinking. I'm a merciful man. I've been forced to make

hard decisions, but I've always acted with the gods' approval. Haven't they blessed me already with an heir? And it seems you're coming to your senses too, at last."

He believed the gods smiled at the slaughter of my family. And my pregnant belly confirmed the truth of it.

He added, as if Aegisthus had been struck deaf, "We needn't spend more time together than we must. Our duties won't cause our paths to cross too often, and it's not as if I'm overfond of your bed. You'll be at my side when I summon you, and I'll expect to hear modest report of you when I don't. As for the child, he'll have a nursery within your apartments till he replaces Aegisthus in the heir's house."

Aegisthus – who'd seemed absorbed in the bard's account of the famous hunt of a monstrous lion, in which Atreus now played a pivotal role, despite the adventure taking place long before his birth – turned quick as a whip to Agamemnon. "You're moving me to the heir's house?"

My thoughts shifted uneasily back to Menelaus. Shouldn't the true-born brother be Agamemnon's natural choice? Had the pair quarrelled?

"Better you than someone entirely outside the family." Agamemnon waved his empty kylix at the wine steward. "Now, as for nursing, a boy weakens when he's kept too close to his mother. My son won't be clinging to any woman's skirts. He'll have a wet nurse and won't be sucking tit any longer than he has to."

"I'll nurse my own child," I cried. Did he think he could break the bonds of nature? He wouldn't tear another baby from my arms.

He took a deep draught from his cup. "How long were you thinking?"

"Three years."

He appraised my breasts through the sheer fabric of my blouse. "You'll hardly have enough for one infant, and by then you'll have another. Give him to your girl – I hear she's pregnant. She seems sensible, not likely to pamper the boy. Modest, too."

Were there no secrets in this palace? Irritated, I snapped, "She can't be that modest. Was she forced by a god?"

He reached out, lifted the seal ring from my chest and studied it coolly. Then he jerked the thong over my head and tossed the ring into the fire. "You won't be stamping your authority here any longer. It's time you understood your place as a woman and my wife."

Aegisthus jumped to his feet, prompting a yelp of protest from the hound leaning against my legs. He glowered at Agamemnon, fists hanging by his sides.

"Sit down, fool," said Agamemnon. "Find a wife of your own and don't concern yourself with mine." He gestured at the gawping bard to continue with his performance.

"As Menelaus has?" said Aegisthus.

"Helen," I whispered in astonishment. Surely the gods couldn't be so cruel? Not Helen too, forced into the House of Atreus? I looked to Aegisthus for confirmation. He watched Agamemnon.

"An excellent match," said Agamemnon.

I covered my face with my hands. Poor Helen. Poor Menelaus. My sister would have no enthusiasm for a husband so meek, so lacking in physical attractions. And my poor father and mother wouldn't have wanted this union any more than mine. Agamemnon must have threatened them with a force they knew only too well he'd use.

"Menelaus was glum enough when I told him he'd be marrying her," said Agamemnon, "but he'll be grinning himself to sleep every night now. With those hips, she'll deliver an army of heirs to our house."

"Mind your tongue and show your wife some respect," muttered Aegisthus.

"Stop telling me how to treat my wife. Get one of your own and get your eyes off mine."

Aegisthus picked up his kylix and nonchalantly swirled the contents. "Didn't follow your own advice, did you?"

Agamemnon lunged at him, knocking the cup from his hand. The hound shot from under the table, skidded across the hall, and tangled itself in the scarlet curtain. My husband leaned across the table, veins bulging in his temples. "How many did you kill when I took back my throne from that usurping little shit? Those bastards weren't even your kin, but you didn't spill their blood – you left it all to me. *Me!* And now you come back expecting to reap the rewards. Well, I'll tell you this, the House of Thyestes is kin to me no more, because it *is* no more. My line will rule till the last stone of Mycenae crumbles. This woman here will have a fat belly from now on, till her womb dries up." He turned to me. "Stop staring at him and get upstairs."

Startled, I glanced at Aegisthus in time to see him shove the table edge into Agamemnon's groin. As Agamemnon groaned, Aegisthus' fist flew at him. Agamemnon dodged the blow. His own fist connected with Aegisthus' eye and sent him sprawling sideways to the floor.

I took a few steps towards Aegisthus, my skirts dripping wine from the spilled cups. Agamemnon seized my arm and dragged me to the doorway. He hauled me into the porch and up the staircase, faster than I could walk.

"You're hurting me," I gasped.

When we reached my bedchamber, he grasped my shoulders and shoved me backwards onto the bed. He stood over me like a man possessed, panting, his face twisted.

My stomach churned at the thought of what he might intend. I curled up and hugged myself. "The child…"

He gave his head a little shake. "I…I won't touch you. I'd never risk my boy. All I want is a healthy heir."

We both turned towards the little idol of Artemis, guardian of all infant creatures, on my bedside table.

"If the goddess delivers my child safely," said Agamemnon, "I'll make her such a sacrifice, the fairest creature born next spring in my kingdom."

A rash promise, since he had little hope of locating this paragon.

I wrapped the bedcovers around me. "Let me sleep, now."

"Yes – good, go to sleep. But tomorrow you'll exercise. Nothing strenuous, just a walk around the palace grounds with your women. It'll heat up your blood and make sure you give me a healthy boy."

CHAPTER 11

Next morning, I rose less refreshed than when I went to bed. I dressed before Harmonia stirred in the adjoining chamber, took an alabastron of salve from a chest and walked to the men's quarters.

The palace was waking. Maids swept the corridors. Savoury aromas of flatbreads and steaming porridge cooking over braziers rose from the courtyard. I didn't linger on the gallery above to watch the sleepy guards break their fasts at folding tables.

Aegisthus had taken a humiliating blow last night. Though I hadn't provoked or encouraged the quarrel, I kept thinking of Agamemnon's warning to him: *Find a wife of your own and don't concern yourself with mine.* I dismissed the insinuation behind those words, but perhaps I'd misjudged Aegisthus as I had Menelaus. Perhaps we needn't be enemies, even if we could never be friends.

He answered my knock at his door at once, already dressed in a white tunic that contrasted with his olive skin. He averted his face.

I strode past him into the bedchamber. "I'm here to tend your injury. I've a lotion."

He remained at the door. "You needn't trouble yourself."

"Nonsense. I grew up with two brothers; I spent half my childhood nursing their wounds. Not that they brawled with each other, of course, but Polydeuces loved boxing and Castor broke horses. I learned to treat cuts and sprains, and worse."

He turned to face me. Interest lit up his eye, the one that wasn't purple and sealed shut. "You have brothers?"

"No." Immediately, I regretted mentioning them. The twins had died years earlier in a fight with our cousins over stolen cattle; so much the worse my family was for their loss. I drew out a stool from under a table, the only furniture in the sparse little chamber besides a bed and some chests. "Sit."

Aegisthus approached the stool sheepishly, his athletic limbs gangling. I pushed back a black curl that fell over his forehead and dabbed the salve over his swollen eye. The eyelid flickered beneath my touch.

"Does it sting?" I asked.

"Quite the opposite. It's the first time you've been gentle with me."

I smiled, and he smiled too.

"A warrior deserves a little kindness after battle," I said, wondering if the jest would offend him.

"Aid me in my battles, and I'll lend my sword in yours."

I smeared the remaining salve over the bruising on his cheekbone. "How silly. Achaean women don't fight, though the bards sing of wonderful barbarian women equal to men in battle."

"Patience is the weapon of Achaean women. It's stronger than any spear. I admire a patient woman far more than a hot-headed warrior."

I drew back to study his expression. Not even Tantalus, with his esteem for me, ever expressed such a sentiment. But of course, Aegisthus was teasing.

"Then you won't be disappointed at failing to return Agamemnon's brotherly caress last night," I said.

"Not at all, though I'll be disappointed if you won't step outdoors with me this morning. A half-blind man needs a guide."

To my surprise, the suggestion delighted me. "Surely you can't get lost in the citadel?"

"Away from the citadel."

"Agamemnon disapproves of pregnant women doing anything more bracing than strolling around the palace grounds."

"Then I'll clear every stone from your path along the wild roads."

I'd forgotten how pleasant it was to laugh. "Why not? Let's hurry, before he can stop us."

Aegisthus' smile transformed his bruised face. He rose and held open the door for me.

*

When he revealed where we were going, I almost changed my mind about accompanying him. But he was so eager for companionship that I pitied him. We made our way along the Crone's Spine, leading a panniered mule laden with offerings, to the hill tomb of Atreus and Pelopia.

Aegisthus hadn't attended the second funeral of Atreus. He'd been absent from Mycenae on some business or other. Unsealing a tomb, a practice decently reserved for new burials, is always unpleasant. Those of my ladies who'd attended the second funeral with their lords described the stench of decay as overpowering. The pine resin torches of the attendants and the burning of woody rosemary incense only added to the oppression.

The decomposing bodies of Atreus and Pelopia, contrary to Agamemnon's suspicions, were richly dressed and surrounded by grave goods of gold, bronze, silver and ivory. Two once-magnificent chariot horses and six hunting dogs lay arranged around the chamber. As fast as propriety allowed, the sallow-faced slaves piled yet more cups, weapons and jewellery around Atreus' corpse and set an ebony-framed footstool at his feet. Pelopia received a trinket box and mirror. Then Agamemnon slid a knife across the woolly throats of a sheep and a goat, and the metallic tang of blood mingled with the perfume and putrefaction as the animals' lifeblood gushed over the floor. While slaves prepared the funeral feast, Agamemnon droned prayers to Mater Theia's daughter, the Lady Who Receives Many.

Afterwards, the slaves refilled the dromos with soil and rubble to guard against grave robbers, leaving the hill to swell above the surrounding landscape like the Mother's breast. Aegisthus stared at it now through his good eye, at the carpet of sun-browned grass. His face was unfathomable.

"Will you make the offerings for me, Clytemnestra?"

"What?" Involuntarily, I took a step back. "Are you afraid of their shades? Atreus and Pelopia were your foster-parents. They won't harm you if your offerings please them."

"Then it's another man's corpse in that tomb. Atreus was never gentle to his sons while he lived."

I considered lending him one of the amulets I wore around my neck, which protected my unborn child, but his mouth was stubbornly set and I knew he'd refuse. Besides, keeping the amulets to myself seemed wise.

From one of the mule's panniers, he took three libation bowls, which he placed on the ground, and an amphora of water drawn from the Perseia Spring. He cleansed my hands and poured the rest of the water into the first bowl, filled a second bowl with wine from a second amphora, and a third with honey. Then he handed me a myrtle wreath and wheat cake. He sliced a lock of black hair from his head with a dagger and dropped the soft curl onto my palm.

"For Pelopia, all of it," he said.

"Very well," I agreed.

I laid the offerings before the mound, poured the libations and spoke a quiet impersonal prayer to the shade of the dead queen.

*

Aegisthus was quieter than ever as we retraced our steps towards the citadel. Given his obvious sadness, I felt a little ashamed of my disappointment at returning so soon.

"You were fond of Pelopia," I said, to gain some time and learn more about him.

"She was a mother to me."

I remembered the story of her intervention after Aegisthus, as an infant, was abandoned outside the palace. He might have died or been reared as a slave, if not for the young queen.

"I'm glad," I said. "Every child should know a mother's affection. Was she close to your foster-brothers?"

"No. Agamemnon was arrogant. He couldn't forget she was Thyestes' daughter."

"And Menelaus?"

"She kept her distance from the family. It wasn't her fault. We were outsiders, she and I. But she called me her strength."

"A gentle goddess surely brought you together. And what about Atreus? Did he have any love for her? I suppose he married her to make sure her sons would be his, so they wouldn't avenge Thyestes' murdered boys." As it came to pass, Pelopia had no children. A blessing.

Aegisthus glowered in the direction of the citadel walls. "Yes, that's about right. He treated her despicably."

"There's no cruelty I'd believe him incapable of. Poor drowned Aerope."

"Aerope was the fortunate wife. Pelopia suffered seventeen years of his brutality. Seventeen years! She couldn't flee. Even his enemies wouldn't risk accepting the wife of the most powerful Achaean king as a supplicant at their hearths. After the revenge he took against his own family, how much worse would he punish a stranger?"

"Didn't Pelopia serve as Athene's priestess before she married Atreus? Couldn't she seek the goddess's protection?" Even as I said this, I knew her situation had been hopeless. Atreus had committed impieties that made gods shudder. He wouldn't hesitate to pollute the Protectress' sanctuary.

"She served Athene as a girl in Sicyon, in a grove, not a sacred house. Olive trees don't offer much protection against rampaging, vengeful husbands."

Like father, like son. My own husband was shaped from the same mould. "How did Atreus force her to marry him?"

"He didn't. When her tenure with the goddess ended, she came to Mycenae to seek her uncle's guardianship, and he married her."

My sympathy for the dead woman evaporated. "The fool! She chose to marry the man who murdered her brothers? She actually sought out the protection of a monster?" Pelopia had willingly married her tormentor, a choice I was never given.

Aegisthus stiffened, indignation flashing in his eyes. Then he sighed. He halted the mule and seated himself on a wide boulder at the side of the road. "She was alone in the world. Her brothers were dead. Her father had fled who-knew-where after their murders. Maybe she went to Atreus for reparation, and he offered it through marriage. Perhaps she thought he'd welcome the chance to redeem himself through kindness towards her. He certainly owed her as much."

Best, I decided, to change the direction of our discussion. "And you, Aegisthus – was Atreus a better foster-father than a husband?"

He laughed and patted the boulder for me to sit beside him. I did so, glad to share his confidences, despite their unhappy nature.

"Atreus thought he could instil in me a sense of loyalty to his house," he said. "He imagined this was something you knocked into a boy. True, he gave me a broad education – arms, administration, the history of his family – but he was a hard, violent man. I wasn't sorry when he died."

"Even though it meant exile for you and your foster-brothers? What happened that day, when Thyestes retook Mycenae? I heard Thyestes' account, of course, but he confused it with Heracles storming Troy."

I thought he might smile at my joke. Instead, a shadow passed over his brow. He took some time before replying.

"Agamemnon captured Thyestes during the battle outside the citadel walls, did Thyestes tell you that? You can imagine how Pelopia's mind worked when she heard. The first time her father took the throne, Atreus believed serving up the meat of her brothers was reasonable retaliation. I went to her apartments and begged her to let me carry her to safety, to some island or foreign city. She said we could never be free of such a family." Aegisthus' jaw tightened; his expression remained as hard as the citadel walls, which he stared at so fixedly. "She kissed my face, called me her darling. Then she snatched the sword from my belt and plunged it into her belly."

I covered my mouth. "Aegisthus, I'm so…"

He shook his head, rejecting any sympathy for himself. "Thyestes' mercenaries had fled. The battle was over. Atreus set out at once to give thanks to his god Poseidon in the poplar grove above the citadel. Unhappily for him, the deathless ones chose the moment of his triumph to undo him. Isn't that their way?"

I shuddered. The gods delight in punishing the arrogant.

"No one found out who struck him down at the Perseia Spring," said Aegisthus. "Perhaps it was a mercenary separated from the pack. At any rate, Thyestes escaped from the palace. He regrouped his warband and returned for the final slaughter. The Followers and palace guards deserted Atreus' sons to save their own hides, and turned the palace over to Thyestes. Before fleeing, Agamemnon and Menelaus asked me to join them, to help gather forces against their uncle, but I went my own way."

He went his own way, grieving for a loving foster-mother, shedding no tears for his foster-father's demise.

"I'd seen enough bloodshed," he said. "I wanted no more. Not that Thyestes didn't deserve to be strung up by his own guts for what he did to Pelopia."

Poor Pelopia, abandoned by her father after that awful supper, left to plead for reparation from the murderer of her brothers. Foolish Pelopia, who believed her best option was to marry a monster.

Aegisthus slumped into musing. After a while, I laid my hand on his arm.

"Forgive me," he said, "I must have worn you out with all this talk. We should get back to the palace." His gaze dropped to my hand, then focused so intently on my face that I wondered if I should take my hand back.

"Yes," I said at last, "we should get back."

"Yes," he said.

We spoke little during the remainder of our walk. I felt as I had when Menelaus confided in me about Queen Aerope's drowning, as if a barrier had broken down. Yet I was less at ease with Aegisthus than with his foster-brother – and this intrigued rather than disturbed me. Quiet, intense Aegisthus was as different from open-hearted Menelaus as night from day.

He gave me his arm as we climbed the cobbled ramp to the palace. I thought of his account of Thyestes storming Mycenae, how different it was from the boasts of Thyestes. Thyestes had indeed made no mention of being taken prisoner by Agamemnon, and he seemed not to know this version of Pelopia's death. He said she'd fallen amid the general carnage, struck down in the confusion.

Perhaps he hadn't cared enough to find out what had happened to his daughter. Or perhaps he didn't care to remember the loss of yet another child.

*

At the palace stables, a flustered, crimson-cheeked groom dashed across the flagstones to lead our mule to an empty stall. Before I could wonder at the boy's agitation, Agamemnon's voice roared above the uneasy snorts of the animals, accusing the groom of neglecting a prize Trojan stallion's hooves. A distressed neigh accompanied his shout, perhaps from the animal in question.

Bulk followed bellow as Agamemnon emerged from a shadowy corner of the stables. His small eyes glittered at Aegisthus. "Back from your outing, I see."

Aegisthus motioned his head at an ass being led by another groom. "And you're just heading out?"

Agamemnon smiled sourly. "Thought I'd catch out these sluggard grooms before they take the horses to pasture. The amount I paid for the Trojans, they should be fanning away every fly and catching each dollop of dung before it hits the floor." He acknowledged me with a jut of his chin. "Well, aren't you two becoming friendly?"

"I'm sure you want your family to get along," said Aegisthus.

"So long as my brother isn't Thyestes."

"We were visiting your father's tomb," I said.

Agamemnon's flinty eyes narrowed. "And why would you go there?"

I smiled very deliberately, straightened my back and assumed a haughty tone. "I might not have chosen to be part of your family, but I'm carrying a child of this house. For her sake – or his – I won't provoke the ancestors' wrath by neglecting their rites. Aegisthus regularly makes offerings at Atreus' tomb, and he suggested I should join him."

Agamemnon's scowl faded. "Sensible woman. Seems my foster-brother isn't so dull-witted either. He knows where his interests lie."

"I do," said Aegisthus.

"Heir presumptive till my son comes of age – not bad for a bastard fosterling," said Agamemnon. "My father always said the gods guided you across his threshold for a reason, so hurry up and show us what it is!"

Aegisthus smiled confidingly at me. "It's true, you know." He patted the eagle-claw hilt of the sword in his belt. "See this? This is no poor man's weapon. I was born no commoner's brat. I was found with this sword laid across my basket, placed there by the Protectress herself. She watched over me then and watches over me still."

Agamemnon had listened to this boast with an expression of indulgent contempt. He pinched the bruised skin over Aegisthus' cheekbone. "She wasn't guarding you last night, though, was she? There's a beauty I gave you!"

*

After that first excursion, I spent many days with Aegisthus. Agamemnon made no attempt to discourage our friendship. He seemed, instead, to view it as a way of securing my acceptance of my place in the family.

Aegisthus and I would sit and talk in the shade of the trees outside the palace, or stroll around the citadel. Sometimes we took a travelling chariot and drove over the plain. We valued our respite from the palace, with its tallow-lamp stink and dreary frescoes of slain beasts and sword-broken men, with its labyrinthine corridors where we held no real power, only the warmth of our titles. We discussed little of consequence, since we had little of consequence to discuss. We shared stories of our childhoods – he of kindly Pelopia, me of my gentle parents and pretty sister. I glimpsed Aegisthus' early miseries: the rough tutors, the frustration of never truly belonging, the casual cruelty of Agamemnon, which often gave way to protectiveness towards Menelaus, but only towards Aegisthus if the family honour was ever threatened.

The remainder of my pregnancy passed as smoothly as it could. Agamemnon summoned me to the hall from time to time, where we sat exchanging mundanities – he covertly drumming his fingers and sighing, both of us preternaturally alert to every crackle from the hearth fire or footstep on the balconies. As the moments crawled by in the hall, my mind drifted to Aegisthus. I recalled his smiles at my carefully chosen witticisms, the way his grave face softened to reveal traces of the child he seemed never to have been. At those times, he reminded me of that other dark-eyed youth I'd held so dear, my lost boy-husband. Bittersweet moments.

My slim frame irritated Agamemnon, who demanded I should eat more, walk less and stop wearing belts. But, by the time of the Festival of the Casting Out of Spirits, my girth delighted him. We stood before the celebrants in an underground cavern, sharing a sacred meal of seed-grain porridge, my face impassive, my ankles swollen and back aching. Afterwards, he rewarded me with a gold armlet and laughed when my arm proved too plump for the bauble.

How could I help remembering Iphitus during those days? Such a short time ago, he'd been the cause of these changes in my body, my cumbersome belly, my breasts filling up in readiness for his hungry mouth. I recalled his kick in my womb, and I wept. But, with every passing day, my love intensified for this new child, for the daughter I was determined she'd be. Months earlier, I would have swallowed Eritha's concoction before the child ever drew breath. Now, she would live, and I wouldn't fail her as I'd failed Iphitus.

*

"You look ready to burst," remarked Agamemnon in the courtyard one afternoon, late in my pregnancy. It was around the time of day when he usually finished his nap, before heading back to the hall to hear any remaining petitioners. Judging by his sweating face and tousled hair, he'd indulged in something more strenuous than napping.

"And you look…rested," I said, concealing my disgust.

He sneered at the blanket draped over Aegisthus' arm, which I'd removed from my loom and given him to carry.

It depicted a family of river ducks in the soothing hues of childhood.

"Sentimental," scoffed Agamemnon. "A hunting scene would suit the lad better. I won't have you turning him into a weakling, Clytemnestra. You'll give me a fat little heir, not some woman's man, like Aegisthus, here."

"My mother gave my father two athletes for sons and two equally healthy daughters. There's no reason I shouldn't have strong children."

"And how many did she lose?"

"Crass!" Aegisthus jabbed a finger in Agamemnon's direction.

A flush mottled Agamemnon's cheeks above his coppery beard. "Crass? You wouldn't buy horses from poor stock, would you? You'd check the pedigree of your hunting dogs. All the more your wife."

"I dropped from a strong tree, as you no doubt knew before you married me," I said. My mother's many miscarriages were none of his concern.

"Your father wasn't its sturdiest branch."

I'd already turned to walk away, but his words halted me. "What do you mean by that?"

He took a few moments before muttering, "Tyndareus has joined his ancestors."

I stared at him in ice-cold shock. "What did you say?"

"Send offerings to Lacedaemon. Tell your mother to pray to Tyndareus and the ancestors to guard over our child."

"When…?" I struggled to find the right words. To place them in the right order. "Why wasn't I…?"

Aegisthus laid a supportive hand on my back. "What happened, Agamemnon?"

My husband glanced towards the hall with an exaggerated sigh. "It was the eve of Menelaus' wedding to Helen. The Laconians have a custom – quite a good one, actually – where the bridegroom has to spear himself a boar before he can marry the king's daughter. Tyndareus' heart gave out during the hunt. Helen was there. The old man died peacefully in her arms, knowing Menelaus would succeed him."

His callousness pierced through the unreality of his news. "My father died during your visit? And you didn't tell me?"

"I thought the news might unbalance you, in your condition, especially after...everything else." He shrugged. "How many men would be so considerate? You can use my herald, send greetings to your mother. And now, I've petitioners to see." With that, he strode off.

My legs threatened to buckle beneath me. Aegisthus placed steadying arms around me. "Send your message later," he said. "First, I'll see you to your apartments."

I let him support me through the palace, numb, trembling, barely able to comprehend that Tyndareus of Lacedaemon, my gentle father, was dead.

CHAPTER 12

y mother and sister would think I didn't care. I hadn't journeyed to Laconia for my father's funeral or to make offerings at his tomb. I'd sent no message of comfort. They'd think I'd forgotten them, forgotten my noble father, absorbed in my miseries here in Mycenae.

The morning after learning of my father's death, I sent Agamemnon's herald, Tros, to Lacedaemon. Not many days passed before Tros' return. He stood before my throne, his grizzled head bowed, while I railed and threatened and pleaded with him to admit his report was mistaken.

Helen had received him on his arrival in Lacedaemon. My mother, she told him, was dead. She had succumbed to grief for our father.

How was it possible, my parents were gone? Gone, like my brothers. Gone, like my sister, who might as well be across the Sea of Aegeus. Helen and I were alone, near friendless, powerless.

I rose from my throne to berate the herald. Pain tore through me. I fell back down and clutched my stomach.

Harmonia, big with child, waddled to me. She took my hand in her own cool one and ordered Tros to fetch Eritha.

"Too soon," I gasped, doubling over.

"The child doesn't think so," she said.

I tried to focus on her voice, on the shape of her words as she gave instructions I could barely comprehend to my women: "…birthing chamber…ready…appease the goddess…" Phantoms of disaster flitted around me. The pangs were coming too fast, too hard. Too soon. So often, this had happened to my mother before me. So many dead babies.

"Come," said Harmonia. She took my arm. One of my ladies took the other, and together they guided me slowly from the throne room.

The palace seers had sworn the child would arrive two new moons from now. I'd planned everything accordingly. Eritha was to lodge in the palace in plenty of time. *Impostors.* I'd strip those seers of their offices, punish them with pains, such wrenching pains. Groaning, I sagged against the doorframe of the birthing chamber, cursing the herbwife for her absence.

"She'll get nothing from me!" I shouted. "Nothing!"

Harmonia instructed me to lie on the bed. Two maids lifted my legs to hold the child in place, while a third raised my skirts and tried to soothe my contractions with an oil-drenched cloth pressed to my belly. My ladies sat in a circle on the floor, legs and fingers crossed, murmuring prayers to divine Eleuthia to delay the birth until Eritha came. I sobbed in fear and frustration. I willed my body to be still, but it betrayed me with every new, tearing spasm. My ladies' voices resonated in my ears, chanting powerful female magic. I knew their efforts were in vain.

An age seemed to pass before Eritha arrived, though Tros surely brought her by chariot. She marched into the chamber, more commanding than I'd imagined possible, and ordered the maids to strip me. They tugged at my damp skirts and hoisted my buttocks.

Eritha felt my belly and said, "Sit her on the stool."

"I'm losing another one," I wept. Two maids were tucking their arms under my armpits and heaving me from the bed. I couldn't bring myself to assist them. "She's gone, she's gone."

Eritha grinned at me and kindled a glimmer of hope. "Maybe not."

I stumbled the last steps to the birthing stool, collapsing as a warm gush burst over my thighs. Three maids stationed themselves around the stool to keep me from slumping. They pleaded with Eritha to give me poppy juice.

The herbwife, crouching beneath me, said, "No time. Push, lady."

Under her guidance, I pushed and breathed, pushed and breathed. The Mother herself came to me then. She possessed me, the goddess whose travails are eternal, invigorating me with her fierce determination.

Eritha cackled when the last agony tore through me. Her strong thin hands drew from my body a slippery scarlet creature far too tiny to have caused such torment. A creature too silent. Iphitus had announced his birth with an indignant howl. His sister appeared lifeless.

"Is she…?" I panted. I couldn't finish the question. My heartbeat had raced during the labour; now, it slowed to a dull thud in my ears.

"She's breathing, maybe not for long." Eritha gave my child's bottom a slap. The baby whimpered.

"Give her to me," I said, my voice between a sob and a warning. My baby needed my arms, my strength. "Give her to me!"

Eritha eyed her doubtfully. "It's not always wise. The king must be told, and then—"

"Then nothing. Give Iphigenia to me!"

Until that moment, I hadn't chosen a name. This was a father's prerogative. But now I knew what she must be called: "Mighty-born". My son, my "Mighty One", hadn't lived to fulfil his name, but this one would live. She must live. I would be her strength. I would protect her. I would strike down any who tried to harm her.

"She will live," I said.

"That's for powers greater than ours to decide, but rest assured I'll do all I can." Eritha placed the tiny creature in my arms. "Your mother reaches for you, little cicada."

A torrent of love surged through me at the feel of my child's sticky, downy red skin against mine. Her birdlike chest rose and fell as hypnotically as a Siren song. I spat on my middle finger and made the sign against evil on her forehead to ward off the malign spirits who creep close during births and deaths.

I even had affection to spare for the herbwife. "Do all you can, Eritha. I'll reward you handsomely – handsomely."

She squatted again and turned her attention to the cord attaching my daughter's body to mine. She gave it a gentle tug. "My only concern is for my patients' welfare. Though, of course, if you see fit to reward a service well done, I'm in no position to object, old and alone in the world as I am."

After delivering the placenta, I lay in bed with my child on my breast, refusing my women's persuasions to take her from me when it seemed she wouldn't suckle. At last, Iphigenia's tiny mouth closed around my nipple, as I'd known it would, and she sucked weakly.

When my daughter had had her fill, Harmonia approached. "Time to wash the little cicada, lady. I promise you'll have her back almost before you notice she's gone." She beamed at Iphigenia with such pleasure, she might have birthed her herself.

"Oh, very well," I sighed, envying her as she took the baby in her arms.

"Hang a fillet of wool on the palace door," she ordered the maids. "A girl-child is born to the king."

*

The maids painted the nursery door with pitch and hung a sprig of pungent valerian from the lintel; on the windowsill, they placed buckthorn branches – precautions to keep evil spirits at bay. Children are at their most vulnerable before their fathers name them at the naming ceremony.

Tomorrow, on our daughter's seventh day, Agamemnon would carry her three times around his hearth. Witnessed by everyone who could squeeze into the hall – family, Followers, officials and priests – he would accept her into his household. I couldn't allow myself to think otherwise.

He hadn't visited her or sent word to me.

His disregard for me was an insult to be stored away, but he hadn't necessarily rejected our daughter. Some men – Tantalus was one – are impatient to view their babies. Others, such as my father, made wise or weary by experience, wait till the naming ceremony or the funeral. My father never rejected an infant, no matter how frail or ill-formed, but Agamemnon wasn't Tyndareus. A knot tightened in my stomach as I caressed the apple-red cheek of the sleeping baby on my breast. Her lips puckered as if she dreamed of nurture.

Shortly after the birth, I'd sent a maid to Agamemnon requesting him to name our daughter Iphigenia. He dismissed the girl without reply. I would have gone to him myself, but I was confined to the women's quarters, along with all the women who'd attended the labour, till the miasma could be cleansed from us. Though I hardly expected Agamemnon to be an affectionate father – indeed, I wanted to spare my child his excessive influence – his neglect would be intolerable. My daughter was a princess of Mycenae, entitled to all the honours of her position.

Eritha's thin hands hovered over Iphigenia. "Come, give her to me, lady. You must sleep. Tomorrow is an important day for you and Cicada both."

"Oh, take her, you nagging old witch," I said, before I could change my mind. "Be careful!"

The herbwife settled her, before lying down in her own bed next to my daughter's. After a while, when my glances towards Iphigenia's cradle had satisfied me that my child was asleep, I fell into a doze, lulled by Eritha's snores – and a goddess visited my dreams.

Which one, I couldn't say. She stood far taller than a man, with a face terrible in its beauty. She loomed over the cradle. Though her lips never opened, her voice filled the room, elemental as fire or water, as earth: *Why does she live?*

Icy sweat broke out all over me. An infant crawled around the goddess's white feet. Iphitus.

Then Iphitus was gone. The goddess was gone. And Agamemnon hunched over the cradle. In the light of his lamp, his face was haggard, baleful as the male lion who devours his cubs. I forgot to breathe. The damp sheet clung to me. My muscles tensed.

He shook his head slowly. "Too soon," he muttered.

He turned away and crossed the nursery. He didn't look back. The door creaked shut behind him.

*

Too soon. What had Agamemnon meant?

The riddle plagued me for the rest of the night. Too soon to survive? Too soon to be his? Had he entered the room at all or had I dreamed his apparition? Perhaps a daemon visited my child in her father's form.

In the morning, I sent a servant to Mater Theia's sacred grove below the citadel to plead for the goddess's intercession. Agamemnon must be made to see that our daughter's tiny limbs could grow strong, that she could survive the dangers of infancy – that she sprang from his seed, however much I might prefer a resourceful god had seeped into me in the guise of my bathwater.

Late in the afternoon, the women who attended the birth gathered around me. I set a flaming laurel branch to fizzle out in a basin of water drawn from the Perseia Spring and spoke a ritual incantation. Then we dipped our hands in the water to purify ourselves from the birthing.

Harmonia dressed me magnificently in a chequered varicoloured skirt, its tiered fringes tinkling with crescent-moon discs. She paired it with a saffron-yellow jacket and tied an embroidered blue apron around my waist. My baby remained naked. Since her birth, I'd refused to let anyone swaddle her tender, downy pink body. Now, trusting no hands but mine, I placed her on a cushion and covered her soft forehead with a gold diadem, tied under her chin. Over her forearm I drew a bracelet barely bigger than a man's finger ring. She didn't protest, though Iphitus would have kicked and bawled. My heart ached with love for this delicate daughter.

Cradling her in my arms, I led my ladies from the women's quarters. We took the lengthier of the two routes towards the king's hall, so we could emerge from the Corridor of the Double Axes into the main courtyard.

Ribbons, garlands and aromatic pine branches decorated the walls, the colonnades and the doorways of the courtyard. Slaves from the palace and peasants from the towns and villages pressed around us. The odours of wine and intoxicating kykeon wafted from their mouths as they cried out blessings to my daughter

above the wail of reed pipes and the knocking of drums. I raised
my child for their admiration, then held her close. She didn't cry.

Spear-wielding guards approached me and cleared a path
to the hall, where more well-wishers had gathered in the
porch. A crush of bodies in the vestibule obscured the griffins
and sphinxes painted on the walls. As we passed through the
curtained doorway to the hall, I cupped my daughter's rosy cheek
and willed her not to fear the smoke and heat and strangers. To
stay silent and strong-born.

The hall was no less packed than the courtyard. Somehow
the guests made way and I carried Iphigenia to the ever-burning
hearth fire, where her father would be waiting. My sister had
secured a place close to the hearth with Menelaus. My heart
swelled at the sight of her, the first since my wedding to Tantalus
– and now she too was a bride. With a pang, I recognised her
skirt and jacket, precious heirlooms once worn by our mother,
passed down from our grandmother. Helen's body had fleshed
out to do justice to the glittering clothes. She was a woman now,
and beautiful. She smiled sadly, holding out her hand as if to
close the distance between us. I gave a small nod, conscious of
the solemnity of the occasion.

Something was wrong. Several of the nearest guests wouldn't
look at me or my child; others stared keenly. Agamemnon wasn't
standing at the hearth or seated on his throne. There was no
sign of him through the smoke and onlookers.

Aegisthus appeared at my side and whispered, "I'm sorry."
He took my baby before I could react.

He turned to the guests. In a voice as resounding as a herald's,
he announced, "Friends, last night Artemis the Huntress came
to King Agamemnon in a dream. She told him to bring down
a great beast today in his daughter's honour. If this sacred
duty delayed him, he gave me permission to act in his place so
nothing mars this most auspicious occasion."

A buzz, both credulous and incredulous, passed through
the gathering. A shadow seemed to fall over the hall, over my
daughter, a chasm to open up before her.

My child was half accepted, half rejected. Her father had gone hunting on her name day. Had he given any such instruction to Aegisthus, related any such dream? Was he, even now, spilling his seed into some other vessel and planting an heir? Or had the goddess or daemon, the one who'd visited my own dreams, schemed to deprive my baby of a father on the day she most needed one?

Sickened, I raised my hand for the rite to begin.

Aegisthus, fosterling of the House of Atreus, ran three times with my daughter around her father's hearth. On the third circuit, he darted me a look as he drew near.

"Iphigenia," I whispered.

He lifted my baby above his head. "I name this child Iphigenia, daughter of Agamemnon. Smile kindly on her, protectors of our house. Grant her modesty, beauty and skill at the loom. May she be a mother of many children and may her life be long."

*

I carried my docile daughter around the hall, introducing her to well-wishers and accepting name-day gifts. Servants bustled around us, setting up tables and stools, placing cooking utensils about the hearth. My heart soared at the praises lavished on Iphigenia and ached at the pitying looks cast her way. I seethed at Agamemnon's treatment of her. And I feared for her. How I feared.

When the cooking was well underway and the savour of roast meats filled the air, Agamemnon, with a band of Followers, trudged bloodied and bedraggled into the hall. He gazed absently around our guests, who gawped back at him. In his arms, he cradled the dappled pelt of a fawn, as though the tender creature still dwelled in it.

His eyes wandered to me and he held out the pelt. "A gift for your child."

"Won't you wash?" I hissed between my teeth.

He thrust the pelt at a passing slave and walked away.

Trembling, unwilling to guess what his behaviour meant, I drew close to Helen and Menelaus and let their bodies shield me and my daughter from the murmuring guests.

Helen wrapped her arm around me and laughed mordantly in my ear. "Husbands!"

I freed myself and held her at arm's length, while she studied me in turn, this gold-glittering woman in our mother's clothes. All too soon, she'd be gone from me again. Was she gone already? Helen had been the spring maiden who longed for summer, a girl who yearned to have suitors more numerous than the stars, yet begged my father for the yoke of marriage. A girl whose beautiful hands preferred chariot reins to a distaff or shuttle, though she insisted otherwise. The gods had granted Helen her desires, and now there was a hardness about her, bitter to see.

I managed a smile for Menelaus. "We never had a chance to say goodbye. I'm so glad to see you again."

He turned pink to the ends of his earlobes. "You're too kind, really too kind."

Helen sighed.

He reached out a clumsy finger to touch Iphigenia's cheek. "She's as beautiful as her mother and aunt, as beautiful as your own mother." He blushed harder at his own gallantry.

"How fortunate she takes after our side of the family," said Helen. Her laughter held an edge that made her husband wince, but I couldn't disagree with her.

I rocked Iphigenia, whose eyelids were fluttering. "She sleeps well. Eritha, my herbwife, says that's a sign of a gentle nature." Though a gentle nature probably wasn't such an asset for one born into the House of Atreus.

A stirring of the guests indicated, at last, Agamemnon's return. He stared at Iphigenia from the doorway. He was oiled and gleaming, as on the night of her conception. I pushed that memory down. He crossed the hall, moving as if his ankle-length, priestly-white tunic chafed him, and sat at the largest table.

Harmonia held out her arms to take Iphigenia to the nursery. My mouth dried up. I stepped back, clutching my child. I shook my head.

"Don't be afraid," she whispered.

Tantalus' voice echoed in my ears: *This heat and smoke isn't good for her.* I looked around, but he wasn't there. My sister squeezed my arm. She pressed her cheek to mine. "Give her to her nursemaid," she said. "She's safe. Your Iphigenia is safe."

Pushing down every throbbing instinct, I let Harmonia take my baby from my arms, as I knew I must. Helen held my hand in both of hers and led me to Agamemnon's table. Menelaus and Aegisthus joined us.

The rest of the guests sat in pairs at small tables inlaid with ivory reliefs, my best furniture, a marriage gift from my mother and father that had remained in storage since my wedding day to Tantalus. Attendants carried silver pitchers and basins around the hall to wash our hands. Wine stewards hurried to fill our cups. Servers spread the tables with baskets of bread, platters of meat, and dishes of olives, oils and sauces.

Agamemnon walked to the hearth fire to offer a libation of wine and morsel of bread. "Lady Who Dwells in the Flames," he prayed, "may you smile on my house and those true-born of my hearth." He returned to the table and clasped Menelaus' shoulder in passing. He didn't acknowledge Helen or Aegisthus, nor they him. When he raised his kylix, the feast began.

Though a boulder seemed to have lodged in my gullet, I made a point of sampling the venison of Agamemnon's fawn. Better to let the guests think I approved of his hunting expedition than have them speculating about his earlier absence. Later, I'd berate him in private for not carrying our daughter around the hearth.

His appetite was no heartier than mine. When a server tried to put a venison brisket before him on the table, he flinched as if it came from Atreus' cauldron. He drank his wine and interrogated Menelaus on Laconia's recent trading activity. Aegisthus added an occasional word or two to their conversation. His dark gaze wandered around the hall, returning often to me.

Helen bent her head close to mine. "How can you stand it?"

The question startled me from my observations. "What?"

"Him – Agamemnon – how can you stand him?"

I wanted to say I couldn't, to nestle my face into the familiar fabric of our mother's clothes. But I too was a mother and must be dignified. "What choice do I have? And now there's Iphigenia."

Helen's laugh rang out. "And what about Iphitus? Tantalus? Even the old man. I don't know how you stand it. If you only knew what he was like when he came to Lacedaemon. What he did to our father, our poor, poor father." Her lovely mouth twisted with hatred, preventing her from finishing.

"Our father?" Would the sinking dread Agamemnon inspired in me never end?

"If he hadn't hounded Father, wanting me for Menelaus, wanting our citadel, our fields, our sheep, our stinking cows—"

"Speak quietly." I darted a look around the table, but no one seemed to have heard us above the roar of conversation. Agamemnon was forcing mouthfuls of minted lamb and spiced chickpeas between his thin lips and questioning Menelaus about the productivity of his palace workshops. Aegisthus watched me moodily; our eyes met and he looked away.

"How cold you are," said Helen. "I'm trying to tell you how your husband bullied our father to his grave. If Agamemnon hadn't tormented him to make Menelaus his successor, Father's heart wouldn't have failed. He'd be here tonight in your hall. And so would Mother."

I snatched Helen's hand from the table and crushed it in mine.

She winced. "Poor darling, forgive me. How cruel I am. You weren't there, you can't imagine how terrible he is."

*

And so the feast dragged on. No one at our table betrayed much appetite, except Menelaus, who enjoyed generous helpings of every meat and side dish set before us. Helen snapped at him whenever he tried to tempt her with a delicacy. His bewilderment was painful to see. Once or twice, I tried to steer the conversation by engaging Aegisthus. My efforts cheered my sister, though not my gloomy friend. Helen flashed us such roguish smiles, I fell silent.

Finally, Agamemnon poured a last libation to the Good Spirit of the Household. The servants cleared away the serving dishes and wiped the uneaten food from the tables. The bard rose from his stool, took his tortoiseshell lyre from its peg on the wall, and plucked out a delicate rhythm. In a voice resonant enough to reach the carousers in the courtyard, he sang of Mater Theia forming the dying ones, the race of mortals, from her dark clay.

"Now I remember you," he sang, "and another song too." He began a longer composition meant for my edification, praising notable feats of motherhood by goddesses and by a few exceptional mortals. This attempt by an unmarried youth to teach me my instincts filled me with scorn. I had to remind myself that the Muses themselves inspire singers to song.

Agamemnon nodded significantly as the bard, changing his theme, waxed on the ideal qualities of wives and daughters; but, after a while, he grew fidgety. He went back to questioning Menelaus about the contents of Lacedaemon's store cupboards, which our guests took as a signal to renew their own chatter. The bard strained manfully to make himself heard.

Helen stroked my arm. "He's watching you."

"Who?" I glanced at Aegisthus.

"He's the best of the brothers. Then again, he isn't really one of them."

"Is Menelaus really so terrible? He's fond of you. And he isn't Agamemnon."

Her lips curled as she studied her quiet, affectionate husband. I could have shaken her. This was what came of yearning for perfection, for love. No man could have satisfied Helen, not even if Dionysus himself carried her off to his woodland lair and made her queen of the revels.

A painful memory came back to me: a mortifying afternoon, four springtimes ago. Helen and I, on one of our chariot rides, had stumbled on some rustics performing their rites. These weren't the solemn ceremonies presided over by our mother and father, but drunken foolery. Cheeks flushed and eyes sparkling, Helen beamed at the rustics, who hopped and gambolled around a phallus pole. They shouted for us to join them – and, to our parents' unknowing shame, the youngest daughter of King Tyndareus and Queen Leda threw herself full-pelt around the beribboned phallus. Helen ignored my demands to return at once to the palace, and I ignored her enticements to balance one-legged on a greasy wineskin. She'd always been too impetuous, and marriage seemed to have changed nothing.

She squeezed my hand. "You have the worst of it, I know. How else could I bear it? If I could free us both, I would."

"I have a child," I said. What did she think I should do? Run off with Aegisthus, endanger him and disgrace myself? Bring shame on Iphigenia as the daughter of an infamous whore?

But surely she meant no such thing. Heat rushed to my face. I waved my kylix at a wine steward to hide my embarrassment.

"We have an uncle in Acarnania," said Helen.

Her words chilled me. A woman might flee, but she could never, never escape. "Don't even say it. Agamemnon will care about Iphigenia in time. At the very least, he'll protect her. If I had to marry him a hundred times to keep her safe, I would."

"What are you women whispering about?" shouted Agamemnon above the din of the guests and valiant efforts of the bard. "Never trust women who whisper," he told Menelaus. He laughed. "Never trust women."

"I'm sure we're very fortunate in our wives." Menelaus tipped his kylix at us.

Agamemnon dismissed the bard with a flick of his wrist and called for dancers. Servants arranged our stools along the four walls and carried away the tables to the storerooms. When we were reseated, pairs of young men and women tripped into the hall, holding hands. To the accompaniment of flutes, cymbals and a rattling sistrum, they whirled and glided around the hall. Two of the youths somersaulted out from the circle and formed a step with their hands for each girl to hop up on, before she flipped backwards into the arms of a waiting boy and rejoined the swirling dance.

The guests roared in approval. Helen clapped. Even Agamemnon seemed to enjoy the spectacle, perhaps hoping a girl's breechcloth would work loose so he could lick his lips and scowl at her wantonness.

He slapped Menelaus' shoulder. "Your wife'll be glad there's dancing boys. So will Aegisthus – he hasn't ploughed a woman since he came back to Mycenae. Not that you can tell what he prefers. Probably takes out his frustrations in the stables."

A muscle twitched in Aegisthus' cheek. He rarely responded to Agamemnon's taunting, though might have won his respect if he had. But I was glad he resisted the bait on this occasion. I could depend on my friend not to cast an ill omen over my daughter's name day, even if I couldn't depend on her father.

At the end of the dance, Aegisthus slipped an amethyst ring from his finger and turned enquiringly to Helen and me. Helen tilted her head and gave the full force of her consideration, not to the dancers, but to Aegisthus. Her lips curved in a beguiling smile. She was so beautiful. My stomach sank.

Aegisthus waited for our answer.

My sister pointed to a boy with glossy black hair, whose sculpted chest tapered down to the narrowest of waists. Judging from his moonstruck expression, he had the audacity to return her admiration.

"I agree," I said. The loveliest boy and his partner were indeed the best dancers.

The youth's partner accepted the ring. She tugged the boy's hand and tried to lead him back to their troupe, but he stood rooted to the spot, staring slack-jawed at Helen. My sister's smile invited him to look and forbade him to look away.

Menelaus smiled too, in simple pleasure at the good fortune of the winning pair.

CHAPTER 13

After Helen returned home with her husband, I sent heralds regularly to Lacedaemon with gifts and counsel. I did what I could to influence my impulsive sister, but, as the days raced by – as the weeks turned into months and the seasons came and went – my concerns for Helen faded. My sister might be a child in wisdom, but my daughter was a child in years. Iphigenia needed all the nurturing Helen and I never lacked as girls. My child became my thoughts, my hopes, my fears.

Her first smile made me cry. Her wordless babbling was poetry. When she began teething and two perfect little front teeth poked through her pink gums, she hardly fussed at all. Every stage of her progress was a miracle, a cause for celebration and thanksgiving, each a stage her brother never reached.

She was my child in every sense. *Mama* was her first word, not *Tata* or *Nurse*. When she learned to crawl, she always made her way towards me to be petted and told what a clever girl she was. She crawled, and eventually toddled, a little later than my ladies' children. Later, too, than Harmonia's boy, Nicandros, who was born two moons after her. This, Eritha said, was due to her early birth.

Eritha dubbed her well: "Little Cicada". Poets say cicadas are immortal, which made the name seem auspicious. They thrive on sips of morning dew, just as the gods drink nectar. "Sing me a song, Cicada," I'd say, and my baby would slap her hands together, chortling.

All the same, I feared for my delicate girl. I sent up countless burnt offerings to Paean the Healer and to every other deity who could deliver her from rashes, aches, fevers and chills, and to those who could prevent illness.

"You fret over her health more than she does," Aegisthus teased me. He fretted only a little less, which was far more than her father, who'd forgotten his disappointment at her sex by forgetting her entirely. When Aegisthus wasn't absent from Mycenae on Agamemnon's business, he brought Iphigenia elixirs and charms. He brought her dolls too, and rattles, balls and spinning tops. For her second birthday, he gave her a wooden cicada, which she mounted and pretended to fly.

By then, I was big again with child. Agamemnon remembered Iphigenia long enough to insist on a son this time, or he'd get one elsewhere. Well, let him. He wouldn't be the first man to appoint a bastard as his heir, but surely no king would put aside his queen and daughters to marry a woman of low status.

*

My second daughter emerged after a two-day labour. I thought I might die during our battle. At times, I even wanted to. But whenever I came close to fainting away, I thought of Iphigenia and of this mysterious child who didn't want to leave me, and I knew I must live.

Following his new daughter's birth, Agamemnon didn't creep into the nursery to gaze at her while the palace slept. He sent no servants to enquire after her health. He fulfilled his duty at her naming ceremony, and named her Electra.

Iphigenia adored having a little sister. She laughed and chattered whenever I held her over the baby's cradle. She loved to tug my ladies' skirts and point at the baby: "Lecta, sis, Lecta." Electra developed more quickly than Iphigenia had. Iphigenia followed her everywhere when the baby began to crawl – and I followed both girls, ready to sweep up my elder daughter, whose tottering pursuit was less certain than Electra's dogged scrambling.

The baby howled in indignation whenever anyone curbed her explorations. She was forever upending my ladies' wool baskets and tripping the slaves. I couldn't produce enough milk for both girls, so Harmonia nursed Electra. Sometimes, it was like a knife sliding between my ribs, watching her sit with

Electra at one breast and her strapping Nicandros at the other, but at least I could still suckle Iphigenia.

All in all, the first few years of Iphigenia's life were the happiest I'd known since Agamemnon shattered my world. No time was ever as peaceful again.

CHAPTER 14

Agamemnon occasionally sent for the girls, to check on their progress. He sat them on his knees in turn, tilting their faces this way and that, testing their small limbs, as his daughters wriggled in ecstasy. Iphigenia, he decided, would be pretty – one day, she'd fetch him a good alliance. Electra had the makings of a fine boy; as her mother, it was my duty to train this out of her.

The girls begged to see him between these visits. Sometimes, I took them to the balcony above the hall, on the condition they kept very, very quiet. With a child on either hip, I let them gaze in awe at their distant idol while he oversaw the business of Mycenae with his scribes, administrators and counsellors. The girls, of course, understood nothing of what was said, but I remained apprised of the production of weapons, jewellery, perfumes, cloth and furniture in the palace workshops, of exports and imports, boundary disputes, allocation of land tenures, and all the intricacies of kingship. Such matters bored Agamemnon, but he was too greedy and shrewd to neglect them. He was a better king than Thyestes, lesser than I'd have been.

One morning, finding him alone with Aegisthus, we lingered on the balcony. Aegisthus was sitting on a stool by the hearth, watching the glow of the fire while Agamemnon glowered at him from the throne. Usually, I took the children away if the hall was almost empty, so they couldn't distract Agamemnon and rouse his irritation. Just this once, curiosity overcame my judgement.

"You might be a bastard," Agamemnon was saying, "but surely there's some noble or another sniffing after you for his daughter? A foreigner? A minor chieftain from some barbarous place – Thessaly?"

I hushed the girls with a clack of my tongue and waited for Aegisthus to reply. Since Electra's birth, I'd seen far less of him.

I often wondered where he was and what he was doing. Busy though I was with my children, my mind would stray back to those days when he and I regularly shared our confidences. Agamemnon had appointed him overseer of wool production, which meant supervising workshops throughout the Argive Plain, as well as monitoring the royal flocks.

Aegisthus chuckled. "Keen to be rid of me?"

"Stay as long as you like, but you won't be taking a wife while you live in my kingdom. You'll serve me better if you're responsible to me alone. Don't forget how much you owe the House of Atreus."

Hearing my sharp intake of breath, the children turned wide eyes to me. So Agamemnon feared Aegisthus as a son-producing rival? His obsession with getting a male heir grew with every passing month. He subjected me to all kinds of remedies and rituals at the hands of his wise men, forgetting that I at least had proved myself worthy, in the goddess' eyes, of producing sons. Mater Theia was snuffing out the House of Atreus as if dousing a rancid tallow lamp. Even Helen, for all her promise, had given Menelaus a daughter.

"You have your distractions though, don't you?" persisted Agamemnon. "I mean, you're a man, aren't you? You've a girl or two in the palace, or among the shepherds' daughters?"

Aegisthus smiled at a coil of smoke curling lazily from the hearth. "If you say so."

Their exchange sickened me. Really, I should walk away before it took a grosser turn. At least the children were too young to understand it.

"By Pan's hairy arse, you're testing me!" bellowed Agamemnon, and the children jolted in my arms. Then he heaved a sigh and scratched his coppery beard. "Come, Aegisthus, we're brothers of a sort, aren't we? Yet you never confide in me. Even the fiercest boarhound turns up its belly sometimes."

"You'd like to share confidences?" said Aegisthus. "Tell me about your own women. You must have a pack of bouncing sons by now."

Agamemnon scowled. "Sometimes I think there's a curse on my house. Daughters, that's all my wife's given me. Two useless daughters. Iphigenia's so sickly, it's a grief to be her father. And as for Electra—'

"Tata!" cried Electra, unable to restrain herself.

Her father glared up at the balcony and caught sight of us. Aegisthus' casual air deserted him; he stared at me, his lips parting.

"What do you think you're doing, spying?" shouted Agamemnon.

"Don't be absurd," I said. "The children just wanted to see you. It's better than disturbing you by arranging a visit."

"Babies belong in the nursery. If I wanted to see them, I'd send for them."

"Children, say goodbye to your father," I told my whimpering girls.

My heart ached for them as I carried them away. Electra squirmed and strained her small body in an effort to keep sight of her tata, even when the hall was far behind us. Only when I'd closed the nursery door did she bury her face in my breast and sob with her sister.

At least, for now, the girls were too young to understand their father's assessment of them. I dreaded the time when this wouldn't be.

*

Agamemnon, it seemed, feared Aegisthus as a potential rival and feared the sons Aegisthus might produce. I needed to know whether my husband would ever get a son of his own, or if he'd resent our daughters for ever. The morning after the incident on the balcony, I woke Harmonia in the nursery and we set out at dawn for the oracle of Great Artemis.

We disguised ourselves in hooded cloaks, since I required a true answer from the priestesses and not one calculated to please their queen. An acolyte met us on the path to Artemis' grove just as the sun split the clouds. She led us to a little pool watered by a brook, took off our sandals, and cleansed our feet and hands. Then we followed her into the fragrant shade of the cypress grove.

Harmonia had gathered a bouquet of wildflowers during our walk. I placed it on an offering table, along with silver votive figurines of a deer and a bear. The offerings were more than sufficient for a priestess to appear from among the trees and invite me to approach the Goddess Tree. I had no difficulty identifying which swaying cypress this was – bright woollen garlands hung from its lower branches. The chief priestess sat below the tree, gnawing mushrooms. Her face, with its meshwork of wrinkles, was tipped towards the branches in contemplation.

The younger priestess explained that I could ask a single question and the chief priestess would interpret the reply through the undulations of the tree.

I held out my hands to the Goddess Tree. "Great Artemis, will my husband ever get a son?" Not, *Will I give my husband a son?* This, I had no wish to know.

The ancient priestess didn't rise or acknowledge me. She remained intent on the shivering dance of the cypress, as if its leaves were emblazoned with those symbols only scribes understand. I was filled with reverence for the goddess. I sensed her near, Artemis the Great One, imparting the truths known to the deathless and the dead.

The crone threw her hands in the air. She cried out in a thick voice, "Beware, the king! On a polluted altar, he will get an unlawful heir. Beware, the one who wants to be king!"

I stepped back and clutched my cloak tighter around me. Harmonia, in the shade of the ring of cypresses, looked as ashen as I felt.

"Why mention kings to me?" I said. "And what's this, an unlawful heir?"

"Only one question," said the younger priestess. She swept her hand to indicate the path leading from the grove.

The crone grinned, gummy as a newborn. "Beware the king – poor king, poor king," she sing-songed. "Beware his heir – poor queen, poor king."

I took Harmonia's arm. Pursued by the babbling and cackling of the crone, we hurried from the grove. Tree roots snatched at our feet. We didn't speak till the cypresses lay far behind us, till the breeze waned and sweat trickled down my back from the heat of the morning sun. I pulled off my cloak and dropped it in Harmonia's arms.

"What could the oracle mean?" she said.

We were passing along a dirt track. A small flock of scraggly sheep trotted across our path, towards a few withered gorse bushes amid a scattering of mud-brick dwellings.

"Who knows?" I said. "At worst, it means what she said. Agamemnon will commit sacrilege on an altar. The resulting child will be his heir."

Harmonia's brow furrowed. "How could that be?"

"He's Agamemnon. He does what he likes."

"But how did the priestess know who you were? We were disguised."

I flicked a buzzing insect from my face. "Because her goddess knew. Oh, cease your prattle, if you've nothing sensible to say."

From one of the mud-brick houses, a man emerged and shooed his way through the grazing sheep. He turned in our direction and raised his hand to shield his eyes from the sun.

"Clytemnestra!" he shouted.

"It's Lord Aegisthus," said Harmonia, as if I'd lost the power of recognition.

The house Aegisthus exited was a poor dwelling, the sort that accommodates a family's animals overnight, along with the family. Aegisthus' manner gave no hint of his business there. No scribe accompanied him, and I doubted such pitiful sheep counted among Agamemnon's meat or wool flocks. He waited for us to catch him up.

"Can I walk you back to the citadel?" he said.

I shrugged. "If you've no affairs to keep you."

"I've been meaning to speak with you. I haven't had the chance."

"You certainly seem busy."

"Could we have privacy?" He tilted his head to indicate Harmonia.

"Her? She's discreet."

He snorted. "Our family's business is none of hers."

Harmonia drew an injured little breath, which pleased me. The oracle had shaken me and I regretted the interest she took in it.

"Walk behind us," I said.

She obeyed, but Aegisthus remained silent even when she fell some way back.

"For someone who wanted to talk, you've not much to say," I told him.

He studied the ground. "How have you been?"

"Oh, quite well. Obviously you couldn't ask such a reckless question in front of Harmonia."

"I've been waiting for the right time to speak. You're always with the children."

"And you have your duties and companions." My inability to hide my jealousy rankled, and my annoyance made it twice as obvious.

"I'd sooner have your family."

"You wouldn't want Agamemnon as a bedmate." With a stab, I imagined Aegisthus with a voluptuous wife, someone like Helen. The father of sons and daughters.

He grimaced. "I hate the thought of him touching you."

Heat flashed through me, disconcerting. "Did you follow me today?"

"I needed to see you – outside the palace." He took my arm. His words came tumbling out, as if he feared the chance to speak wouldn't come again. "I need to make you understand, Clytemnestra. All the times we spent together, our walks, our confidences…the only peace I've ever known is with you—"

"Aegisthus…" I tried, not too strenuously, to free myself from his grip.

"Please, listen. You gave me no reason to think…but I did think, and now I believe. We should leave together, go abroad, take the children. I have allies. Where do you think I was all that time while Thyestes ruled?"

His words hit me like a sweet blow, an ache for what might have been, for what could never be. And with a thrumming clarity, I understood the danger he posed to my daughters. When I was sure of my voice, I said, "I would never – *never* – ruin my children's lives, not for you, not for me. Why would you even think it? Who'd marry them if I disgraced them? They'd be lucky to find labourers for husbands."

"I have allies," he said again.

"Do you actually believe those allies would defy the most powerful king in Achaea for your sake? Agamemnon would forbid any kindness to my daughters, just to punish us."

Us.

He said, "Then I'll kill him."

I jerked my arm from his grasp. "Insane! Would my children be less shamed by having their father's killer for a stepfather? Would I be less shameful?"

"Your husband's killer shares your bed. Your children call the killer of their brother 'Father'. You refuse to avenge your dead. I'll avenge them."

His accusations scalded. "What business is it of yours? My dead were nothing to you."

"For you. I'll do it for you."

"I want nothing from you."

He groaned, bowed his head. I focused on the looming citadel.

"I didn't mean to suggest any of this is your fault," he said softly.

Yet he had blamed me, accused me of failing in my duty to my dead. He was as blind as Helen to my predicament.

He half-heartedly kicked a rock from my path, just as he'd done the day we first walked together, after I'd soothed his bruised eye with salve. After he fought Agamemnon for insulting me. "You shouldn't have to live like this."

"Let me make it plain," I said, weary, as if trying to tell Electra why she couldn't have everything she desired. "I hate my marriage, but the gods don't. The gods hate disorder. They hated Thyestes for seizing the throne. They allowed his poor innocent sons to be punished for his crime. They elevated the sons of Atreus. Should I fight the gods? Would you fight the gods? Would you ignite a feud between our sons, and those of Menelaus and Helen, who'd be obliged to avenge Agamemnon?"

At this suggestion of our imagined children, Aegisthus' head snapped up. His eyes were painfully bright.

I cut him off before he could speak, before my own words could be softened by pity and regret: "Besides, I value your friendship too much to have you under the illusion I share your feelings."

He flinched. After a moment's pause, he said, "As you wish, lady. You should call to your woman, let her catch up. Can't leave her for the beasts, I suppose."

I forced my unwilling body to step away from him and made Harmonia a signal. She caught it, despite the distance between us. Aegisthus fixed his absent gaze on her.

CHAPTER 15

I saw Aegisthus only a handful of times after his proposition. With a word, I could have mended things between us. I could have told him…what? I could have told him nothing, so I said nothing, and he left Mycenae.

No one could tell me where he'd gone. Agamemnon didn't seem to care, though apparently no quarrel had taken place between them. So I put Aegisthus from my mind. Whenever he intruded on my thoughts, as the days passed and the seasons changed, I reminded myself he didn't belong there. A queen doesn't mope like a serving girl. Dreams are for slaves; queens have destinies. Even if my destiny was an ill one, my duty was to lead my daughters safely to theirs.

Iphigenia was my greatest comfort, affectionate and undemanding. She loved to "help" me and my ladies while we sewed, handing out glittering discs to decorate our materials. She stood at her toy loom and pretended to weave, copying us with all the gravity of her tender years. She played well with my ladies' little ones, unlike her sister, who depended less on others, or liked to think so. Electra would sit in the corner of the room, setting up building blocks and knocking them down. She had a fondness for other children's toys and a reluctance to share, a trait that reminded me of her father.

Sometimes I caught Agamemnon appraising our daughters when he passed them in the courtyard. He boasted about the brilliant matches he'd make for them; already, he'd mentioned them in the messages he exchanged with the Great Kings of Hatti, Egypt and Troy. I suspected his motives whenever he ordered me to bring the girls to supper in the hall, but I resolved to let them take whatever happiness they could from those rare occasions. Afterwards, I reminded him that our daughters were far too young for their marriage prospects to be seriously considered.

One morning, he sent a servant to the nursery with a summons to bring the girls to supper that evening. I'd been teaching Iphigenia and Electra simple steps from the dances to the goddesses, which in time they'd lead. To avoid overexciting them, I didn't mention the invitation until later that evening. They skipped away to be bathed and perfumed, holding Harmonia's hands and chattering in delighted anticipation.

The time for supper approached, and still Harmonia didn't bring the girls to the throne room, where I waited for them.

"Sorry to disturb you, lady," said a breathless maid, hovering in the doorway.

"Disturb me? What's wrong?"

"Nothing, it's just that Princess Electra asked permission to wear a necklace, and when her nursemaid refused—"

"She can wear the necklace." The request, I suspected, hadn't been made politely, but it was a welcome one. Only yesterday, Electra had indulged in a boisterous solitary game of pretending to be Heracles and the entire crew of Jason's *Argo* – and now she wanted to be a pretty queen. "I'll chastise her later for any bad behaviour."

"Yes, lady, it's just that the nursemaid said the choice was unsuitable. So the princess ran away, and now we can't find her."

I sighed and made my way to the nursery.

*

Slapping footsteps and piping squeals sounded through the nursery door, indicating Electra's return.

When I entered the room, Iphigenia skipped towards me for my admiration. Though she was too little to require clothing, Harmonia had dressed her in a short tunic since it was past harvest-time and winds gusted through the shutters and chimneys of the palace. The maiden lock over her brow, and the longer braid at the back of her otherwise shaven head, gleamed with perfumed oil. On the day of her wedding, she would dedicate this forelock to Great Artemis, as all girls do, but thankfully that day was far off.

"Very pretty, dear," I said.

A maid stood close by the wall, concealing a hopping, jumping child behind her back.

Harmonia cast the maid a frosty glare. "This stupid girl let Electra out of her sight while I dressed Iphigenia. The princess ended up in your room, lady."

"Let me go," grumbled Electra, behind the maid.

"Show me my daughter," I said.

The maid hung her head. Her arms dropped to her sides.

Electra darted out from behind her. The child's face was smeared in red kermes paste and she'd draped herself in one of my blouses, which trailed and billowed around her. For jewels, she wore several strings of carnelian and lapis beads, and a casket worth of armlets. She held up her arms to keep the armlets from falling off.

"I visit Tata," she declared.

"Not till we've stripped you and cleaned your face," I said.

"No!" Her feet caught in the blouse as she tried to run. She pitched forward, armlets clattering to the floor. I caught her before she fell. She tried to dive from my grasp, either to evade me or gather up the armlets, or both. I held her fast and removed the necklaces while she writhed and raged.

Harmonia and I changed her into a tunic and wiped kermes paste from her face, then I carried her from the nursery. Iphigenia trotted at my side, casting sympathetic looks at her bawling sister.

"Hush, Electra – do you want your father to hear you?" I said. "Weren't you playing brave Heracles yesterday? And today you're crying like a little girl."

"Tata like me," she gasped between choked breaths. "Tata like girls."

Where had she heard that?

"He cares for you very much," I said, "and for you, Iphigenia."

"No Ipheege!" screamed Electra.

Iphigenia's bottom lip wobbled. I clasped her little hand.

Though Electra should be punished, I had to restore calm, for both girls' sakes. If our lateness didn't test their father beyond his endurance, tears certainly would.

"He cares for you both, and that's why he sent for you tonight. And here we are, children. Tata's hall."

In the porch, a single sentry guarded the bronze door to the vestibule. He said nothing as we passed him. No aroma of cooking greeted us when I drew back the scarlet curtain. No servants turned spits at the hearth or stirred cauldrons. Lamps and wall torches were lit, but no table had been set. The throne was unoccupied.

"Is Tata hiding?" asked Iphigenia. Her eyes brightened with a spark of hope and the threat of tears.

"Hide pillar!" yelled Electra, trying to wriggle from my arms.

Iphigenia dashed off to investigate. She circled each of the four bronze-ornamented hearth pillars in turn and scampered twice around the last. She froze. My heart ached at the bewilderment in her voice: "Mama?"

"Tata! Where my tata? No, no!" wailed Electra, as I turned around and carried her back to the porch. She swallowed her sobs to listen while I asked the sentry where the king had gone.

"He was called away," the man replied. "He said to tell you, 'The princesses are too young.'"

I bit back my anger. "Is he in his apartments?"

"Can't say, lady."

I smiled in fury. "Oh, can't you?"

But what did it matter whose bed Agamemnon fornicated in? He'd raised my daughters' hopes, only to crush them. The tears Iphigenia had been holding back burst from her, prompting an answering howl from her sister, who slapped at my chest with her sturdy little hands. I placed my palm on Iphigenia's head and guided her upstairs, all the way back to the nursery.

Once the girls were in bed, Iphigenia gulped down her tears and curled herself around her sobbing sister. Electra made a half-hearted effort to squirm away, before sagging into Iphigenia's thin arms. I stroked the downy softness of my daughters' heads till both girls whimpered themselves to sleep. I kissed their faces in turn. Iphigenia's eyelids fluttered. Electra groaned.

I should have known their father would let them down. They were "too young", not yet useful to him. But, if the notion took him to raise their hopes again, how was I to protect my girls?

*

Next morning, I returned to the nursery to find Electra wriggling on a stool while an ashen-faced maid, supervised by Harmonia, passed a razor over the fuzz on the child's scalp. Iphigenia sat on the floor, playing with Harmonia's son. The pair were freshly shorn.

"You're too little and I'm busy," said Iphigenia, trotting a terracotta doe across the floor. "Come back when you're a big dolphin."

Nicandros frowned at the wooden fish in his hand. "What do I do now, Genia?"

"Cry," she laughed.

"I never cry." The boy's declaration sounded less like a boast than a simple assertion.

"That's because you don't have a tata," said Iphigenia.

"Enough, children," chided Harmonia. The contented smile, which she always had around her solemn boy, didn't falter.

Electra bounced on the stool. "No maiden lock. I hunter!" She reached in front of the maid's obsidian razor to pluck at her forelock.

"Careful!" I cried.

Electra yelped as a thin red rivulet opened on her scalp.

The maid gasped. "Oh, Queen Clytemnestra! I didn't mean to. It's just that she won't sit still."

"Calm yourself," I said. "The cut isn't serious, and I'm sure you came prepared."

The maid had indeed brought a cloth and salve. Sniffling, she tended to Electra's injury. The child glowered around the room, her lower lip trembling.

"What game are you playing?" I asked Iphigenia and Nicandros.

"Hunting," whispered Electra.

"Not hunting, silly," giggled Iphigenia. "Tata and the men are hunting. Nicandros saw them leave. We're playing palaces, but Nicandros doesn't know how."

"He no prince," said Electra. She winced as the maid pressed the cloth against her cut.

"I'm going to be a warrior when I'm big," said Nicandros. He dropped his gaze. "If the king lets me."

Poor child. Slaves didn't serve in royal warbands, even slaves whose mothers were nursemaids to kings' daughters. He had more chance of becoming Zeus' cup-bearer.

"Whatever service you perform for the king, I'm sure your mother will be very proud," I told him.

Harmonia preened her already perfect hair.

"Thank you, lady," said Nicandros. "I want to be a hero and have adventures like Heracles and Jason."

Electra snorted. "You ba-bas- You baster! Basters can't hero."

"That's unkind," I said. "Say you're sorry at once to Nicandros." Try though I might, I couldn't think of any bastard heroes of lowly stock to correct her with. True, Heracles' parentage was disputed and he'd served for a year as Queen Omphale's slave, but that wasn't a tale for young ears – and Heracles' two potential fathers were a king and a god.

Electra pressed her lips in a stubborn line.

Iphigenia took Nicandros' hand. "You're our friend. I know you'll be a great warrior."

"Thank you, Genia," said Nicandros, shyly returning her smile.

*

Though I threatened Electra with a beating, nothing would induce her to apologise to the slave boy. When the nick on her head stopped bleeding, I led my daughters by the hand from the nursery, ignoring Electra's struggles till she twisted her body so far around that she discovered, with a yelp, the limits of her arm socket.

My turn came to cry out, more from surprise than pain, as small teeth nipped my wrist. I released Electra and slapped her across the cheek. Her face turned scarlet. Her breath came in bursts through her nose. Iphigenia reached out to her, and she dodged away.

"Don't try to comfort her," I said. "She's a naughty little girl, aren't you, Electra?"

"No!" Electra blurted.

I dragged her resisting body downstairs to the first floor of the palace and into the Gallery of the Tapestries, the long, narrow room decorated with frescoes of tapestries and of curtains. Unlike my throne room, the gallery has a fixed central hearth, which makes it a pleasant place to sit with my ladies in cooler weather. Fighting back her tears, Electra met my ladies' curious looks with gulps, gasps and scowls.

"Are you sorry now?" I said, so all could hear.

"No," she whispered.

I instructed Iphigenia to card wool with another child. Electra, I ordered to stand in front of me while I sat on one of the stone benches along the walls and spun wool on my distaff. No one would speak to her, I warned her, until she apologised to me and Nicandros.

After a while, her limbs started to tremble from the effort of remaining motionless, but she pretended not to notice when I raised an eyebrow in silent enquiry. I allowed a maid to give her water, but permitted no other indulgence. Eventually, she slumped onto her bottom. I shooed away Iphigenia, who approached with a cushion.

As time wore on, I dismissed my ladies. Electra, by then, was sleeping on her side, her cheek pressed against the cool gypsum floor. I ached to bundle my wayward girl in my arms. A tugging sound roused me from my contemplation of her. Iphigenia hadn't left with the ladies as I'd instructed. She was trying to pull a square of weaving from a loom.

"What are you doing?" I said.

"A blanket for Electra."

"Take Princess Iphigenia to the nursery," I told the remaining maid.

Iphigenia tiptoed around Electra, laid her little hands on my knees, and turned up her face for a kiss. I pressed my lips to her forehead. How was it that so small a creature could so often be the source of my strength?

The maid took her away and my thoughts returned to Electra, asleep on the floor. Was this one really mine, or a true child of the House of Atreus? I chided myself inwardly for such a treacherous thought.

Her father strode into the gallery, noticed her on the floor and narrowed his eyes at her. "Is she a hound, now?"

"She was misbehaving. She'll stay there till she apologises."

"Women's business." He waved a dismissive hand, but continued to regard Electra sidelong. "I suppose you're wondering what happened last night. The fact is, I made a mistake sending for your daughters – and this behaviour confirms it. It'll be a while before they can wait on my guests and sing pleasingly."

"Quite some time."

"Still, I'd have expected more progress. I'm thinking of their futures, you realise." He sounded accusatory, as if he suspected me of ever thinking about anything else. "They won't be marrying petty Achaean chieftains. I want Hatti or Egypt. True, I already enjoy profitable relations with the Great Kings, but imagine how much more we stand to gain when my grandsons number among them. And such brilliant marriages will of course benefit the girls, too."

"Will you be acquainting yourself with your children before sending them to the Land of Hatti?"

"What would I do with them? Sew? Pick flowers?"

"My father told us stories." I laughed at the absurd notion of Agamemnon doing the same.

He gave me the same withering look he'd given Electra. "Perhaps I'll find them each a blathering old husband who'll bounce them on his knee. At any rate, they're young yet, but who and when they marry is my concern. Your concern is to prepare them, and I suggest you make a better job of it." With a last grimace at his daughter, he walked on through the gallery.

I leaned back against the wall and gave way to a crushing fatigue. When I finally forced myself to rise from the bench, I saw that my daughter's eyes were squeezed shut.

"Electra," I said softly.

She gave a choked gulp.

I lifted her and folded her in my arms as she burst into frenzied sobs. She buried her face in my chest. Her hands scrabbled around my neck.

"Breathe slowly," I said, as she gasped for air. I cupped her grimy cheek in my palm and rubbed her sturdy little back.

"He's…sending me…away," she panted.

Would he hurt all of my children?

I kissed her shorn head. "No, darling. No one is sending you away."

"He said! Want Tata!"

Hatred filled my heart as I held her to me.

When her emotions were spent, I carried her limp, clammy body to the nursery and instructed a servant to fill a bathtub. I hummed a lullaby as I bathed Electra, massaging her tense shoulders and back till she could no longer fight the drooping of her eyelids. Gently, I lifted her from the tub, dried her and laid her beside her sleeping sister.

Heavy with weariness, I stood in the doorway and watched my two girls at peace in the oblivion of sleep. I crept out and closed the door.

"Clytemnestra," said the voice I most longed to hear.

Aegisthus stood before me. He tentatively held out his arms and I sagged into them.

CHAPTER 16

N ever again, Aegisthus swore as we clung together outside the nursery, would he leave me friendless – a promise he repeated over the following days. He had returned, and he was resigned. And, though I could offer him no more than friendship, he swore to cherish all I could give.

Just once, he asked, "And when the girls are grown and you're still Agamemnon's wife?"

"You think that would be the time to disgrace them?"

He didn't raise the subject again.

We talked of his self-imposed exile, his wanderings from stranger's hearth to stranger's hearth, of the friendships he'd forged among the Achaeans and friendships he'd renewed. In turn, I confided my concerns for my daughters and my frustration over Electra's defiance. He suggested appointing a new nursemaid. Harmonia, he said, was too preoccupied with her own child to devote herself to mine. This seemed unfair. I wondered at his dislike of her, but I didn't wish to dwell on the reasons that might lie behind it, perhaps a friendship badly ended. Sometimes, I studied little Nicandros, his dark complexion…

I wondered whether I was making Harmonia redundant by being over-attentive to my children, reducing her to the role of their serving woman. But I continued to guide and educate them – and Electra continued to grow more distant. Surrounded by my ladies and their little ones, she shrouded herself in a cocoon, and emerged, startled and resentful, only when her name was repeated over and over. I hoped this was a childish phase and feared it was not.

Iphigenia remained as gentle and obedient as ever. As the anniversary of her sixth name day drew near, I planned to present her with a gift Helen had given when she was born: a beautiful gold armlet embossed with lilies and bees. Aegisthus

suggested having a similar armlet made for her sister, to raise
Electra's spirits. I agreed, though we both knew we were trying
to prevent an envious outburst by pandering to the worst in
Electra's nature. But I wanted to make sure nothing marred
Iphigenia's delight in her special gift.

Instead of summoning the master goldsmith to the palace,
we decided to take the children on an outing to his forge outside
the citadel, to be measured for the resizing and fashioning of
the armlets. When we went to the nursery to collect the girls,
Electra was still curled up beneath her bedcovers. Harmonia
frowned down at the child's burly little form.

"Up." I pulled the covers aside.

"Sick," murmured Electra, burying her face in the cushions.
Feigning illness was her latest tactic to remain in the nursery,
with Harmonia waiting on her.

"Nothing fresh air won't fix," I said. "Come, we're visiting a
workshop today."

"Too hot."

I tucked my hand between her forehead and the cushion. Her
mildly raised temperature probably resulted from burrowing
under the covers.

Iphigenia rose from a stool in the corner of the nursery
and tiptoed past Electra's bed. She went to Aegisthus, in the
doorway, and hugged his legs. "Please may we go now, Uncle?"

Electra drew her a sidelong glance.

"You'll be too warm," I told Iphigenia. Sunlight beamed
through the window shutters, though it was barely spring; yet
Harmonia, for some reason, had chosen to dress the child in a
long-sleeved tunic.

Iphigenia's gaze dropped to her sleeve. "It's pretty."

"It's plain, dear. You'll have much prettier clothes when
you're older. Why did you dress her, Harmonia?"

"I didn't, lady. She dressed herself before I woke," said the
nursemaid.

Aegisthus and I exchanged surprised smiles. Iphigenia was
rarely so assertive. Such a show of independence was to be
encouraged, though of course not overindulged.

"I'd like to go now," the child said.

"Once Electra gets out of bed." I briskly tapped my younger girl's arm.

"What's wrong, little one?" said Aegisthus, tipping Iphigenia's chin.

She tugged at his kilt. "We shouldn't make Electra come if she doesn't want to."

Electra giggled and buried her face deeper in the cushions.

My skin prickled. Suddenly, separating Iphigenia from her sister seemed more important than forcing Electra to obey.

"Very well," I said. "Harmonia, Electra says she's ill. Make sure she stays in the nursery all day and doesn't leave for any reason."

*

Most smiths work in the artisans' wing of the palace, producing items for export and domestic use, but the master goldsmith had earned the privilege of working unsupervised. He lived in his own forge, where he crafted prestige items.

His assistant welcomed us at the door and led us to a bench in an anteroom. We listened briefly to the tap of a hammer before the master emerged from the inner forge. He spread out his muscular arms, which gleamed with his wares, and thanked us for the honour of our visit. Iphigenia shrank a little, between me and Aegisthus, but returned the man's warm smile.

I took the armlet from the cloth I'd wrapped around it. "I'd like to have this resized, master goldsmith. And tell me, could you fashion another just like it?"

"Oh…" murmured Iphigenia as the smith studied the armlet and rubbed his thumb over the honeybee finials. "Oh! Who is it for?"

Aegisthus gave her maiden lock a gentle tug. "Who could it be for? Perhaps a very small girl with very small arms?"

A half-incredulous, wholly delighted smile lit up her face. "For me?" She clambered up on the bench and threw her arms around Aegisthus' neck. "Thank you, Uncle."

He laughed. "No, Cicada, you must send thanks to Aunt Helen. Though I won't refuse your hug."

"It was Aunt Helen's name-day gift to you," I explained, recalling with an ache Aegisthus carrying our beloved girl around the hearth at her birth celebrations, slipping so easily into the role of her father.

Iphigenia clasped my neck and showered my cheek with kisses.

"I'm glad you like it, my darling," I said. "Now, lift your sleeve so the master goldsmith can measure your arm."

She stiffened. "I'll get cold."

"Don't be silly," I said.

She stared down at the floor.

With mounting disquiet, I took her thin arm and turned up her sleeve. A series of fresh bruises mottled her skin. Aegisthus swore under his breath. I turned her sleeve back down.

"Excuse us, master goldsmith," I said. "We'll be back in the coming days."

Iphigenia's hand was cold in mine as I led her back along the main thoroughfare to the citadel. White-faced, she asked, "Mama, are you angry with me?"

I stopped walking. "Iphigenia, you must tell me what happened."

"Nothing, Mama."

"Would you lie to me?" My tone was sharper than I meant.

She bit her lips and blinked back tears.

Aegisthus hunkered down beside her. "Cicada, never be afraid to tell your mama the truth. She and I will always protect you."

"I don't want to get my sister in trouble."

I knelt beside Aegisthus and raised the hem of Iphigenia's tunic. Another bruise disfigured her shin. I gathered her in my arms and pressed her to my breast, as much to hide my anger from her as to comfort her. The anger was for myself.

"My darling, understand this," I said. "No one will love Electra when she's a grown lady if she's a bully. If you want to help her, you must tell us exactly what she did to you."

Iphigenia broke into sobs. "She didn't mean it, Mama. Not really."

She admitted that Electra had struck and kicked her on a number of occasions. To my shame, I recalled various bruises and Iphigenia's explanations of clumsiness, which I'd accepted. Electra believed Iphigenia had angered their father and was to blame for his lack of interest in his daughters.

"She says he hates me," Iphigenia sobbed. "He thinks I'm a silly, weak girl."

"That's not true. He's just very busy," I said.

Aegisthus snorted.

"Isn't that so, Uncle?" I said. "And now, darling, Uncle Aegisthus will take you to the orchard. The apple trees are blooming and they're very pretty. Would you like to see them?"

"Yes, Mama," said Iphigenia quietly. She slipped her hand into Aegisthus'.

*

I left Aegisthus and Iphigenia and continued to the palace. In the main courtyard, a rabble of small, stick-wielding slave boys had formed a circle around two little warriors duelling in their midst. I stood watching them from beneath a colonnade as they yelled encouragements and battlefield taunts. My mind was elsewhere, on my daughters.

The reigning champion, Nicandros, won his foe's surrender and faced up to the next contender from among the whooping boys. The two grim opponents were so absorbed in ducking and dodging, and thrusting their makeshift weapons at each other, they didn't notice their friends' shouts die out. Agamemnon and a greybeard counsellor had emerged from the Corridor of the Double Axes. They smiled at the boys' antics, before continuing to the hall.

In the nursery, I found Electra indulging in her own thuggish stick-game. She raced around the chamber, jabbing at tables and chairs with a broom handle. "Birds will eat your liver!" she shrieked. "No grave for you. No mercy from the warrior queen."

She sprang at Harmonia and struck her across the back of the calves.

"Stop it, naughty child," chided Harmonia.

"Naughty indeed," I said.

Electra's arm, stretched back for another strike, went rigid.

"The laundry women will be on their way to the Perseia Spring," I told Harmonia. "Join them. Perhaps you'll be more skilled at washing than managing infants."

Harmonia's lips parted, then pinched together. She bobbed her head and left the nursery.

Electra gaped. "But that's my nanny!"

"Vicious little warriors don't need nannies, do they?"

She scratched her nose uncertainly. "No…"

"Look at this." I unwrapped Iphigenia's armlet. "Today, I was going to ask the master goldsmith to make one just like this, for you. But not anymore."

Electra dropped the broom handle with a clatter and reached out. "I want it!"

"It's far too pretty for a warrior." I traced my fingertip over the granulated stripes on an embossed honeybee. "If you learn to behave like a princess, I might change my mind. You'd have to prove you deserve something so lovely."

She took a few steps towards me, hand outstretched. "I *am* good."

"Have you been good to your sister?"

Her maiden lock bounced with her emphatic nod.

"Is hitting your sister what good girls do? Is kicking?"

Her eyes darted in calculation. "I didn't do it. She did."

"Oh, she kicked her own leg and hit her own arm?"

"Y-yes?"

"I heard a different story."

Fire flashed in Electra's eyes. "She's a liar! I hate her."

I slapped her face. "How did you like that?"

She thrust out her lower lip. Her breath came hard – as much from fury, I suspected, as from a desire to cry.

"You didn't like it, did you? Then why did you strike your sister?"

"She's stupid. She makes my tata hate me."

I sighed and motioned her to a stool. For a moment, she remained mulishly unmoving, then obeyed and sat cupping her pink cheek.

I drew up a stool opposite hers. "Electra, listen carefully. You're very young, and you don't understand the responsibilities grown men have. Your father reigns over Mycenae and the Argive Plain, and over everyone who lives there, not just his own family. That's why he can't see you often. And he's a man. Women spend their days with children, men with other men."

"Uncle Aegisthus must be a woman."

"Uncle Aegisthus isn't a king. Your father wishes he could spend more time with you, but he's very, very busy." I remembered Aegisthus snorting when I told Iphigenia the same lie.

"He has time to hunt."

"Hunting keeps him practised for battle and puts meat on our table."

"Why can't I hunt? Why can't I fight?"

"Because you're a child and a girl. Hunting is dangerous. When you're older, you can drive after the men."

"I am not little!"

I tilted her chin with my finger. "Electra, when I say something, you'll accept it and not argue. You can't go hunting and your father can only see you when he has time to spare. I know this makes you unhappy, but it's the way of things. Now, you'll apologise to your sister."

She jerked her chin free. "Didn't do anything!"

I clasped her hands in mine to hold her captive. "I'll tell you a story, Electra, about another naughty princess who wasn't sorry for her wicked deeds. Her name was Medea." A disturbing tale, but she only needed to hear the parts that fit the lesson. "Medea did many bad and selfish things. And, with each wicked deed, her heart grew harder. Soon, she no longer cared about how much she hurt her family, though she ought to have loved them. But there was someone Medea did love – a man named Jason. You've heard of him, haven't you?"

The hero's name caught her attention. The tip of her tongue peeped through her lips.

"Jason himself was hard-hearted," I continued, "but Medea was so far gone in her wickedness, she couldn't tell good from bad. She and Jason stole the treasure from her father's palace and ran away together. Her angry father gave chase, and, to stop him from catching her, she seized her little brother. She chopped the child into pieces and threw each piece, one by one, to the ground. Her father had to pause to pick them all up for burial. Medea hurt her family, Electra, and you are hurting your family. If you don't mend your ways, you'll become as wicked as Medea. The more naughty things you do, the harder your heart will grow. Do you want this to happen?"

"Did Medea steal an armlet with the treasure?"

"No, she did not. The gods wouldn't let her have any armlets. She was too wicked. Gods never forgive people who hurt their families. Do you know how they punished Medea? The dove goddess Peleia made Jason desire another lady, one who was sweet and gentle. He cast off Medea and married this lady. Cruel Medea lost everything: her husband, palace, treasure and family. She yearned to return to her father's kingdom, but he hated her for her wickedness to her brother. So she fled to the mountains and lived a sad and lonely life."

"But she sent the new lady a poisoned dress," said Electra. "The new lady died."

I hadn't expected her to know this part of the story. "Wherever did you hear such a thing?"

"The bard sang it."

"Bards make up stories to entertain their audiences, but that's not what happened. Besides, Medea still lost everything she loved. Would it be worth losing everything you love just to hurt your sister?"

Electra pondered. "No…I don't want to make my tata angry. I want to live here for ever and ever."

Not the reasoning I'd hoped for, but it was a start. "Then you'll apologise to Iphigenia, and afterwards prove you deserve a pretty armlet."

"Yes, Mama."

I held out my hand. Electra slipped from her stool, and we set out for the orchard.

*

Electra apologised to Iphigenia with good grace. She hugged her beneath the blossoming apple trees and afterwards was gentler around her and more considerate. I suspected this new manner wouldn't last. So, it seemed, did Iphigenia. Though Iphigenia made no complaint against Electra, she found excuses not to wear the resized armlet, except at my insistence during festivals and ceremonies. On those occasions, sometimes I caught Electra sidling up to her to touch and stroke the golden band.

Once, I overheard Iphigenia offering to share the armlet between them.

"No, it's yours," I said, batting away Electra's outstretched hand. "Your sister will earn her own, if she's very good."

Electra's eyes followed every movement as Iphigenia slipped the armlet back onto her arm.

For a time, Electra managed to restrain her avarice. She had new distractions. I was teaching my daughters simple skills such as basket-weaving, and letting them watch me manage the slaves and household. With Agamemnon as their father, they were never too young to prepare for their future roles, even little girls who yearned to be Amazon warrior queens. Iphigenia flourished under this instruction and brimmed over with questions. Electra thought the womanly arts could be mastered without effort, and she seethed in frustration whenever her error was put to the test.

One afternoon, the girls and I were returning from taking stock of fruits drying on the palace roof. Iphigenia chattered about the gods' bounty, while Electra sighed and yawned, brightening only when we reached the balcony over her father's hall. Agamemnon, attended by his greybeards, was granting an audience to a gaunt young petitioner who complained of a neighbour stealing his land by moving the boundary stones between their adjoining fields.

"And when I asked Archelaus to stop, he said he'd burn down my house," said the petitioner, gesturing helplessly with his hands.

Electra peered through the wooden balusters at her father. Agamemnon was picking his fingernails, which were doubtless filthy from the funeral games he'd held the day before for a favourite Follower, fallen to the tusks of a boar. He remained silent.

"I appealed to the District Guardian, but he says he'll get his quotas just the same, whoever has the bigger field," said the young farmer. He seemed not to have considered that Agamemnon too would receive his quotas just the same.

Agamemnon shrugged. He scratched his armpit with his newly preened nails.

A shrill note crept into the petitioner's voice: "Things are hard, lord. Our last harvest would have been poor enough, even if Archelaus hadn't stolen the best of it. But now I've eight to feed, including my parents. My wife, you see, she's just had twins."

This sinister latter revelation drew a shudder from Agamemnon. "Then stand up to him, man. Or have your mother do it."

"Lord, forgive me, but I thought..." The farmer wrung his hands. "I thought...well, you're the king."

"If you think a king has nothing better to do than resolve petty disputes, think again. Come back when Arche-Archidamus has stolen your wife along with your cabbages, raped your goats, and poured libations to your ancestors from his bowels. Go!"

Pale-faced, escorted by a scribe, the young farmer left the hall.

*

The girls wanted to know what the petitioner had done to make their father angry. Since the man acted properly, I explained instead the injustice of his neighbour's behaviour. Iphigenia offered to give up her meals and send them to the man's family.

Electra asked why the two neighbours didn't fight a duel for ownership of the fields.

My mind lingered all day on the farmer. I imagined his half-starved wife trying to nurse her lean and quiet babies. At least my own children never lacked necessities, nor indeed luxuries, despite being burdened with a brutish father.

After sending the girls to their nursery, I instructed a servant to load a cart with provisions. The scribe on duty earlier in the hall might know where the farmer lived; failing that, the servant need only ask around the farms for Archelaus' neighbour, a father of newborn twins. I might have no power to gain justice for the farmer, but I could ensure his family didn't go hungry for now.

For the night's entertainment, I'd invited Aegisthus and some of my favourite ladies to hear a bard who'd arrived at the palace that afternoon. Itinerant singers are welcome at any hearth, since they bring news from their travels, along with their songs, in return for a meal and a place to sleep. My pleasure, however, was cut short by a maidservant, who entered the throne room and stood before me, anxiously plucking at a loose thread on her tunic.

"Well?" I said.

"Lady, I've come from the nursery."

The glow lingering from my earlier good deed, and from amusement at the bard's bawdy couplets, extinguished. "Electra?"

"Both girls. Princess Electra has set Princess Iphigenia crying. Forgive me, lady, but you said you wanted to be told if Princess Electra did anything especially naughty."

"What is it this time?"

"The princesses have been excitable, talking about the king and his petitioners. Princess Electra wouldn't settle. She became angry at Princess Iphigenia. She…she said…"The girl dropped her gaze to the floor.

"Speak freely."

"She said Princess Iphigenia is greedy, that she keeps everything to herself and gets all the attention."

"Return to the nursery. I'll visit shortly."

During this exchange, my ladies had pretended to be engrossed in the bard's song, while darting looks my way. Aegisthus, seated on the bench beside me, turned to me with a raised eyebrow.

I reached for my cup of wine on the bench, discovered I'd no appetite, and pushed the cup away. "Electra has her father's nature."

"She's just a child. Children fight," said Aegisthus. "Girls too."

I laughed, remembering the arguments Helen and I used to have, yet we were always fierce allies beneath it all. My daughters, not so much.

I said, "She's greedy and spiteful. She's Agamemnon's heir."

Aegisthus frowned. "She's your daughter too. How can you speak about her like that? You are everything those two girls have."

This observation shamed me; it would have rankled, too, if Aegisthus weren't my friend, kinder to my daughters than their father ever was. How draining this strife had become.

Upstairs, we found Electra hurtling through a corridor in the domestic quarters. On seeing us, she clasped her fingers around her arm but couldn't hide Iphigenia's armlet. The gold band sat snug around her brawny little forearm, instead of the upper arm, where her sister wore it. She howled when I seized her shoulder and forced her into the nursery.

Iphigenia sat cross-legged on the floor, clutching Raggy, her favourite blue-and-yellow ragdoll. Her eyes were round and staring. Harmonia fussed over her.

I released Electra. "Return the armlet to your sister."

Electra glared a challenge at Iphigenia. "She gave it to me. It's mine."

"Did you, Iphigenia?" I asked.

Iphigenia hugged Raggy and blinked rapidly at Electra. She whispered, "No."

I reached for Electra's arm. She dodged away and broke for the door, where Aegisthus caught her and swept her up. She pummelled his chest with her fists.

"Stop that." He took her wrists in one hand. She squirmed, swivelled and almost slipped to the floor.

"Let me go!" she yelled. "It's battle spoils. I'm Archelaus."

He raised her to eye level. "How could you steal from your own sister? Sisters and brothers are sacred. The gods punish our mistreatment of them. You should defend Iphigenia and never harm her."

"You can't tell me what to do!" she shouted. "You're not my father. You're just pretending." And then, she spat at him.

My first instinct was to strike her. I stifled it and even managed a smile. "Electra, dear, didn't I once promise you your own armlet, if you were very good? Well, the master smith has made it. If you're silent for the rest of the night, we'll go tomorrow to see it."

Her eyes widened. Her lips parted, before curving into an amazed grin. She removed Iphigenia's armlet from her arm and held it out to her.

When I'd tucked Iphigenia into bed and kissed the child and her doll goodnight, Electra marched to the bed and tugged at the covers.

"You'll sleep beside your nursemaid," I said. "She'll make sure you don't stir – and, if you do, I won't take you to the forge tomorrow." Aegisthus offered me his arm; I took it gladly. "Now, I'm going to listen to the bard without any more interruptions."

*

The next day, Electra wept as the master goldsmith melted her armlet in a crucible and poured the molten metal into a little ingot mould. He looked almost as miserable as Electra.

Once more, he asked, "Lady, are you sure I can't recast the gold into something you'd like better?"

"Your craftsmanship was faultless, master goldsmith. Keep the gold as payment for a job well done. When Princess Electra learns that a loving heart is the most precious thing a girl can own, she'll deserve the treasures mortal hands can make."

I ordered Electra to thank the goldsmith, and we left the forge. She sighed like a weary hound all the way back to the palace.

CHAPTER 17

armonia, as Aegisthus once warned me, was unfit to be my daughters' nursemaid. Any woman could have managed Iphigenia, but Harmonia had failed entirely to discipline Electra. Her nurturing instincts were for her son alone. She had, however, once been my most efficient handmaid, and I decided to reappoint her as the most senior among them.

My new choice of nursemaid was a woman recently captured during a raid on the island of Anaphe, who'd taken to suckling the slaves' little ones after her two infant daughters were traded abroad. I waited until I'd heard enough satisfactory reports about the woman's character, before summoning Harmonia to dress me in place of my usual maid.

"Your daughters are used to me," said Harmonia, tightening my braided belt. "Can't you keep us both, lady?"

"Two nursemaids in one nursery? Bad as two master smiths at a furnace or two kings on a throne." I shook my head to dispel an unbidden memory, Thyestes and Atreus, warring kings, been and gone.

"Electra will be upset," said Harmonia.

I selected a jewelled headband from a casket on the table. "She'll adjust."

"Still, I expect it makes sense, given your condition."

The headband slipped from my fingers. "What?"

Harmonia stepped back to study me. She loosened my belt. "Should I send for Eritha to examine you, or would you prefer the palace herbcutters this time?"

Though I'd missed four bleeds, my belly barely showed. I still hoped to miscarry, as I'd done numerous times. The prospect of giving a son to the House of Atreus, a boy to be moulded into the image of those violent men, jolted me awake at night, soaked in sweat, like Thyestes haunted by his murdered boys.

Every bit as much, I feared losing the child or having another girl. Agamemnon was furious at his lack of an heir. What would happen to Iphigenia and Electra if I failed him again? My daughters were safe for now, but what if the notion struck their father to take a new royal bride and put us aside? As Jason did with Medea, Heracles with his faithful Deianira – and those women had lavished devotion on their husbands, as I never had.

"I'll send for Eritha closer to the time," I said, "if I must."

*

Now that my secret was known, I had little choice but to tell my husband. First, I broke the news to Aegisthus, seated together on a bench in my throne room.

"I suppose it had to happen sooner or later," he said, grimacing. "What now?"

I laid my hand on his. For a startling moment, I felt the life force swirling within him, within his veins, this man who might have been mine. "What can I do?"

The question required no answer, but he turned his face to mine with such vehemence that I drew away. "What can you do? What can you do? You should have escaped while you could. Taken your daughters. You'll never take a son from him."

"Of course not," I said, stunned.

"He'd never let you. Oh, what've I done?" He squeezed his temples between clenched fists. "I should have stopped this. I could have stopped it. I knew it could happen and I refused to believe it."

I edged away from him. "What are you talking about? He's my husband. No one can stop him from claiming his rights."

He groaned. "Will it be a boy?"

"How should I know?"

"Better it's not. Better for all our sakes." He jumped up from the bench and reached the door in a few strides.

I ran after him, cursing myself for breaking the news so bluntly. His pride was wounded, his foolish hopes, impossible hopes, sweet fruits forever dangling from a branch beyond his reach. He hurried through the courtyard towards the hall, where Agamemnon had spent the last several days with the officers of his warband, planning harvest raids on distant neighbours.

"I should've stopped it, I could've stopped it," he mumbled.

Dismayed, I reached for his arm. He was too quick and seemed oblivious to my pursuit. He passed the sentries guarding the porch, threw back the scarlet curtain in the vestibule and strode into the hall.

"Get out of here, get out!" he shouted, shoving one of Agamemnon's gaping officers. "I'll talk to you alone, Agamemnon."

My husband's startled face settled into a sneer. "Finally, he's lost his wits. All right, gentlemen, I'll handle the madman. We're clear on tactics, anyway."

I slipped into the shadows of the vestibule as the muttering officers left the hall.

"You dare force her to take your herbcutters' poisons…" began Aegisthus, before the officers were even out of earshot. He left the threat hanging. "Girl or boy, the gods will decide, not you."

"So you've heard?" said Agamemnon.

The ice in his voice returned Aegisthus to his senses. "Yes… her…her woman told me."

"The nursemaid?" said Agamemnon. "Funny, she told me too."

Aegisthus barked a laugh. "Yes. Funny, that."

Harmonia had informed Agamemnon of my pregnancy? This revelation, coupled with Aegisthus' scorn, gave me a sickening jolt. In a calmer and more detached part of myself, I resolved to take care of her later.

"I'll have a son this time, whichever medicines the doctors have to prescribe," said Agamemnon. "She owes me that. Don't presume to tell me what I can and can't do with her."

"Why does she owe you anything, after what you did? You killed her family."

"Never mention those names to me."

"What names? Tantalus? Thyestes? The infant Iphitus?"

Agamemnon bellowed like a bull calf mid-castration. He jabbed his finger towards Aegisthus. "Listen here, you snivelling bastard. I spared that woman when I took Mycenae. I could have sold her, but I spared her, though she'd been ploughed by that usurping little shit. I pitied her, a woman whose father colluded to deprive me of my throne."

"You saw to your own interests."

Agamemnon turned crimson with fury. "And why wouldn't I? The throne's mine – it always was. It'll be my son's too, the child in that woman's belly."

"With the pressure you put on her, she'll probably miscarry."

I thought Agamemnon would strike Aegisthus. Instead, he said, "You hope so, don't you? You want to remain heir, that's why you're hanging around. If she loses my son, I'll fill her back up. I'll fill her every night till her womb shrivels. She owes me a son, and she'll give me one if I have to break her back to get him."

"Don't speak about her that way."

"She's my wife and I'll speak how I like. Save your concern for whatever beasts you mount. But I'll tell you this – and you can run off and tell her the same – if she won't give me a living son, I'll find a woman who will. I'll take a woman who has. She and her daughters can beg at some other man's hearth."

Bile rose in my throat. Nauseous, I turned away.

The bronze-plated door to the porch was ajar. A woman stood behind it. My head took a few moments to clear, before I realised she was Harmonia. Her eyes gleamed with an intensity I'd never before seen in her. We held each other's gaze for a long moment, then she walked away.

*

She might have thought to escape my wrath, but I wasted no time in summoning my daughters' treacherous nursemaid to my throne room. In a brief, frigid interview, I ordered her to gather whatever possessions my husband had paid for her services, along with her son, and leave Mycenae.

Instead, she appealed to Agamemnon. He stalked that night into my bedchamber to declare that he would never – *never* – discard his son – that Nicandros was indeed his. The veins bulged in his forehead and bull neck as he bent over me where I lay. Little flecks of spittle flew from his lips, landing on my face, as he shouted that he'd never give up Harmonia. He'd never cast out his mistress, as he now threatened to cast out me and my daughters if I failed to give him an heir.

He gripped my wrists and hauled me to my knees, levelling his twisted face with mine. His breath reeked of wine. "If the slightest harm comes to my boy or his mother, be sure of this: you and yours will suffer the same and more."

He'd already proved himself capable of all manner of cruelty whenever he considered himself justified, yet I couldn't believe he'd wilfully ruin his own daughters – and I couldn't afford not to believe it.

I freed myself from his grasp and lay on my side, facing the wall. My flesh crawled as he bent over me to bite the side of my neck in a loveless kiss.

And so the faithless bitch Harmonia remained in the palace, tasked only with serving in Agamemnon's bed and rearing his son.

CHAPTER 18

I berated Aegisthus for his outburst, which had plunged me and my daughters deeper into danger. He listened, head bowed, then entreated my forgiveness and withdrew himself from me. Whenever our paths crossed, he acknowledged me politely and said little. To my dismay, he took to arming himself again in the palace, carrying his eagle-claw sword in his belt for the first time since he returned from exile after Agamemnon seized the throne.

He wasn't the only one unhappy at my pregnancy. Electra scowled and watched me like a raptor whenever she was present during my consultations with Eritha. Iphigenia, conversely, asked the herbwife so many questions that Eritha vowed to make an apprentice of her.

"He'll be strong as an ox," Eritha declared, withdrawing her hands from beneath my skirt after one such examination, "just like his father."

"He?" said Electra.

"Of course. A brother for you, dear," replied the old woman, and Iphigenia clapped her hands in delight. "In the early months, your mother was vomiting like a virgin at a drunken orgy of Dionysus. That's a sure sign there's a boy in there, eager to burst into the world and make his name. And her size too, and the way he sits in her womb – she'll give the king a son this time. No more disappointments."

"What do you mean, 'disappointments'?" demanded Electra.

"Hold your tactless tongue," I told the witch as I wrapped my skirt around me.

Eritha tittered. "Oh, I didn't mean…Quickly, girls, would you like to touch Mama's tummy before she hides your brother away?"

"No," growled Electra.

Iphigenia handed her sewing to her new nursemaid and ran to the bed. For the past few weeks, the woman from Anaphe had been helping her to embroider large messy stitches into a blanket, a gift for the baby, in a design intended to be floral. I loosened my skirt, and an almost painful love surged through me as my daughter's fingers lighted like a butterfly on my belly.

"Would you like a boy, Mama?" she said.

Indeed, I needed a son.

"So long as the gods grant the child good health, I don't care," I said.

"Why? Could it die?" asked Electra.

Iphigenia gasped, her eyes stricken.

"There, there, little dove," cooed Eritha, patting Iphigenia's head. "Nothing'll happen to your brother if I can help it. Not that I work miracles, mind, but no one's brought more seedlings to bud than I have. That's why my ladies never scrimp on paying me my worth."

My younger daughter had crept to the table where Eritha's paraphernalia lay. "Electra!" I shouted, and she jerked her hand from inside the herbwife's bag with a yelp. Some of the bag's contents spilled over the table: several charms, an alabastron painted with evil-looking weeds, and a smaller bag.

"Was only looking!" Electra pointed at the alabastron. "What's that for?"

"Ah, that's a precious lotion prized by wealthy ladies. It preserves the skin's delicacy from the ravages of childbearing." Eritha grinned obsequiously at me. "No price is too high to keep a husband's affection."

"And this?" Electra picked up a grey, disc-shaped amulet.

"Oh, that's not something your mama would want. See the symbol painted on it? It's the magical sign for 'woman'. These are used by ladies who want girl children."

"Perhaps I'll buy it for next time," I said.

"Put that far from your mind," said Eritha. "Such powerful magic shouldn't be trifled with. If this amulet remained near you overnight, a daemon could gain passage through your dreams and alter the little prince in your womb. Electra, dear, slip it back into the bag, or your mother might birth a strange one."

I shuddered to think what Agamemnon would make of a "strange one".

"Quickly," I said, "put it away."

*

After dismissing Eritha and the children, I went early to bed but barely slept. A confusion of dreams shattered my peace: Eritha soothing me, tipping poppy juice between my lips…the pains of the birthing stool, tearing me apart…my women's encouragement… their cries of shock…Harmonia holding up a child.

A girl, lady, your son.

A boy with the breasts of a woman.

Look at her phallus! See it swing!

The phallus of a bull. A swinging axe. A bull at the altar.

The sound of insistent knocking brought me to groggy half-consciousness. A beam of moonlight pierced through the narrow window and cast the room in grey half-light. A man's voice whispered my name through the bedchamber door. I moaned, unsure whether I still dreamed.

"Clytemnestra," the voice came again, harsh. Aegisthus.

Afraid he'd be overheard, I called to him to enter. Though my throat was parched and my voice croaky, I feared I too might have spoken too loudly.

He came into the room and stood over me, his eyes lustrous in the darkness. "Well? What did the herbwife say?"

He'd woken me in my chamber to ask such a thing? I laughed involuntarily.

He flinched. "You're well, aren't you? And the child?"

Before I could answer, he touched my cheek. I laid my hand over his, meaning to lift it away. Instead, I held it in place. His palm was soft as a boy's. The fingertips of his free hand trailed down the side of my neck, sending heat through my flesh. I leaned back against the wall. The warmth spread in waves, flushed down through my swollen belly.

He bent his head, his breath against my lips. "Is this how our lives are meant to be?"

I took his hands and placed them by his side.

"Will you give him child after child, till he wears you down?" he persisted.

Hadn't he promised to cease this mad talk? Had he forgotten what happens to those who fight against the order set by the gods?

"I don't have a choice, Aegisthus. Mortals don't get to decide the way of things – don't you know that by now?"

"No, we decide. We could leave now. Tonight."

Had he forgotten the fates of Tantalus and Thyestes? The fate of my innocent son, punished for the deeds and ambitions of men?

"We can't fight what the gods ordain."

His jaw clenched. "How do you know the gods haven't ordained *us*?"

"If they have, it's with a will to destroy us."

He dropped to his knees and pressed his cheek against my hand. Protests and endearments murmured from his lips. I longed to soothe him, to stroke his dark hair. "Leave with me now," he pleaded. "Or after the birth, immediately after. Just swear."

Heartsore, I smiled to take some of the sting from my words. "Aegisthus, be sensible. Where could we go? What would we do? Everything you own comes from Agamemnon, and my dowry wouldn't last for ever, even if we could carry it from the palace. You've no ship to go raiding and nothing to trade. What would you do? Be a mercenary? You rarely practise arms. An adviser in a foreign court? What king loves you enough to risk Agamemnon's anger and army by appointing you? What, then? Hire yourself out as a labourer, be that most despised of men, landless and distrusted, selling your services to anyone who offers shelter for a season or for an odd job that needs doing? What of my daughters? What of the child I'm carrying? What of me? I won't let your folly sweep us all to disaster."

He rose to his feet. "You think I can't take care of you?" He gripped the eagle-talon sword hilt in his belt. "This is my flesh. This weapon decided my fate long ago. It made me who I am."

I glanced at the sword dubiously. I'd never imagined he'd ever had occasion to use it. If we took away Agamemnon's heir, my husband would fight Aegisthus all the way to Hades.

"You said yourself, Agamemnon will never let a son of his go," I said. "And what would he do once he retrieved him? Humiliate him to punish me? Torment him with the threat of Harmonia's bastard?"

"He already means to raise Nicandros up. He wants me to begin overseeing the boy's education, guide him in the princely arts. He's keeping all options open, whether you give him a son or not."

Shivering, I pulled the bedcovers over my shoulders. "Enough. I want you to go, now."

"You won't be moved?"

How could he believe I was unmoved?

I said, "Just go."

For a while he stood, sighing in frustration. I turned to face the wall, and at last his footsteps retreated.

I drew up my knees as far as they'd go, as far as my belly accommodated. For a while, I allowed myself to imagine Aegisthus as my husband, my lover. Sleeping every night in his arms. Waking by his side in a little house, somewhere far from here, a farm. Electra and Iphigenia playing. Warriors breaking down the farmhouse door. Our family fleeing, forever looking over our shoulders. My children homeless and rootless, forced into exile by their own mother.

Little by little, I became aware of something beneath me, prodding into my hip. I tried to slip a hand under me and failed. Angling my ponderous body, I drew out the object: a small disc. I held it to my eyes in the dim light. A symbol was inscribed on its surface: a short line, curved like a waning crescent moon; beneath it, two dots, side by side; then a continuous loop denoting a skirted body and two arms. The magic symbol for "woman".

As if scalded, I pushed myself upright. As fast as my pregnant gait allowed, I crossed the chamber, threw open the door and flung Eritha's amulet into the corridor. A servant answered my shout.

"Take this cursed thing outside, straight away," I ordered her. "Take it from the citadel. Bury it."

For the remainder of the night, I didn't close my eyelids, for fear of a dangerous spirit entering my dreams.

CHAPTER 19

As Eritha foresaw, the child in my belly was indeed eager to join the world of men.

After a short labour, he tore from my body in a rage and bellowed like a bull calf. Eritha grinned up at me from the floor; I almost saw the gold ingots glinting in her eyes. I sagged on the birthing stool, propped up by my ladies, and peered through beads of sweat at the wrinkled red creature in the herbwife's arms. No other eyes than mine did I trust to confirm his maleness.

Agamemnon didn't wait for the purification rites. He swept into the rank, polluted birthing chamber, with no glance or kindly word to spare for me as I lay exhausted in bed. He flexed his muscular arms to snatch my squalling son from Eritha, who was washing him. I jerked upright; a scream caught in my throat. Agamemnon's voice echoed back to me from a distant time: *Look away.* Then that awful final sound, the dull thump which wakes me so often from nightmares.

My ladies fussed about me as I slid back down on the bed.

Laughing, Agamemnon held the baby above him, face down. "My son – he's perfect. Your first boy, Clytemnestra."

Tears pricked my eyes. I turned away, remembering my first-born's smell and soft hair. His little skull. *Agamemnon's skull, smashed. Agamemnon's legs, staggering beneath him. His bulk collapsing like a bull beneath the sacrificial axe. My fingers in his blood-matted hair.*

But it was too late, too late. *Forgive me, Iphitus.*

Agamemnon carried our child to the narrow window, which looked out over the citadel. "This is your inheritance, my son – this and more. You'll never be cast from your homeland. You'll never need to fight for what's yours. I'll make sure of it." The corners of his eyes glistened when he turned around to yell at my women, "Get out of here, all of you. Bring Aegisthus and my daughters."

Appalled at the prospect of Aegisthus seeing me lying here, weakened, in a chamber fetid with my own blood and sweat, I ordered my maids to sponge me down, pin up my hair, and set incense burners throughout the chamber before departing.

Aegisthus gave a dazed apology for the intrusion as he ushered Iphigenia and Electra into the chamber. Shyly, holding hands, the girls approached their father, who stood splay-legged, clasping his son proudly. Iphigenia hesitated at my bedside, but Electra pulled her forward. A few paces from their father, they halted and darted bright anxious glances at their new brother.

Agamemnon lowered the baby for the girls to admire. "Daughters, greet the heir to Mycenae."

The girls drew closer, still clutching each other's hands. When Iphigenia rose on tiptoes to peer at her brother, Agamemnon granted her an indulgent smile.

"He's so small and pretty," she whispered, as if afraid to disturb the grizzling baby.

Her father raised a scornful eyebrow. He turned to Electra. "And what do you think?"

"I like him if you do, Tata."

Agamemnon snorted. "Not before time, the gods gave me this boy. Now, listen to me." He swept his arm to indicate all of us. "Each of you will honour this child. He's far above you. One day, he'll wear the sacred fleece of kingship, his hand will hold the sceptre of Mycenae. Today, I'll make a great sacrifice of thanksgiving – and you, Aegisthus, will swear the oath of the slaughtered horse. You'll promise to defend my heir for as long as you live – an oath my father should have made his brother swear."

The colour drained from Aegisthus' face at the mention of this most terrible oath. It required the oath-taker to stand on a lump of flesh hacked from the sacrificial beast and call out dreadful curses to rain down on himself if he ever broke his vow.

"The gods smile on our union," said Agamemnon, turning at last to me. "I swear to you, no man shall ever harm our son. He'll never suffer as I did in exile. As you did too, doubtless, brother." He removed one of his hands from the baby to punch Aegisthus' shoulder. Aegisthus gaped at him in sickly astonishment.

Hoarse with unaccustomed feeling, or perhaps from the incense smoke, Agamemnon went on, "I'll never forget how it was. I never told you, Clytemnestra, of the suffering I endured because of those usurpers. There was nothing to gain from making you ashamed."

"Be careful, Agamemnon," I warned him. I scrutinised my daughters' faces as they gazed at their father and brother in bliss and bewilderment. The girls knew nothing of my earlier marriage or their lost brother. For as long as was humanly possible, I intended to keep them ignorant of the horrors that had taken place within these walls, within this family.

Agamemnon didn't seem to hear me. "May those usurpers have no rest and no comfort, no libations to their thirsty spirits."

"Yet they were your kin," said Aegisthus.

Agamemnon was too immersed in memories to take offence at the reminder. "How can those who've lost nothing imagine what it's like to have your birthright stolen from you? Menelaus and I, fleeing Argolis with just the clothes on our backs, no time to collect our belongings. I, the rightful king of Mycenae, having to persuade lesser kings to give me arms and warriors, with nothing to offer in return except promises. The two of us, surviving by my cunning and courage. Sometimes I despaired of ever regaining Mycenae." He fell silent, staring moodily at the child in his arms.

"Who stole your throne, Tata?" asked Electra.

"Be quiet," I said.

When no one else ventured to speak, Iphigenia said, "Uncle Aegisthus, what did you do while Father and Uncle Menelaus raised an army?"

Agamemnon roared with laughter, his softer feelings forgotten. "Him? Who knows? Skulked around like a vagrant."

The child knew her mistake, even if she didn't understand it. She tried to change the subject. "Don't you think the baby's lovely, Uncle? Wouldn't you like a son?"

"If the gods intend me to marry, they'd best grant me a daughter like you," said Aegisthus.

"Agreed," said Agamemnon.

He approached my bed and placed the baby in my arms. I cupped my son's head in my hand. *Safe now, little one.*

Agamemnon walked to the door, paused and said, "Daughters, come to me. Kiss your father."

The girls approached him bashfully. He lifted Iphigenia to accept her kiss on his bearded cheek. Back on solid ground, she stood frozen with rapture.

Next came Electra. She flung her arms around his neck and kissed his face over and over. He chuckled and tried gently to prise her from him. Her grip tightened as if to the mast of a sinking ship.

"Let go!" he said.

"No, Tata. Stay, stay!"

He laughed again. "Enough, now."

"No, no!"

He wrenched her hands from him and dropped her to the floor, watching as if she were a peculiar little insect as she reeled backwards, whirling her arms to keep her balance.

"What manners she has," he said. "If she can't curb her wildness, it must be smacked out of her."

The child had almost won her battle to remain upright. Now, she fell on her bottom. Tears welled in her eyes.

From the corridor, her father shot out a parting remark: "Gods, spare this family any more women."

*

Agamemnon didn't see his son again until the birth festivities, when he carried him around the hearth and named him Orestes Agamemnonides.

While pregnant with Iphigenia, I never imagined I could feel again such devastating love as I had for Iphitus. I dreaded to feel it. But, from the first moment she lay on my breast, then Electra after her, I'd have faced down armies for my daughters. It was different with this new son. Sometimes, when he lay in his cradle, I yearned for him so much that I wept. Yet I felt like a stranger when I held him, or at best an aunt or nursemaid, permitted to dandle him on her knee before he must be surrendered to his rightful parent. I was his temporary custodian, and he was his father's son. To love him too fiercely would damage us both.

His father visited the nursery every day, lingering long enough to pass judgement on Orestes' progress and rapid growth, and to toss him in the air. Then Agamemnon would stride off to indulge in more pressing matters – hunting or games, or a bout with a bed-slave. My daughters gazed at their father as he caressed their brother, waiting for him to notice them, their small bodies tense, their upturned faces eager – their expressions crumpling every time he walked away without a glance in their direction.

The entire palace pampered Orestes in a manner my girls could only dream of. He was the most fortunate of children, blooming with health and, even more importantly, his father's attentiveness. The gods' altars brimmed over with offerings for his well-being. Agamemnon even rewarded me with gifts when Orestes gave his first smile and learned to sit unaided. When the baby began to crawl, he took him into the hall to dazzle the Followers and greybeard counsellors with a demonstration. Even still, I couldn't entirely shake off the fear that he was filling the palace with unacknowledged boys, in case anything happened to Orestes. I interrogated the pregnant slaves and scrutinised the faces of every bastard boy.

"My young Heracles," laughed Agamemnon, sweeping Orestes up from the rug where the sturdy baby sat knocking down wooden bricks, which Iphigenia piled high for him.

"My Heracles," whispered Electra. Her thoughtful expression turned to a frown when I cupped her shoulders and drew her to me.

Agamemnon set Orestes back down. The baby swayed for an instant on his little feet, before his pudgy knees buckled and he flopped forwards.

"How much longer till he can stand on his own?" asked Agamemnon. No time soon, I hoped, but before I could answer he quipped, "He'll soon grow tired of rug burns on his buttocks.

Only girls enjoy that." He slapped Orestes' upended bottom, prompting an indignant squeal from the infant. "Before we know it, he'll be walking, it'll be time for his education."

"He's just a baby," I said, keeping my voice low to avoid giving Orestes' nursemaid fuel for tattle of a rift between mistress and master. Not that I distrusted her. Agamemnon had appointed the kindly woman from Anaphe as Orestes' nursemaid, after reappointing Harmonia to look after my daughters at the bitch's request. I consoled myself with the fact that at least he wasn't foolish enough to trust the mother of his bastard with the well-being of his heir. I limited Harmonia's influence over my girls to sleeping in the nursery, and I kept her son away from my children to prevent him from acquiring notions above his status – if he hadn't already. To my chagrin, Nicandros was already training under the sword master and spear master, alongside the sons of the Followers. Aegisthus, additionally, was preparing him for an education in administration and economics.

"Grant our son his infancy, at least," I said.

"I won't have you gelding him," said Agamemnon. "His destiny is the throne and battlefield, not the loom. You can have him for as long as he sucks tit. After that, he's mine."

The baby, yowling at Iphigenia's attempts to help him, succeeded at last in uprighting himself. Wide-eyed, he watched Agamemnon stalk from the nursery. He wobbled a little on his bottom, as if the sight of his bronze-haired giant of a father overawed him.

I called to Iphigenia, who trotted to my side, and I held both daughters close. Iphigenia embraced me around the waist; Electra grumbled.

If Agamemnon must have my son, our daughters at least were mine. Our children knew a semblance of security and would do so for as long as I could help it.

CHAPTER 20

As Orestes grew, he kept the rare fair colouring of his father, though he was lighter than Agamemnon. The stubble on his shaved head was fiery blond, and his complexion the sort that flushed in violent betrayal of his every emotion. His hazel eyes, and soon his stocky limbs, followed Electra wherever she went. She responded with exasperated sighs and steered her brother towards Iphigenia, who delighted in mothering him. Iphigenia soothed Orestes when he was cross, tended to him when he bumped his head or cut his finger, and told him stories about gods and heroes, which he was far too young to understand.

But the first word he uttered wasn't some approximation of "Iphigenia", nor "Mama" or "Tata". It was "Lecta".

As soon as Orestes could walk without teetering, Agamemnon presented him with a tiny leather helmet adorned with a pair of wooden tusks above the brow.

"How much do you admire your brother?" Agamemnon asked my girls as he set the helmet on Orestes' small head. Bewildered and proud, the boy tried to peer up at the curling tusks.

Iphigenia giggled at the fiercely blushing little warrior, but sobered when her father scowled at her.

"It's too big. It would fit me better," said Electra.

"Nonsense, girl – he's growing fast." Agamemnon clapped his hands and a servant, hovering in the doorway, entered the nursery with a toy spear and miniature leather shield with bronze boss. Agamemnon snatched the round shield and slung the strap over Orestes' shoulder. He directed the child's chubby fingers to clasp the handle and curled Orestes' free hand around the shaft of the blunt spear. A stab of grief pierced my heart, but my son must of course one day become a leader of men and make us all proud.

Orestes drew back the spear to tap it against his chest in salute, as he'd seen the guards do. He misjudged, clunked the blunted tip against his helmet, and caught it in one of the horns. He yelped in confusion. Electra threw back her head in gales of laughter.

"Quiet, little bitch," snapped her father. "He's a baby yet, but you women won't be babying him for ever." Electra watched, blinking through her tears, as he took the spear and helped Orestes find a comfortable grip. To me, he said, "I see you still haven't taught the girl any manners. If you can't manage a daughter, how can I trust you with my son?"

Orestes glanced at me, then at his father. Under the lopsided helmet, a faint line puckered the soft skin between his eyebrows.

*

A wooden sword was Agamemnon's next gift to Orestes. Then a breastplate and greaves. A toy axe. A slingshot. Every miniature weapon except a bow and arrow, the weapon of cowards. He was arming Orestes for a departure the child was far too young to make. In turn, I encouraged Orestes to join in the make-believe games of the Followers' sons, who played in the palace. My son had a poor imagination. He always wanted to fight – and to win, which his playmates usually permitted. He was never happier than when his father heard of his prowess and, if the mood took Agamemnon, celebrated by swinging him by the arms in a laughing, wheeling dance.

More often, Agamemnon bemoaned his lack of progress. Orestes was slower on his feet, at the age of five summers, than Nicandros had been; Nicandros had vanquished boys two or three years older. Though Orestes grew tall and robust, he was always smaller than his father's ambitions.

"Servants' brats brawl, they have to grow up fast," I protested. "Princes can learn at a more natural pace."

Agamemnon ignored me and crooked his finger at Iphigenia, who approached him with bowed head and obedient step. We were in his hall for one of his increasingly regular inspections of our daughters. Iphigenia stood shyly before him. Small and slender though she was, she was blossoming into a young maiden as pretty as springtime.

"Where's the other one?" asked Agamemnon.

"Poorly," I said. Electra was in fact recovering from an earlier misadventure, wiser not to relate.

Agamemnon pinched Iphigenia's arm and turned her about. "Still young for the marriage bed, but she could be betrothed. How would you like to be a princess of Troy, girl?"

My heart ceased beating.

Iphigenia turned to me, blinking in confusion. "I think…I think I'd rather—"

Despite his question, her father wasn't interested in what she thought. "Old King Priam has plenty of sons."

"You hate Priam," I said. "Don't you?"

To my shock, I realised how hazy my grasp of the world beyond the nursery had become. I could scarcely believe Tantalus used to sit me by his side and ask my advice, that I'd deliberated and given it. I envied the boy-king's lost queen. Yet surely the world couldn't have changed so much that Priam of Troy would betroth even the least of his sons to an Achaean?

"Of course I hate him," said Agamemnon. "He's a spiteful old man, who can't get over his sister's abduction back in Heracles' day. And what use would the old woman be to him now? There's no profit in sentimentality."

Heracles. Like so many Achaean feuds, the animosity between the king of Troy and the lords of Achaea could be traced back to the strongman of seven-gated Thebes. Heracles had led an Achaean coalition against Troy in retaliation for a personal insult from the then king, Priam's father. He killed the king, slaughtered every one of Priam's brothers, and gave Princess Hesione to a comrade as battle spoil. Young Priam escaped and afterwards succeeded to the throne. Ever since, he'd levied punishing taxes against all Achaeans accessing the vital sea and land routes to the East. He continued to demand the return of his now aged sister.

"Only the pragmatic prosper," said Agamemnon. "I'm keeping all avenues open, or should I say trade routes? But that's men's business." He tilted Iphigenia's chin this way and that, as if she were a hunting dog he was considering purchasing. "What's wrong with the other one, anyway?"

"Just a sniffle," I said. "Best to keep her in the nursery until she recovers."

Iphigenia gave a shocked giggle at my lie.

Her father gripped her jaw. "What's that? Why's she laughing?"

"She's nervous," I said. "Will you check her teeth next? Inside her ears for ticks?"

He brought his stony face level with hers. "Your sister is sick and you find this amusing? An unnatural woman you're turning into. I thought Electra was the savage, not you."

Iphigenia blinked at him, too stunned for tears. "I…I don't find it amusing, Father."

"Then why aren't you looking after her?"

"Father, you sent for me. And Electra doesn't like to be crowded. She already has our nursemaid and Orestes."

With a curse, Agamemnon leaped from his throne and bounded across the hall. I hurried after him, protesting that Electra's condition wasn't contagious, but he paid me as much mind as he would wind whistling in the rafters.

We found Electra seated cross-legged on the nursery floor, making two dolls fight. Harmonia sat on a chair opposite, mending a rip in one of Electra's tunics. Orestes was nowhere to be seen. Electra gaped at her father's sudden advent. The long scab above her upper lip had peeled away. It dangled over her cheek, revealing a shiny pink line of new skin.

"It's just a scratch," I said. "It's beneath your concern."

"Why would I be concerned?" Agamemnon strode to the child and tipped her jaw to examine the injury.

"Tata," Electra breathed. "Tata, it hurts."

His eyes narrowed. "How did she do this?"

The poor child beamed with foolish pride. "With your razor. I saw your servant shave you. Your door was open. And

I thought I'd show you, Tata, I'm just like you. I can do all the things boys do."

The incident had occurred three days earlier. Harmonia, ashen-faced, alerted me after Electra went missing and a search party of maids had failed to find her. Aegisthus discovered the child cowering on the floor in Agamemnon's bedchamber. A wickedly honed obsidian blade and a blood-smeared mirror lay beside her. He bundled her into a blanket and carried her to me. When I lowered the blanket from her face, she glared at me, blood flowing freely over her mouth, then burst into a fit of sobs.

Agamemnon released Electra's chin. His lips curled. He stepped back. "She's mad."

I ached to defend her, to make him see there was nothing she wouldn't do to win a glance from him, a smile, a kindly word. For him to pick her up by the arms and swing her in a wheeling, laughing dance. He'd neither understand nor care.

"Her nursemaid failed to supervise her," I said. "I've admonished them both. It won't happen again."

"The girl could have sliced off her lip. What man would want her then? You're wild, all of you women. If you aren't tamed while you're young, you're ruined. The girl needs a whipping and I'll see she gets one."

He dismissed my protests that the children were mine to chastise, and vowed to give Electra five lashes. The child's brow puckered. She rubbed her tender arms as though they already prickled from a lash, whose touch, I feared, would be lighter in her imagination than in reality.

"And where's my son?" he demanded, turning to Harmonia, who was still pretending to sew. "He's the reason I'm here."

The bitch smoothed her skirts and peeped up at him with a coy smile. "Prince Orestes is practising arms with his half-brother on Arachne's Peak, supervised by Lord Aegisthus. Shall I send for him?"

"Have a room prepared in the men's wing. You women have corrupted my son for long enough. From now on, he'll be in the charge of men."

He left the nursery, followed by Electra's tragic gaze.

Half running, holding my skirts so I wouldn't stumble, I chased him through the palace. I kept my voice steady, though my nerves felt like strings stretched too taut over a lyre: "The children are my responsibility. Orestes needs my care and the care of his nurse. He's too young."

"You won't ruin him the way you've ruined those girls," Agamemnon shouted over his shoulder.

The strings snapped. "*I've* ruined them? Electra only wanted to impress you. She scarred herself so you'd notice her. The children want you to love them. Even Orestes wants you to love him."

He squinted at me as though he thought me as mad as Electra. "Absurd. What father loiters around nurseries?"

"My father."

He snorted.

Trembling with fury, I followed him through the Corridor of the Double Axes, where double-headed ceremonial axes hung in pairs along the length of the wall. I could have torn one down and hurled it into his back. Not enough, to destroy my Iphitus and Tantalus with his own hands, to destroy my father through the shock of losing both daughters to the House of Atreus, to destroy my mother through grief for my father. Not enough to break my daughters' hearts. Now, he'd snatch my son too soon. Orestes would never be mine.

"You'll take no more from me!" I screamed.

Through the sheer force of desperation, I grabbed his arm and succeeded in jerking his bulk around to face me. My wrist gave. He drew back his arm and smashed his fist into my breast. I doubled over, clutching my breast in agony.

"Wild, the lot of you. Perhaps that goat-fucker Aegisthus has the right idea. At least his wives won't give him any worse offspring than mine."

Gasping, I stumbled after him, out around the back of the palace and through the Perseia Gate. Orestes was on a low scrubby slope of Arachne's Peak, lashing out with his wooden sword while Harmonia's bastard, seven years the elder, effortlessly blocked him with a shield. When Orestes heard

Agamemnon call his name, he dropped the sword. His face crumpled as if he feared he'd been caught out in a shameful deed.

Agamemnon placed his hand on the child's fiery-gold head. "Enough, now. A boy can't fight before he's taken his first steps."

My son spared no backwards glance for me as his father led him away. The rage that had propelled my limbs left me, like breath passing through a conch. I pressed my palms to my bruised breast, aware again of how it ached.

"What's happened?" said Aegisthus.

"He's taken my son. He's giving him over to men." I clutched Aegisthus' arm. "Watch over my boy. Be kind to him, for my sake at least."

He bowed his head.

I returned to the nursery to make sure the slaves packing Orestes' belongings didn't forget his favourite toys.

CHAPTER 21

Agamemnon remembered his threat to whip Electra. Afterwards, she returned to the nursery hugging herself and moving crablike to hide her injured, naked back. She expressed no curiosity at the absence of her brother and his possessions. When Iphigenia asked if she was in pain, she answered, "Father hates me."

This of course was untrue. His feelings for her weren't so strong. I assured her he merely wanted her to grow into an obedient young woman who'd make a modest bride. This at least was no lie.

The lash hadn't broken Electra's skin – her father would have ordered its wielder not to spoil her looks. I told her to lie on her front so Iphigenia and I could smooth salve into the faint pink stripes. While we worked, I wondered whether there would ever be any relief from the mundane disharmony of our lives.

In the months that followed, Electra thwarted any hope of peace. She longed for what she could never have and could never be. The harder she strove for her father's affection, the deeper she antagonised him. She teased and baited Orestes during the precious moments we shared with him. She stole his training weapons and broke his toys. In response, I scolded her, ignored her, smacked her or taught her moral tales, and she resented me. I tried to push down the guilt of loving my daughter but of so often disliking her.

Iphigenia was my blessing. With mingled pride and trepidation, I guided her into maidenhood. She cheerfully learned the household and religious duties she'd one day perform. Even I could see she'd never excel at womanly crafts, but she was anxious to please and always willing to be instructed. Though the weeks crawled by, their passage brought ever closer the time when she must leave my arms and go to a husband as yet unknown. This, I could hardly bear to consider.

Aegisthus remained distant, watching my little family with the look of a man who was nobody's husband, lover or father. And I watched my son, who stood in the shadow of Harmonia's gifted bastard, under the bewildering onslaught of Agamemnon's praise and put-downs. The world of men was swallowing Orestes, and he was its floundering, eager victim.

And so our days drifted predictably by, until something unexpected happened. A Trojan prince visited Mycenae.

*

The prince's four heralds arrived ahead of him at the end of a particularly long, dry summer. They rode in ivory-inlaid chariots more suited to a master than his messengers. Their robes were impractical for travel: ankle-length and dyed with the wildly extravagant purple obtained from murex shells. I could only wonder how their lord would compare with his magnificent servants. Remembering Agamemnon's suggestion of a Trojan bridegroom for Iphigenia, I prayed King Priam's son would be noble and wise.

Prince Paris arrived later that evening with his oversized retinue. He was quite a vision, in a multicoloured, ankle-length, long-sleeved tunic, set off by a rich woollen cloak as sumptuous as anything in my clothes chests. A conical hat crowned his head, and gold dripped from his arms and neck. He later began to dress in the Achaean style, but Paris drew mesmerised stares whether he was overdressed or near naked. His black hair shone, his skin was smooth and tawny, his waist was narrow and his shoulders broad. He had a boyish face above a man's body, with dark eyes that might have laughed or wept in a heartbeat, before misting into daydream.

Throughout Paris' stay, Agamemnon treated him as a brother – not a "brother" like Aegisthus, but one he actually liked. He never missed an opportunity to throw his arms around the affable Trojan, while they laughed together at some private joke. Nor did he stint on wine, food or entertainment at the nightly feasts he lavished on Paris. Dancers, tumblers and musicians competed to please the Trojan – and, ultimately, their king. The most exquisite were paraded for Paris' selection to warm his bed.

Agamemnon flaunted our children too. On the day of Paris' arrival, Iphigenia bathed and anointed him, and, with Electra, waited on him at supper. Such customs had made me uneasy when Helen and I performed them as girls for my father's guests. How much worse, watching my virgin daughters attend a virile young man.

Paris shared Agamemnon's table that evening, while I sat adjacent to the Trojan at a table with Orestes. Aegisthus, on my other side, sat with the bastard Nicandros, as if a slave's boy should take precedence over our nobly born guests. Agamemnon had summoned so many Followers and dignitaries that my ears pulsed with the din of conversation and the slaves struggled to negotiate paths between the tables. The air was thick with the aroma of meats turning on spits over the hearth or bubbling in rich sauces in tripod cauldrons, enough food to feed the guests twice over.

Feigning interest in his conversation, I scrutinised the expressions flitting across Paris' handsome, guileless face. My stomach knotted whenever his gaze lingered on my daughters, but he paid them no more than the friendly interest of a guest for his host's family. He told me of his ambition to see something of the world and have an adventure before taking on the responsibilities his father intended for him. He planned to call on various Achaean kings and had already visited several on his way to Mycenae. I wondered at the foul-tempered Trojan king giving Paris permission for such a tour, despising the Achaeans as he did for Heracles' long-ago raid on Troy. Doubtless Paris had charmed King Priam into agreement. I wondered if Menelaus and Helen would fall under Paris' spell too, if he visited them in Lacedaemon. Now that my sister was a mother, to little Hermione, I hoped she'd outgrown any foolishness.

"What do you think of our new guest-friend?" asked Aegisthus quietly, forcing a light note into his voice.

Electra sidled up behind him. In a voice like a shepherd's horn, she said, "He curls his hair like a girl. Iphigenia wants to marry him." She grinned at her sister, who was too absorbed in waiting on Paris to notice.

The Trojan prince pretended not to hear Electra's remark, or really was engrossed in Agamemnon's monologue on the superiority of Achaean guard dogs over eastern breeds.

"Don't be so rude," I whispered. "We're the prince's hosts, and he's our guest. That is a sacred relationship. He's to be esteemed."

Aegisthus stabbed his knife into the lamb haunch on his table.

Iphigenia, without needing a signal, refilled Paris' wine and earned the full radiance of his smile. She blushed and dropped her gaze, before darting another look at him. Electra trotted off to offer him an over-spiced relish for his meat.

Our guest-friend raised his kylix. "To the womenfolk of my host's family, the three fairest ladies in Achaea."

I smiled in acknowledgement of the banal compliment.

Agamemnon snorted. "Ah, but you haven't seen my wife's sister. Now, there's a beauty."

If given a choice, I'd rather my daughters and I were praised for our accomplishments and good character than our appearances, but Agamemnon's crassness in front of our royal guest stung. Aegisthus exhaled in disgust; the Trojan prince grimaced; Orestes fidgeted uncertainly on his seat.

Paris took my hand and bowed his head over it in that curious eastern way. "Any sister of Clytemnestra must be enchanting, though I can't believe Helen's lovelier than my hostess."

"Helen?" Aegisthus stared at our linked hands. "You know her name?"

Such an easy smile Paris had. "Of course. My host is the most famed Achaean of his generation. We in Troy hear news of his exploits and his family. Why, my bard sings a stirring song of his valour during the great siege of Mycenae, when Agamemnon won back his throne against his uncle's massive forces."

Agamemnon laughed, as well he might. "A stirring tale indeed. Drink up, my friend, drink up!"

Our bard sang his own rendition of that lying song after the feast concluded and the tables were folded away. His silvery

words spun a fantasy of Agamemnon coaxing the traitorous
Tantalus and Thyestes to leave the safety of the citadel walls
and duel with him, two against one, on the plain below the hill.
As ever, the singer made no reference to Tantalus' baby son or
bride.

Despite Paris' declared fondness for the song, he seemed
more entranced by the "Hymn to the Nymphs of Taygetus",
which praised the alluring female spirits of that famous
mountain range of my homeland. Quite the devotee of poetry,
he smiled dreamily while the singer likened the charms of
the mortal women of Laconia to those of the breathtaking
nymphs.

Agamemnon winked at Paris. "Excellent hunting to be
had in Laconia, if you enjoy the chase. My brother would be
delighted to welcome you, as would his lovely wife. In fact, as
your host, I insist you pay your respects." He chuckled, then gave
a long sigh. "Ah, my friend, the Trojans and Achaeans have years
of ill-feeling to overcome, we both know it, but your visit has
allowed me to dare hope...Paris, might you and I build a bridge,
so to speak, across the Sea of Aegeus? I've always dreamed of
the Mycenaeans and Trojans becoming allies. Your city and
mine, buttressing each other's sway over western Asia and all
the islands in between."

Judging from the surprise on Aegisthus' face, he and I were
equally ignorant of this ambition.

Paris shrugged ruefully. "There's little I wouldn't do to please
you, if it were in my power, but my father will never reconcile
with the Achaeans – any Achaeans – unless Telamon of Salamis
returns my aunt. Father made it a condition of my tour that I
appeal to Telamon."

Agamemnon scowled at our guest-friend. "The storming
of Troy had nothing to do with my family. That warmongering
wine sack Heracles was only a distant relative. Listen, Paris,
I'm not a persuasive man. I don't have the arguments to move
Telamon from his hard-heartedness. My brother Menelaus is
the one with the honeyed tongue. Appeal to Menelaus. He'll
know what to say. With Princess Hesione returned, Mycenae

and Troy can be allies and together dominate the coasts and sea."

Once again, Aegisthus' expression reflected my own astonishment. I might have laughed, too, to hear Menelaus' eloquence so described, if Agamemnon's motives didn't trouble me so much.

Paris assured Agamemnon he'd visit Lacedaemon, since his host desired it. He smiled lazily as the bard wove the names of my sister and mother, along with my own, into his song of the beauties of Laconia.

"Is my cousin Hermione pretty too?" asked Iphigenia, who sat at my feet with Electra while I absently caressed her braid. "Will my brother marry her?"

I tried to conjure up an image of Helen's daughter in my mind, though I hadn't seen her since a brief visit to Lacedaemon two springtimes ago. Surely any daughter of Helen would grow into a dazzling woman, however plain the child. Not that Hermione's looks would influence the possibility of a marriage between her and my son – an unlikely prospect, given that Agamemnon had already wrung from my birth family all he could.

"Your father hasn't discussed it with me," I said.

"Anyway, Orestes would bore her," said Electra. "He's not very clever."

My son reddened and glanced at Paris, who pretended to be engrossed in the bard's ridiculous song, "The Labour Pains of Heracles' Mother".

"You little bi—" began Agamemnon, but Iphigenia cut him off before she could help herself: "Our brother is brilliant!" Her hand flew to her mouth.

Orestes held his head higher. He smiled at the antics of the bard, who was thrusting his pelvis as he sang of Zeus' cuckolding of Heracles' father.

Agamemnon nodded. "You must wish you had a son like mine," he told Paris, "a legitimate one, I mean."

"He's a fine boy," said Paris.

"Of course he is – daughters of Tyndareus make excellent breeders." Agamemnon guffawed, knocking Paris' arm as the bard danced past our seats in a squealing impression of a violated woman.

*

I cared little for Paris's company, but I dreaded his departure. He intended to ride without delay to Lacedaemon. As a precaution, I sent a herald ahead of his party to remind Helen of her responsibilities as a wife, mother and the daughter of our exemplary parents. I feared for my sister around such a man, and I feared for the Trojan around her.

Despite Paris' impatience to leave, Agamemnon delayed him until after the Festival of the Striking of the Clods. He wanted to show off his children as they enacted, for the first time, the roles of the gods during the rites.

On the morning of the festival, I dressed Iphigenia myself in a saffron-yellow skirt, its fringed tiers tinkling with gold discs shaped like grains and flowers. I curled her maiden lock over her forehead, plaited her ponytail and crowned her head with a garland of dried asphodel. She was lovely as the wildflowers of spring. A lump ached in my throat as I studied her at arm's length. On her fragile shoulders lay her people's hopes for the coming harvest.

"Beautiful," I said. "My darling child."

She smiled up at me. "Will I always be the Spring Maiden, Mother?"

I waited until sure of my voice. "At least while you're unmarried."

"Then I want to stay a maiden for ever." She twirled away, laughing. The fringes of her skirt flew out, the discs pattering like tiny cymbals.

But her wish could not be. She'd lately budded into womanhood, a transition I hid from her father till one of her women, doubtless the treacherous Harmonia, informed him. At least the betrayal meant we could celebrate the crossing-of-the-threshold rites with the palace women, out on Holy Mountain, as was proper.

It also meant Agamemnon wouldn't be slow in arranging a marriage alliance. Sure as corn ripens and the reaping follows, so a bridegroom would shatter our peace and carry off my Iphigenia.

*

She and I – as the Spring Maiden and Mater Theia – led the procession from the citadel to the plain, accompanied by the shrilling of pipes and beating of drums. The inhabitants of the lower town flocked out from behind their walls to join us. We sang hymns and danced in solemn celebration past grazing pastures and freshly sown wheat fields.

From the opposite direction, a box-chariot with a single driver rode towards us. The driver reined in his team and jumped down from the hide-covered, flame-patterned car to confront us. His hooded lion-pelt cloak flew out behind him, lending him the illusion of nobility. I clasped the Spring Maiden to my breast while the driver, the Keeper of Riches, tried to prise her away. All around us the celebrants shrieked.

Gently, inexorably, the Keeper of Riches parted me from my child and ushered her into his chariot. He touched his lash to the horses and sped away, handling his team as skilfully as any charioteer twice his age. I turned to see Harmonia smiling after him with a mother's pride, when she ought to have been tearing her garments like everyone else.

I led the wailing procession along the chariot tracks to a field where the vehicle and horses stood in the care of a groom. The Keeper of Riches, levelling a spear, waited for us at the edge of a yawning chasm. A circle of maidens, highborn playmates of Iphigenia, danced around the chasm to the mournful melody of flutes and a kithara.

The music ceased on a cymbal clash. The maidens fell to the ground.

I approached the chasm and announced, "I have lost a precious seedling. O Keeper of Riches, let the seedling rise from the earth that covers her."

The Keeper brandished his spear. "I have put a crust over the earth. Mother, she shall not rise."

I knelt to touch his feet and reminded myself that today he was a god, not my husband's bastard. "Lord, be not unkind. Let the seedling rise from the earth that covers her."

"Mother," he said, "she shall not rise."

His eyes, haloed with red sunrays, moved from me to the Earth Encircler, who stepped out hesitantly from Agamemnon's side at the forefront of the celebrants. Orestes was far too young for such a role, but Agamemnon hadn't been able to resist impressing Paris by elevating both sons to the status of gods. My husband's gaze flicked sidelong to the Trojan, whose handsome face made an appropriate expression of admiration.

The Earth Encircler piped, "Keeper of Riches, Giver of Wealth, let the seedling rise from the earth that covers her." He looked so vulnerable, standing before the older boy, his chest naked and soft above his river-blue kilt. He needed both hands to hold his three-pronged spear, which was taller than him. He peered up at the Keeper of Riches from under a bronze helmet topped with bull's horns.

"Earth Encircler, she shall not rise," said the Keeper of Riches.

I returned to stand with the celebrants as the Earth Encircler and Keeper of Riches began to dance a duel. They swayed from side to side to the rhythmic piping of an aulos, aiming mock strikes whenever the cymbals clashed.

No effort had been spared on training my son, yet he threw continual glances of appeal at his callous father, who responded with scowls and muscular stabbing gestures. The stonier Agamemnon's face grew, the more the Earth Encircler slipped out of time with the music. My stomach tightened as the little god's lunges grew wilder. He seemed desperate to strike, in earnest, his far more dextrous opponent. His attacks drew gasps from the celebrants, who witnessed the ritual yearly, but never where one opponent meant the other real harm. Tears of frustration mingled with the little Earth Encircler's sweat. Crimson-faced, panting, he jabbed his trident upwards in an attempt to catch the neck of the Keeper of Riches. His opponent skipped aside.

I edged closer to Aegisthus, who watched the duellers through narrowed eyes. I nudged his hand to indicate that he should make whatever covert signal he'd taught the boys during practice bouts, that he should stop the fight. He seemed not to notice me.

The Keeper of Riches, as if sensing my wish, held out his arm to meet a clumsy thrust from the Earth Encircler's trident. A prong scored his flesh. He danced away and dropped into the chasm.

The celebrants milled around and muttered while we waited for the next part of the rites. Agamemnon glowered at me over the heads of those standing between us, as if I were somehow to blame for the combatants' ill-omened performance. Harmonia had crept up behind him, but a peasant woman's arms, not Agamemnon's, had steadied her as she swayed in fear for her son. Though I spared no pity for her, I'd shared every moment of her anxiety.

The maidens resumed their dance around the chasm, raising their voices in hymn to the bountiful goddess of spring. We celebrants linked arms, I with Aegisthus and a stranger, and danced in concentric rings around the girls. We called on the Spring Maiden to rise from the earth. We called on the Keeper of Riches to release her.

A swarm of naked children darted beneath our arms, giggling and wielding mallets. The boys wore grinning satyr masks and felt hats with horns; garlands of flowers wreathed the girls' heads. The children hurtled through the circle of maidens and leaped around the chasm. Electra, most enthusiastic of all the sprites, tested her mallet with swings. Her maiden lock bobbed over her eye. She scampered so close to the chasm, I feared she'd topple in and join her sister.

We celebrants stamped our feet harder and raised our voices louder to the absent spring goddess, while the maidens screamed obscenities at us for our lack of devotion. We shouted harder to the Spring Maiden, our voices soaring above the flutes and kithara. We quickened our sidesteps to the beat of the drum. Our controlled movements contrasted with the gambolling of the mallet-swinging sprites, until the drum beat so fast we could no longer keep pace with it. At the edge of my vision, I saw celebrants collapse – an old man and a woman big with child. I dreaded falling and being trampled. Yet my body tingled with exhilaration. Laughter burst from my throat. I grinned at Aegisthus, who laughed back at me, sweat pouring from his brow. I became aware of my own damp brow, of my jacket soaked and sticking to my back. The kohl, carefully applied by my maids, would have pooled under my eyes; the red dots of kermes paste would be smeared over my cheeks. This thought made me laugh all the more.

When the drumbeat stopped, people cried out in shock. Unlike many, I kept my balance, though I swayed like a drunkard. Aegisthus wrapped his arms around my waist and a lightning bolt flashed through me. Whether he meant to steady me or himself, or held me for some other reason, I didn't know.

The Spring Maiden, aided by her unseen abductor, rose from the chasm. The Earth Encircler reached out a small hand to assist her, but she pressed her palms into his shoulders to lever herself onto solid ground.

In a howling mass, the sprites flew at her. A sharp breath caught in my throat. I almost started towards her but knew I must not. Their attack was in play, I reminded myself – but she bruised so easily. With each clash of cymbals, a sprite darted from the pack to deal the Spring Maiden a single imitation of the farmers' mallet-blows that flatten clods of earth so seeds can sprout through. She flinched at the first strike, then endured the following serenely.

Until Electra's turn.

Cruellest of the sprites, Electra swung her mallet with a grunt. The Spring Maiden's silent lips parted; her hand flew to her arm where the blow landed. Electra struck again, on the hand that touched the bruised skin. The Spring Maiden winced.

I stepped forward. Aegisthus held my arm and shook his head, pained, impotent. The spectators muttered. Agamemnon glared at Electra, who seemed to be weighing up whether to deal the Spring Maiden a third blow.

Then the unthinkable happened: the Keeper of Riches returned above earth.

He bounded up from the chasm, snatched Electra's mallet, and threw it away. He drew the Spring Maiden behind him as if to carry her back underground, to deprive the land and condemn the soil to barrenness.

The celebrants wailed. Veins bulged in Agamemnon's temples.

The Keeper of Riches led the Spring Maiden to me and uttered words never heard before in any ceremony: "I am banished, I am defeated. Into the earth I drew the Spring Maiden. To the land above, I return her."

This improvisation soothed the celebrants enough for them to raise their voices in the final hymn to the reborn Spring Maiden, though in more subdued tones than was customary.

As we returned across the fields towards the citadel, Agamemnon turned to me, scarlet with fury. "That jumped-up son of a whore could have ruined the harvest. I'll stripe his back even worse than I'll stripe Electra's."

I said nothing. Over my shoulder, through the crowd of weary celebrants, I saw Harmonia and knew that the same dread filled our hearts.

*

We waited in the palace courtyard while a servant fetched a whip. Iphigenia pleaded with her father that Nicandros had only been trying to protect her. She begged no mercy for Electra, who glared at her before kneeling to receive the lash.

Fortunately for Electra, I'd reminded Agamemnon during the walk to the palace that scars enhance a man's reputation but hurt a woman's. At his whispered command, the servant took care not to damage our wayward daughter.

Harmonia knew better than to plead for Nicandros. Agamemnon took the whip from the servant and laid into the boy himself.

Next morning, a scowling Electra, sombre Iphigenia and respectful Orestes joined the nobles bidding Paris of Troy farewell outside the palace. Paris presented Agamemnon with gifts of decorative swords, rolls of coloured cloth and caskets of Eastern jewellery. Agamemnon matched Paris' generosity with eight heavy tripods and twelve pithos jars, as tall as a man, each filled to the brim with wine or perfumed oil. He gave Paris extra mule carts to transport the loads. The vehicles were rickety and the beasts feeble.

We watched from the citadel walls as Paris' party wound its way down the slope from the citadel. Crowds of cheering well-wishers pursued the Trojans, no doubt expecting and receiving largesse. More than a few of the women, I didn't doubt, would have followed pretty Paris all the way to my sister's palace in Laconia, if their feet could have carried them along the many stony roads and rutted highways.

The glimmer of a smile twitched Agamemnon's lips. "Well, that's done with."

Aegisthus had climbed the wall to join us. "Is it?"

Agamemnon merely chuckled.

CHAPTER 22

I expected peace and quiet, of a sort, to return with the Trojan party's departure. And for a while it did.

Agamemnon decided Orestes was ripe to learn the art of kingship in earnest, as if our son's immature display at the festival had never happened. He divided Orestes' time between practising arms under the direction of masters and learning diplomacy and justice, so far as Agamemnon could teach those skills, in the hall.

On the rare precious occasions we spent together as a family, I found few topics of conversation to engage a child who understood little of the world into which he'd plunged. I was conscious of Agamemnon watching us like a raptor – conscious too of his bastard, who, far from remaining in disgrace, spent more time in the hall than Agamemnon's legitimate daughters. The bastard's mother was no less of a fixture, at least in the women's quarters. From time to time she melted away, but, like one's own shadow, Harmonia always returned.

"Tell your mother what progress you've made since you last saw her," said Agamemnon to Orestes, at one of our family suppers. "You might even catch up with your brother before your hair turns grey." He fixed Orestes with a hard stare over the rim of his kylix.

My son grimaced at Nicandros, who shared his table. He scratched the fiery-gold stubble on his scalp, a new nervous gesture. His fingers were dirty from his meal of blood pudding.

I smiled. "Go on. I'm always interested in what you're doing."

"Of course you are," said Orestes with startling condescension. "Very well. I've been listening to my father deal with petitioners. There was a farmer yesterday…" His brow furrowed with the effort of recollection. "Something about a neighbour moving boundary stones between fields. Turns out, he's been pestering Father for years about the same thing – the nerve."

"He should leave Father alone," said Electra. Her mouth fell open, as if amazed to find its owner agreeing with Orestes. I tapped myself under the chin to remind her not to gape.

Agamemnon spat a bone shard to the floor, where the hounds fought over it. "Quiet, girl. Only men and grown women can speak without invitation. I see she still hasn't learned any manners, Clytemnestra."

Crestfallen, Electra stared at the embroidered rows of rosettes and doves on her lap. I'd instructed my daughters' maid to dress both girls in matching woollen tunics. Electra had demanded to know why she couldn't wear a kilt such as Orestes sometimes wore.

"Besides, Electra is misguided," I said. "Tell me, Orestes, who else should the people turn to for justice, if not their king?"

Orestes watched Agamemnon while he replied, "The king has much to do, Mother. You can't imagine. He hasn't time to listen to peasants' squabbles – and the peasants squabble a great deal, my father says."

Agamemnon roared with laughter. Orestes paled, but a timorous smile quivered his lips when his father said, "Just so – just so."

The boy continued, emboldened, "The farmer grumbled that his neighbour tried to…to—" the next word was clearly new to his tongue; I doubted he understood it – "cuckold him with his wife. Father says wives must remain in their places – isn't that so, Father?"

"Very much," said Agamemnon.

"And the silly peasant needs to work on his speaking." Orestes plucked a piece of wheat bread from the basket on his table. "My speaking is very good. I have a tutor who teaches me. If the peasant spoke better, he could sort out his own squabbles and not pester my father."

"Farmers haven't the means to employ tutors. You have many good things, Orestes." I swept my hand to indicate the baskets piled high with cheeses and breads, and the bowls of rich condiments. "This is your due as the prince of a great house, but you must never take the Lady of Fortune for granted."

Orestes rubbed at his scalp and frowned. He snapped his fingers at a hovering server and selected a fat slice of pork belly from the server's platter.

Agamemnon smacked the server's arm to express his own disinclination for more meat. "Why are you troubling my boy? Do you want him forgetting his status? You know nothing of men's affairs. Keep it that way."

"Really? She ruled well enough, once," said Aegisthus.

This caught me unprepared. So too did the rush of memories, quick and crystal as a series of splashes from the Perseia Spring: Tantalus and I hearing petitioners in this hall; my little husband turning to me, asking my opinions; informing me of the day's events, in the privacy of our bedchamber, whenever Thyestes grew exasperated by my participation in the realm of men.

To my surprise, Agamemnon said nothing. He drummed the hilt of his knife on the table and watched the children from beneath lowered eyebrows.

Orestes dropped his slice of pork. "Mother ruled with my father? That's impossible! He'd never allow such a thing."

Forgetting Agamemnon's warning against speaking, Electra bounced on her stool. "Is it true, Mother? Did you rule, like a man?"

Iphigenia knocked Electra's arm with a discreet elbow.

"What an absurd question," I said.

"Of course it isn't true." Orestes' face quivered in disdain. "Women can't possibly rule. Besides, the wicked kings Thyestes and Tantalus ruled before father. And Mother couldn't have ruled before them. She isn't *that* old."

Another server approached with a bowl of pickled cabbage. The acrid stench of vinegar caught in my nostrils. I waved him away.

My children still knew nothing of my first marriage to the father of their murdered brother. They knew nothing of their murdered brother. The truth couldn't be hidden for ever, I knew, but, even if Agamemnon hadn't forbidden it to be mentioned, I'd have shielded them. Let them be spared the shame and horror of discovering their father's crimes, at least until childhood lay

behind them. If I could help it, Orestes would never take up the
duty of avenging his brother. No mother would desire her child
to be tormented by the terrible goddess Erinys for the crime of
spilling a parent's blood.

"Perhaps, children, your uncle thinks my father consulted me
over the affairs of Laconia," I said, "but I was just a girl in those
days. More often, he consulted my mother. Electra, dear, close
your mouth unless you're about to put something in it."

Electra shook her head as if to clear it. A righteous gleam
came into her eyes. "Did you…Mother, did you have a husband
before Father?"

Agamemnon's fist crashed onto the table. Plum sauce shot
from a serving bowl and spattered his tunic. "Just what are you
trying to prove, Aegisthus?"

Aegisthus popped a mushroom into his mouth with his
knife. "I simply thought Orestes could benefit from listening to
his mother. He has to learn wisdom and justice from somewhere.
Or perhaps I could teach him? I'm trying to bring out those
same qualities in Nicandros, who, after all, is just a slave's boy."

The slave's boy bowed his head. Iphigenia stretched out her
hand to him, but he sat too far away to reach.

The veins stood out in Agamemnon's forehead. "Orestes
learns well enough from me."

"It's kind of you to take such interest in my children," I told
Aegisthus, smiling coldly. "Rest assured, they'll hear nothing
from me that they wouldn't benefit from hearing."

Supper continued in silence.

*

Aegisthus had attempted to betray me in the most underhand
way: through my children. He had no right to decide if and
when they should learn of their father's crimes. What did he
hope to gain from tearing open the wounds of the past? Or did
he simply wish to torment us?

A chance to berate him came the following day. I was placing
a honey cake at the Protectress' courtyard shrine when, from

the corner of my eye, I glimpsed Aegisthus stealing towards the Corridor of the Double Axes. I called to him and he halted. He turned slowly and approached me.

I smiled for the benefit of the guards who paced the courtyard, placed a hand on Aegisthus' arm, and drew him to a bench under the colonnade, where we wouldn't be overheard. Still smiling, I warned him never again to allude in front of my children to my former life, never to hint at their father's brutal deeds – unless he yearned for my everlasting enmity.

"There's no such thing as a secret when it's known to the world," he said.

"My children don't live in the world, not yet."

He listened without further comment as I vowed to seek his banishment from Mycenae with just the clothes on his back, if he ever defied me.

"Such an affectionate brother as Agamemnon won't be hard to persuade. He'll forbid every lord and peasant in Achaea from sheltering you, or they'll face the wrath of the Mycenaean warband."

Aegisthus rose and made a mock Trojan-like bow. "What a loyal wife. As you wish, Clytemnestra."

An image flashed through my mind: the eagle-claw hilt of Aegisthus' sword striking his cheekbone. Before I could turn this fantasy into reality, Agamemnon's herald Tros approached from the hall and beckoned us to follow him. Never, when I set eyes on this hunched, elderly messenger, did I fail to shudder at the memory of his breaking the news of my mother's death. I kept him several paces behind me as we walked into the porch, while Aegisthus followed at an even cooler distance.

Thick smoke curled low over the hearth in the hall, too lazy to escape through the chimney, high above. A scattering of greybeard counsellors, seated on high-backed chairs in front of Agamemnon's throne, peered at me through the swirling haze. More counsellors huddled together like twitching rabbits near the curtain, bobbing their heads together in wordless conference. A sweating youth in the knee-length blue tunic of a Lacedaemonian herald stood opposite the throne. If he backed

away any further, he'd end up in the hearth fire. He wasn't
Helen's usual man; Menelaus must have sent him.

My heart knocked to a curious rhythm as I crossed the floor
towards Agamemnon's throne. Only a few weeks earlier, my
sister's herald had brought greetings and bland news, saying
little of Menelaus' Trojan guests, though the foreigners still
lingered in the palace. So much for Paris' desire to see the world.
I had sent Helen a message in return, asking after her daughter.

Agamemnon, with a jut of his chin, motioned for the cringing
herald to speak. The youth opened his mouth a few times, trying
to summon the sonorous voice so prized in his class.

I gripped the curved backrest of an empty chair and
manoeuvred my way to the seat, willing the news to be of little
Hermione, not Helen, however ill it might be. A shameful
desire, since the child too was my family.

"That bitch Helen," spat Agamemnon when the herald
remained wordless. The greybeards seated before him murmured
and sighed like breezes in the rafters. "If you ever betray me as
your slut sister betrayed my brother, I'll toss you to my slaves.
Your children will be nothing."

I leaned into the backrest of my chair to keep from sagging.
"What are you saying?"

"That Trojan degenerate didn't just get his feet under my
brother's table. He got his cock into Menelaus' wife. She's
brought shame on this family. If you ever do the same to me,
I'll kill you."

A peal of mirth almost escaped me at the notion of shaming
the blood-soaked House of Atreus, as if it had ever been clean.

Aegisthus came to stand behind me. I was grateful for his
nearness. "Don't speak to her that way."

Several twittering counsellors drew him scandalised looks.

"Who are you to say how I should speak to my wife?"
demanded Agamemnon.

"You don't need to threaten her. She's virtuous as Athene," said
Aegisthus. "She's had a shock, Agamemnon. Let her take it in."

"No – no, I understand," I said. "What does Menelaus intend
to do, Agamemnon?"

"Get her back, of course. The whore's run off to Troy."

I felt Aegisthus' fingers clutch the back of my chair. My head swam. My skin turned cold and clammy, despite the heat of the crackling hearth fire. I held my face in my hands.

Not enough for Helen to snatch kisses in the corridors or be discovered romping with her lover in her bed; she and Paris had eloped. This was a calamity I'd never foreseen. Foolish, reckless Helen. She had indeed brought shame on her house, the House of Tyndareus. Such an offence could no more go unpunished than if I'd deserted Agamemnon for Aegisthus' bed.

I forced down my emotions and focused my thoughts. "You'll send envoys to King Priam, of course?"

Agamemnon shrugged. "Doesn't protocol demand it? But he'll never return her willingly. He'll keep her in revenge for his dried-up old sister."

The breath left me in a giddy laugh. I clapped my hands. "Then persuade Telamon of Salamis to return Princess Hesione. Threaten him with your warband."

The tight mask of fury slipped from Agamemnon's face. His teeth flashed through his beard in a grin. "Why would I do that when they could be sacking Troy?"

CHAPTER 23

Agamemnon's plans became clearer in the following days. My ladies and I listened from the balconies above the hall while he held councils with his Followers and greybeards.

He intended for Troy's riches to be my son's inheritance. For its wealth to buy Orestes a vast army, the fiercest mercenaries from around the world. To equip and maintain a domineering navy. To furnish a huge merchant fleet, with crews equally skilled in bartering and raiding, who'd voyage ever further in the endless quest for copper and tin to turn into weapons of bronze.

Agamemnon would raze the famous towering walls of Troy to the ground and raise the walls of Mycenae to the heavens. Orestes would sit so securely on the Mycenaean throne, no one – brother or stranger – would ever dare challenge him as Atreus, Thyestes, Tantalus and Agamemnon had each been challenged. Our son would never face exile and humiliation. This, the destruction of Troy would ensure.

Tros the herald moved around the hall, passing the beribboned staff of his office to whoever wished to speak. Aegisthus took the staff and scoffed at the ability of Agamemnon's warband to sack Troy, even if it enlisted every last Mycenaean farmer who could wield a sickle.

Agamemnon bobbed his head in agreement. He grabbed the staff from Tros. "It's true, Mycenae alone can't bring down Troy. But Achaea can. Friends, I intend to unite the squabbling tribes of the Achaeans and bring them under my command. Unite them by friendship…or by force."

He raised the staff to silence the storm of exclamations.

"No other man could achieve such a thing. I will lead the Achaeans in the greatest enterprise they've ever known. For a share of the pickings, they'll swear the loyalty of their houses to me and my descendants for all time. And they'll be eager for a share all right. They've raged over Priam's treatment of them, over the crippling taxes he levies on Achaeans for granting access to the Hellespont and the eastern land routes."

He scanned the hall, watching his words sink in. "I tell you this: Heracles' raid on Troy will look like a children's stick-fight compared to what Priam has coming. We'll carry off more than a few trinkets and a screaming princess. We'll take everything. And we'll take back that bitch Helen too, for the sake of my brother's honour and for his poor abandoned child."

My knuckles turned white as I gripped the balcony rail. I hadn't believed Helen's actions could be any more appalling. She'd deserted her daughter, like a careless girl who tires of a ragdoll?

Aegisthus gazed up at me with pity in his eyes. I wondered what sort of light flamed in Paris' eyes when he looked at Helen, a light that could make her leave her own child. Sometimes, when Aegisthus watched me in a certain way, a sensation long slumbering stirred in me. I woke in the night, convinced he was beside me, felt his breath on the back of my neck, his hands caressing me. If I asked, he would be mine: his touch, his whispered words, his desire, perhaps even his love. I had only to give the sign, the one Helen had given Paris.

"She must have had her reasons for leaving the child," Aegisthus was saying.

Agamemnon snorted. "An itch between her legs."

That sign, I'd never give. The safety of my children came before any lover.

A greybeard began praising Agamemnon's warmongering as the gift of a devoted father for a beloved son. Ah, noble Agamemnon! Who else, more than he, understood the pain of having one's inheritance torn from one's grasp? Dear Prince Orestes must never suffer such a calamity.

Agamemnon nodded gravely and motioned for the staff. "Those who've never known the grief of losing their birthright can count themselves fortunate. There's treachery everywhere, and usually with a woman at the heart of it, a false bitch setting men against men. This time, it's Helen. In my father's day, it was my own mother. Atreus set an example, and so must I."

My stomach sank. I'd been so dismayed by Helen's transgression, I hadn't considered how Agamemnon might punish her. When his army left for Troy, I must offer a hecatomb to the Lady of Love, beg her not to forget her most ardent devotee.

Aegisthus, Agamemnon announced, would remain in Mycenae during the sacking of Troy. He was no warrior; he'd serve best as temporary Guardian of Mycenae. This proposal brought indignant squawks from the greybeards, who'd probably imagined one of their number would be chosen.

"Now, now," chided Agamemnon. "No one respects age more than I do. I've always said time grants a man wisdom, if it doesn't take away his wits. But it also slows him down. Perhaps I overestimate Aegisthus a little, but I suspect he can blow his nose without holding a day-long debate on the benefits of emptying his nostrils. All the best men will be in Troy, but at least he has no ambition, and that makes him more trustworthy than most. He can't bring Mycenae to its knees in the course of a few weeks, and he'll have you greybeards to guide him. As for the queen, she'll be under his authority until I return. He'll rule the kingdom, and she'll rule the nursery. You greybeards needn't concern yourselves there."

A ripple passed over the hall, not quite laughter, a slight easing of tension. I bowed my head so the women around me, and the men below, couldn't read the emotions swirling within me: humiliation, exhilaration, hope. Agamemnon was leaving, Aegisthus was my friend – wasn't he? – and, for a few weeks, the palace would feel like home.

Despite my sister's betrayal of his brother, Agamemnon was leaving me in the care of another man. He trusted me more than he knew. He understood that I was no Helen to be tempted by a winning smile or a pair of shapely calves.

Aegisthus glanced up at me. Unlike the gloomy faces of the greybeards, his expression was inscrutable.

*

Heralds were dispatched throughout Achaea with promises of the glory and easy riches to be won in Troy. Kings, princes and chieftains began arriving from near and far for a war council. The first chariot to rumble through the Gate of the Sacred Lionesses was Menelaus'. Then came King Odysseus, crafty husband of my cousin Penelope, from the rugged island of Ithaca – a suspiciously swift arrival. Wealthy King Nestor of Pylos followed, a greybeard famed for wisdom. Over the next several weeks, a multitude of lords descended on our palace from their mountain strongholds, distant coasts, fertile plains and uncountable islands.

Early arrivals and unapologetic latecomers threw themselves on Agamemnon's hospitality, which he lavished with a smile fixed on his lips and veins throbbing in his temples. Our guests hunted in the forests till it seemed no boar, deer, wolf or bear could remain. By night, they guzzled on their kills and on the provisions from our depleting larders. They pawed at the slaves, tested each other's prowess in practice combat in the courtyard, and brawled in the corridors in pious memory of feuds inherited from forefathers.

Agamemnon's patience had almost evaporated when the last of his guests arrived: Achilles, prince of the minor Thessalian citadel of Phthia, and Achilles' cousin Patroclus. Achilles was a golden giant, easily the handsomest of the Achaeans, though his eyes and mouth were the most implacable I ever saw. He was the nephew of King Telamon, captor of the Trojan princess Hesione. Telamon's ox-like son Aias, also present, was Achilles' only rival in stature.

Achilles made an impression on everyone. Iphigenia flinched whenever he so much as glanced her way, though she beamed and blushed around the slender, mild-mannered Patroclus. Electra never missed an opportunity to fawn over Achilles. He patiently answered her naive questions about war and glory with replies that would have sounded boastful from any other man, but seemed from Achilles to be scrupulous honesty. Here was a man who never doubted his excellence and never knowingly told a lie. Admirable, if unwise.

Agamemnon hated him. He sneered whenever Achilles reached for the herald's staff to pick holes in the Trojan proposals, which was often. But what did that signify? Agamemnon hated many men.

After the arrival of Achilles and Patroclus, the Achaeans spent weeks debating their plans for raiding Troy. In the evenings, my daughters and I attended their feasts and entertainments. Agamemnon wanted to display the girls to future suitors, though to my relief he glowered whenever any but the elderly Nestor of Pylos spoke to them. More accurately, he glowered when the girls replied.

He showed off Orestes and Nicandros too, seating them together and bragging about their promise. At least he did until I corrected Nestor for assuming Nicandros was mine. Flustered, the old king responded by pointing out that his own bastards never sat so near his table, since he considered slaves' offspring unequal to legitimate sons. After this, some of the Achaeans took to calling Nicandros "Glorious Bastard", which caused sniggers. Agamemnon began frowning at Nicandros and excluding the already quiet boy from conversations. Eventually, Nicandros and Aegisthus ate at a table among the lesser Achaeans.

"Perhaps you could speak for Nicandros to my father," Iphigenia asked me as we listened to the bard regale the Achaeans with yet another version of Heracles' sack of Troy. Her voice betrayed little hope.

"Why would I do that? If you care about your brother, you'll never ask me such a thing again." I indicated my son with a tilt of my head. Orestes' confidence had soared since the bastard's slip from grace. He was, at that moment, telling Odysseus of Ithaca about the feats he'd one day achieve, which would surpass the pending sack of Troy. Perhaps Orestes' time to shine really would come, one day.

Iphigenia stared into the shadowy corner of the hall where Nicandros and Aegisthus sat. "I do care about my brother."

"Hush," I told her. Child that she was, she couldn't understand why Nicandros was not to be pitied. The Glorious Bastard had far too many admirable qualities.

*

Though I'd no reason to regret Nicandros' fall from favour, there was another whose condition disturbed me: Menelaus was no longer the man he'd been. Dark shadows rimmed his listless eyes, lines furrowed his pale forehead. He only became animated when speaking of his desire to avenge his wife's dishonour on Paris. He made no other mention of Helen. Sometimes he joined Nestor, Odysseus and Agamemnon at their private councils and fumed that Paris went unpunished while these three endlessly talked and the Achaeans hunted boar. But more often he brooded alone. The gentle man who'd advised me long ago in the Circle of the Ancestors to accept the gods' will, who'd confided his childhood torment, was gone.

My son, too, occasionally sat in on these meetings, at Agamemnon's insistence. His eyelids would droop and his red-gold head would nod from the heat of the hearth fire and the drone of men's voices. Agamemnon would startle him back to the present with a barked reprimand, while old Nestor chuckled indulgently.

Usually, however, Agamemnon, Nestor and Odysseus met alone. On one such afternoon, I stood concealed on the balcony above the throne, listening to Nestor's high-pitched melodious voice regale his audience with a tale from his youth. The Pylian king loved to provide edifying examples to the less glittering younger generation.

"Ah, yes! Ereuthalion, godlike champion of the Arcadians, stood over eight feet tall. From head to ankle, he wore bronze armour, and he wielded a mace of that marvellous and indestructible metal, *iron*, as if a blow from his massive fist wouldn't knock the wits from a man larger than either of you.

No one among the hardened warriors of Pylos dared to accept his challenge of single combat – until a brave stripling stepped forward, the youngest in the Pylian army, untried in battle."

"Is that so?" said Odysseus.

"Yes, indeed. And the stripling's comrades took him by his hairless chin. They begged him not to risk himself – he was the dearest of Neleus' twelve sons – but the boy remained undaunted. He marched out to meet the giant, naked, armed only with a slingshot. With a single stone, that young hero dashed out the giant's brains. What man today could perform such a feat? And I saw it with my own eyes. You see, my friends, I was that stripling. And so ended the glorious war between Pylos and Arcadia."

Though I couldn't see Nestor from where I stood, I imagined his bald head bobbing merrily. He paused, allowing his companions to reflect on the lesson of his tale, then explained, "You too, Agamemnon, are daring to face the giant, King Priam of Troy, whose city the Achaeans thought was unconquerable. You will be Boy Nestor to Priam's Arcadian Ereuthalion. You are Achaea, and Achaea will topple Troy as we three have long desired."

"How wise you are, my friend," said Agamemnon. "If only you were of an age to fight by my side, but your counsel is as peerless as your right arm."

"I still say Troy won't fall as easily as you both think," said Odysseus.

"Here he goes again," said Agamemnon. "Don't let me down, Ithacan. Look what it's taken for you to see things our way – the abduction of Menelaus' wife!"

"I'm rather fond of my own wife – my son too, and my home," said Odysseus. "Rest assured, I'll do everything I can for a swift victory so I can get back home to my quiet little island."

"And return richly rewarded," said Agamemnon. "Don't pretend you aren't as hungry for wealth and fame as any other man. Didn't I promise you we'd one day unite the Achaeans, that we'd—"

A scream cut him off, followed by a roar and the thud of boots. A woman dashed through the doorway, chased by a crimson-faced guard.

"Lord, she pushed past me," blurted the guard. "I told her you weren't seeing petitioners. I'll fling her out on her ear. Here, you!"

He grabbed the woman's arm and jerked it behind her. She stretched out her free arm to Agamemnon in supplication, though the massive hearth lay between them, and fell to her knees on the hard floor. She raised her tear-stained face to her king. She was quite lovely, wide-eyed and black-haired. Her patched and faded tunic only enhanced her natural beauty.

"Why, what's wrong with you, sweetheart?" said Agamemnon.

The guard dropped the woman's arm but remained poised over her.

"King Agamemnon, noble lord," she said, voice trembling, "I've been begging for an audience for weeks. Your guards say you've more important things to deal with."

"And so I have. Come, come, I haven't all day."

"I beseech you, lord, have pity for a widow with no grown sons or brothers to protect her. My neighbour hounded my poor husband to an early grave. For years, he shifted the boundary stones between our fields, and no one would help us. We asked the District Guardian to do something, but he said he got his taxes just the same."

Agamemnon tutted.

"Then Archelaus began stealing our livestock and poisoning our crops. He beat my Polites with a club for protesting. He threatened to—" the woman covered her mouth and choked back a sob – "bash our little ones' heads in. And he said he'd do terrible things to me, but his wife was alive then, and she was fiercer than him. But now she's in the earth and so's my Polites."

"You poor lady," said Nestor.

"Why didn't your foolish husband appeal to me?" said Agamemnon. "So this…this Archilochus has been shifting the stones again since your husband's death, is that it? If I had a sack of wheat for every time I've heard that one!"

The farm wife bowed her head. "The stones are gone. He's taken the field, and now he says…he says he'll take me too." She drew a fold of her tunic over her face to hide her humiliation.

"But it's the children I'm frightened for – my children, oh my poor children…"

"…will have a new father," said Agamemnon. "It's a solution of sorts, though not one that pleases you, it seems. Well, stand up, turn around. Let's see what pleases me."

The woman stared at him.

"Go on," he said.

Stiffly, hesitantly, she obeyed.

Agamemnon grunted in appreciation. "Can't blame a fellow for wanting to sow her field, eh, Nestor? What do you think? You've always enjoyed lovely women. And you, Odysseus, surely my wife's cousin isn't all you have warming your bed?"

The two kings remained silent.

"Over here, let's see you close up. There's more than one way for a pretty woman to earn her rations, you know."

The farm wife's gaze darted around the hall. It fixed on a fresco on the north wall, of women watching from the windows of a besieged palace while warriors fought on a red hill above. Those women might as well have been the farm wife, at the mercy of any man who wanted to conquer her. They might have been Helen or me, waiting for the sons of Atreus to snatch us from our chosen husbands. They might have been women as uncountable as grains of sand on the shores of Troy.

The farm wife stood rooted to the spot. Shrilly, she said, "Surely a noble man like you would hate a woman who forgets her husband's memory?"

I heard a chair scrape on the floor. Odysseus said, "Should we leave you?"

The woman turned as if to flee. The guard grabbed her and pinned her arms behind her back.

Agamemnon laughed. "Of course not. What sort of king lets his cock get in the way of a council? The woman can wait. Guard, tell the bath girls to prepare her."

The guard struck the shaft of his spear against his chest and led the sobbing woman away.

*

Rows of three-handled hydriai lined the benches of the Red Bathroom, along with smaller vessels of perfumed oil. Attendants had carried several off to heat their contents – water from the Perseia Spring – for the farm wife's bath. One bath girl remained behind, seated on a bench with the sobbing farm wife. She patted the woman's back and assured her the king took his pleasure quickly, which made the farm wife weep all the more.

They rose when they saw me in the doorway. I handed the bath girl a new tunic, which I'd taken from the linen storeroom, and told her to dress the farm wife. The two women gaped at me when I informed them that a pair of Aegisthus' henchmen were waiting outside the bathroom to take the farm wife home.

"They'll give Archelaus a beating," I said. "Make sure they do it well enough, so he won't trouble you again."

I walked away, aglow with invincibility. If Agamemnon remembered his supplicant after he finished with Nestor and Odysseus, I'd tell him I met her in the palace and took pity on her. Let him rage. He had no shortage of pretty slaves to console himself with, who were more resigned to their sad fates.

My mind returned to his conversation with Nestor and Odysseus. He'd mentioned them long desiring a pretext to invade Troy. This came as little surprise, but he seemed to suggest something else too, something which had troubled me for some time: surely not even Agamemnon could stoop so low as to encourage the cuckolding of his own brother? Not that he'd scruple to use my sister as the spark for his conflagration.

If I really were invincible, a goddess and not a mere queen, I'd show him no mercy for the destruction he'd heaped on my family.

A clamour, from the foot of the staircase to the porch, announced my youngest daughter. She attempted to hurtle past me on the stairs, like an ill-judged cast of a javelin.

I caught her by the shoulders. "How many times have I told you not to run in the palace?"

Electra raised her dirty, tear-streaked face. "Why can't I? Why shouldn't I do all the things Orestes would do if he wasn't such a baby? I hate him. I hate Uncle Aegisthus. I could have hunted with Achilles today!"

Suppressing a sigh, I coaxed from her the reason for her distress. The child had stowed away in the food chest the Achaeans were taking on the day's hunt, first feeding the contents to the boarhounds. The driver of the provisions wagon heard her scratching at the lid of the chest during the ride to the forest. When he opened it, he found Electra hoarse and panic-stricken from lack of air. Aegisthus had taken her back to the palace.

"He should've let me stay!" she shouted. "Achilles would have thought I was so clever. Iphigenia would never have done what I did, even though she follows silly Patroclus everywhere. I might never get the chance to hunt with Achilles again."

If Agamemnon found out, her punishment would be far worse than losing an imaginary privilege. Her antics had shamed him before his allies, the most desirable potential bridegrooms in the land.

"Come with me," I said, and after a moment's hesitation she obeyed.

I led her through the palace till we reached her bedchamber. The girls now occupied separate rooms, decorated at my orders with frescoes of girls engaged in such suitable activities as carding and spinning wool, gathering saffron, and dancing for the goddesses in circles cut into turf. For too long, I'd told myself Electra would learn to tolerate her lot, as I tolerated mine. In a few years she'd marry, and her husband would expect a wife, not a little boy. Yet dolls still littered her bedchamber floor – bowmen, slingers and spearmen – playthings discarded by Orestes.

I drew two wicker chairs together and we sat facing each other. Electra flinched as I took her hand.

"We've spoken many times of a daughter's duty," I said. "Tell me again what your father and I require of you."

Woodenly, she said, "I must obey you in all things and treat my siblings with respect."

"And what do we require when you're a grown lady?"

Her fingers wriggled like vipers in my grip. "I won't leave my father! Don't make me. I can take care of him when he's old. He'll need me then."

Poor foolish headstrong child. "Listen to me, you cannot remain at home – you're not a peasant, Electra. You'll marry and forge a bond with a famous house. There's no greater service a well-born girl can perform for her father." I softened my voice at the misery in her face. "My darling, I'll do my best to make sure he finds you a kind husband. Once you have your own household, you'll be happier than you are now, I'm sure of it."

"As you are, Mother?" For a child so naive, she saw more than I wanted. She glared at a fresco of two women working at a loom. "I don't want to be a woman. Women are sluts."

"What did you say?"

"Whores," she added quickly, her eyes widening.

I kept my voice light. "Wherever did you hear such a thing?"

"It's what Father says. He makes them do what he likes, because he's a man and king. They squeal like pigs and he gives them jewellery. I wouldn't squeal like a pig for jewellery. Why does Father like that?"

"Do not repeat this, Electra, and you must never spy on your father again. Put this far from your mind."

She reached under her chair with her bare foot and kicked an archer doll across the floor. "Will he get another son? I don't want him to. Orestes isn't clever, and he can't fight with a spear – but I could, if Father would give me the chance. It isn't fair. Orestes doesn't need to do anything, and I try so hard."

"Too hard. If your father says nothing to you or about you, he's pleased with you."

She peered at me. "Like he says nothing to Iphigenia?"

"Exactly."

"Iphigenia doesn't do anything. And yet she is so very, very loved."

"What? Well, certainly your father's pleased with her, and that's enough to expect." I rose and smoothed my skirts. "Now, you'll stay in your chamber and think about what I've said. Do you understand?"

Her shoulders slumped. "Yes, Mother. I understand."

*

I mused over how to reach my unhappy child, but Electra's nature was what it was. No punishment or reasoning ever succeeded. I thought she might settle a little once the Achaeans were gone. In the meantime, now that she could ignore Nicandros without offending her father, she perversely decided to form an attachment with her half-brother.

Agamemnon had stopped Nicandros' arms lessons, and the boy began spending long mornings in the courtyard with Electra, patiently teaching her to cast a javelin and block sword-blows with a shield. Such activities were far from appropriate, but Nicandros seemed to be a steadying influence on my daughter. Old Nestor, who was mooting the possibility of a future betrothal between his own baby daughter and Orestes, found the arms practice charming, so Agamemnon let it continue. Nicandros at least kept Electra from worse mischief, and I saw little danger now in their relationship.

Electra spent more time with Harmonia, too. It gave me no pleasure to spot them chattering in the corridors or under the colonnades, or strolling around the grassy terraces of the citadel, but Harmonia had no real influence anymore. She'd fallen from Agamemnon's favour along with their son. Though I instructed my ladies and servants to tell me of any conversations they overheard between the woman and my daughters, I no longer tried to keep the girls away from her.

Agamemnon still permitted Harmonia and Nicandros to take part in the rites and celebrations that higher slaves could attend, and so they were among those who joined the Followers and counsellors for the Achaeans' departure ceremony.

This ceremony began auspiciously. In return for the Achaeans' safe homeward journeys by land and sea, Agamemnon sacrificed a ram and a young bull over the hearth in his hall, to Hermes the Guide and Poseidon Who Secures Safe Voyages. Next came the gift exchange, always a careful business, where host and guests swap gifts of binding friendship and equal value. Agamemnon and his guest-friends exchanged all manner of fine things: beautifully wrought tripods, silver cauldrons, gold beads, bronze cups, tall Cretan vases, bales of rich fabrics…

It was all tedious, except for one incident.

This involved Aias of Locris, a short, stocky man, known as "Little Aias" to distinguish him from Achilles' cousin, Great Aias of Salamis. Throughout his stay, Little Aias had lived up to his lesser name. He was close-fisted, a braggart, and scornful of the conventions that allow such men as the Achaeans to gather under the same roof without hewing each other's brains out. When Little Aias' turn came to exchange gifts with Agamemnon, he serenely deposited a paltry linen cuirass on the dais, before Agamemnon's throne, and returned to where he'd been standing. He said nothing about forwarding substantial gifts from Locris. Agamemnon sneered at him. Several onlookers tittered or muttered.

Orestes, seated to one side of the dais, curled his lips in imitation of Agamemnon. "The Glorious Bastard could wear it for his courtyard combats with my sister."

"Indeed? And what will we give Little Aias in return?" said Agamemnon.

Orestes' quivering face betrayed his pride at being consulted. "Give him…give him the bastard's mother."

Laughter filled the hall. Teasing hands nudged Nicandros, who wrapped his arm around the pale-faced Harmonia. Seated to the other side of the dais, Nestor chuckled sheepishly. He'd long regretted, I suspected, the trouble his flustered remarks about his own bastards had caused Nicandros.

"What do you think, boy?" Agamemnon asked Nicandros. "Is she a fair exchange for your fine new cuirass?"

Nicandros' square-jawed young face barely moved as he spoke: "Sire, I can't give or take what's yours."

Little Aias grinned. "Oh, I don't care who wears the cuirass, Agamemnon, but I'll gladly have the woman if you're finished with her." Whether in mischief or earnest, he seized Harmonia and tipped her over his shoulder.

Quick as an arrow, Nicandros snatched an ornamental gift-exchange sword from its startled new owner. Aias dropped Harmonia at once, but Nicandros, who stood as tall as the Locrian, seized him from behind and held the blade across his throat.

Gasps met this sacrilege. Kings might decorate the walls of their halls with shields and with frescoes of war, but no human blood may be spilled there. No stranger can be threatened, unless the gods' demands are especially cruel.

Agamemnon leaped from his throne and bellowed at Nicandros to release his guest-friend, which the boy did at once. He commanded his henchman, Talthybius, to take Nicandros away and beat him bloody. Harmonia fell to her knees, wailing, pleading for her son.

"Get up, slut, and go to your new master," said Agamemnon.

Nicandros had been allowing Talthybius to lead him towards the scarlet curtain. Now, he flung him off and hurtled back the way he'd come. Whether he meant to throw himself at Little Aias, at Harmonia or even Agamemnon, we never discovered. Talthybius dealt him a punch to the back of the head that sent him sprawling.

Electra and Iphigenia screamed, clinging to each other. I laid my hands on their shoulders. "Hush, girls, hush," I whispered.

As if Agamemnon's mood could get no fouler, Achilles of Phthia shouted over the heads of the Achaeans, "She's his mother, Agamemnon. The boy acted well."

A number of Achilles' friends cheered. The Achaeans by no means disliked Nicandros – the boy's nickname was a jest aimed at their host. Few men consider bastardy to be shameful, especially those who share it and whose fathers never let it stand in their way.

Agamemnon flushed crimson. "Forget the beating, Talthybius. Throw the bastard out on his ear. Drive him from the citadel. Get out of here, you little shit. You've dishonoured me and my hearth."

A fleeting astonishment passed over Talthybius' face before it resumed its habitual hardness. He raised Nicandros. The swaying boy tried to walk a straight path through the incredulous, murmuring Achaeans, who parted for him. As he staggered past Achilles, the Phthian prince clasped Nicandros' shoulder.

"Travel the world and make a name for yourself. A son must strive to be greater than his father," said Achilles.

At this, Electra hid her face in her hands and shook with sobs.

Agamemnon did not seem to hear Achilles. Slack-mouthed, eyes unfocused, he watched the scarlet curtain close behind his son.

*

I was as glad to see the Achaeans depart as they, it seemed, were eager to leave.

Agamemnon, Odysseus and Nestor had carefully planned the order in which each man would drive his chariot from the outer court. This way, they might avoid a conflict erupting before the Achaeans even set foot in Troy. Accordingly, Nestor's chariot, with a legitimate son at the reins, was first to rumble down the great ramp to the lower citadel. No one objected, since he was eldest. Nor did anyone seem offended when Menelaus departed next. The cuckolded husband leaned from his chariot to give Agamemnon's shoulders a farewell buffeting that drew obscenities from my husband in the names of several gods. Plenty of scowls followed each succeeding chariot with its handsome, plumed horses, with its princes in shining ostentatious armour, clasping spears as if already heading out to war.

Orestes held his arm in taut salute to the departing Achaeans and wouldn't let it fall, even when it began to tremble. He flushed with pleasure at the answering salutes from his father's guest-friends, though many seemed more interested in taking a last speculative look at Iphigenia. Their stares made me nauseous. When Iphigenia bowed her head to hide her blushes, her embarrassment only encouraged them. I'd have taken her indoors at once if such an action wouldn't be interpreted as an obvious snub, to be stored away and perhaps later recalled.

Gradually, I became aware of Electra's absence. I spotted her quickly enough, standing beside Achilles' chariot while he held his horsehair-plumed helmet over her head. Achilles had declared that, if he couldn't be first of the Achaeans to depart, he'd leave last. It meant the same to him as ranking anywhere in between. Electra and Orestes heard this pronouncement with open-mouthed awe.

Finally, when the most influential men except Achilles had gone, I could no longer endure the rivalry of the Achaeans or the discomfort of my eldest daughter. Let the rest of them take offence all they wanted. I led Iphigenia and Electra back to the palace and retired alone to my apartments to sort through a casket of ornaments for decorating clothes and hangings.

Before long, however, I shifted to a window seat. It seemed I could not, after all, resist the disturbing allure of those men who would wage war for my sister's return.

CHAPTER 24

Over the following months, Agamemnon threw himself into the preparations for his assault on Troy. He ordered repairs to his fleet and built new ships. He scrutinised scribal inventories of greaves, arrowheads, chariot wheels, medicines, bandages and everything else an army required. He and his officers mulled over how much food would see his Mycenaeans through the sea voyage and the assault on Troy – or, at worst, a siege that might drag on for weeks. He consulted oracles with questions about strategy. He heard omens from Calchas, a shifty-eyed itinerant seer who'd arrived in Mycenae shortly before the Achaeans. He intended on taking this man to Troy.

At other times, he brooded alone in his apartments. Natural enough, to feel some foreboding about the challenge he'd set for himself, but I preferred to imagine him consumed by self-loathing and grief for banishing his eldest son. How devastating, to lose one's child and know that the blame is entirely one's own.

I passed the days weaving a saffron-yellow bridal veil. Soon enough, I too would lose another child. I couldn't pretend otherwise. The interest the Achaeans had shown in Iphigenia, and the shy curiosity she paid one or two in return, was as obvious to her father as to me. She must have the finest clothes to take to her husband's house. Sorrow and pride mingled in my heart as I imagined her on her wedding day. With every cast of my shuttle, I wove a mother's love into her veil.

After removing the veil from the loom, I spent an evening sewing rows of silver moon discs along the hem. I worked till the flickering of the table lamps in my bedchamber grew dim, long after the light of the moon ceased to filter through the narrow window. Pleased with my handiwork, I spread the veil across a table to keep it from creasing, then undressed for bed. As I removed the last of my skirts and folded it on a chair, the chamber door flew open.

The wine fumes on Agamemnon's breath reached me before he did. He shambled past the table, snared his leg in the veil and stumbled. He kicked out to free himself.

"Spying slut!" he mumbled. "Spying for that whoreson. Bitch!"

"I've no idea what you're saying," I said, unwilling to let him provoke me.

"Achilles! Spying for that dogface. Listening from the balcony." He grabbed my shoulders. "You're just like your slut sister. Whore!"

Before I could utter my contempt, he shoved me onto the bed and loomed over me. I flinched from the hot, reeking blasts of his breath: "That he-whore Paris had you first! I trusted you. You sent heralds. Told Helen how good he was!"

I struggled to rise, but he pinned me down. "I sent heralds to warn her against him," I said, keeping my voice calm, trying to soothe him. "Agamemnon, I've never deceived you. You must realise how ridicu—"

His hand cracked against my jaw. He lifted his kilt to reveal his half-erect manhood. I ignored the stinging in my face and braced myself for the invasion no woman can refuse her lord. His fingers groped between my legs. His clammy member prodded my inner thigh. Let him foul my body. I'd retreat to my mind, where he couldn't touch me.

He was weeping. Mucus dripped from his nose and pooled between my breasts. "I'll have any woman I want, you frigid bitch. You drove her away! You drove away my son."

He tried to ram himself into me. I squeezed my eyes shut.

The goddess must have pitied me; he soon wearied of flopping in and out. He rolled off me and lumbered towards the door, colliding with a chest, then a chair. I willed him to stagger off down the corridor so I could wash out any seed that might have leaked from him.

When he finally managed to open the door, he shouted, "Icy bitch! A cock could snap off inside you. Too frigid to fuck willingly, I'll grant you."

*

As soon as the thud of his footsteps faded, I picked up the saffron veil from the floor and scoured it for damage. A small tear, repairable. I threw on a tunic and hurried to the Red Bathroom, where I flushed myself out with cool water from a hydria.

Back in my chamber, the stench of exhaled wine and male sweat hung thick in the air. I lay on my bed, still dressed, skin crawling from the feel of Agamemnon. Sleep, I knew, wouldn't come for me tonight.

Was my protectress angry with me? I'd neglected her shrine while weaving Iphigenia's veil. I'd forgotten my need of her. Agamemnon's pending departure had made me complacent.

I rose, took a trinket from a jewellery casket – a shield-shaped brooch for the shield maiden – and left the chamber.

The palace was deserted, until I reached the stairs to the porch.

"Clytemnestra!"

At the shock of hearing my name, I almost turned back. Aegisthus stood at the foot of the stairs, in the flickering light of the wall torches.

He bounded up the steps to meet me. "You should stay in your chamber. He's in a foul mood. I saw him earlier, he's drunk." He sucked in his breath and touched my bruised jaw where Agamemnon had struck me. "I'll kill him. Give me the sign and I'll kill him right now."

I leaned into him from the step above. He smelled of hearth smoke and horses, and of himself. My hand, of its own volition, reached out to mirror his, to touch his jaw. His dark eyes widened. I tipped his face and crushed my mouth onto his.

And he was kissing me back. He pushed me against the wall. I wrapped my arms around his neck as he pulled up my tunic. His hands ran over my thighs, my hips. He raised my leg in the crook of his arm. Desire stupefied me, such as I'd never known, not even with Tantalus, sweet childhood love. Not even when I lay awake in bed and imagined this man beside me. He didn't ask if I was ready. He knew the answer. He tugged up his tunic with his free hand, the one not jammed between the wall and my buttocks.

The words hovered on my tongue, threatening at any moment to erupt from me in a rush of desire: *Kill him.*

Kill him. And what would become of my daughters, my son? Wards of Aegisthus...loyal children of a murdered father...loyal to their uncle...to vengeful Menelaus.

"Madness," I murmured, still kissing Aegisthus, hardly recognising this thick voice as my own.

He held me more desperately as I tried to wriggle free, half lost to lust, half hiding from comprehension.

I shoved him from me.

His eyes were stricken. He stood motionless as I turned from him and hurried back upstairs.

*

The next morning, Agamemnon seemed almost abashed when we passed each other in the courtyard and exchanged stilted pleasantries. He didn't mention his drunken assault on me, nor did he ever again accuse me of misdeeds, imagined or real. Aegisthus, less forgetful, sought opportunities to speak with me alone. I surrounded myself with my ladies.

During the last weeks before the Mycenaeans' departure, Agamemnon threw himself into the final preparations for raiding Troy. He cast off his grief for his rejected son as only a man could. Perhaps his new seer Calchas cured him with assurances of the victory to come. This straggle-haired devotee of the god Paean claimed to be a master of every arcane art. He was a prophet, priest, magician and healer, an indispensable intermediary between gods and men. He claimed to have once served the Trojan king and to know Priam's weaknesses. Agamemnon was a fool to trust the gangling vagrant.

From reading a sheep's entrails, Calchas had divined that early spring would be the most favourable time to sail for Troy – something any sailor, poet or child could have confirmed. Countless songs are sung of unwary travellers falling foul of the summertime rages of Boreas, the north wind, on the Sea of Aegeus.

The Achaeans were to assemble at the harbour town of Aulis. On the day of Agamemnon's departure, his Followers, counsellors, administrators and the higher slaves gathered at first light for the guardianship ceremony. Various commoners – representatives from among the farmers, herders and artisans of various professions – stood in the hall in awe-stricken silence, stealing glances at their king and their surroundings. Docile though these men were, reports had reached us of villagers and townsfolk who already grumbled that the Trojan adventure had bled them white in taxes. I only hoped the attack on Troy would be as swift as Agamemnon believed.

He and Aegisthus faced each other, five paces from the throne, with Calchas standing between them like an adjudicator at a wrestling match. Agamemnon wore the gold-flecked fleece of kingship and a floor-length robe dyed with the priceless Trojan purple obtained from sea snails. A leafy diadem of thin beaten gold gleamed on his sweating brow, and costly silver and bronze armlets covered his biceps. He eyed Aegisthus like a rival rutting stag as he gripped the sceptre of Mycenae, his knuckles white beneath the ornament on its tip, the twin lioness guardians rearing at an enamelled altar. Aegisthus stood empty-handed and bare-armed, in a white linen tunic. A serene smile played about his lips as we waited for the climax of the ceremony.

Calchas raised his bony hands and droned a prayer: "Hear me, Father Poseidon. If the Mycenaeans ever wrapped the thigh bones of bulls in glistening fat and burned them for your delight, then grant to Aegisthus, Beloved of Atreus, the wisdom of kingship." At Agamemnon's loud sucking of breath, Calchas added, "Do this, so the true king's deputy may govern justly in the true king's absence. On Agamemnon's return, you shall receive the finest bull in all of Argolis, a beast in the pride of its prime." He poured a wine offering into a libation channel in the floor.

An acolyte approached me with a bowl containing powdered earth. I scooped out two handfuls and walked towards the throne, sprinkling the powder as I went.

Aegisthus, barefoot, followed the trail of earth. He paused at the dais for Calchas to place a saffron-dyed lambswool cloak around his shoulders (Agamemnon had earlier made it clear that he wouldn't part with the golden fleece). When Aegisthus sat on the throne, wrapped in the yellow mantle, my husband looked ready to choke. From another acolyte, Calchas took an ash-wood replica of the royal sceptre and set it in Aegisthus' right hand.

Agamemnon snatched my arm and spat out the words of bestowal: "I entrust to you the guardianship of my kingdom and with it this woman. Do you accept?" He thrust my arm towards Aegisthus.

Aegisthus gently clasped my wrist. "I do accept, son of Atreus."

Heat came to my face.

A sulky huddle of Agamemnon's counsellors, standing in front of the scarlet curtain, shifted to let my children enter the hall.

Iphigenia walked ahead of her siblings, who followed side by side. Agamemnon bristled like a hound at the sight of his eldest daughter taking precedence over his son. An unnatural stillness fell over the hall, except for the crackling branches of cedar and thyine that sent up clouds of spice and sweetness from the hearth fire.

Silence, broken by several sharp intakes of breath.

Agamemnon spluttered, "What…by the dew…of Peleia's crotch? He looks like one of the Lady's harlots!"

This was an exaggeration, since the Lady of Love's holy prostitutes were usually female and old enough to serve at her shrines.

Orestes' eyelids were powdered green with malachite. His lips had been reddened with the same paste used to paint suns on his cheeks, chin and forehead. Red rosettes patterned his chest and the lengths of his arms. Even his tiny nipples were red. My ladies decorated me in similar fashion when I presided over festivals, but men rarely used so much paint and powder, except the soft natives of Crete.

Orestes' solemn expression dissolved. "She swore you'd like it, Tata!"

Electra hovered behind her brother, as if debating whether to stay or flee. She gave a strangled giggle and threw a kermes-stained hand over her mouth.

"There wasn't enough time to wash him," Iphigenia whispered to Agamemnon.

His fists clenched. I knew he'd never do something so ill-omened as to hit his children during a ceremony, but Iphigenia did not. She darted between Agamemnon and her siblings and dropped to the floor, clasping her father's knees as a supplicant. He kicked at her with the toe of his sandal as the onlookers gasped.

I wrapped my arms around Iphigenia and raised her, darting Agamemnon a warning glare. He recollected himself enough to seize Orestes' shoulder. With a shudder, he drove him towards Aegisthus.

"Why doesn't he rise, Tata?" said Orestes, as Aegisthus reached down from the throne to clasp my son's hand.

Aegisthus pretended not to hear. "Orestes, son of Agamemnon, heir to Mycenae. The king has appointed me as your guardian. I vow to treat you as I would my own blood."

An acolyte led a white kid to a sacrificial table, where Calchas offered it to Zeus Horkios, Punisher of Broken Oaths. The acolyte caught the kid's blood in a basin and presented it to Iphigenia and Electra.

The girls dipped their fingers in the warm blood and followed their father to the throne. Iphigenia swore to obey her guardian in Agamemnon's absence, or suffer the god's wrath. Electra muttered the same promise, though with an ominous glint in her eyes.

The greybeard counsellors came next, one by one, to dip their fingers in the blood and swear loyalty. I trusted their glowering faces even less than Electra's. Then came the administrators and the commoners, the guards having sworn loyalty over the previous days, unable to leave their posts for such a long ceremony.

I might have found the oath-taking tiresome, if not for a compulsion to study the expressions of every taker. Perhaps more than ever, we'd need the Mycenaeans' loyalty during the weeks of Agamemnon's absence. Those lords of Achaea who weren't joining the Trojan expedition might be casting covetous glances towards the citadels of absent kings, and Mycenae was the richest prize of all.

We broke our fasts on the roasted goat, along with cold meats, eggs, cheeses and bread, before Agamemnon took a curt leave of me outside the palace. He embraced Orestes, whose skin now glowed pink from the scouring of sponges. I'd sent him to the bath girls during the oath-taking.

Agamemnon released him and held him at arm's length. "Don't let me down, boy. Aegisthus is temporary Guardian of Mycenae, but you will one day be king."

"I swear I'll never disappoint you." The child rubbed his rosy arms. "Again."

Agamemnon tilted Orestes' chin. "Listen to me. You've no time to be a child. Understand this: I go to Troy to unite the quarrelling Achaeans, so you can become their overlord. The throne of Mycenae will never again be challenged. I risk my life for you, and you alone." He blotted a tear on Orestes' cheek with his thumb. "Be a man. I'll win Troy for your sake, and, if I'm killed in the effort, you'll continue my work. Mycenae will be the strongest city that ever was."

Solemn, miserable, Orestes nodded.

Aegisthus laid his hand on my son's shoulder. "Don't worry, Agamemnon. I'll take care of your interests."

With a brusque nod, Agamemnon climbed into his chariot beside his henchman Talthybius, who stood holding the horses' reins. The chariots of the Mycenaeans began their descent from the palace. From the citadel walls, the children and I watched with Aegisthus till the king was no more than a distant speck on the Argive Plain.

PART THREE

CHAPTER 25

Aegisthus lost no time in trying to persuade me to overthrow Agamemnon. We could raise an army from among the common folk and guards who harboured disloyalty to their king. Recruit the allies Aegisthus made during his self-imposed exile. Make new allies from among Achaeans not participating in the Trojan expedition. Strengthen the garrison to defend the citadel against the king. Station forces at strategic points about the Argive Plain. We must hurry, before the signal fires announced Agamemnon's imminent return.

Orestes would remain heir, Aegisthus assured me, and rule once he came of age. My children wouldn't be fatherless – he'd treat them as his own. And they needn't seek vengeance for a father who died not by ambush, but in noble battle for the throne.

I told Aegisthus he was a fool. Why would I seize the throne my son was already destined to inherit? Was I another Helen, to hurt and humiliate my children for the sake of a man?

Coolly, he reminded me that he might have raised an army long before now to attack the citadel, as Thyestes and Agamemnon did before him. For my sake alone, he hadn't done so. He had waited till he could have me by his side, and would wait even longer if he must, for as long as it took to convince me. But no better chance would come again.

"Do you really think you're doing what's best for the children?" he said. "Look at what he's doing to them. No child was ever more confused than Orestes. Except Electra."

This stung, the insinuation that I'd failed my children, when I only ever strove to protect them.

"And Iphigenia?" I said.

"Granted, she's a happy child. She has your love."

"They all do!"

"First-born children have a special place in their mothers' hearts."

"You know she isn't that."

He looked away. Then he began to speak of the past as a justification for seizing the throne. Mycenae was never Agamemnon's to inherit, nor Atreus'. The former king, heirless nephew of Atreus and Thyestes, had consulted an oracle to ask who should be Guardian of Mycenae while he waged war on Athens. The oracle told him to entrust his throne to a son of his grandfather. Since it didn't specify which one, he offered Atreus and Thyestes joint guardianship. And, when the king died in battle, Atreus claimed Mycenae for himself.

"No law requires the elder to succeed," said Aegisthus.

"True," I said, "but the Mycenaeans wanted Atreus to rule alone."

Or at least they had, till Thyestes persuaded Atreus' wife, Aerope, to steal the golden fleece of kingship. When Thyestes threw off his cloak on Atreus' coronation day to reveal that same fleece draped around his shoulders, the unhappy Mycenaeans saw fate at work and let Atreus be banished.

But Zeus set a portent in the heavens, the sun reversed its course, and the Mycenaeans brought back Atreus.

Later, of course, Thyestes retook the throne and ruled with Tantalus. And, to my grief, the gods let Agamemnon reclaim Mycenae and wreak destruction on Thyestes' house.

"Don't you see? The gods favour the House of Atreus." My defence of Agamemnon's blood-soaked family sickened me, but they were my son's family too.

Aegisthus sounded like a man who'd swallowed wine mixed with gall: "Do we ever truly know what the gods want? But this much I do know: they've turned their faces from those they once favoured. They're sick of the spilling of blameless blood, the blood of innocent children. Atreus spilled it first, then Agamemnon ripped open the wound."

"What has any of this to do with you?" I demanded. A dull ache throbbed in my temples. Why must he remind me of a past I could never change? Was he blind enough to think I wouldn't change it if I could? But I couldn't. I *couldn't*. Iphitus was dead. Tantalus, dead. Nothing could ever bring them back.

To dwell on grief and horror can drive a person mad. Didn't he understand what he was doing?

"You profited by Atreus," I told him. "He took you in, raised you as his foster-son. Have you no loyalty? Do you actually believe you've a greater claim to the throne than the son of his blood? You dredge up the horrors of the past to justify your envy and greed. You care for nothing except power."

I turned from him, appalled. Suddenly, the truth was startlingly clear. All these years, I'd believed Aegisthus to be my friend, believed him unambitious. And all the while he'd skulked around the palace, waiting for his moment, waiting to take my son's inheritance. Waiting.

"You're mistaken," he said quietly.

*

After this conversation, I avoided crossing paths with Aegisthus whenever possible. How foolish I'd been to imagine Agamemnon's absence would bring respite to my family. I stopped taking walks in the courtyard and no longer played games with my ladies in the Gallery of the Tapestries, since Aegisthus needed no pretext to pass through those places whenever he chose. Instead, I kept to my private apartments or worked wool in the throne room with my daughters.

Often, Aegisthus sent servants asking me to join him and his counsellors in the hall, or inviting me to take air with him in the citadel. I feigned headaches or pressing duties. Occasionally, when his demands grew insistent enough to make tongues waggle, I took the children and joined him. Surely he wouldn't speak in front of them of deposing their father.

"Eat," I commanded Electra as we sat one evening with Aegisthus at supper. "Silly girl. Do you think your father's wearing himself into a shadow moping over you?"

Her face darkened. She crammed a hunk of bread into her mouth and stared at me without chewing. Her sister, with forced gaiety, began chattering about a race the girls had run that afternoon with some of their friends on the track below the citadel. Orestes listened with the same enthusiasm he had for his supper – very little. He chewed his food and drank from his cup, mechanical as one of the smith god's automatons.

"The sword master said your practice went well this morning. You'll be a warrior before long," Aegisthus said to Orestes.

"Better than listening to petitioners while the men sack cities," said my son.

Aegisthus smiled coldly. "Someone has to govern. A king can't leave his kingdom in the care of a mere child."

Orestes flushed and stabbed his dagger at the meat on his table.

Electra smirked, cheeks bulging with uneaten bread. "Couldn't you govern in Father's place, Mother? You ruled once, remember? Guardian Aegisthus said so. Didn't you rule Lacedaemon with Grandfather Tyndareus?"

"Don't be silly," said Orestes. "Women don't rule. A king's daughter might bring a throne to her husband, but she can't sit on it. That's why Father has to bring back our wanton Aunt Helen, so no one can challenge Uncle Menelaus. But our aunt never ruled Lacedaemon, and neither did our mother. And Mother couldn't have ruled Mycenae either. The usurpers ruled before Father, and Grandfather Atreus ruled before them. So there wasn't time for a woman to steal the throne."

He leaned back on his chair, smiling at Electra, pleased with his logic. She ignored him.

"That's enough idle chatter," I said. Since Aegisthus' earlier allusion to my brief former power, the children hadn't dared raise the subject. Anger flashed through me at the memory of his betrayal.

No one had much appetite. I signalled for a servant to clear and clean the tables. Aegisthus called for Iphigenia's favourite tumblers, who came dancing into the hall, seven couples accompanied by a flute player and drummer. Iphigenia alone clapped and smiled as the girls and boys somersaulted and cartwheeled around the hearth, though she darted nervous glances our way.

Electra yawned and ceased to watch the acrobatics. She picked at her teeth, a pleasant after-supper habit copied from her father. "Orestes is right, I suppose. Women aren't clever enough to rule. All they can do is clap their hands, or weave, or squeal for jewellery."

Her brother nodded.

"But, if Mother really did rule," she continued, "it must have been with the usurpers. She was too young before, and it couldn't have been after."

Before I could reprove her, the tumblers formed a line and flipped past us to the drumbeat, following each other so quickly that the air split around us. The skin prickled on the back of my neck.

Aegisthus waited till the last tumbler passed. "True. Your mother's first marriage was to King Tantalus."

The children gasped, all three of them. Orestes' mouth fell open. A furrow appeared between Iphigenia's eyebrows.

I rose and glared at Aegisthus. "What nonsense is this? Up, children. It's time to retire."

Electra pointed a quivering finger at me. "How could you, Mother? My father's enemy!" Indignant though she was, she couldn't hide her curiosity. "How *could* you?"

"I wanted a great kingdom for the children I'd bear. None is greater than Mycenae. And that's all you need to know."

From the half-buried past, memories flooded back to me: Father and I, seated in his hall; an emissary arriving from Mycenae to pledge King Tantalus' suit; Father telling me in private what he knew of Atreus and Thyestes' battles for the throne, ignorant of that gruesome feast. Despite my parents' reluctance to accept the match, I had all the certainty of youth. Atreus was dead, so the rule of Tantalus and Thyestes must be the will of the gods.

"You wanted to rule. You wanted to know how it felt to be a man," said Electra.

"What a preposterous thing to say," I said.

"Tantalus respected your mother's counsel," said Aegisthus. "And there's something else you should know. Your mother gave him a son."

I shoved the table so hard, the edge caught Aegisthus in the ribs. "I curse you!" My voice rang out above the din of the drum and flutes. "I curse you to the last of your line!"

Orestes dived from his seat and flung himself at my feet. He seized my legs in violent supplication. "Where is he? Is he in exile? Will he come back? Will he steal the throne like Thyestes did?"

I sank back down, suddenly drained, and touched the red-gold fuzz on this living son's scalp. "He's dead. Your brother drew breath for a short while, and now he's dead."

"Oh, Mama," whispered Iphigenia, covering her mouth. "We'll make dedications at his tomb. We must pray to him."

"Yes…yes, make dedications," mumbled Orestes. He scrambled up from the floor and stumbled back to his seat. "I had a brother, and now he's dead. Let's not forget him." He pretended to focus on the acrobats. His naked chest heaved.

The tumblers, for their part, carried on as if nothing was amiss. Only when Tros the elderly herald entered the hall and blew the horn of his office did they falter in their timings. The music stopped. The tumblers thudded to a halt.

"A messenger from the king," announced Tros.

Talthybius, Agamemnon's hard-faced henchman, entered the hall and approached the table Aegisthus and I shared. He made me a curt nod before addressing his message to Aegisthus. "Guardian, King Agamemnon wishes you to know that the Achaean fleet remains in Aulis harbour, delayed by gales. He orders you to send further provisions." He rattled off a list of supplies required from the palace stores and to be appropriated from the villages and towns.

"So be it," said Orestes.

"He took supplies enough to see him through two expeditions," said Aegisthus. "How can he be running short already? Tell him to practise moderation."

Orestes stiffened. "Well, really…"

I said, "The cereal harvests were poor this year and the people have to eat too. Agamemnon will have what we can spare from the palace. I doubt he'd thank us if he returned to a rioting populace. We have to be cautious, with most of the army gone from Mycenae. Did he have any further message?"

The henchman turned his stony face to Orestes. "Prince, he wants to assure you of his deepest affection. He instructs you to practise arms every day. You must heed the Guardian of Mycenae and the venerable counsellors in affairs of the kingdom, and guide your sisters with a firm hand."

"What's his message for me?" said Electra.

Talthybius took a moment too long to reply. "Why, he passes on his regards to his dear daughters and esteemed wife."

I dismissed the man with a flick of my fingers. He waited till Aegisthus confirmed the gesture.

"Can I visit Father in Aulis?" cried Electra, bouncing on her seat.

"A warriors' camp is no place for a girl," I replied. This was far from accurate, but it was no place for a daughter of mine.

"Then we should all go." Some of the sparkle left Electra's eyes. "Father will be pleased to see Orestes."

"I'd dearly love to see him," said her brother, "but I've promised to watch over the kingdom."

Before Electra could hurl an insult at him, I assured them none of us would be making the long journey to Aulis. At my signal, the tumblers resumed their performance.

*

Aegisthus believed the predicament of the fleet was a sign of the gods' disfavour, and I too sensed their hands at work. I feared Agamemnon would return home in humiliation, defeated not by the clashing of swords, but by raging, contrary winds. The Achaeans, cheated of their promised easy victory, would curse the sons of Atreus and seek compensation – and this would spell disaster for my son's inheritance.

I ordered the high priestess of the winds to call on her deities to let the Achaeans sail, yet still the fleet remained stranded. So I arranged a costly sacrifice and walked with Aegisthus and my daughters to the Tower of the Winds, a short way south-west of the citadel, on the appointed evening. Not a blade of grass stirred on the plain; impossible to believe that storms could be raging in Aulis. Orestes and the greybeard counsellors went ahead of us in mule carts, a mode of transport my son considered marginally more dignified than walking. Electra lagged behind, grumbling about leg cramps and aching feet. She still sulked over my supposed betrayal of her father through my earlier marriage.

Neither Electra nor Orestes had enquired further about their lost brother. Their disinterest saddened me, but it was better for them to forget what they'd heard. In answer to Iphigenia's delicate questions, I'd told her that Iphitus died during the confusion when her father's men stormed the palace. She'd gain nothing from knowing the full truth. She wanted to make libations to her brother's shade, so we'd returned to the cave shrine for the first time since I carried her in my womb. Thick foliage grew over the cave's entrance. I stared at it remorsefully, a heavy weight pressing on my chest. Iphigenia tore at the leaves and creepers with a tenacity I hadn't imagined she possessed. She turned to me and held out her grazed hand. Inside the cave, the clay warrior still guarded Iphitus' musty swaddling. I hardly knew whether to be sorrowful or glad that Tantalus and Thyestes' hair cuttings had disintegrated. We placed dolls and other toys around Iphitus' stone cradle, and smiled and sobbed as I told Iphigenia my few precious anecdotes of her seven-day-old brother.

"At last, Mother," said Orestes at the foot of the rocky hill where the mud-brick Tower of the Winds stood. One of the drivers helped me and my daughters into a wagon, and we let the sturdy mules convey us the remainder of the journey.

A sacred slave met us at the gate of the rubble-walled temenos, the holy precinct, of the Tower. The woman washed our hands and feet with water poured from a ewer; then, to the music of flute players, we followed a little maiden through the temenos. We stopped before a long, wide altar piled high with blazing wood, where the high priestess waited. A large pit yawned next to the altar.

We participants – my family and the greybeards – each took a handful of barley from the maiden's basket. We threw it over the first of the two sacrificial beasts, a majestic night-black stallion adorned with garlands and ribbons. The high priestess sliced a few hairs from the stallion's forelock and cast them into the altar fire. She implored Boreas, the furious north wind, to return to the Palace of the Winds high in the mountains of Thrace, from which he'd stormed forth too soon. His brother Zephyros, the gentle west wind, she begged to leave off the pleasures of the feasting table and blow kindly so the king's fleet could sail to Troy.

An assistant stunned the stallion with a blow from a double-headed axe, severing the sinews in the proud beast's neck. My daughters and I raised a mournful wail while the priestess slit the victim's throat.

The second stallion, white as milk, went the way of the first. The sacred slaves set about dismembering the black stallion and smearing its fat over its former companion. They heaved the white stallion onto the blazing altar to burn through the night as an offering to Zephyros. The black stallion was cast into the pit for Boreas. The priestess peered up at the motionless clouds in the darkening sky. Perhaps she yearned, as I did, for a gust to reach us from far-off Aulis to waft away the stench of slaughter and smouldering horseflesh, as much as for the west wind to launch Agamemnon's fleet. Not a leaf fluttered on the sacred oak tree.

"Lady, lord. May I speak with you in private?" she said.

"As you wish," said Orestes, starting forward from among the greybeards.

Aegisthus raised his palm to check my son's progress.

Orestes' voice, childish and piping, followed us as we walked with the priestess towards the Tower of the Winds: "Am I not heir? My father commands the Achaeans!"

The greybeards perked up from their bumpy journey and the lengthy rites. Old eyes brightened; bowed backs straightened.

Aegisthus glanced over his shoulder at Orestes. "And I am Guardian of Mycenae. When you're a big lad, you can talk to priestesses. Not now."

"I'm the man of this household," shouted Orestes, "and you're a man too scared to fight Trojans!"

This brought murmurs of shocked delight from the greybeards, even some mutters of agreement.

Aegisthus' lips curled. "I don't care for the glittering prizes of Troy. And let me remind you, boy: if your father fails to return from his adventure, it won't be your rump sitting on the throne. He gave me the guardianship of you and Mycenae both. I'll rule in your stead till you reach manhood, so best learn some respect."

The greybeards scowled. I didn't contradict Aegisthus. He was correct, and Orestes needed a lesson in humility.

We entered the Tower, followed by the sound of my boy choking back angry sobs.

*

The high priestess had little enough to tell us. Despite her failure to move her deities with spells, rites and offerings, she'd discovered that a higher god commanded Boreas to set his breath against the Achaeans. Who that god was, and why he was angry, she didn't know. Perhaps she was trying to deflect attention from her incompetence, but it would be no surprise if Agamemnon really had offended more powers than the winds alone.

We returned to the palace and waited once more for the beacon fires to signal the Achaeans' departure. And still no news came, either by flame or by herald, until one evening when my daughters and I were working in the Gallery of the Tapestries. We'd been copying Iphigenia's favourite tapestry from among the vivid frescoes on the walls around us. Iphigenia was separating the warp threads so I could cast the shuttle, while Electra stood sighing behind us like an old mare. A servant entered the gallery to tell me a messenger had arrived from Aulis.

I found Aegisthus swapping stilted pleasantries with the messenger, Talthybius, in the hall. Judging from his tense face, he already knew the message.

Talthybius turned at the sound of my footsteps. He tapped a ribbon-adorned herald's staff against his breast. "Greetings, lady, on behalf of your noble lord. Agamemnon sends his most affectionate regards to you and his dear children. He enquires particularly after his modest and obedient daughter, Princess Iphigenia." His words were honey, his smile stone.

My stomach tightened. Why would Agamemnon enquire after Iphigenia?

"The delay in Aulis has given him the opportunity to strengthen his alliances with the famous princes under his command," continued Talthybius.

I meant to say, *Is that so?* The words never left my throat. I folded my arms across my chest as if in challenge. It hid their trembling. Aegisthus, seated on the throne, watched me with an anxious frown.

"Yes, indeed. Your lord has chosen to grant the highest possible honour to one of Achaea's most promising young warriors. He has decided…"

The rest of Talthybius' words swirled around me, muffled yet terribly near, as though I were submerged in shallow water: "…young man with a destiny…a glorious future ahead of him… carving out a brilliant reputation…what a blessing from the gods, what a gift from a loving father. What glorious sons for Iphigenia."

My gentle child, my strength, my Spring Maiden, was to be the bride of Achilles, warrior prince from distant, barbarous Thessaly.

Aegisthus came to me and placed a supportive hand on my elbow. In his free hand, he held the replica sceptre of Mycenae; he never appeared before visitors without it.

"She's barely fourteen. She's so young," I heard myself say. The smoky hall was airless.

Talthybius chuckled like the rasp of scraping swords. "How like a mother. But her father is resolved. It's vital he secures Achilles' loyalty, and the prince would be offended if Agamemnon refused him the girl. He'd return to Thessaly and take the morale of the army with him. The men's spirits are low enough already, with the delay of the fleet."

I could no longer restrain my emotion. "Must I sacrifice my daughter to Agamemnon's ambition? She's a child!"

"He insists, and he's your husband and king. Rejoice, lady. The marriage will be as much an honour for the princess as for

Achilles. What girl wouldn't dream of marrying a young warrior poised to become one of Achaea's most celebrated heroes?"

"Wouldn't he prefer Electra?" I blurted, and immediately burned with shame. But hadn't Electra admired Achilles? And he'd been so patient with her, strange little creature though he must have thought her. If he waited just a few more years...I passed a hand over my eyes, which stung from the garish colours of the wall frescoes and the painted floor. "And if I refuse to send my daughter?"

Aegisthus, I saw, gripped the sceptre so tightly his knuckles were pale.

Talthybius said, "Then my men and I will take her without your consent, on the king's orders. But your husband is sure you'll want her departure to be as painless as possible."

I lowered myself onto a stool beside the hearth and asked dully, "And if I agree, when does he expect us in Aulis?"

Talthybius' eyes never left me, like those of a hunter approaching cornered prey. "He requires you to remain in Mycenae to care for your younger children. Iphigenia will leave with me tomorrow morning."

I started towards him, shouting, "Am I not to conduct my own daughter's wedding? He'd rob me even of that?"

All those years of nurturing Iphigenia, of preparing her for the destiny of every daughter – of preparing to lose her. I'd tended her like a jealous gardener, and now came the culmination of all my care, the most sorrowful and joyful day of our lives together. It was my duty, my right, to hold high the wedding torch that would guide her across the threshold from maidenhood to womanhood. Was Iphigenia to be motherless on the day of her rebirth?

"Your husband of course regrets your absence, but he insists on it," said Talthybius. "Iphigenia may take one virgin maid to prepare her for the wedding, but no mature woman may enter the camp. The seer Calchas, you see, has discovered the reason for the fleet's delay. Boreas doesn't act alone – the goddess Artemis commands him, that mighty and terrible virgin. An altar was built to her on the beach in Aulis, but some of the camp women defiled it. They performed lewd acts before it with the men. So Great Artemis commanded us to cast out every unchaste woman, which meant expelling all the females. And now she requires the purifying rite of a marriage to be conducted at her altar, but she won't tolerate the marriage to be consummated."

"Not…consummated?" I said.

"Not consummated. Your daughter must be returned to you as a virgin and remain for two more years in your care. This is as much Achilles' wish as the goddess's. He's far gentler than many assume. He considers the girl too young for the marriage bed and he's anxious not to separate her from her mother."

Aegisthus glared at Talthybius. "Why didn't you say so at first?"

His displeasure struck me as a betrayal. My child was to be spared for two more years. Couldn't he be glad for her? She'd return to my arms, a virgin. In two years, Achilles might have forgotten her and she could consummate a true marriage with some other. But was he really so undesirable a match? He was courageous, honest and already winning fame. He'd shown kindness to Electra. And he was young, beautiful. Withered old hands wouldn't caress my daughter's soft flesh.

Aegisthus, it seemed, wanted to see me cornered with nowhere to flee except over the sheer cliff edge of rebellion.

"I'll prepare her," I said quietly, though my heart was still heavy. "Talthybius, convey my respects to her bridegroom."

He struck his chest with his staff. His smile did nothing to soften his face.

CHAPTER 26

I insisted on keeping Iphigenia with me for one day longer, before she must depart for Aulis. After her wedding, she'd return to Mycenae to remain in a strange suspended state between maidenhood and womanhood, until her husband claimed her. I wanted her to know one last carefree day as a child in the land of her birth.

No day since her naming ceremony had been more bittersweet. We left the citadel in the morning, along with her siblings and Aegisthus, to enjoy the gifts of Mater Theia. We climbed low foothills of mountains, rambled through woods and rested in clearings. The air was clear, bright and full of promise, warm as a loving father's embrace. If our spirits were sometimes sombre, they were more often light. Whenever Electra and Orestes ran ahead, Iphigenia would venture a question about her looming marriage and future home. Aegisthus and I answered as best as we could, but no more than we must. My child had two more years before she'd be a wife in truth – time enough to learn of the mountainous land over which she'd one day be queen.

Orestes kept us entertained. He forgot his princely burdens and skipped around like the small boy he was. He chased after a moth, whose brilliant wings we didn't recognise. Iphigenia and Electra wondered whether a god had sent the tiny portent and what it meant. They agreed it was a happy sign. Perhaps I'd ask a seer later.

My son stretched out his arms and hopped up and down as the moth fluttered from his reach. Thwarted, he turned to his sisters and yelled, "You can't catch me!"

"I don't want to," said Electra. She slipped her hand into mine and sighed contentedly. I squeezed her fingers and tried to banish the memory of offering her to Talthybius in Iphigenia's place.

For an instant, Orestes hesitated, then cried, "Catch me, Guardian!"

Aegisthus had been strolling at Iphigenia's side, identifying the names of wildflowers at her request, though she was the Spring Maiden and knew every one. His eyebrows shot up. He glanced about, as if expecting to see another "Guardian" Orestes might be challenging. Iphigenia giggled, nudging him. He lumbered a few steps after my son, before casting us a sheepish look over his shoulder.

"Quick! He's getting away!" shouted Iphigenia.

Electra caught her sister's enthusiasm. "Get him!"

Aegisthus made a pretence of running at full speed, but he wasn't used to humouring small boys and his long legs quickly caught up with Orestes. He threw out his arms as if to catch my son, who whooped in delight. Aegisthus' hands fell back to his sides. Orestes made a half-hearted swerve, which was no longer necessary, and the pair waited stiffly for us to catch them up.

*

In the evening, the girls and I played knucklebones and board games in the Gallery of the Tapestries – Iphigenia's favourite pastimes. Electra chattered and laughed, and seemed reconciled to the fact that her hero was marrying her sister. If anything, Iphigenia had risen in her esteem. When I told Electra to go to bed so Iphigenia and I could have one last private conversation, she rose without complaint and sprinkled Iphigenia's face with kisses. To my astonishment, she clung to my neck and pressed her cheek to mine.

"Goodnight, dear one," I whispered, with a guilty twinge. I held her close, this daughter I'd offered to give away.

Iphigenia seated herself on a cushion at my feet. In a tumbling torrent, she confided all the hopes and fears she'd suppressed since learning of her impending marriage. The formidable reputation of her bridegroom filled her with pride, as Talthybius had suggested – and, as I'd known, with dread. She was glad her husband wouldn't be an old man, gladder still that she needn't become queen of Phthia for perhaps many years, till Achilles' father, King Peleus, died. She had time to learn to love her new land.

Achilles' cousin Patroclus had told her stories about Peleus, who'd numbered among Jason's Argonauts. The king's adventuring days were long gone and he was now as mellow and kindly as any elderly Thessalian warrior might be. Iphigenia smiled wistfully as she spoke of Peleus. She didn't want an elderly husband, but she was still young enough to yearn for a father.

She hung her head and plucked at the fringe on my skirt. "Mama, when you said Father had ordered me to marry, at first I wished Electra was leaving instead of me. Perhaps I still do."

"I admit, I had the same desire. There's no sense feeling ashamed, dearest." I could feel contrition for us both.

I kissed the crown of her head and pushed down the bitter regret that I wouldn't be with her on the most important day of her young life. Wouldn't see her in her scarlet dress or set on her head the bridal veil I'd weaved with such care. Wouldn't share in her marriage feast or light her path with the wedding torch, whose flame wards off the daemons that threaten brides poised on the threshold of womanhood.

One day, though, I might perform this last duty when her bridegroom came to carry her from Mycenae. The thought made me weep. We wept together.

*

At dawn the next morning, we descended the cobbled ramps from the palace towards the houses of the gods in the lower citadel. Iphigenia glowed with nervous excitement. Her favourite maidens from among the daughters of the Followers danced around us and sang songs to Virgin Artemis, while Orestes played the double flute. Electra, to my bewilderment, lagged behind, stiff and silent. I ignored her. Her surliness would not spoil Iphigenia's last hours in Mycenae as an unmarried girl.

We made our way to the House of Many Goddesses in the sacred quarter. In the forecourt, Iphigenia accepted a spouted silver vessel from one of her friends and poured a libation of honeyed oil over the circular altar of Artemis.

"Dear Lady Who Tames Wild Beasts," she prayed to the goddess, "accept these gifts. Lay your hand on my head and guide my path."

Her eyes shone with bright unshed tears as she piled her most treasured childhood possessions on the altar: a pretty blue skirt I'd woven for her; Raggy, her ancient and tattered doll; a flute given to her by Aegisthus; and the gold armlet name-day gift from Helen. This last, I felt uneasy about consigning to the flames, but Iphigenia feared to deny the goddess. I gave her my torch to light the kindling and woollen materials. Electra stared at the armlet till it was lost behind the flames.

Another girl handed me an obsidian razor. I lifted the maiden lock from Iphigenia's brow and we gazed into each other's eyes. She trembled like a lamb at the altar, who understands something of its fate but cannot control it. I understood too, and always had: I must let her go, let my child become a woman. Marriage is the destiny of every girl, giving life to children is her purpose. As Iphigenia's mother, I mustn't wish to deprive her of that. I must be proud – and I was. I must beg the goddesses to make her marriage happier than mine.

For the last time, I caressed my daughter's precious glossy maiden lock between my forefinger and thumb, then sliced through it with the blade. Iphigenia choked back a scream. I folded her palm around the shorn curl, willing her to be strong-born, to be worthy of her name. She stifled her sobs and threw this last token of her girlhood into the flames.

All that remained of her wedding rites, for me as her mother, was the procession to the Perseia Spring to draw water for her nuptial bath. If she couldn't be purified in her own bedchamber on her wedding day, she would at least have water from home. The honour of carrying the loutrophoros of lustral water hadn't fallen to Electra. It must be carried by the maiden who'd bathe the bride in Aulis – and Agamemnon had ordered that Iphigenia's family must remain in Mycenae.

I led the children from the citadel, holding my torch high to chase away the spirits and shadows. Orestes piped a wedding hymn to the accompaniment of the girls' tambourines and

castanets. Iphigenia and her maidens danced and sang in honour
of the goddesses, all the way up the hill, past the poplar woods
and onwards to the Perseia Spring. And they danced and sang
all the way home.

*

I'd instructed Talthybius that Iphigenia's departure procession
would begin at the palace. She'd descend the grand stairway and
continue through the citadel by the main ramp, watched by her
people.

Yet, on our return from the spring, his chariot waited inside
the Gate of the Sacred Lionesses. A mule cart stood behind it,
loaded with Iphigenia's clay bathtub and the chest containing
her wedding dress, veil and jewellery. A sentry on the buttress
overlooking the gate blasted a horn, and to my chagrin the
citadel-folk began pouring from mansions, workshops and the
houses of the gods to line the streets and walls. There could
be no returning to the palace now. Iphigenia's departure must
proceed with dignity.

At my nod, the water-carrier gratefully loaded the
loutrophoros and herself into the mule cart. I tapped Iphigenia's
back to remind her to stand straight. She must appear strong
and assured before the people – and even stronger when she
stood beside Talthybius in the chariot that would carry her far
from home. Once the citadel walls were a distant speck, she
might rest her weary feet in the cart.

The sentry on the buttress sounded the approach of
Aegisthus and the counsellors. In ordinary circumstances, the
wedding party, not these men, would proceed down the ramp
from the palace, singing wedding hymns to the music of flutes.
I'd lead the way, holding the torch. Iphigenia and her husband
would follow, while well-wishers showered them with nuts, figs
and dates. Instead, the bride stood like an onlooker, waiting for
the Guardian and greybeards. In place of nuptial finery, she wore
a practical tunic, which was neither too warm nor too cool, dark
enough to hide travel stains. Not until her return from Aulis

would I see her, for the first time, in the dress of a grown woman. How proud she'd make me; how proud I was.

When Aegisthus reached us, he took Iphigenia's hands in his. He spoke in a voice powerful enough to satisfy the onlookers, but his gaze was for my child alone:

"Iphigenia, daughter of Clytemnestra, may the gods be with you on your journey. Soon, you will fulfil your mother's great care of you. You are everything any parent longs for, the gentlest of children, loyal and virtuous, patient and generous. If you could play with your dolls a little longer, we'd wish it so, but your father summons you. So let me say this: you are the daughter I would have wished for. You are the pride of your mother and the joy of your guardian. You are loved."

My girl pressed her lips together and threw herself against his chest. He folded her in his arms, kissing the shorn stub of her maiden lock. Slowly, he released her, giving her time to wipe away her tears. She held out her arms to Electra.

Electra ignored the gesture. "Why are you crying? Don't you know how lucky you are? You're serving our father."

Iphigenia blinked wordlessly at her.

"You're even more of a baby than Orestes," added Electra quickly, as I reached for her. She cowed her brother with a flash of her eyes before he could protest. "But at least he knows his duty to our father."

I dug my fingers into Electra's arm and drew her to my side. She turned up her face to mine, and the accusation I saw there took me aback.

Mastering her dismay, Iphigenia walked to the mule cart. She asked the driver to open the chest and select the most beautiful piece of jewellery inside. The man took out a golden armlet shaped like a coiled snake, symbol of rebirth and fertility. He placed it in her cupped palms.

She slipped the armlet over Electra's arm. "Wear this to remember me while I'm gone. Think of me as the sister who loves you, not as Achilles' bride. Wish me well and let's part as friends."

Electra had the grace to drop her gaze. She mumbled an almost inaudible farewell. Instinctively, I wanted to make her return the jewellery, so Iphigenia's arm wouldn't be bare of this talisman on her wedding day, but I would not have the gesture tainted.

Iphigenia turned to Orestes. "Farewell, brother dear."

Orestes held out his arms and kissed her. "Safe journey, gentle sister. Be sure to pass on my highest regards to noble Achilles."

She smiled and sniffed.

Then she turned to me and melted into my arms. "Mama, I'm frightened."

I clasped her more tightly. "We must accept our fates," I whispered. "This is your duty, my darling."

I held her for a long time, caressing her, my eyes prickling from holding back tears while she quietly wept. The onlookers, I hoped, would not consider her grief ill-omened. Any modest, sheltered girl would dread to leave her mother and home.

I kissed her wet eyelids, placed my hands on her shoulders and held her away from me. "Farewell, most beloved of children."

She turned from me with a visible effort and faced the Mycenaeans. Her voice, though tremulous, carried across the utter silence: "Good people who serve my father, I know my duty. I go to do as my father bids. I go to marry the great Achilles and make my mother proud."

A sombre cheer greeted this. On her return, I'd ensure the most joyful of celebrations. Singing, feasting and dancing.

Talthybius helped her into the chariot. I reached up to clasp her hands one last time, and she pressed her lips to my forehead.

My throat pained me almost too much to speak: "The Spring Maiden goes into the earth for only a little while, then returns to her mother's embrace. You'll return to me, dear one, when I can bear your loss no longer."

The herald on the buttress called for the guards below to raise the crossbar on the Gate of the Sacred Lionesses. The bronze-plated doors swung slowly open. Talthybius saluted me and touched his whip to the horses' backs. With dry, burning eyes, I watched his chariot carry its precious load from the citadel.

CHAPTER 27

My daughter had made a brilliant match and would soon return to my arms, yet my heart was like a seed crushed between two millstones. I tried to concentrate my thoughts on Orestes, whose education mustn't be neglected in Agamemnon's absence, and on Electra, who'd retreated behind her walls after sallying out so briefly. I wore all outward signs of care, made all necessary arrangements – and Iphigenia filled my every moment.

Iphigenia, in an unfamiliar tent in a wind-blasted camp, her heart full of dreams and dread.

Iphigenia, taking her nuptial bath in water carried from the Perseia Spring.

Iphigenia, fumbling with her wedding finery, no one to help her except one little maiden.

Iphigenia, seated among strangers at her marriage feast, no loved ones gathered around her, no one to celebrate this most momentous transition of her life, just her dour father.

I thought of her bridegroom, fierce Achilles, who might insist on his right to carry her to his tent. Talthybius had sworn she'd return to me untouched, or I could never have let her go. Was I foolish to trust him? To trust Achilles? Was I mistaken in not warning my child about the pains of the marriage bed? I hadn't wanted to frighten her.

Aegisthus tried to distract me. He asked me to help him set taxes with the district collectors, agree production targets with the overseers of the palace workshops, go over inventories of imports and exports with the scribes. I told him Orestes should be at his side, learning. My son spent too long practising with the spear and sword, obsessed with gaining skills beyond his years and ability, to the neglect of his mind.

"He's just a little boy," said Aegisthus.

"A little boy who'll one day be king. He can't learn quickly enough."

Aegisthus fixed me with a penetrating look. "His youth isn't the only reason I value your abilities above his."

"Then you should be realistic," I said.

*

As the days passed, I spent my time weaving, sewing and waiting. Aegisthus continued to request my assistance: priests were demanding more honey for their deities, more incense, oil, fat sheep and spotless goats; petitioners needed arbitration to settle feuds and redress murders, ravishments, abductions, land grabbing, livestock rustling, sorcery…there was no end to the misdeeds of the Mycenaeans. I saw nothing to gain by my participation, so kept to my throne room.

Though Iphigenia occupied my waking thoughts, at night I dreamed of my other absent child. I tossed and turned, the bed sheets sticking to my skin. Sounds echoed in my ears, distant yet forever near; visions flashed beneath my eyelids: Iphitus' wail, his tender face, his eyes of newborn blue. His swaddled weight in my arms. Torn from my arms. A wall, shrouded in darkness. A woman's screams, my screams.

Except this time, I wasn't in bed. Aegisthus shook me gently. I sat slumped on a bench in the courtyard, in the shade of a potted myrtle tree. I must have dozed off, and Iphitus' shade had visited my dreams. The Mother had let my lost child rise; she punished me for allowing Agamemnon to take another of my children. But my daughter, unlike my baby son, would return to my arms, if only for a short while.

She was late already, by my reckoning. Her escort must be afraid of tiring her after the emotions of the wedding day. She was still so delicate. Was she sick?

"What's wrong?" asked Aegisthus.

I held my face in my hands.

"Achilles will be a kind husband," he said. "Who could fail to love Iphigenia?"

"Her father."

"Agamemnon and Achilles couldn't be more different. Take your mind off things. I came to find you – it's a thorny one, another endless feud."

I'd supposed the day's business to be finished and had waited till the courtyard was empty before venturing from the throne room. But of course Aegisthus spent longer with petitioners than Agamemnon did.

"Oh, very well," I said.

With a sigh, I followed him into the hall, where two peasants in short rough tunics glared murder at each other in front of the empty throne. One had a scar curving from the outer corner of his eye, down around his cheekbone and turning back to meet his mouth. I wondered if it was a gift from the other petitioner, a russet-haired man. The seated greybeards paid the pair no attention, muttering among themselves and casting sullen looks my way.

Aegisthus set a stool next to the throne for me and remained standing. "Tell your story to your queen," he ordered the petitioners.

The peasants hesitated for a surprised moment, before launching into their shared history with the gusto of bards competing for an olive wreath.

Their feud had originated with two brothers – the peasants' great-grandfathers – over the ownership of a prized ewe. The great-grandfather of Lyceus, the scarred fellow, had tried to retrieve the animal from his brother's flock, believing it to be his own long-lost ewe, and met with fatal resistance from the great-grandfather of Elatus, the russet-haired man. Inevitably, Lyceus' grandfather exacted vengeance by killing Elatus' great-grandfather. Elatus' grandfather killed Lyceus' grandfather, in turn; then all the sons, uncles, nephews and cousins joined in. On and on, the feud went.

"And you want the bloodshed to stop," I told the two men.

Elatus wrung his hands like a laundry woman at her sheets. "Lady, I'm the last of my line, and same with him. Who'll make libations to my ancestors if Lyceus kills me? Who'll pour to me?"

Aegisthus regarded both men sternly. "You've a duty to avenge your dead. Do you imagine you can absolve yourselves?"

"There is another way," I said. "Take a ewe to the farm of the last man who spilled kindred blood. Spit your inherited offences on her head and sacrifice her to Alastor, daemon who inflicts blood feuds on the generations. Bury her far from your farms and don't be tempted to save any portion for yourselves. Do this, and your family's crimes and obligations will pass from you. The curse will lift."

"Can it really be true?" said Lyceus.

"If the queen herself says so…" said Elatus, stealing a glance at his enemy.

"Go now. End your feud," I told them. "Afterwards, pay some attention to your wives. If they're as young as you, the goddess might bless you yet with children to remember you."

The greybeards eyed me with varying degrees of resentment and suspicion, as a guard led the peasants away. This didn't surprise me. What did puzzle me was the grimace on Aegisthus' face. He, after all, had persuaded me to arbitrate…

*

Whether such a horror could be purged by laying the guilt on a ewe's head, I didn't know, but the rite was as powerful as any.

Despite his lack of enthusiasm for the solution, Aegisthus asked me to hear more petitioners over the following days. I agreed, if only as a distraction while waiting for Iphigenia's return. I had sent a herald to Aulis to find out what delayed her and to bring her home.

As I sat dispensing justice and unpicking knotty problems, I recalled how I felt as a young woman by Tantalus' side in this same hall, so full of expectations, never faltering in my self-belief. Aegisthus, like Tantalus before him, conferred with me, listened carefully to my decisions, nodded in approval and spoke encouragements. The gloomy greybeards reminded me of the Followers who'd always resented our rule.

My days passed swiftly in the hall, and the nights dragged in my chamber. At last my herald returned.

He described arriving in Aulis to find the beach deserted. The tents and shelters were gone; the rubbish of occupation, gone; even the latrine trenches had been filled in, though the stench lingered. All that remained were some fire pits and altars. The herald had stayed on in Aulis to question the townsfolk. He learned that the fleet set sail the day after Iphigenia's arrival and she was presumed to have left with it.

A cold, clammy fist closed around my vitals. "Why would they take her to Troy?"

The herald shook his head. "Perhaps her husband couldn't bear to part from her?"

This seemed unlikely. Surely Achilles was too noble to carry his young bride into danger, just to avoid a few weeks of loneliness while the army laid siege to Troy?

"Bathe and eat, get some rest," Aegisthus told the herald. "In the morning, you'll set out for Phthia. Achilles might have sent Iphigenia to his father's palace to prepare for his homecoming." He squeezed my hand with only a little more conviction than I felt.

The herald averted his gaze from the gesture of familiarity. "Yes, Guardian."

*

So the herald set out for Phthia in search of my missing child, while I remained in the palace, sick with misgivings, impotent. Over and over, I brooded on every possible explanation for Agamemnon's silence. I brooded till I almost despaired. I conjured up Iphigenia, saw her standing before me, heard her soft voice; but these apparitions offered no sign of where she might be. I yearned to leave the palace, to search the length and breadth of Achaea, as the Mother did for her own absent Spring Maiden, but where would I begin? Instead, I waited for my herald's return.

After a while, there seemed no reason to leave my chamber. I couldn't concentrate on daily tasks, could no longer pretend interest in the cares of others. Orestes and Electra were, shameful to admit, far from my thoughts.

One evening, Orestes knocked at my door, the first time he'd deigned to visit the women's quarters since Agamemnon removed him from the nursery. He asked me to take supper in the hall.

"I've no appetite," I said.

He rubbed at the overgrown fiery gold fuzz on his scalp. "You do understand, Mother? My sister has married well. Achilles is very skilled in arms. We can be proud of our connection to him."

I tried to pat his shoulder. He was just out of reach and my hand fell away. "I expect you're right, son."

He left the room. Afterwards, I couldn't remember if I'd said goodbye.

The next day, his sister jostled past me in the corridor without breaking her stride. I'd summoned the energy to step around the chamber door and call for a maid to heat some bathwater.

"Don't be so rude," I told Electra.

She stopped. Slowly, smiling, she turned around. "Rude, Mother? I didn't think you'd notice me."

"Of course I noticed."

"You haven't noticed anyone since Iphigenia left."

My mind felt hollow as I groped for a denial. The effort was too wearisome. Electra was a child – I wasn't obliged to defend myself to her.

Her hard smile twisted downwards. "Why didn't you send me to marry Achilles? I could have served Father in his army. I'd have fought like an Amazon. Achilles would have taught me." She glared at me, as if expecting me to laugh.

"Ridiculous," I said.

"I could have! Harmonia taught me about the Amazons before you chased her away. They're the only women worth their fathers' trouble getting them. I could have proved myself. Father would have seen how good I am. But you sent my sister."

"Your father summoned Iphigenia, not you. But your turn will come too, little girl. He'll take all of my children. So, off you go, weave yourself a bridal wreath."

I ducked back into the bedchamber, slammed the door, sank nauseous to the floor. From the corner of my eye, I saw the chest that so recently held Iphigenia's veil. I clambered towards it on my knees, hoping the veil might somehow still be there. I threw open the dust-covered lid, clung to the empty, gaping chest. My shoulders heaved. No tears would come.

I'd wept no tears since Iphigenia's departure. I'd weep none until she and I were once more reunited.

*

The days dragged painfully by, and still no word came from Agamemnon or Achilles.

At last, our herald returned from the citadel of Achilles' father in wild Thessaly. I hurried to the hall, where he and Aegisthus were waiting for me.

King Peleus had treated the herald with impeccable courtesy. No news, Peleus assured him, could be more welcome than that of a marriage between his only child and the daughter of King Agamemnon of Mycenae. Old Peleus described Achilles as a devoted and respectful son, who never failed to seek his permission and blessing when correct to do so. Achilles also took care to delight Peleus with regular messages about his adventures whenever he was abroad.

He'd sent no herald to announce his marriage to Iphigenia.

CHAPTER 28

Once my shock from the herald's revelation passed, a simmering anger replaced my blind fear. There was now only one place Iphigenia could be. Agamemnon and Achilles had indeed taken her to Troy.

For reasons I couldn't fathom, they'd carried her off as though she were a camp whore, made her suffer a long journey across wind-lashed seas in a ship full of coarse soldiers, without privacy or comforts. Many a grown man sickened during such a voyage, let alone a fragile girl who'd never so much as viewed a ship from the shore. Was it even safe to sail, with Great Artemis and Boreas so recently furious? And now she must endure weeks in enemy territory, in a camp full of warriors whose wives were far across the sea.

Was Achilles so besotted with his bride that he couldn't bear to part from her or even wait for his trusting father to grant him permission to marry? More likely Agamemnon had given him no time to inform King Peleus, impatient to seal the alliance and set sail. Or had Achilles perhaps considered it unwise to spare a herald, now that he was going into battle? Or had the herald been waylaid on the way to Peleus' palace? Thessaly was, after all, a land of bandits.

Achilles' thoughtlessness was bad enough, but Agamemnon's failure to send me word of Iphigenia's departure and her safe arrival was inexcusable.

"If he lacks the decency to send a herald to us, we'll send one to him," I told Aegisthus.

"His behaviour doesn't surprise me, though I'll admit I'd thought better of Achilles," said Aegisthus. "But Iphigenia's safe, I'm sure of it. Achilles is too proud to let any harm come to his bride. Take your mind off things, Clytemnestra. I'm hearing petitioners tomorrow. Assist me."

I laughed. "How can you possibly think I'd care for their petty problems?"

"I thought Agamemnon was the one who considers their cares petty. Sit with me, hear your people. I've no desire to do this alone."

I studied his face. Power sat well enough with him, for a man who claimed not to hunger for it. Sometimes I wondered whether Aegisthus really did wish to share his authority, or whether my value to him – as twice queen of Mycenae – lay in my ability to provide a veneer of legitimacy to his ambitions.

"I won't," I said, rising from the courtyard bench where we sat. My ladies, by now, would be arriving in the throne room to begin the day's work. We were making garments for Iphigenia's return, suitable for a young bride.

Let Aegisthus enjoy his position while he held it. Soon enough, the beacon fires would announce Agamemnon's return – a joyful sight, since it would mean the return of my daughter. For two more years, she'd remain at my side. Or, as the whims of her husband and her father dictated, she'd gather her belongings and take a proper leave of her family as a married woman.

*

So, I busied myself in making clothes for Iphigenia, Aegisthus busied himself in the affairs of Mycenae, and we both waited for our herald's return from Troy.

The greybeards, I learned, had become mellower now that they no longer saw me except when I passed by on the balconies over the hall. They were, however, obliged to tolerate Electra's presence, if not mine. I'd dismissed my daughter from my throne room after she proved more of a hindrance at the loom than a help. At first, Orestes protested when she wheedled her way into the men's company. He'd begun to spend more time in the hall, basking in the praise of the greybeards, pouting and fretting when Aegisthus ignored his less-than-sage counsel. Aegisthus allowed Electra to sit to one side of the scandalised greybeards, as long as she remained quiet. At suppertimes, he encouraged the children to talk about what they'd heard that day – a transparent ploy to prick my interest.

One afternoon, passing by the hall on my way to inspect some newly dyed fabrics drying on the roof, I overheard Electra scoffing at a petitioner. The woman knelt on the floor, touching Aegisthus' knees in supplication.

"Rise. I'm listening," said Aegisthus.

Electra arched a scornful eyebrow and flicked her gaze over the petitioner's tousled hair and frayed woollen tunic. Her brother was absorbed in picking at his fingernails. The petitioner struck me as familiar, though peasant women looked much alike after a few poor harvests: thin, tired, coarsely dressed. This one was pretty enough, despite her obvious misfortunes. The wide, tear-bright eyes in her gaunt face might have appealed to a compassionate man – or a predatory one.

"I came here once before to beg the king for justice," she said. "He wasn't…he didn't…Oh, Guardian, I've nowhere else to turn. My neighbour made me his wife, though I didn't want him, and I can't escape while he lives. And now he's threatening my three boys. He says, why should he rear brats that aren't his. And my little daughter, the way he looks at her…What can I do, Guardian? What should I do? Help me – please, help me." Convulsed by sobs, she fell to the floor again and clasped Aegisthus' knees.

Electra's voice rang out, cold and clear: "Why don't you stand up to him? Don't you live on a farm? You must have a tool you could use."

The woman had fought visibly to compose herself while Electra spoke. Now she stared at her, open-mouthed.

"Quiet, child, you understand nothing," said Aegisthus. He took the petitioner's hands and held them. "What would you like me to do? Speak up, don't be frightened."

I held the balcony rail and leaned forward to catch the petitioner's reply, but she was weeping too much to speak, overwhelmed by such a sympathetic hearing. She needn't have been so grateful. Aegisthus sighed. He let his gaze drift around the hall while the woman sobbed.

"Enough; stand up," he said. "This gets us nowhere. As a man, I can tell you that few men delight in their predecessor's offspring. Your new husband is probably trying his best. If his words are a little gruff, I'm sure he means no harm. Be patient. Count yourself lucky. Your children have a new father and won't starve."

For some moments, the woman remained on her knees, stunned by his indifference. I considered making my presence known and reproving him. Did he care so little for justice when I wasn't seated beside him, observing his behaviour?

The petitioner dropped face-down on the floor and seized his ankles, the most abject form of supplication.

He shuffled his legs in discomfort. "Guard, take her away. She's not the only one waiting to see me today."

As the guard led her off, I remembered why she looked familiar. Agamemnon had once granted her an audience, with Nestor and Odysseus present. He'd shown as little interest as Aegisthus in protecting her from her bullying neighbour. I'd intervened by instructing Aegisthus' men to beat the man, a remedy which I now saw had failed.

The guard was pushing her into the vestibule.

Aegisthus called out after her: "Come back five days from now. You might find a more sympathetic audience."

He glanced up at the balcony, to where I stood.

*

Though I resented Aegisthus' attempt to manipulate me, I couldn't help brooding over the unlucky petitioner and the brute who'd killed her husband, molested her and now threatened her children. She might be a poor farm wife and I a queen, but our similarities weren't lost on me. We were pieces on a gaming board to be claimed, manoeuvred, and discarded by men. Rich or poor, famous or obscure, men made the rules that ordered our lives, and they broke them. She and I were women.

There was a time, it's said, when goddesses and their priestesses ruled this land. A time before the warlike Achaeans came. With power comes responsibilities to those made powerless, and if the harassed widow cannot expect justice from her king, what right has he to wield a sceptre? If a woman receives only cruelty or indifference from her husband, father, brother or son, why should she trust her well-being to any of them?

Today, I'd be king to that forsaken petitioner. I'd send some burly fellows to hang the man who raped her and menaced her children.

This I did, and I was elated when I sat down that evening at supper. Aegisthus spoke of the affairs of Mycenae, oblivious to the fact that I'd thwarted his scheme to lure me into the hall. Electra watched us suspiciously, in between mocking Orestes over his boredom during the morning's proceedings. Her brother blushed, blustered and claimed that a mere girl couldn't understand the techniques men employed to keep commoners in check. Electra responded with laughter, and I scolded her with only the mildest of reproofs.

Pleased, drowsy, I returned to my apartments and stood motionless while a maidservant undressed me. Then I lay on my bed, closed my eyes, and descended to the Underworld.

I walked through the Asphodel Meadows. Hermes Pompaeus must have led me there, the god who delights in bearing away mortals in sleep. Sturdy stalks and scentless white petals brushed against my bare legs. Gibbering shades flitted past me. They could not see me or hear me – I'd made no blood libations to animate them; I hadn't known I'd come here. Still, I called out for my lost ones in the hope that they'd found their way here at last.

Tantalus drifted towards me through the pallid flowers, hazy and indistinct, yet I knew it was him. His shade drew close. I held out my arms, and he smiled in his sweet familiar way. He cradled a baby, rocked the swaddled bundle gently as a woman.

"Iphitus," I whispered, though my throat tightened painfully. Longing ached in my breasts.

Another shade drifted behind my little husband and son. Love washed over me for black-haired Thyestes as it never had beyond Hades. His night-dark hair caught fire with sunrays that did not shine over this foggy meadow. The flame-haired shade pointed at Tantalus.

But it wasn't Tantalus. It was Aegisthus, and Aegisthus was weeping. He placed Iphitus on a bed of asphodel petals, then knelt, scratched at the earth with his fingernails. He paused from time to time to ask, "Little Cicada, who broke your wings?" He dug a hole, deep and wide. "And now your song is silent." He took the swaddled bundle and dropped it in the hole.

The breath tore in rasps from my lungs. Sweat slicked my skin from scalp to thighs. I sat upright in bed, with the cushions scattered around me. Fingers were gripping my forearm.

"Pompaeus?" I cried.

Aegisthus, pale as asphodel in the lamplight, released his convulsive grip on me. He slumped to the floor, glassy-eyed.

I scrambled to my knees and crouched over him. "What's happened? What's wrong?"

He said nothing.

I grabbed his hair and jerked his face to mine. "Tell me!" I screamed.

In a cracking voice he said, "The herald returned from Troy. There was an accident, your husband said. Trojan bowmen. The fleet was beaching, the bowmen attacked. She was struck. Fell overboard. Washed away. Your husband said."

Washed away? My ears rang. Washed away? *A lie.* I grasped Aegisthus' shoulders. I shook him with all the rage of grief long suppressed. *A lie.* His face swirled before me. *A lie.* I opened my mouth. I screamed from my stomach. *A lie.* He tried to hold me, to still me. I clawed at his chest and tore my hair.

My daughter was dead. And her father lied.

Sobs replaced my shrieks. I heard them as if from a distance. My body was numb, I no longer felt. I drew Aegisthus to me. Blood streaked his cheeks, ran down his chest. I gripped his face. I forced his mouth to mine, gnashing my teeth. Our faces were wet, our mouths were wet. Numb. My palms came away from his face, bloodied.

I sank onto him. I needed to feel. I needed to feel. My child was dead. The Spring Maiden was dead. I needed to feel. We clung together, we moved together. We scratched and tore.

Iphigenia was dead. We wept together. Our tears mingled. We clung.

Afterwards, we whispered in breaking voices of our love for Iphigenia, till my throat closed up.

Aegisthus echoed my unspoken words: "I've failed her. I failed them all."

CHAPTER 29

During the grey-black hours of morning, Aegisthus and I went down to the courtyard and had the herald brought to us. A guard held him, while another pressed a knife against his throat. Tears squeezed from beneath the herald's closed eyelids. Mucus pooled under his nose. If he admitted the truth, I told him, his ordeal would be over. He gibbered like the shades in Hades.

"The truth," I demanded. "You know the truth."

From the moment he'd entered the courtyard, I hadn't the slightest doubt he knew what had really become of my daughter. At first, he stood yawning like a hog while sweat trickled down his brow. His eyes darted in every direction but mine. His hands fluttered nervously with his denials of further knowledge. I had them bound behind him.

A foolish part of me dared to believe my child still lived, a hope as faint as a hairline crack in a cyclopean wall. If so, why had Agamemnon lied? She must be in danger from her father, her husband, or both. And if she was really gone, I had to know the truth.

"Cut off his earlobe," I said.

The herald managed a scream before the guard who held him clapped a hand over his mouth. The other guard pinched the herald's earlobe between a thick finger and thumb and waved the knife in his face, while the captive squirmed like a speared fish.

"Uncover his mouth. Speak!" I said.

The restraining guard slid two fingers aside to reveal the herald's compressed lips. At my nod, the knife-wielding guard sliced off the earlobe. A herald's person might be inviolable when he travels abroad; at home, not so much. Besides, what did laws matter now?

A rivulet of blood poured from the maimed ear and curved under the herald's chin. It continued downwards between his palpitating pectoral muscles, before splitting into channels over his stomach. I waited until whines replaced his roars.

"Take off the other earlobe," I commanded.

This threat broke him. Through bubbles of spit, he begged me never to reveal that he was the one who'd told me what happened on my daughter's final night. I snatched the bloodied knife and rammed the hilt into his mutilated ear to warn him how much worse it would be if he held anything back. The blade slit my palm. I didn't feel it at the time.

On arriving in Troy, the herald sought out Agamemnon, who'd given him a terse account of Iphigenia's drowning. Miserable, he made his way back through the camp to the spot where his shipmates were setting up a temporary shelter. A young man, Achilles' cousin Patroclus, approached him and asked him to visit the Phthian prince's shelter. As soon as the herald crossed the shelter's threshold, he was the recipient of a blistering tirade against Agamemnon.

"Tell Queen Clytemnestra I knew nothing of this," shouted Achilles, his handsome face and implacable lips twisted in fury. "Never would I have given my name to such an abomination. I'd never have allowed the child to suffer and her mother to mourn."

Achilles told the herald that my daughter and I had been deceived, and his own reputation had been stained with infamy. He'd known nothing of the proposed marriage until, on a fatal wind-torn night, he'd stumbled on the celebrants performing their rite on a bluff above Aulis bay. Dressed in her bridal gown and veil, Iphigenia had approached the altar of Artemis with faltering steps. Her stony-faced father waited for her there, with wily Odysseus and Calchas the straggle-haired priest. Odysseus removed Iphigenia's veil. Calchas lifted her over the altar.

Aegisthus' arms kept me from collapsing when the herald revealed what happened next.

Calchas opened my daughter's throat as if she were an animal. Achilles stood rooted to the spot, dumbfounded by horror. By the time he recovered his wits, only Odysseus remained of the murderers. Achilles flew at him, intent on breaking Odysseus' neck. Before he reached him, Odysseus explained that Achilles' elderly father had hired mercenaries to guard Phthia palace in place of those warriors who'd left for Troy. The men were in Odysseus' pay. If any harm befell the perpetrators of the night's evil, they'd murder Peleus. Thwarted, furious, Achilles sank to the bloody earth as Odysseus walked away.

Next day, the north wind ceased raging. The Achaeans set sail. My daughter had died in exchange for a fair wind to carry the fleet to Troy.

*

Aegisthus carried me back to my chamber and tried to comfort me while I rocked back and forth on my bed. My breath came in gasps; the more I gasped, the less I could breathe. The room drifted away.

When I came to, a healer stood beside the bed. I screamed at him to leave. Over and over, I screamed. He couldn't bring back my child. He couldn't heal me. He scuttled off.

For days, a fever consumed me. I heard Iphigenia weep at the foot of the bed, but when I murmured her name and opened my eyes I saw only Electra, and moaned in grief. Another time, I heard my son say, "Really, Mother. You must rise. You're the queen."

When the fever passed, the maids filled a bathtub and half lifted, half dragged me into the herb-scented water. Afterwards, they spooned broth into my mouth and wiped the spillage from my chin with a piece of bread. I shuddered, remembering Harmonia's ministrations during those dark days after Agamemnon murdered Iphitus.

Aegisthus visited me every day and night. He held my hand, spoke of mundanities: Orestes had developed an interest in beekeeping and was training with the keeper of the palace hives; Electra had devoted herself to a pup rejected by her father's favourite boarhound bitch, a limping runt Agamemnon would certainly have drowned. The children knew nothing of their sister's death. Aegisthus thought it best if they heard it from me, their mother, when I felt stronger.

Iphigenia lay in a lonely grave in Aulis, and her brother and sister knew nothing. How utterly I'd failed them all.

I sat up in bed. "I must tell them…I must tell them…" Groaning, I caught my face in my hands. "What can I tell them? What can I say?"

"Why, you'll tell them the truth, of course," said Aegisthus. "Won't you?"

"That the father they worship murdered their sister, their own flesh? How could they live with such knowledge?"

Aegisthus stared at me for a long moment. "You must tell them what he did. He must be punished." His mouth set in a hard line while he waited for my reply.

I pushed myself from the bed and paced towards the window. "Of course we'll punish him. He'll never sit on the throne again." My thoughts worked quickly, forming visions of the future, of Agamemnon thin and pale, clothed in rags. "Send for reinforcements, every ally you can muster from your time in exile. Agamemnon will never set foot within the walls of his beloved Mycenae again. We'll fight him. We'll overthrow him. We'll hold the throne for Orestes."

Aegisthus' eyes glittered. "You can't mean such a thing. He deserves to die."

"You think I don't know that? But, if I destroy him, I'll destroy the only children left to me. Yes – yes, they must learn the truth. I must tell them. But, if I execute their father, their curses will rain down on me. They'll excuse him anything, even this. Me, they'll never forgive. They love me little enough already, how well I know it."

"You know that isn't…" He didn't finish his lie.

"If they despise me, what's left for me?" I ignored the flicker of pain on his face. I loved him well enough, but no man has the same claims on a woman as her children. "They'll resent me when we banish him, it's true, but even they couldn't expect me to forgive him." I laughed in sudden merriment. "How he'll enjoy exile! Don't you see? Losing his throne will be the slowest torture of all for him, as it was once before, worse than all the torments of the sinners in Hades. Think of all the times you've heard him wailing about his years of being nothing, no one, landless, an outsider."

"If we'd killed him years ago, Iphigenia would still be alive."

I could have lunged at him, but the power left my limbs. I sank onto a chair by the window. A memory returned to me, Agamemnon creeping into Iphigenia's nursery the night before her naming ceremony, leaning over her cradle, muttering, "Too soon."

Another memory, sharp as an obsidian shard: the evening of Agamemnon's return from my father's citadel, after he'd given my sister to Menelaus. He'd quarrelled with Aegisthus. In his fury, he dragged me to my chamber. I begged him to remember the child in my womb, and he swore, if the goddess gave me a healthy child, to deliver to Artemis the fairest creature born that spring. I'd forgotten his promise, supposed it fulfilled.

Now, I understood: Agamemnon never forgot; nor had Artemis. The first perfect creature was no spotless lamb or kid. It was our daughter.

All these years of trying in vain to protect my children. All these years, a filthy shadow hung over us all. Our house was cursed. Atreus' abominable supper had plunged us into madness, into self-annihilation. And now another child was dead.

With an effort, I summoned my voice: "Let my children despise me for banishing Agamemnon, but I will not have them hate me to destruction."

"Justice!" shouted Aegisthus. His voice startled me from my torpor. In a few strides, he crossed the distance between us. He seized my shoulders. His fingers dug into my skin. "You owe them justice, damn you."

Hatred burned in his eyes. After a few startled moments, I realised his gaze was turned inwards.

His shoulders slumped. His hands fell to his sides. "Forgive me. I've failed you, my love. I failed them all."

"Tell me truly," I said, "what my dead were to you."

Aegisthus lowered himself onto the crumpled blankets on the bed. He closed his eyes and drew a laboured breath. "You know I hated him, hated my foster-father."

"Your foster…?" I fell silent, not wishing to distract him.

"Yes. It wasn't just his heartlessness and brutality to me. It wasn't just his brutality to Pelopia, though that was it too. It was who he was. Who I am." He stared down at his fists clenched in his lap. "Atreus wasn't like Agamemnon, whatever you might think. Your husband fears offending the gods with each crime he commits. Atreus had no such qualms. He even boasted of slaying the sons of Thyestes, of serving those innocent boys to their father. *Boasted.*"

A truly evil man. And his son was no less a child-killer.

"Sometimes, after supper, Atreus forced the bard to sing of that banquet." Aegisthus grimaced at the memory. "The bard would peer down at the floor and up at the ceiling, as if he thought he'd be sucked into the earth or struck by lightning for his impious song. Pelopia cringed to hear those sordid accounts of her father feasting on the flesh of her brothers. And every time the bard reached the part about Atreus drowning Aerope in the bath for her adultery, Atreus' eyes never left Pelopia's face."

Aegisthus' own eyes, unexpectedly, lit up. "But Thyestes got his vengeance for those dead boys in the end. He returned once more to besiege Mycenae and destroy Atreus, who was just as eager to end their feud one way or the other. He hurried to the citadel walls with Agamemnon and Menelaus, and I went to the armoury for a spear. I might have had no love for my foster-father, but I was loyal to my friends and home.

"Pelopia called out to me as I passed the throne room. I went to her, since no one else would have bothered to tell her what was happening. We'd always been close, she and I, outsiders as we were – the unloved foster-son and the niece Atreus married to ensure her offspring would be loyal to their father. She begged me not to fight. She wept and told me she couldn't bear to lose me if I fell in battle. What would be left to her? I was too young, she said. I was untested. I was her everything."

Aegisthus bowed his dark head, caught up in memories of his gentle foster-mother, one of the few people to ever truly love him.

At length, he said, "She didn't say so, but I knew she hoped Atreus would be killed and her father would retake the throne. I couldn't blame her. But it seemed her wish wouldn't be fulfilled. Atreus summoned me from her side to tell me the fighting was over and to berate me for not playing a part in it. Agamemnon, he said, had captured Thyestes. My foster-brother stood among the Followers, looking proud and bloody and contemptuous.

"'If you want to prove you're no weakling who hides behind women's skirts,' said Atreus, 'take your famous sword and go kill Thyestes.' He meant the sword I kept locked in a chest in my room, the one I was found with all those years ago as a baby outside the palace. Godless though he was, he apparently baulked at spilling such close kindred blood as his brother's. While he might think nothing of butchering his nephews, he wouldn't risk his sons committing the reverse act on their uncle.

"I'd little enthusiasm for slaying a defenceless captive, and Pelopia's father at that. Atreus interpreted my distaste as cowardice – or worse, treachery. If I refused to kill Thyestes, this would be evidence of a plot, he said, between me, Thyestes and Pelopia. He'd hang us all as traitors. I didn't doubt his threat; he'd no love for any of us. I often supposed the only reason he fostered me was to menace Pelopia through her fear for me, subjecting me to whippings and threatening much worse. Not that he was gentle to Agamemnon or Menelaus, but he had a proud sort of loathing for them. They could rise after he beat them; I crawled.

"So I went to my chamber, took up my sword and set off for the prisoner's room. I drew back the bolts on the door. Thyestes was sitting on the floor of his cell, bound hand and foot. One of his eyes was half closed and purple. Cuts criss-crossed his face. I wondered how many of his injuries were inflicted after leaving the battlefield. Despite his obvious pain, he grinned up at me with chipped teeth and declared himself delighted to meet me. I warned him not to speak too soon, which made him chuckle.

"'That's a fine sword you have, lad,' he said, nodding at the eagle-claw hilt rising from the sheath on my belt. His good eye twinkled. 'Will you do me a last kindness before running me through? I'd like to see my daughter one more time. Bring Pelopia to me, won't you, son?'

"I didn't trust him, but how could I refuse such a request? If Pelopia asked me afterwards whether her father had asked to speak with her before I sliced open his helpless body, how could I lie and pile hurt on hurt? So I went to fetch her – and that was my mistake."

Aegisthus stared into the middle of the room like a hound who sees and hears things invisible to men, as though the shades of those who lived and died so unhappily in this palace still lingered. As though the palace were a tomb that trapped us all, the living and the dead alike.

"Pelopia gasped to see her father so battered. She wasn't close to him, hadn't seen him since long before her marriage, but kin is kin. She fell on her knees and burrowed her head in his shoulder. He moaned, perhaps in two kinds of pain, then growled at her to rise.

" 'The sword the lad carries, I know where it came from,' said Thyestes. Pelopia frowned and told him I'd been found with it. 'Yes, and I know where it came from,' he repeated. 'The man who got him on his mother left it for him. She was a priestess of Protectress Athene in Sicyon. She'd been performing the nocturnal rites of her goddess. Her dress became bloodied, so afterwards she stripped to wash it in the stream near Athene's sacred grove. She never saw the man who crept from the bushes and pushed her face-down onto the bank. He covered her head with the sopping dress. That man got her with child and left behind his sword, so he might one day make himself known by it.'

"This story of my conception, if true, appalled me. And a chill dread told me worse revelations were to come. Thyestes bowed his head and said quietly, 'That sword was mine. I was the man who raped the poor girl. I did it because the gods fated it. I had no choice. It wasn't through lust, my daughter, never through lust.'

"Pelopia had listened ashen-faced to her father. Tremors convulsed every visible part of her body. She gave a cry, somewhere between a moan of despair and an animal scream. Then it happened so quickly. She snatched the sword from my belt. She seemed about to swing it at Thyestes. Dumb, frozen, I couldn't react. She turned the blade around. She plunged it into her belly.

"My limbs unlocked. I screamed. I grabbed her as she fell. I sank down with her and laid her across my thighs, crooning to her, berating her, begging her not to die. I demanded to know why she'd done such a thing. How could she leave me? How could she take away the only person I ever loved, the only one who loved me? The hateful truth stared me in the face as starkly as her glazed eyes, but I couldn't admit it.

"She was trying to speak. Her bloodless lips moved. They called me her beloved brother, her light. Her son. I bent over her and touched her mouth. I pressed my lips to her sacred lips to silence her, to silence those monstrous, beautiful words. Her son, I was her son. She was the one who'd arranged for me to be left outside Atreus' palace as a baby. For my sake, she became brutal Atreus' bride. My mother hadn't abandoned me. I wanted to drown out her terrible words with my tears, as rain smothers the murmurs and groans of Mother Earth. I begged her to be silent, to speak, to never leave me, to call me her son. Her son. The life was ebbing from her. I cradled her till she died.

"I laid her on the floor and turned to Thyestes. Bound though he was, he threw himself sideways as I lunged at him. If I killed him, he bawled, I'd be cursed for all eternity: he was my father. I laughed and told him my begetting was curse enough. I fell on him, seized his beard, jerked up his chin to expose his hairy throat. But I had no sword. I couldn't touch my sword. I pummelled my fist into his eye, the undamaged one. I swore to kill him.

"He hadn't wanted to defile Pelopia, he screamed, but what was one more crime – against a daughter, at that – after Atreus made him cannibalise his sons? Following the murders of those boys, my *brothers*, he'd consulted an oracle to ask how to get vengeance. He learned it would come through a son he fathered on his own daughter. 'The thought of it made me sick,' he whined, curling his face into his chest to evade my blows. 'But I hardly knew her. And what's a rape? Worse if it's your own flesh, granted, but she hardly seemed like a daughter to me. And I hid her face.'

"I wanted to smash his face against the wall, to crush it into pulp. But he was my father – my sire twice over, father and grandfather both. And Pelopia, sweet blameless Pelopia, was my sister-mother. I tipped back my head, as if the ceiling of Thyestes' cell were the heavens, and roared from the bottom of my lungs.

"I slumped back down beside Pelopia's body. When Thyestes dared speak again, he told me that I, as his son, had no choice but to avenge my dead brothers as the oracle foretold. To leave those boys unavenged would be worse than spilling their killer's blood, even though Atreus was my uncle.

"I promised him nothing. I untied his ropes and told him to play dead. Then I lifted my mother's corpse, still with the sword in her belly, and left the cell. I told the sentries standing at the end of the prison corridor that I'd strangled Thyestes – he certainly looked broken when they peered around the door at him. Pelopia, I said, killed herself out of grief for him. I commanded them to follow me to her apartments, out of respect for their dead queen, and guard her till burial. When they tried to protest, I assured them Thyestes was going nowhere. His filthy carcass, of course, took care of itself.

"After laying Pelopia on her bed, I took back my sword—" Aegisthus winced – "and wrapped her in a sheet. I returned to the hall to give a version of events to Atreus, but Agamemnon told me he'd already left to make a thanksgiving sacrifice in Poseidon's poplar grove above the citadel. Obscene haste, considering Thyestes' carcass was still warm – very warm. So I set out after my foster-father, my *uncle*, without a clear plan. Yet surely I must have known what I'd do.

"I slipped out through the sally port to avoid the guards on the Perseia Gate and made my way to the Perseia Spring. Atreus, I knew, would go there first to purify himself before honouring his god. I found him on his knees, scooping handfuls of water over his head like a joyful boy. He must have thought his troubles were over: his brother was dead and he knew of no surviving nephews. His troubles were indeed over. As he bent to splash glittering water up at his face, I crept behind him and stabbed him through his bull neck.

"Agamemnon was in a rage when I got back to the palace. Thyestes had flown, he roared, and I was a callow fool for imagining I'd killed the old fox. Unlike Atreus, Agamemnon's troubles had only just begun. A priest of Poseidon reported having discovered the king's corpse at the Perseia Spring, cut down by an unknown assailant presumed to be Thyestes.

"When Agamemnon finally lay against his cushions after the disasters of the day, no doubt he took consolation from dreams of golden fleeces and lion-topped sceptres – till a servant roused him a little before dawn. Thyestes, at the head of the earlier-routed warband, had returned to storm the palace. Agamemnon and Menelaus' losses were terrible. Most of the guards and Followers went over to Thyestes, and the sons of Atreus fled for their lives.

"As for me, I'd no desire to remain in King Thyestes' palace. I gathered a few possessions and set out along the opposite road to Agamemnon and Menelaus. Later, I learned I had a last remaining brother, the shepherd boy Tantalus. Thyestes had brought him to the palace to keep him safe from the vengeful sons of Atreus, to protect any sons Tantalus might father. But he failed, as you know too well, and I failed to avenge their deaths on Agamemnon.

"So there it is, Clytemnestra. Now you understand everything."

CHAPTER 30

N ow I understood everything. Brother to my murdered husband. Uncle to my murdered son. Last surviving son of a murdered father. Now I knew who Aegisthus was and why he wanted Agamemnon dead. Long ago, he'd avenged the three small sons of Thyestes, slain by Atreus, but Atreus' eldest son had heaped crime upon crime.

Aegisthus remained seated on the bed, watching me with anxious glittering eyes. I turned away, so my face wouldn't betray my horror. I looked through the window towards the night-shrouded outline of the Mother's sacred hill. My stomach roiled. Brother to his mother. Son of his grandfather. Born of a union forbidden to mortals, a coupling that begets monsters and madmen.

"Clytemnestra..." he whispered.

Gods might join together, brother with sister, parent with child – the deathless ones are immune to pollution. Beasts lie with kin, too ignorant to recognise their own lack of divinity. But mortals are punished for imitating gods.

The floorboards creaked behind me. I turned slowly. Aegisthus knelt at my feet and touched my knees. "Purify me," he said softly. "For too long I've carried my secret, my stain. Who could I tell? You alone know who I am. Only you can help me, Clytemnestra."

My horror dissolved, swept away by a wave of pity – of love. Truly, I loved this man, this brother of my sweet Tantalus. I took his head between my hands and kissed the tumbling forelock on his brow. How alike they both were, their black hair and olive skin, their sense of justice, of decency, and yet Aegisthus was so entirely himself. He was my friend, my ally, my lover. He was my children's kin and as much a victim of the House of Atreus as any of us.

And he needed me.

"I'll purify you," I said.

I knew no rites to wash away such a pollution as his. The hero Oedipus, king of seven-gated Thebes, chose banishment for committing unknowing incest with Jocasta, his mother-wife. Queen Jocasta, like Pelopia, saw no other way to purify herself except suicide. Thebes – its women, livestock, crops and plants – suffered sterility until the royal couple atoned for their polluted bed, yet Aegisthus' presence brought no such blight to Mycenae. He was the product of the sin, not the perpetrator.

I could cleanse him. I would find a way.

Another matter gave me pause. "Why didn't you kill Agamemnon long ago, if you wanted to avenge our dead?"

His supplicating embrace tightened around my legs. "I never forgot them. I always knew I'd get vengeance, however long it took. The thought of how he'd suffer kept me going. If only I'd killed him sooner, for the sake of the living. Forgive me, Clytemnestra, forgive me. And may Iphigenia's shade forgive me." He laid his cheek against my knees.

I stroked his soft hair. "You're not to blame." We both had to bear our share of regret, but only one monster bore the blame. Agamemnon alone, of our generation, had the gore of children staining his hands.

"I'll consider myself blameless once he's dead," said Aegisthus. "After he stole the throne, I meant to kill him at once when I returned to Mycenae. But dread tormented me. What if Agamemnon's crimes against my family – your family – were the gods' punishment for what I'd done to Atreus? I'd spilled kindred blood, though I was right to avenge my murdered brothers. What knots the gods tie us in. Then I learned Agamemnon had married you, and I saw a way of arranging his death without further polluting myself."

"You left a dagger in my throne room," I said.

"I thought your duty to your dead was as great as mine, and you at least weren't kin to Agamemnon. You weren't even, in truth, his wife – a fact he promised he'd soon remedy. I knew you'd want to strike the blow for your child. I hadn't any qualms about your being punished. Forgive me, but I didn't love you yet, though I'd have asked Menelaus and the Mycenaeans to show as much mercy as they could, in pity for all you'd been through. And the cycle of vengeance would have ended with you."

The cycle would have ended with my execution. No one would have granted me mercy. No one would avenge a female regicide and husband-killer, whose death was publicly enacted justice and not private revenge. I'd yearned for such a death, considered it my duty.

I touched Aegisthus' cheek. There was nothing to forgive.

When his feelings for me began to change, Aegisthus had once more determined to get vengeance with his own hands. He couldn't have trusted the deed to a henchman: kin, not strangers, should get the blood-price for kin. He decided against committing the deed openly – he wanted to avoid continuing the cycle of vengeance between himself and Menelaus, and any as yet unborn kin. Agamemnon's death must seem to be an accident or a mysterious killing, like the murder of Atreus.

"I don't believe Menelaus would've killed you if he'd known you were Thyestes' son," I said. "He considers you his brother, and you really are his family. He'd have understood your duty to the dead. He'd have settled for banishment."

"I'd have had to kill him to make doubly sure," said Aegisthus. "But it's too late now to ponder these things."

A new plan had formed in Aegisthus' mind. He had tried to persuade me to elope with him. Together with my daughters, we'd find refuge with one or another of the allies he'd made during his self-imposed exile. He'd declare himself to be the last surviving son of King Thyestes, raise an army, and slay Agamemnon in fair combat for the throne of Mycenae.

I, however, hadn't proved amenable.

But now we had no need to storm the citadel. We needed only to defend it against Agamemnon's return. Aegisthus had already made approaches to those Achaean leaders who hadn't joined the Trojan expedition. He'd also sent men far and wide to gather an army from among the labourers who wandered Achaea in search of work, and from the slaves who'd fled the palaces of absent masters to hide out in the mountains.

"It's time to declare the truth of my birth," he said. His face gleamed with zeal. "I'm the heir of Thyestes, true king of Mycenae. I'll claim the throne as the son and brother of kings, with you as my queen. When Agamemnon returns from Troy, we'll be ready for him. There can be no exile for the murderer, only death."

No exile. Only death. Aegisthus could accept no less, our dead could accept no less, and neither, I knew, could I.

"And Orestes?" I said.

He locked his earnest eyes with mine. "He'll be my heir, if the Mycenaeans consent. I'll swear an oath. If we have more sons, they'll inherit after Orestes. I'll never harm him in any way. He's your child and you've suffered enough."

For my sake, if not for that of Orestes, he'd never harm my son. I understood. And, as for the Mycenaeans, they would of course gladly accept Orestes as heir. King Aegisthus and Queen Clytemnestra they'd accept whether they liked it or not.

I held out my hands to Aegisthus, and he rose from the floor. We had much to do. We must consult the priestesses of Peleia to discover which rites could purify a man born of incest. I must speak, also, to Orestes and Electra. For too long, they'd been ignorant of their sister's fate. Later, Aegisthus and I would leave for Aulis to look for Iphigenia's grave. We'd pour libations to her shade and raise a grave marker. On that hallowed ground, he and I would swear a binding oath – to slay her murderer on his return from Troy.

*

I left Aegisthus and set out to find my children.

They were playing with Electra's new boarhound pup on a grassy terrace below the palace, oblivious to the threat of unseasonable rain from the ash-grey clouds gathering over the peaks of the Mother's Bosom. Orestes wore a loincloth such as a slave might wear; Electra, a boyish kilt. Their bodies were sun-browned. Really, I must speak to the woman from Anaphe. It didn't do to have the children running around like farm boys. I rubbed at the back of my neck, at a prickle of guilt.

Orestes threw a stick and slapped the boarhound's scrawny rump. The pup scampered a few steps on gangling legs, then returned to cower against Electra's shins. My daughter punched Orestes' shoulder. She scooped up the dog under one arm and stroked its oversized head.

When I called out, the children raised their right arms in a disconcertingly formal greeting. The armlet Iphigenia had given her as a parting gift, the serpent of rebirth, gleamed against Electra's tanned skin. Tears pricked my eyes. Electra held the pup between my body and hers as I drew her to me. She slipped free and fussed over the animal as if I'd injured it. I embraced my stiff-backed son.

"Children, it's good to see you," I said. "Yet, it pains me."

"You've woken, Mother," said Electra.

I touched their shoulders to indicate that we should sit on the grass. My mouth was sour with the news I must impart. "Yes, I have. Orestes, Electra, I've something terrible to tell you."

Electra kissed her puppy's nose. "Iphigenia's dead."

Stunned, I watched her set the animal down and seat herself on the grass. She gathered the pup into her lap and arranged its frail limbs to her liking, while crooning a song. Orestes watched her, as if waiting for instructions. Receiving none, he stretched out his legs and turned his bare toes in circles.

During the brief walk from the palace, I'd groped in my mind for a sequence of words to reveal the devastating truth as gently as possible. Now, I forgot everything as I sank between my last remaining children, these strangers, onto the sharp, dry grass. Electra tickled her dog's ears. Orestes twisted an unshaven tuft of hair at his temple.

"An archer shot her when the fleet beached in Troy," said Electra. "I overheard the herald tell Guardian Aegisthus. She fell into the sea. There's no better way a girl could die than in her father's army. How lucky she was. How fortunate."

"She died serving our father, when you think about it," said Orestes.

Fortunate. They believed their sister's death was fortunate? How had their minds become so warped? The sound of a pounding hammer carried down to the terrace from a workshop in the palace. Each stroke matched the umbrage rising in me; I pushed it down. Electra and Orestes weren't to blame for their delusions. Their father taught them to disdain women. And they still didn't know what he'd done.

I said, "Listen to me. This will be hard for you to hear, as it is for me to say. But you must learn the truth. Your sister never left Aulis. The promise of marriage to Achilles was a lie to lure her from my arms. Children, Iphigenia died as a sacrifice so the fleet could have a fair wind to sail to Troy. Do you understand? Your father killed his child. For a wind."

It was said. The case for his death was made.

Fear glimmered in their eyes. Fear that their father wasn't the idol of their imaginations. Fear, perhaps, for themselves.

In Orestes, doubt swiftly replaced it. In Electra, defiance.

"Even if it's true, she was lucky. Lucky, I tell you," cried Electra. "She was nothing before, and now she's everything. Father chose her, and men will remember her. He chose her to help him win his war. He *wanted* her. She did the most brilliant thing a woman could do. She served her father and died for his cause. I wish it was me!"

Orestes tried to pat her hand. She slapped his fingers away.

He turned to me. "She died for a noble cause. You should be proud."

I struck his cheek. How dare he, a child, tell me what to feel? He gaped and scrambled away from me, backwards, on his bottom.

I shook Electra's shoulders. She struggled, and I shook her harder, ignoring the feeble growls of the pup in her lap. "He killed my daughter!" I shouted, bent on making her understand. "Killed her for his war! Killed her so he wouldn't be humiliated in front of the Achaeans. He didn't have to fight. He chose to fight. Would he have sacrificed Orestes? Iphigenia was my child. She was my flesh – your flesh."

Electra pushed the dog from her lap and jumped to her feet. "I wish it was me! If it served his purpose, I'd have offered up my throat. Why not? I'd have let him dash my brains out."

With a sickening lurch, I wondered if her sister went so willingly to the altar. Did Iphigenia stretch out her neck for the knife? Did she value her life no more than a beast's? I'd coddled her, made all of her decisions, raised her to meekness as her nature inclined and as custom dictated. She'd put the desires of everyone else before her own.

"Look at me!" yelled Electra. "*Me.*" She dragged Iphigenia's armlet from her forearm, leaving white trails in her skin. With a sob, she hurled it into a clump of thistles.

The little hound turned its head once towards her. It gave a quizzical yip, before limping after the armlet and plunging face-first into the thistles. Electra screamed. The hound retrieved the armlet, dropped it, and sank whimpering onto its belly. My daughter ran to the animal and threw her arms around its neck.

Over her shoulder she shouted, "You wouldn't have cared if I'd gone in her place. No one else mattered to you."

"That's not true," I said.

"Then why did you tell the herald to take me to Aulis instead of her?"

My mouth went dry. "How...?"

"Then you *did* tell him." Her lips twisted into a smile or a grimace. "Just as you told Iphigenia you wanted to send me away instead of her. I was listening."

My mind flashed back to Iphigenia's last days in Mycenae, Electra's light-heartedness, how she'd clutched my hand as we wandered over the hills and through blossoming meadows, how happily she'd played games and chattered. Next morning, sullen and puffy-eyed, she'd refused to sing the bridal songs.

"I thought you preferred Achilles," I said dully, but there was no defence.

Electra's fire extinguished. "It was always her. Always her." She rose and walked away, followed by her faithful hound.

I hugged my knees to my chest and stared at the high walls and battlements of the citadel, overcome by weariness. All of these years I'd struggled in vain to protect my children from Agamemnon. I never imagined they might need protecting from me.

Orestes coughed, a little distance behind me. "Never mind, Mother. The important thing is, Iphigenia was a hero – as much as any girl can be. She was almost a hero."

I pushed myself to my feet, my arms and legs like stone. "Don't spend too long outside. The weather's turning."

CHAPTER 31

Aegisthus and I spent the beginning of the rainy season, such as it is, in Aulis. We arrived at dusk, just as the heavens broke, and made our way to the tumbledown fort of the chieftain, Alegenor, whose two sons were fighting in Troy.

The old warrior's watery eyes showed no curiosity when a herald announced us in his draughty hall, though we'd sent no word ahead of us. Alegenor proved to be an indifferent host, never asking about our daily absences from his fort. He had few wits left to him, which at least made him less likely to send report to Agamemnon of our visit.

His sparsely populated town sits on a rocky peninsula between two bays. Its inhabitants, mainly poor fisherfolk and potters, shied away from our questions. They seemed benumbed from the recent occupation by Agamemnon's army. We quickly decided that the northern bay was too small to have accommodated the Achaean fleet, but the circular southern bay offered harbourage for beaching many ships. On the grey bluffs above this vast bay, in the shadow of towering pine forests where the legendary huntsman Orion killed his first stags, we began our search for my daughter's grave.

When we found the altar, I didn't weep. It was a rough-hewn granite block, unembellished except for a pair of sacral horns. I ignored the trembling in my legs and walked around the altar once, twice, in silent communion with the stone. I urged the dumb rock to speak, as though it could tell me if this was where my daughter died.

Something tiny and metallic glittered at the base of the altar. My insides turned to ice. I dropped to my knees, scooped the object up on my fingertip: a silver disc shaped like a crescent moon. Other tiny discs lay scattered about the grass. I snatched them up like a starveling gathering bitter-vetch in a famine.

These were the ornaments from Iphigenia's bridal veil. This altar, still stained with the blood of sacrifice, could be no other. I rubbed my knuckles against a rusty smudge at the foot of the altar. Precious blood. Blood that screamed for vengeance, as surely as her last breath begged for mercy and received none. Here, Agamemnon took our daughter's life.

The discs pressed into my flesh as I ground my clenched fists into the earth. Never, I vowed to the Mother and to She Who Receives Many, would I weep again, not until I stood over Agamemnon's corpse shedding tears of joy. From now onwards, my heart would be like this granite altar where Iphigenia died, the heart of a goddess, unrelenting.

Several paces from the altar, Aegisthus hunched over a rectangular plot of earth inside a scanty border of pebbles which the grass almost concealed. The plot measured the length and breadth of a larnax, such as people might use for their bathtub and coffin. Such as Iphigenia took to Aulis to bathe in on her wedding day.

I reached my daughter's grave just as my legs buckled. I sank to the ground, scratched my cheeks and tore my hair. Screams burned in my throat but didn't pass my lips. My body convulsed. My eyes remained dry, my vow to the Two Queens unbroken. But at last, my Iphigenia, your mother crouched over you in mourning, as was your due.

The driver of our ox cart unloaded the grave marker, which I'd ordered a master mason to carve under my supervision in a workshop in the palace. I'd known Agamemnon would leave our daughter's grave unmarked. The lower panel depicted Mater Theia holding my child in an eternal embrace. Sparrows, Iphigenia's favourite birds, filled the upper panel against a field of crocuses.

When the little stone was installed, Aegisthus and I picked our way down to the beach to purify ourselves in the chilly water, while the driver dug a libation trench. Every day of our search, we'd loaded a piglet and three amphorae of liquid offerings into the cart. Now, on returning to the burial place, I poured a bowl of honeyed oil over Iphigenia's grave marker. To her thirsty spirit, and to the daemon Erinys who avenges the murdered dead, I poured two bowls into the trench, of wine and water. I lay down to whisper prayers as the libations sank into the earth.

The time had come to swear our oath, the one we should have sworn all those years ago when Agamemnon committed his first atrocities. Aegisthus cut the piglet's throat and I caught its blood in a bowl. By the Two Queens, we vowed to destroy the murderer on his return from Troy. We dipped our hands up to the wrists in the bowl and implored the terrible goddesses to submerge us in our own blood if we failed in our duty.

Before leaving Aulis, we set up a new shrine to Artemis. We transferred the altar to this place, since I couldn't bear to leave it overlooking Iphigenia's grave as a memorial to her murder. The shrine can be found beneath a shady plane tree beside a clear-running spring. The goddess is surely content, for the spot is beautiful indeed.

*

I wasted no time in returning to Mycenae. Unwise, to leave a kingdom too long without its king – a lesson Agamemnon will learn.

And so I sit in my hall, governing my land, dispensing justice. The scribes and administrators are no longer surprised by my grasp of affairs. Petitioners forget I'm their queen and not their king. The greybeard counsellors still grumble, of course, but this doesn't trouble me: old men who swim against the tide are soon overwhelmed by it. I've replaced the surliest with younger men, who claim my wisdom is praised throughout the kingdom. They lie; I'm not loved. The world admires brilliant men and tolerates modest women.

Aegisthus has been travelling throughout Boeotia, Euboea and Argolis. He is recruiting an army from among the landless, fugitive, mercenary and disaffected, while his henchmen recruit in southern and western Achaea. A messenger arrived this morning to announce his imminent return. Aegisthus and I made a pact at Iphigenia's grave: he will head the army and I will rule our kingdom. He has much work to do, training our new warriors and strengthening their loyalty to our cause. We've longer to prepare than we thought. The gods are dragging out the siege of Troy.

Above me, footsteps patter on the balcony. I glance up to see Electra and Orestes glowering down into the hall. They huddle together like refugees at the cold ashes of an unwelcoming hearth. They've barely spoken to me since I told them the truth about their sister's death. Soon, I'll find Electra a suitable prince from another city, somewhere far from this land where she can never be happy. Orestes, too, will go abroad. Perhaps he can learn charioteering and martial techniques in the Land of Hatti, but only once his father is dead and no longer at war with an ally of the Great King. Better to let Electra and Orestes go than to condemn them to haunt the palace like the shades of so many other lost children.

Their cousin Hermione hovers behind them, a plain, freckle-faced little girl. I return her shy smile. Menelaus sent her to me, now that he's lost hope of returning soon to Laconia. I pity the poor child, who couldn't inspire her mother's love. I will love her. She'll remain with me if Menelaus fails to retrieve Helen. Perhaps I'll keep her even if he does. Hermione was so traumatised by her abandonment that she couldn't speak when she first came to Mycenae. Now, early every morning, when the palace is as quiet as the child herself, she lingers by my side while I work at my loom. I'm weaving a purple carpet, which I will roll out for Agamemnon's arrival. This time, when he tramples on the wealth of our house, our people will witness the act.

A guard draws back the scarlet curtain and announces, "Aegisthus, Guardian of Mycenae."

My lover strides into the hall, flushed with success and vigour, almost as youthful as the day I met him outside the Circle of the Ancestors. Electra and Orestes mutter on the balcony as I rise to embrace him. My love for Aegisthus has grown with every day of his absence. I've missed his support and our shared confidences. I've missed his smile. I've missed him in my bed.

"Welcome, dear friend," I say.

His lips linger on mine for longer than is wise. I allow it.

When Agamemnon is food for the dogs, we'll announce the truth of Aegisthus' parentage. Our army will crush all dissent against us. Posterity will judge us harshly – a king's desire for bloody war outweighs a mother's need for justice for her children. So be it. Our troubles will pass, in time. We will begin an era of peace that no glory-mad king ever imagined or desired.

Aegisthus claps his hands and a servant appears in the doorway. With a stir of triumph, I see that the man holds the sceptre Aegisthus promised to bring me on his return. My lover places it in my arms. I have no need for a presentation ceremony, which might encourage questions about my right to rule, might remind onlookers of two brothers who laid claim to a single throne. I need no coronation. I have always been queen, whether I had influence or not.

The sceptre is solid gold, surmounted by a coiled serpent swallowing its tail, emblem of renewal. A worthy replacement for the sceptre Agamemnon took to Troy. This one was made for my hand and for those of my heirs.

The old authority is gone. A new era has begun.

I, Clytemnestra, daughter of Leda and Tyndareus, will rule justly over the living and exact justice for the dead. The shades of murdered children will be at peace at last. Avenging Erinys can sleep.

CHARACTER LIST

Mortals

Achilles – warrior prince of Phthia

Aegisthus – foster-son of Atreus and Pelopia

Aerope – first wife of Atreus; mother of Agamemnon and Menelaus

Agamemnon – second husband of Clytemnestra

Agathos Daemon – house snake; Good Spirit of the Household

Aias of Locris – Little Aias; warrior prince

Aias of Salamis – Great Aias; warrior prince; son of King Telamon

Archelaus – farmer who persecutes his neighbour, Polites

Alegenor – chieftain of Aulis

Argonauts – heroes who sailed aboard the *Argo*

Atreus – father of Agamemnon and Menelaus; brother of Thyestes

Calchas – itinerant seer

Castor – deceased brother of Clytemnestra and Helen; twin of Polydeuces

Clytemnestra – Queen of Mycenae; narrator of the story

Elatus – farmer feuding with his kinsman, Lyceus

Electra – youngest daughter of Clytemnestra and Agamemnon

Eritha – herbwife

Ereuthalion – champion of the Arcadians

Harmonia – nursemaid to Iphigenia and Electra

Helen – sister of Clytemnestra; wife of Menelaus

Heracles – hero from Thebes

Hermione – daughter of Helen and Menelaus

Hesione – Trojan princess; sister of Priam; slave of Telamon

Iphigenia – eldest daughter of Clytemnestra and Agamemnon

Iphitus – son of Clytemnestra and Tantalus

Jason – leader of the Argonauts

Leda – mother of Clytemnestra, Helen, Castor and Polydeuces

Lyceus – farmer feuding with his kinsman, Elatus

Medea – Jason's spurned wife

Menelaus – brother of Agamemnon; first husband of Helen

Nestor – king of Pylos

Nicandros – Harmonia's son

Odysseus – king of Ithaca; husband of Clytemnestra's cousin, Penelope

Omphale – captor of Heracles

Orestes – son of Clytemnestra and Agamemnon

Orion – famous hunter

Paris – Trojan prince; second husband of Helen

Patroclus – cousin of Achilles

Peleus – king of Phthia; father of Achilles

Pelopia – second wife of Atreus; daughter of Thyestes

Penelope – cousin of Clytemnestra, Helen, Castor and Polydeuces

Polites – farmer persecuted by his neighbour, Archelaus

Polydeuces – deceased brother of Clytemnestra and Helen; twin of Castor

Priam – king of Troy

Talthybius – henchman of Agamemnon

Tantalus – first husband of Clytemnestra; son of Thyestes

Telamon – father of Great Aias; captor of Hesione

Thyestes – brother of Atreus; father of Tantalus

Tros – herald of Agamemnon

Tyndareus – father of Clytemnestra, Helen, Castor and Polydeuces

CHARACTER LIST

Divinities

Alastor – avenging daemon of generational blood feuds

Artemis – Huntress; Lady Who Tames Wild Beasts; goddess of the hunt and of wild animals; guardian of all infant creatures

Athene – Protectress; goddess of the household and of battle strategy

Boreas – god of the north wind

Dionysus – Young God; god of wine and revelry

Eleuthia – goddess of childbirth and midwifery

Erinys – avenging daemon of murder victims

Hades – Keeper of Riches; Giver of Wealth; god of the underworld

Hermes – God of Wayfarers; Pompaeus; guide of the living and the dead; protector of heralds

Hymen – god of weddings

Hypnos – Giver of Sleep; god of sleep

Mater Theia – Mother; Lady of the Black Earth; Lady Who Gives Life; She Who Brings to Blossom; earth goddess

Mater Theia's daughter (whose name is never spoken) – as goddess of the underworld, she is She Who Reigns in Her Mother's Womb, Lady Who Receives Many, She Who Reaps; above ground, she is Spring Maiden, goddess of spring

Paean – god of healing, disease and song

Pan – god of the wilds

Peleia – Lady of Love; goddess of desire; associated with doves

Poseidon – Earth Encircler; He Who Secures Safe Voyages; god of water

Python – serpent guardian of the Delphic oracle

Spring Maiden – see Mater Theia's daughter

Two Queens – Mater Theia and her daughter, together
Zephyrus – god of the west wind
Zeus – Sky Father; Horkios, Punisher of Broken Oaths; god of
    the heavens

ABOUT THE AUTHOR

Susan C Wilson has a degree in journalism from Edinburgh Napier University and a diploma in classical studies from the Open University. She has worked in such environments as the Scottish Courts and the Scottish Parliament. As a writer she loves to explore what makes us human: the eternal motivations, desires and instincts that cross time and place. She also aims to make ancient stories resonate with a modern audience, through historical fiction and contemporary retellings.

Her debut novel, *The House of Atreus: Clytemnestra's Bind*, was longlisted pre-publication for the Mslexia Novel Competition in 2019.